SARAH'S
CHILDREN

SARAH'S CHILDREN

Anne Cameron

HARBOUR PUBLISHING

Harbour Publishing
P.O. Box 219
Madeira Park, BC
Canada V0N 2H0

THE CANADA COUNCIL | LE CONSEIL DES ARTS
FOR THE ARTS | DU CANADA
SINCE 1957 | DEPUIS 1957

Website: www.harbourpublishing.com

We acknowledge the financial support of the Government of Canada through the Book Publishing Industry Development Program for our publishing activities. We further acknowledge the support of the Canada Council for the Arts and the Province of British Columbia through the British Columbia Arts Council for our publishing program.

Printed in Canada.
Cover type design by Martin Nichols.
Cover photograph by Steve Mason/Photodisc.

National Library of Canada Cataloguing in Publication Data

Cameron, Anne, 1938–
    Sarah's children

ISBN 1-55017-274-3

1. Problem families—Fiction. I. Title.
PS8555.A5187S27 2001   C813'.54   C2001-910911-3
PR9199.3.C353S27 2001

For my children:

Marianne (YanYan)

Alex (Waxpa)

Erin (Missy)

Pierre (Pepe)

For my sister Judy and my cousins Fran and Roberta, who have been close friends for most of my life and all of theirs, and who amaze me. For my Uncle Tom, who should be declared a living national treasure.

And especially for Eleanor: two decades and still counting.

Whatever your little heart desires, kiddo.

1.

Sarah Carson could no longer kneel in her garden; years and mild arthritis had put a stop to that. She could, however, put a thick, dry square of rubber matting on the earth and awkwardly lower herself to a sitting position. Her rows were wider apart than most people's, but not entirely because of the rubber pad. For years she had spaced them far enough apart she could take her Troy Pony Rototiller between the carefully tended beans, peas, onions, leeks and garlic. Sarah's spud patch was off by itself, beyond the corn and squash beds. She had a plow attachment for the Troy Pony, and she could go back and forth between the mounds, turning up and hilling at the same time she fought the weeds. Pigweed, mostly. And wasn't that a bugger! Tasty when young and still small, but if you left it unchallenged it could grow up past your shoulders and choke out just about anything you planted, up to and including pumpkins.

Sarah's pumpkins might have been a source of pride if she'd been into such competitions. She'd been the first in town to send off for Giant Pumpkin seeds. Now, just about everybody and his dog had them, but few managed to grow them the size or shape of Sarah's; the secret, she believed, was getting them up off the ground onto an old tire, where the bugs and damp couldn't mar or discolour them, or start a patch of rot. Heinrich Mueller rigged canvas slings for his and even made a device with laths that forced one pumpkin to grow long and slender, but Sarah wasn't about to try that. A half dozen or so good-sized Giants were all she needed or wanted.

She had two grandchildren living out of town, miles and miles and yet more miles up in the Interior—practically, for crying in the night, over the border and into Alberta—and the most she could do was take photographs and mail off copies of what the kids called "their" pumpkins, but she had no trouble finding homes for the surplus. The transition house raffled one off every year, the store down the road a piece bought one, carved it and set it up on top of the recycling bin where it reigned over the parking lot and invited the ghosties and ghoulies to come visit. She gave one to the Catholic church for their Hallowe'en party, and one to the Protestants for theirs, not because Sarah was in any way religious but because she approved of the parties. They got the little ones off the streets and having a wonderful time before the yahoos and morons went out with their booze and their fireworks and their souped-up cars and pickup trucks. She supposed they had another term for it now, she supposed souped-up showed just how far in the past her vocabulary concepts had been cemented.

Sarah didn't grow carrots or cabbages. She had tried, year after year, but the clubroot stunted the cabbage, cauliflower and Brussels sprouts and the root maggots got into the carrots. No use flogging a dead horse or dragging it to water and trying to make it swim. Aggie McNeill grew gorgeous carrots and had no luck at all with corn, and if it was any of the cabbage family a body wanted, well, Bruno Radonovich was the man to see.

The clubroot didn't seem to bother the ornamental kale, though, and Sarah had put in kale plants along her fence, where they seeded themselves every fall, new ones coming every year. Few people she knew considered them food, but Sarah enjoyed them with a dab of margarine or, if she was feeling as fancy as Madam PooBah, a mild cheese sauce. The collards did well, too, and could be counted on for most of the sog of winter. And why not, she had lath-and-plastic frames she put around them, to protect them when the frost came. Annie Cameron had Brussels sprouts all winter and all she did was put plastic bread bags over the plants.

But right now the garden was mostly freshly turned earth, and the bounty Sarah envisioned was in her memory and her imagination. Almost May, and still too cold to put in anything but the hardiest of plants. She had two good-sized rows of spuds in the ground, but no sign of them unless you counted the string marking the furrows, held in place at the ends by wooden stakes. She had her peas planted and they had begun to grow up the netting, but only because of the cold frames she used at night. It was a bother putting up the frames and then taking them down again in the morning, but what was a body to do? The CBC weather forecaster announced, as if it were something to be proud of, that the weather was five to ten degrees below normal for the time of year. Also announced April had been the wettest on record, nearly twice the normal amount of rainfall. Sarah supposed it was the greenhouse effect and global warming; as near as she could understand, the scientists were warning that whatever you usually got by way of weather, you'd get more of it, and lord knows there were good reasons they called this the temperate rain forest. Temperate means only a few degrees difference between winter and summer. Until recently Sarah had figured that made for mild winters. Now it seemed it was apt to make for cold summers too.

She was willing to try to adapt; humans were supposed to be the most adaptable of the animal species. Still, she could remember the spring twenty-one years before, when they'd been eating fresh peas for the twenty-fourth of May. That was the year they had green onions for the first of May, International Workers Day. Her geraniums had been blooming, too. Not this year. But people propose and the creator disposes, and you take what you're given and make the best of it. And the work would be worth it. She'd get her beet seed in today, and maybe the anasazi beans and scarlet runners. She might even take a chance and put out a few of the lettuce plants she'd started in flats in the greenhouse. She liked the kind with the red fringes to the leaves.

Sarah couldn't believe the beauty of a garden. She had never been able to really grasp it. The wonderful green of bean leaves, the clarity of the red stalks of the rhubarb, and the scents and perfumes could make a person feel drunk. Especially the anasazi beans. They smelled like something she couldn't quite identify, almost but not quite like coconut oil, almost but not quite like marshmallow.

She couldn't believe the severity of the pain when it hit, either.

Bruno Radonovitch found her. He wanted to borrow her Rototiller while his own was in the shop being fixed. Most of what went wrong with it Bruno could repair or adjust himself, but when metal cracked or broke, it was into the shop because Bruno knew bugger-nothing about welding and he didn't have the tools to do it anyway. So probably Sarah's life was saved by the broken tine on Bruno's machine. As it was, she'd been lying in the garden for several hours, unable to move. She could hear but she couldn't see anything—her eyes were closed and she couldn't seem to open them. She'd lain there listening to birdsong and wondering how long it would be before she died, and then she heard Bruno, and he was saying things like ohmigawd Sarah, and you just stay calm, the ambulance is coming, as if she were having hysterics instead of plunked there like a jellyfish. In fact the strain in Bruno's voice made him sound like the one apt to take the shrieks. Sarah wanted to tell him to calm down himself, but she couldn't make a sound.

She heard the siren coming closer and closer, and then she heard a sound like tinkling bells, like bits of ice rapping against each other, making music of a kind she had never heard before, not even in her dreams. She had no sensation of any kind, not even of losing consciousness, she only knew that when she was aware of sound again she missed the crystal music. Instead she heard bustle and talking she couldn't understand and then, as clear as clear could be, a male voice saying, "Call the code again, we have pretach."

The crystal music returned, an entire symphony orchestra. Sarah didn't recognize one single instrument in it but the sound called her: she had a mental picture of a violin made of crystal, with silver strings, a silver bow with hair from the tail of a snow-white unicorn, and then, all too soon, too suddenly, the bustling sounds were back and she could feel, actually feel, tears streaming down her face.

"Don't cry, dear." Sarah knew that voice. She tried to open her eyes, and couldn't, tried to move her lips, and couldn't, but she knew that voice, and the frustration of not being able to speak, to acknowledge, was so strong that the flow of tears grew. "Just relax, Sarah, we'll have you stabilized and then we'll work on helping you talk. Don't strain yourself now. If you can, you might go to sleep, you'll be safe, I'll be here. You'll be safe, dear. That's it." The voice kept talking, soothing, and Sarah knew there was nothing she could do to stop herself going to sleep. She surrendered to it. At least the dreadful pain had stopped.

Christine Carson sat on the deck of *Sealkie* with a cold can of beer in her hand and Minnie curled beside her. The Lund Hotel stood to her right, a huge, rambling old wooden structure built in the days when Lund was a destination on the west coast, not a pimple. Tied to the wharf with her were a few other working fish boats and more flotsam than you'd want to see, and tupperware yachts, both sail and powered, speedboats, motorboats, outboards, you name it. Early tourists walked around in bright-coloured printed shirts, looking puzzled because wasn't this supposed to be the Sunshine Coast? So why was the wind off the ocean so cold, and why were their bare feet in their expensive imported sandals starting to turn a pale shade of blue? Overtired kids whined or complained they were cold and wanted a jacket, wanted hot chocolate, wanted to go home, and dogs of every size, shape, colour and description roamed at will, not a licence in the pack. A working prawn boat, the deck heaped high with traps, rocked with the gentle swells, bumped against the bright scotchmen, and the prawner, sitting out closure days the same way Chris was, lolled in the shade with a cup of coffee. He saw her looking over and his grin split his beard. He raised a hand lazily and waved. Chris waved back. No need to say anything, it was all understood. Each of them knew where the other was, stuck between a rock and a damn hard place.

Chris sipped her beer. Well, everyone had known it was coming, had to come. There had even been meetings. She had gone to them, presented a written brief, agreed with the recommendations presented by the fishers and shoreworkers. Drastic measures, they'd said, reduce the catch by a third or there won't be any catch at all. They were willing to bite the bullet and take the loss of thirty-five hundred jobs, because you'd be a fool, worse than a fool to hang on until the last dog was hung, the last breeder caught and canned. So the suits in their infinite ignorance had chosen to mis-understand the wording and intent of the opinions of those most closely involved and handed down their law. They'd have written it in flames across the sky if they'd had any idea how to do that. Instead of reducing the catch by a third they reduced the fleet by a half. Said they'd have a "reverse auction" to buy back licences, and what did that mean but skin the desperate? The small boats, like *Sealkie*, would be forced out, the licences bought up by guess who—the ones with money, the fish companies, the high liners, the dentists, lawyers and doctors who never set foot on a deck unless it was a cruise line, with shuffleboard and a pleasantly heated pool. The volume of catch wouldn't change one bit; it would just be divided among fewer and fewer boats.

And what the hell was Christine Carson going to do in all of this? Where was she going to get seventy or eighty thousand dollars for another licence? And if she took the buy-back and sold her present licence, what the hell would she do with *Sealkie*? Without a licence the boat was nothing but wood, nails and an engine. And even eighty thousand wasn't going to put her in the category of those rich souls who could take the work rigging off, dump some money into refit or overhaul and turn a good solid work boat into a pleasure craft for weekends, high days and holidays. Maybe she could drag 'er to her mom's place, set 'er on the front lawn, fill 'er with dirt and plant petunias. Every six or eight feet she could put in some ornamental gourds, and when they were ripe she could harvest them, scrub them, dry them for a while, then shellac them to keep them from rotting. Eventually they would dry so well their seeds would rattle and she could paint something on them, something tacky, an elf or a few musical notes, and sell them as maracas.

Minnie growled deep in her throat, and in a flash she was on her feet, raising hell.

"Here, you. You're breaking the calm of the day, again. Shattering it, in fact," and Chris put her hand on the Jack Russell's nose. Minnie stopped barking and Chris could hear the echo of footsteps along the wooden planking.

"Chris?"

"Yeah. I'm here. Can I help you?"

"Phone for you at the wharfinger's shed."

"For me? Jeez, maybe it's Johnny Christian phoning to tell me I just won a federal contract worth a million a year."

"If that's what it is," the prawner called, "don't be a cheap shit and forget your friends, okay?"

"I guarantee you," she laughed bitterly, "if that's what it is you'll retire right alongside of me."

She drained her beer can, tossed it in the bucket on top of several others and stepped from the deck to the dock. Minnie was right there with her, as if velcroed to her heel. Chris followed the wharfinger back to the shack and the waiting phone call. If you were in a retreat in the highest slopes of the Himalayas, someone would find a way to reach you by phone. Probably someone trying to get you to sign on to a plan where you paid twice what you should for a no-name freezer so you could fill it with a couple of hundred pounds of frozen food, the kind you never eat anyway.

Lorraine Carson McKye finished hanging her laundry on the line and headed into the house to mix up food for the puppies. From out back, almost but not quite out of earshot, came the sound of traffic. Car after car after car after truck after van, and if a person were standing on the side of the highway the sound would be a near roar. Here, however, it was background noise, easily ignored most of the time.

She had no idea where Wayne was. She hadn't seen him in three days. Which meant that once again she had to feed his pit bull and her seven pups. And Lorraine was afraid of her. Even if the dog had never so much as looked sideways at Lorraine or the kids, she was afraid. There had been so many warnings, so many newspaper reports of people bitten, mauled, even killed by pit bulls, and the scars that crisscrossed the bitch's head told how many fights she'd been in. The fact she was still alive and healthy meant she was an extremely good fighter—savage, quick, and relentless. Who in his right mind would keep a creature like that in a pen in the same back yard where his children played? Well, Wayne McKye, that's who. Wayne Franklin McKye, whom everyone in her world had told her not to marry, Wayne Franklin McKye, who once had curly blond hair and a body that could make your mind go blank. The curl was gone now and so was at least half the hair, and the sand in the hourglass figure had shifted drastically, gathering near the belt, which he now hitched low so his spare tire overhung it. Sometimes, and thank God so far it was still only sometimes and not all the time, his jeans were hitched down so low to make room for his growing belly that when he bent over you could see the start of the crack of his ass. Didn't he *know* how disgustingly gross that was? Didn't he care?

Three days and four nights and not a sign of him, which had to mean he was off on yet another bender, slurping it back as if it cost nothing, or as if the cost didn't matter because he was independently wealthy. Playing the part as if the motel were a thriving success instead of being what it was.

She hadn't wanted the damn thing in the first place, but if there was one thing Wayne did better than party, it was silvertongue. Steady annual income, he'd said, and they could save on what the retiring owners had paid out in wages because they were both young, and strong, and she could do out the units, do the laundry and make the beds, nothing to it, really. He would do the odd jobs, the chores, the upkeep and the scrubbing of floors, washing of walls and such. The retiring owners were old. They couldn't do it any more, they'd had to hire others, year-round, but Wayne and Lorraine would hire women or high school girls to do the units in the summertime when they were sure to be full to capacity and busy, but the rest of the year, hell, they could handle it themselves.

And look at the books, see, even with the cost of wages they're bringing in nearly as much as we get between us. So subtract what we'd save on wages the six slow months of the year and there you have it, no arguing with the figures, look, we're way ahead, and once they widen the highway we'll be laughing all the way to the bank, have the loan paid off in probably five years.

Well, it was closer to ten and still not paid off, and they hadn't widened the highway, they'd rerouted it and built a brand new one. The westbound lanes took people so close to their destination that they just pushed on, why pay for a motel out here in the middle of nowhere when in a few hours we'll be near a fair-sized town, with a decent restaurant and maybe even an indoor heated pool? People driving the eastbound lanes, faced with a long and boring stretch of next to nothing worth mentioning, might have been interested, but the motel was on the other side of the westbound lanes. They'd have to go three miles farther, then get on the cloverleaf, double back the three miles and turn off along the old highway to the motel. And of course they didn't bother.

So what the motel got was exactly what Lorraine didn't want: rent-a-pillow customers, too many thirty- to thirty-five-year-old married men out for a few hours with some airhead of a nineteen-year-old who probably believed the line of guff about the harpy wife and the impending divorce. She and Wayne had argued about it so often Lorraine didn't even bother any more. "Who are you? The self-appointed guardian of the morals of the entire damn country?" She hadn't even argued when he'd put the condom machines in the bathrooms of the units. "A penny saved," he'd laughed in her face, "is a penny earned."

Everyone knows the first rosy blush of romance fades. For the lucky few it becomes a strong and steady glow that warms heart, soul and life for years, making hard times endurable. But who are we to dare think we are so special as to qualify as one of those few fortunates? The mad, hot passions had chilled, the silvertonguing charm had become hot air and bullshit, the sensitivity revealed itself to be spoiled-brat bad temper, and Lorraine wanted out.

And with every three- or four- or five-day bender she wanted out more certainly, more quickly. She'd wasted several years worrying about the kids, my God what would their life be like without a father? Well, they hardly had one. Everything had changed when Sally arrived. Lorraine had expected change, but she had thought it would be for the better, that she and Wayne would become even closer. Instead it was as if a wedge had been rammed between them, hammered and bashed until it spread them so far apart they barely spoke the same language any more. By the time she realized it she was pregnant again, with Franklin-called-Lin-because-who-wanted-to-be-called-Frankie. By the time Lin was two the wedge had grown, fattening itself on resentment and disillusionment and puzzlement.

And here she was, with a line full of wash and a belly full of fed-up. She'd rented out three cabins last night and this morning she'd had to strip off the tattle-tale stained sheets and throw them in the wash. In one of the bathrooms two used condoms lay wrinkled and ugly in the wastebasket. Just looking at them made her feel insulted. Her hands were sweaty in her rubber gloves but she had to wear them—you just never know what in hell germ, bacteria or virus is lurking in the stains, in the wastebasket. And of course Wayne wasn't around to do any of the work. Even when he was home he didn't do much except look after his dog and her pups. Pare his toenails once in a blue moon. Nag at her. Yell at the kids. Fill the yard with boys' toys, then trade them, sell them, whatever, and never a sign of any profit from all the wheeling and dealing. Second-hand motor homes, boat trailers miles from the sea, racing motorcycles, even a parasail, out here where the land was so flat there wasn't a hill to climb let alone a cliff off which to jump. And cars. Oh dear God yes, the cars.

You'd think a person as angry and depressed as she was would have sense enough to hit the road. After all, the highway was just over there, beyond the rim of stunted trees, so why was she here listening to the sound of it instead of over there, adding to it?

But who would feed the dog? Besides, Wayne had the only dependable vehicle with him, wherever he was. The others, in the side yard, were "on the drawing board." Every time Lorraine asked him about fixing at least one of them, he'd laugh and tell her he'd put it on the drawing board. Once, before she got smarter, she'd let herself fall into the Carson bloody-mindedness, and when day followed day and began to form weeks and still her vehicle wasn't roadworthy, she'd phoned the tow truck and had the jalopy hauled in to Roger's Repairs. True, Roger had the thing fixed, tuned and on the road by noon the next day, and true, it hadn't cost a lot of money, but Wayne just about got a hernia from pitching his fit. "Don't you *ever* make me look bad again! You do, and however bad I look, you're gonna look worse because I'll feed you knuckle sammich until your own mother wouldn't recognize you." And she knew he meant it. He'd never really hit her, not really, but he would if he wanted. No gentle sensitive new-age guy for him, you'd be lucky if you got civilized, let alone polite.

And yet, he could be charming, when he wanted. He wore his manners well, when he wanted. When he wanted, life was all sugar. And when it wasn't, it was all shit.

She heard the near-new pickup. Wayne was home, finally. Think of the devil and he appears. But when he walked in, he didn't look like the devil. He looked like someone just about ready to fall flat on his face. He also looked as if he might bleed to death from the eyeballs. He gave her the look that said "don't get started," and she made herself smile—not much, but enough to tell the lie that she was glad to see him. He accepted the lie because he wanted, maybe needed, to believe.

He stepped out of his work boots at the door, padded to the table in his heavy woollen work socks and managed to land in a chair.

"Coffee?" she dared. "There's a fresh pot."

"No thank you, darlin'." That meant he was going to work at being nice; meant, too, he'd probably pulled some kind of a dumb stunt while he was gone. Butter her up before she found out he'd goofed up again. He pulled his trucker's wallet from his back pocket, unsnapped and opened it and fingered the money inside, his lips moving as he counted. "Here." He put money on the table. "Sold the black pup. Prob'ly sold another one, too, but it's not for sure. The guy'll come take a look."

"Want something to eat?" she asked, wishing she had the money in her hand.

"Later maybe. I'm whacked out. I think I'll have a bath and then a bit of a lie-down. Eat when I get up."

She heard the water running in the tub, heard the splashing as Wayne climbed in, imagined she heard him sigh wearily. It must have been a real wingding of a party. She wondered whose smell he wanted to wash off his body.

When the water stopped running she went to the doorway of the bathroom and peeked in. Wayne was lying back, arms half floating, eyes shut, dozing or sleeping. It was safe. She walked to the kitchen table, picked up the money and counted it. Three hundred and fifty dollars. And he had more in his wallet. He must have sold more than one pup and told her the story about the guy not having his mind made up so he could keep most of the money himself. This money plus what Lorraine had from the three cabins would fill the cupboards.

Sally and Franklin-called-Lin would be out of school in another hour and a half. If she finished up here she could be waiting when they came out, take them with her, maybe even splurge on hamburger and fries for supper. They needed shoes, too, but she couldn't do that and get the groceries too.

The phone rang and she hurried to catch it before it rang again and woke Wayne up. If she was quick she could be out of the house and gone in his pickup before the water cooled off enough to wake him. Sometimes he was like a bear with a sore paw when he woke up and she didn't want him demanding "his" money back.

Sarah surfaced from the fog and managed to half open her eyes. Annwyn Daniels was looking down at her, smiling.

"Sarah? It's me, dear, Annwyn. Can you speak to me? Can you say 'hi'?"

Sarah tried. She got the "h" but couldn't get the "i." She tried again and Annwyn patted her hand, then stroked it, her touch gentle. "That's my good old woman," she said, deliberately copying her grandmother's Welsh lilt. "It's not that long ago tha' couldn't say anything and now, just listen to thee."

"Th—" It wouldn't come out. All she wanted to do was tell Annwyn she was thirsty, but part of the word was lost. Sarah tried again, and felt the tears welling.

"So, is there another word would tell me what you want? Try again, Sarah. I know you can get this business of language back again. I *know* it."

"Dr . . . nk." It was like a full day's work. A long, hard, hot, full day.

"Drink? So it was thirsty you were trying to say? Well, I can fix that. Do you want water? Or juice? I have some nice chilled orange juice."

"J . . . s."

"Juice it is. Let's see if you can suck on a straw. And don't you get upset if you can't, because it's not the end of the world. You're very weak, Sarah. But you'll get stronger. And when you do, we'll work together and get back everything."

Sucking the straw was more than work, it was hard labour, but Sarah managed, enough that the tang of the juice cut through the other, dry fuzzy taste in her mouth. But she was too tired to try for more. Again, tears welled.

"Why don't I just spoon some into your mouth? I don't want you doing too much all at once. Open up, dear. That's it. Here it comes, a dribble at a time."

Nothing had ever tasted so good, felt so good, been so welcome. But Sarah had trouble swallowing, felt herself choking. She knew she had dribbled on her nightgown, but Annwyn lifted her head and the choking stopped. It wasn't thirst that needed quenched, anyway, it was just that her mouth was dry, so damn awfully dry.

"Good try. Now, I want you to listen to me." A warm, damp cloth touched Sarah's face, washing off the sticky juice, washing off the tears. "I know you're scared, and I understand why. I'd be scared, too. And I don't think I'd handle my fear as well as you're handling yours. What has happened is awful, and it isn't fair. But you know what Grandma Daniels said about life being fair. Sheep shit, she said. And you're going to weep, I know, and that's fine, it's only to be expected, and any of us would do it. But don't you give up! You hear me? You're a tough old bird, and we both know it. Fight this, Sarah, please. Get angry. This is a bloody insult! Get angry, so angry you can taste it!"

Sarah reached up to touch Annwyn's face. Only one hand moved. The other lay on the bed as if amputated. Sarah tried again, and then her fury flared. She lowered her good hand and slapped at the frozen arm, as if beating it would make it obey.

Annwyn laughed softly. "Right. Up and at it you lazy lump."

Sarah wanted to tell Annwyn she was absolutely beautiful, and knew she'd never get it all out. But it was true. Gorgeous. Had been since she was a little girl. Hair didn't get any blacker and eyes didn't get any bluer. Sarah knew why Christine was fond of her. They'd been friends since grade one, walking, skipping, laughing proof that opposites attract. Sarah knew there were rumours in town and she supposed she ought to care, but rumour is another way to say hot air and ignorance.

"I've phoned Lorraine, and Christine is on her way. And all you have to do, my good old woman, is close your eyes and sleep. Time enough to stay awake when Chrissy gets here. And until then . . . here . . . a little concoction inspired by my grandma. Glycerine to keep your mouth from getting dry, and a shot of brandy in it so's it tastes good."

Sarah couldn't feel the swab, but she could smell and taste the brandy. She laughed, and she knew it wasn't just a thought in her head, knew she had actually managed a laugh. Who else's concoction would it be but Annie Daniels'? Brandy was Annie's cure for everything from sciatica to post-partum depression. Good for what ails a woman, Annie would cackle, and if there's nothing wrong with you, well, it'll fix that, too. Seventy-five if she was a day, our Annie, and if you went by the way she moved around you'd think she was no more than fifty. It was Annie who had snapped Sarah out of her grief after Angus died. Waited two weeks, then showed up at the back door with a brand new bottle of Liquor Control Board Portuguese brandy. I'm here, she said in her heavy Welsh, to put the fire back in your belly. Angus, she said, is dead. He isn't passed away, he hasn't crossed over, and I doubt he's gone to glory. He's dead, Sarah, but you aren't, so let's us tie on a good one and dance the widow's waltz together. Here, she said, never mind the damn glass, drink!

Sarah smacked her lips together, even managed to lick weakly. Then, with what strength remained in her body, she spoke. Inside her head the words echoed clearly: thank you, dear, but what came out of her disobedient mouth sounded like nk a dur.

"You're very welcome, Sarah. Now go to sleep and I promise you when Chrissy gets here, we'll wake you up. I promise."

Sarah let go. It was so hard to stay there, she wouldn't have been able to hang on much longer anyway. Still, it was nice to have permission. No wonder Chris loved Annie's granddaughter so much. And Rainey on her way, too.

That single peal of the phone bell wakened Wayne enough to pull the plug, step out of the tub, more or less dry himself, drop the towel to the floor next to his dirty clothes and stumble to bed. When Lorraine checked on him he was belly down, naked, and uncovered. She pulled the covers out from where they'd been tucked under the end of the mattress and folded them over him. He snuggled, and she couldn't help but remember how cuddly he had been when they were first married, how he would spoon around her back, nuzzling his face into the back of her neck, breathing in the shampoo scent of her hair, and sighing contentedly before plummeting into a deep sleep. What had been lost, where and how?

And where did he ever get the idea all a person had to do with his clothes was step out of them? Presto—the filthy things vanished from sight, only to reappear later, clean, folded and wait-ing in a dresser drawer. When Lorraine picked up his jeans a fine dust settled to the bathroom floor. She checked his pockets and put his comb, small change and jackknife on the counter. She pulled his belt from the loops and put it beside the pocket contents, then pulled his trucker's wallet from his back pocket. Ordinarily she would have put it with his belt without looking at it. But there was nothing ordinary about today. She did something she had never done before: she opened the wallet and looked in it.

The very first things she noticed were the condoms. That told her more than words would have. For how many years now had she been altering her body chemistry, swallowing birth control pills, walking the razor's edge of God alone knows what kind of after-effects. The only reason Wayne would need condoms was because he was stepping out on her. But she wasn't surprised, and she wasn't disappointed.

The next thing she saw was the money. Sold the black pup, had he? It looked as if he'd sold all the pups, their mother, and most of the junker cars in the side yard! If she confronted him he'd tell her that he was going to surprise her, that he'd come up lucky in the Keno game or won four or five numbers in the 6/49. Or per-haps it would be the poker game story, or the surprisingly accurate shot in a pool game story. Well, she'd leave him twenty and he could figure out how best to spend it. If she ever felt the need for an excuse, there were always the condoms. Pussy bandit, that's what they called them when she was a kid.

Less than half an hour later she was driving away from the Bide-a-Wee Motel in Wayne's pickup, in the back of which were sev-eral black plastic garbage bags containing her clothes and the kids' clothes, their sleeping bags and the handmade quilt she treasured, all sitting on the piece of light green foam that fit into the bed of the truck, under the aluminum canopy. The foam was big enough for all three of them to sleep on, and sleep comfortably. Wouldn't you think a man who had bought and measured and cut the foam pad would have thought twice about buying a motel? Couldn't he see every pickup, every van, and most any jeep-y vehicle could be similarly fitted? The foam and the sleeping bag together cost less than a night in the Bide-a-Wee. And for that matter, why hadn't she herself been able to see exactly that?

The kids ran over to the pickup, puzzled, but glad of any change in their routine. They climbed in beside Lorraine, did up their seat belts, pushed down the snickey on the door to lock it, and all the time they were chattering at her, how come you've got Dad's truck, where's Dad, what's up, Kevin Fogarty got a home run but he hit the ball so far it went over the fence into the toolies and we haven't found it yet.

"Your grandma is in hospital," she told them, driving away from the school and heading for the highway. "We're going to see her, to cheer her up and maybe help her get better quicker."

"Does Dad know?" Sally blurted.

"Your dad is in bed, catching up on his sleep, but I left him a note and there's a casserole in the microwave he can warm up when he gets hungry."

"But does he *know*?" Sally persisted.

"Of course he does, dear," Lorraine lied.

"All the way to Grandma's?" Lin laughed suddenly. "If she wasn't sick, this would be like a holiday!"

"Even if Grandma isn't feeling well we can still make it a holiday." God, she sounded so calm, so unafraid, so ordinary. Where had she learned to lie with such conviction? Some holiday. She was petrified with fear, could hardly believe she could actually watch the road, keep her foot to the gas pedal, steer the truck, stay within the speed limit, while every cell in her was shrieking *What if she dies before we get there?* Maybe she should have just driven to the airport and flown. Chris would have met them, driven them to the house. Except that would have eaten up almost all the money and then where would they have been? Probably exactly where they were going to be before next month, anyway. On welfare.

They stopped for gas and while the attendant was filling the tank and checking the fluids and tires, the kids went to the washrooms. By the time they were finished reading the uninspired graffiti on the washroom walls, Lorraine had bought several bags of chips, a cold six-pack of Orange Crush, some Nacho Grande corn chips and a jar of medium salsa, a pack of Player's filters and a Bic lighter, and paid for it all with some of what she thought of as Wayne's money, the neatly folded bills she had stuck in her right front jeans pocket.

"Cigarettes?" Sally reacted as if she'd seen a bottle of rat poison.

"Don't start, Sally. Unless you want to ride in the back."

"I might."

"You can if you want."

"No radio there," Lin warned. "Maybe no chips, either."

"Oh, she can take a bag of chips, or whatever else she wants. It wouldn't be fair otherwise." Lorraine checked the traffic and pulled onto the highway.

"I'll sit here for a while," Sally decided. "But I want to change places with Lin so I can sit by the window. And have it open, too."

"Lin?"

"Fine by me. The one in the middle holds the salsa, right? So's everyone can reach it, right?"

They squirmed and wiggled, one under, one over, then settled themselves and got their seat belts done up again. Lin turned on the radio, found a mouldy oldies station, and tried to get the lid off the jar of salsa. He couldn't, and neither could Sally, so Lorraine managed it, steering with her elbows on the wheel, warning them both that at any moment they could hit the ditch.

"You guys are going to have to send off for one of those courses from Charles Atlas or Arnie Schwarzenegger, build up some muscles before we wind up smeared."

"Who's Charles Atlas?"

"Right. Another relic from my past. Here, it's open."

The light held until nearly seven o'clock, the highway stretched ahead and Lorraine couldn't decide if it was like a promise or a challenge. But there it was, and she kept the truck moving at just barely under the speed limit. She wanted to floor the gas and speed to Sarah, but she didn't want a patrol car pulling her over and she sure as hell didn't want an accident.

At nine, in spite of chips, Nacho Grandes, salsa and pop, the kids were making noises about starvation. Lin was actually starting to get snarly—small wonder, he'd been in the truck for almost six hours. She took the turnoff to a Wendy's and followed the arrows.

To watch them, a person would think they hadn't been fed for a week. Lorraine didn't feel hungry but she knew it was stupid not to eat. She got a big burger inside herself, washed it down with her first cup of coffee and pinned it in place with her second. She waited until Sally had finished eating before she brought out her cigarettes. Sally pulled a face, hurriedly finished her dessert, drained her paper cup of pop and excused herself, heading for the bathroom. Shortly after, Lin left the table and went to the men's. Lorraine sipped her coffee, smoked her cigarette and thought about how stupid she had been not to bring the thermos with her. She could have it filled here and put the kids in the back. They'd fall asleep in minutes and she could drive until who knew what time she would feel tired enough to stop and sleep. When the kids came out of the washrooms, Lorraine fished in her pocket for Wayne's money and slid from her chair. She had the bill paid and the change in her pocket by the time the kids got to the door.

They weren't convinced they were sleepy; they didn't want to climb into the sleeping bags yet. Lorraine didn't argue with them. They were probably safer up in the front seat with her, even if they fell asleep. What if they woke up in the back and didn't know where they were, what if Lin had to pee and thought he was home, just walked to the tailgate, tripped and fell out onto the highway, head first? What if the sky fell? What if Chicken Little or Henny Penny suddenly went crazy, turned savage, pecked holes in everybody's heads?

Instead of driving back to the highway immediately, she went looking for an all-nighter with a thermos for sale. The first two were busts, but in the third she found what she was looking for. She even got it filled with fresh coffee. The night clerk seemed glad of a little company. She smiled easily, chatted with Lorraine, gave her a dozen little creamers and as many paper packets of sugar, put them in a small brown paper candy bag. "We've got some fresh homemade donuts, too," she suggested. "They're good, and made from scratch, not some kind of pre-mix or anything."

"I'll take six of them, please. And a package of gum."

"You okay for gas and such?"

"Maybe I should top up, heaven knows where the gas stations are when a person really needs them."

Then she was back in the truck, heading for the highway, and something that had been nagging at her ever since Wendy's made her pull to the side of the road. Lin didn't even open his eyes. Sally did, but yawned and leaned against the locked door, pulling at her jacket, obviously chilled. Lorraine didn't want to turn on the heater, in fact what she wanted to do was crack her window, get a cool breeze on her face, and drive, drive, drive until she had Sarah in her arms. She got out, went to the back, climbed in and got the quilt, spread it over both kids, making sure the end was nowhere near the pedals, not even close to where it could tangle up her feet. Lin slumped sideways, his head at an awkward angle. Lorraine tucked her jacket under his head and patted him. Then, standing beside the half-open door of the pickup, she pulled Wayne's money from her pocket and in the overhead light tried to figure out what had been bothering her. It took her several long moments of riffling from one twenty to another before she finally realized what it was. Every bill had exactly the same serial number.

Christine sat by Sarah's bed and watched the erratic up and down of her mother's chest. There was a rhythm to Sarah's breathing. She would gasp deeply, struggling, and like a marathon runner would take anywhere from eight to a dozen incredibly deep breaths, her chest heaving. And then, apnea, and for almost as long again, the sheets would be still. The colour of Sarah's face would change, a red blush would begin to form, and then, suddenly, blessedly, the deep gasping would begin again. Chris was afraid one time soon—God, not too soon, not now, not yet—Sarah would forget to start breathing again. She could almost see the fight going on in her mother's head. Was it worth the struggle? Or should she just forgo the whole thing and check out here and now?

"Come on, Momma." Chris was surprised at how loud her voice sounded. She had thought she was practically whispering. "Come on, suck it in and shove it out. Rainey's driving down with the kids, you can't very well not be here when they arrive. Remember what you always told us, there's no excuse in the world for bad manners. Keep breathing, Momma."

"T . . . k." The whisper was soft, but unmistakable.

"What's that?"

"T . . . tk."

The good hand flapped, an impatient gesture, and at first Chris wasn't sure what Sarah was trying to say. Tk? It was like that old Celtic writing, Ogham, where they only used the consonants and you had to guess what vowels had been discarded. Well, why not, how many of the damn things are there, anyway, five? The rest of the words, all the words, are consonants. Tk had to be either tak, tek, tik, tok, tuk, or maybe tyk. Tak? Scots for take? Or ta'k, with an l missing, too? Why not, it's silent. Not tak, but talk.

"Anything special you'd like me to talk about? There's always the weather, I guess, but you know as much about that as I do, and anyway, you know what they say, we talk talk talk about weather and never *do* anything about it."

The hand moved, but not impatiently, more like a circular "keep going" motion. Chris would have given ten dollars for the chance to smoke a cigarette but no hope of that, every alarm in the building would have gone off and who wanted to try to explain that?

"You're doing well, Mom, but you have to concentrate on your breathing, okay? Right now you sort of put it off until you're all out of puff, then you have to suck in like mad. That's probably not good for your heart, and *it* has kicked up enough of a stink already. Try to get a rhythm going here, okay, steady on, and regular. If we knew anything at all about chanting, we could try that, but what I know about it you could shove in your om mani padme om and not really feel it. I'll bring in a tape deck and some tapes next time I come, you can breathe in rhythm to your favourite tunes. Who knows, maybe by then I'll walk in with the music and you'll be sitting on the edge of your bed, ready to dance with me." Sarah's lips moved, and Chris heard a breathy sound, formless. Not a laugh but a word, maybe several, which had escaped any form at all.

"Yeah, it'd be a sight," she babbled on, "you as short as you are and me as tall as I am, Mutt and Jeff do the pavane."

She poured some juice into a glass and placed the straw at Sarah's lips. "Can you suck on this? If you'd rather, I can hold the glass up for you and you can take a real live drink. Would that be better? Let's try it, and don't worry about dribbling, there are some towels here, I'll make a bit of a bib for you. Sort of turnabout being fair play, you did it for me."

The smile flickered, and Sarah's eyes opened. She focussed on Chris, then looked at the glass. Chris took out the straw and held the glass to her mother's lips, and Sarah sipped. She swallowed, smacked her lips appreciatively, and sipped again. Then she burped, a loud, explosive sound that made both of them grin and Chris laugh. "Manners, ya pig," she scolded.

Sarah's eyes closed. The effort of sipping several ounces had been monumental.

Chris put down the glass, wiped Sarah's face with a damp cloth, then sat and held her mother's hand, the lazy one, the one with the IV connected to it, stroking it, concentrating on it, trying to will the hand to do what it was supposed to do. "Two more days of closure," she said, her voice steady, her sobs suppressed. "But I'm not sure I'm going to pretend to go back out again when they reopen. It's not worth it. I was talking to Jeannie Pritchard this morning and she said she wasn't even going to buy lottery tickets any more because she figured she'd used up her full share of luck. When Mark headed off to school again, Jean thought it over and sold the *Lazy Daze Two*. Got a damn good price for her licences and it was a seller's market for boats at the time. Now the whole damn world is out picking the bones like buzzards, cruising around looking for the biggest and best bargoon. Boats are going for a third what they were worth two years ago. But even so, I'm beginning to think I'd be better off either selling or beaching it. When I look at the books I can feel my hair start to go greyer. Hell, it's spring and already the proof is there, if I keep making money at this rate I'll be so broke by the end of summer I won't even be able to buy diesel to keep the prop turning. They've cut the catch quota so much a person would have to rob banks to break even. I figure once I've discounted the operating costs, I've done it to my hands again for the chance to make six cents an hour. I'm thinking of writing the government and pointing out to them they've got a minimum wage law in effect and it's their regulations getting in my way so they have to subsidize me at least to the poverty level."

Sarah nodded, turned her head and looked expectantly at Chris. "M'rrk?"

"Mark? He's doing real well, Jeannie says. Making top grades, just like we figured he would. He's a damn hard worker and it only stands to reason you aim all that energy at the books and the exams will be easy. And would you believe it? That Charlene has actually got a job! I thought Mark had as good as signed on for a batch of grief when he took up with *that* prime prize, but it just goes to show you, I guess. She's slingin' beer in a pub. He looks after the kids, does his homework at the kitchen table while they do theirs, too, then they go to bed and he can really crack the books. 'Course Jeannie's leg's no better and she's still got her granddaughter living with her, that must seem like a load at times, but she's doing okay. I saw Devon Crowley, he sold his boat and now he kind of hangs around the dock lookin' like a lost dog, waitin' for someone to take him him home and give him a warm corner to sleep in, but he looked like that a lot of the time, anyway. Funny how some people never quite seem to make a place for themselves, isn't it? Well, he lived 'er up all over the coast, floozie at every gas stop, and now that game's finished and he's at a loss. At least he's not drinking, guess there's some good in the world."

By the time Sarah's breathing changed again and signalled that she was asleep, Chris's voice was hoarse. She'd gabbed and yapped about the next best thing to nothing at all, trying to weave her words into a cord strong enough to keep Sarah firmly moored to this world, to this life. And Sarah was asleep, properly asleep, not wavering in and out of something that seemed like sleep but was more dangerous. Her breathing was smooth. No more gasping, no more apnea.

Annie came into the room, smiled at Chris, then went to check Sarah's pulse. She had a hypodermic in her hand, the needle covered by a plastic tube. She removed the plastic, cleaned off the connector on the IV with a swab and injected something clear into the rubber bubble.

"She'll sleep for several hours," Annie said gently. "It's safe for you to leave now. Go over to my place, I'll be there in about a half an hour. There's food in the fridge and I'll be starved when I get there. And there's some beer, but you be sure you leave a couple for me because if I get there and the place is dry I promise you I'll kill every living thing in a two-block radius."

The pickup swallowed the miles like a turtle with a minnow, steadily, the headlights carving a path through the night black. Lorraine sipped thermos coffee and aimed the truck, her mind snapping from worry about her mother to the money in her front pocket. That was why Wayne had been so careful about the bills he'd taken from his wallet. The money in her purse, which he'd given her, was ordinary, each bill used and worn, with its own number. The bills in her pocket were not like that. How long had he been passing counterfeit? Was that how he got the toys he brought home, then sold a month or so later? Rowboats, outboard motors, snow tires, you name it. No wonder the side yard looked like Louie's Second-hand!

She thought of the all-nighter, the pleasant woman who worked there. Obviously a family operation. Would they be out the value of the bills she'd left? Probably not. Probably they'd make their bank deposit and the busy tellers wouldn't even notice. Probably the counterfeit wouldn't be discovered until later, or never. So who was going to lose out? Wendy's? The PetroCan? If she had any reason at all to think any of them would wind up the poorer, she'd turn this truck around and go back, trade them the phonies for some real money. But instead she convinced herself *they* weren't going to get the short end, it would be the bank.

Maybe even all the banks. The Royal Bank, after tax profit up eight percent, top CEO take-home two-point-twenty-eight million dollars. *Nobody* was worth two-point-twenty-eight million dollars a year. *Jesus* didn't get paid that kind of money! The Canadian Imperial Bank of Commerce, after tax profit one-point-zero-two *billion*, up fifteen percent. The Bank of Montreal, after tax profits up twenty percent, the sixth straight year of record profits, less than six percent of their income gone to taxes. Hell, ordinary people paid closer to forty percent. Toronto Dominion Bank, up twenty percent profit, top CEO compensation three-point-one-five million, less than four percent of their income taken for taxes. The Bank of Nova Scotia, after tax profit up *eighty-two percent*. And foreclosure rates higher than they had been in years, more and more people turfed out of their homes. Government budget cuts so drastic that in Ontario the impoverished had begun to turn their kids over to the welfare, to be fostered with strangers because they could no longer feed them. And she was supposed to feel bad about the banks losing out on the funny money? In a pig's baby blue eye. She would borrow Alfred E. Newman's motto.

At two in the morning she pulled into the provincial campsite at Old Woman Creek, hoping she would be able to doze, if not actually sleep. If she roused the kids and moved them into the bed of the pickup, the effort would jar her wide awake, so she left them as they were and tried to doze behind the wheel.

Half an hour later she was sitting on the bank of the creek, smoking a cigarette and listening to the chatter of the water as it coursed around stones, some of them moss-covered. When she finished her cigarette she lay on her belly, dipped her head and face in the chill torrent, then, refreshed and more awake than she'd been all day, she went back to the truck and drove on through the night. She stopped twice more, briefly, to drain her bladder, thought of stopping at an all-nighter to refill the thermos and, instead, pulled into a truck stop to fill the gas tank. She paid with Wayne's money, then took her toothbrush and toothpaste into the women's and scoured her stale-tasting mouth. She was just coming from the washroom when Sally got out of the truck and looked around, totally puzzled. No sooner had Sally gone to use what Sarah called "the facilities" than Lin was awake, or at least awake enough that he could be led to the door of the men's and trusted to get rid of his load of pop.

Lorraine tried to get the kids to climb into the bed of the truck and stretch out, but they wanted none of it. Both of them looked just about ready to cry. If Wayne had been there neither of them would have refused, certainly they wouldn't have pulled the old Rain in the Face trick. But Wayne wasn't there and Lorraine still didn't feel secure about leaving them alone in the back. They climbed into the front, Sally in the middle this time and Lin by the door. A couple of miles later they were both sound asleep again, snug and cozy in the patchwork quilt. And in Lorraine's left front pocket was the change from the money she had used to pay for the gas.

She found a country and western radio station, not exactly her favourite but the announcer seemed to be as fond of Bonnie Raitt as Lorraine was. Amazing how some people could establish a place for themselves and then move beyond the boundaries. Here was Bonnie, singing what anyone would think of as blues, accepted on a C&W station lineup. When you're good, you're all the way good. But there was something more, something almost indefinable. Lorraine had thought, at first, she would probably wind up buying every CD put out by k.d. Lang, but very quickly she got bored. What was that? k.d. had one hell of a voice, but Lorraine could play—and had played—the same Raitt record over and over and over, all day long, and not been bored, and no sooner did she hear k.d.'s voice than something in her head clicked off, she didn't even listen to the song. Or maybe it was k.d.'s silly clothes and the cavorting around on stage like a discombooberated mannequin.

God in heaven, how peaceful they looked, snugged together,

sharing the quilt. How must a person feel when push came to shove, the options were gone, and handing them over to foster care was the only way to ensure they would be fed? Who was to blame for that? All those jobs, gone as if they had never been, the ink not yet dry on the NAFTA bullshit and the unemployment lines swelling. Wayne, now, he said it was no skin off his nose. It was Quebec and Ontario voted Conservative and who were the ones got hit hardest if not the ones who had as good as voted for the deal? But still, who could have known? Weren't they supposed to be good jobs, skilled jobs, in manufacturing and technology, and some of those people had held those jobs for fifteen or twenty years, and held them well? And then *poof*. What did a person do then? You can't *buy* a job if you're over forty, and you have, what, a year of UI. When that's gone and there is still no job, what do you do? Living in a dump. Looking at the last cup of oatmeal. Two or three kids to feed, and how many meals of oatmeal had they had already? Is the entire country supposed to get up in the middle of the night, go to the bedroom, and gently, lovingly, slit the kids' throats? No, it's down to the welfare and sign the papers and Bobby and Carol and Ricky get taken to strangers, the government willing to pay more to shatter a family than to keep them together.

The kids wakened early, not a smile between them. Then the pushing and shoving started, with more whining than anyone should be required to endure. Lorraine pulled the truck over to the side of the highway and turned off the motor. The kids stared, puzzled and sulky.

"Behave yourselves," Lorraine said. "Before this gets going, turn it off, because I have been driving all night and I'm three times as tired as you are. You think you're cranky? Push me and find out what cranky really is."

"Well, he—"

"Shut up."

"But he—"

"I said shut up, Sally. And don't bother crying, it doesn't impress me at all. I know you're underslept, but who wouldn't go in the back and stretch out? I know you've been cooped up in this truck for hours and hours. Well, so have I. So just shove a mitten in your mouth and pretend, just for a while, that you know how to behave. And you, mister, just pay attention here. You are not a baby, don't act like one. One more shove, one more push, one more sneaky little pinch and you're going to have trouble sitting on that seat because your arse is going to be bright red."

Lin started to cry. Lorraine ignored him. She put the truck back on the road and drove on, looking for green and white highway signs. Maybe, with any luck at all, dear God this is your child appealing to you, there would be a diner open. If she could get some food into them they might stop acting like enraged ferrets.

They found a Smitty's, and the sulkiness ebbed away with each bite of food. Lorraine ate hungrily, even managed a third cup of coffee, feeling as if the children's lives were safe for another couple of hours at least.

"We're almost there," she assured them. "Just a couple more hours and this safari is done. Before we head off, we'll go in the back of the truck and you can paw through the bag of stuff. There are some books there, and some word puzzles, maybe find something to take the edge off this last bit of road. I really think we should win the lottery so that if we ever make this trip again, we can make it in style. Fly, maybe, in our own helicopter."

She didn't put them back in the truck right away. She walked them around town, hoping some fresh air would soothe the grouchies and some exercise would calm them down. As soon as the stores opened, Lorraine hit them with the kids. She bought new sneakers in one, new spring jackets in another, jeans in a third. When they finally got back in the truck, the last of Wayne's money had been turned into safe, smaller bills and the kids had new clothes and a Game Boy each to keep them occupied. Lorraine drove out of town with her guts in a knot, afraid one of the store clerks would come racing after them, waving the funny money; scared the cop cars would converge, lights flashing; terrified the cops would pile out, guns in hand, and start blasting.

Just before noon she pulled into the hospital parking lot and breathed a sigh of relief.

"Okay, kids." She knew they could hear the shakiness in her voice. "Let's check and make sure all the tags are gone from your new clothes, then . . . in we go."

"Is Grandma dead yet?"

"I don't know. I don't know anything. But if she is, I'll probably start bawling like a two-year-old, and if I do, don't get scared. Just bawl along with me. And if she's not, don't bawl. Okay?"

"How sick is she?" Lin worried.

"I don't know. Would you rather stay here in the truck?"

"No."

"Okay, in we go."

They got out of the truck and stood patiently while she checked them for errant price tags. "Before we head in, there's something I want to say to you guys. With one minor exception, which I'm sure we can all overlook and forget, you've been bricks. It's a *horrible* drive, and we did it almost non-stop, with no chance for you to get out and stretch your legs or run around for a while. You did well. You did *good*."

They looked up at her and she almost went weak with the power of her own emotions. Neither of them would ever get called beautiful, or gorgeous, or even exceptionally good looking, but their hair shone, their skin was smooth and clear and they had straight, strong teeth. Plain, yes, but so what? There was no law said every child had to be a Gerber ad, no law saying they all had to grow up to be Richard Gere or Raquel Welch.

2

Christine wakened slowly, and before her eyes opened she knew where she was. The perfume told her she was in Wee Annie's bed. Nobody else in the whole world smelled like Wee Annie. She breathed deeply and smiled, the other scent coming to her from the skin of her own face, more musky, more elusive, the slightest hint of it cramping her belly and making her shiver. Nobody else in the whole world smelled like that. Only Annie, with her incredibly white skin, her almost too-black hair, and those eyes, God, so blue a person could dive in and drown, lay aside all sense and reason and perish in a blaze of joy.

She slid out of bed carefully. Annie was still sleeping. Chris wanted to stroke her, wanted to kiss her, wanted to insinuate herself between those unbelievable legs and bury her face in bliss, but instead she padded barefoot to the kitchen and turned on the coffee maker. She felt loose and full of yawns. And she'd had the day off, sitting on deck, sipping suds as if she were one of the rich and lazy, while Annie had afternoon shift, had been on it for six days now. No wonder she was still sleeping. Chris knew that kind of fatigue, bone deep and almost paralyzing, God damn shift work anyway!

Minnie sat expectantly, watching every move Chris made, and when the coffee was ready and Chris headed for the back porch with a full mug, Minnie was right beside her, almost dancing, but not barking or whining. No sooner was the door open than Minnie scuttled out, bouncing down the stairs and racing across the close-cropped lawn. She stopped suddenly, squatted, peed, then was up and whipping in circles, chasing what was left of her tail. Chris lowered herself into a porch chair, lit a cigarette and watched as the dog went nuts. Everything had to be sniffed, some fallen leaves had to be grabbed and thrown in the air, then chased. And finally, the entire house had to be secured in place, corralled and kept stable for the coming day. Minnie raced around the front, up the side, around the back and down again, not even glancing at Chris as she whipped around for the second time. Sometimes it took half a dozen trips around the house to make it know its place. Sometimes it took twice that many, and the entire job done without any yapping or barking.

Chris listened to the spring songs of the birds, the loud buzz of a hummingbird at the feeder suspended from a branch of the apple tree. She imagined she could still feel the silver traceries of Annie's touch on her skin, the slow stroking of fingers down her legs, the golden warmth of firm palms on her back, the incredible heat of those lips on her throat, her breasts, her belly. There had been others, many others. Sometimes Chris thought of them and wondered where she had found the energy, and not one of them had filled her life so completely. So much was unique with Annwyn; sometimes just the thought of her made Chris's belly lurch. She might be doing something totally unromantic, nothing to do with sex or love, like gutting fish or scrubbing the deck, and suddenly her pelvic muscles would clench as if she were on the steeply rising slope toward orgasm, and clearer than any photograph she would see Annwyn's face. None of the others had ever done that to her, none of the others had made her feel so willing to be at their mercy. You have to trust someone with your body, your life, your heart, your very soul before you can put aside all the defences of a lifetime and stand so exposed. The greatest thing about it was that Chris felt no risk at all. She knew, the way she knew the sun had its own routine, that there wasn't a mean or vindictive bone in Annwyn's gorgeous body, there wasn't any risk, really, because Wee Annie would bend over backward not to be a mean shit. And in return, Chris would willingly, even eagerly, turn herself inside out to be as decent a person as she could, never knowingly to do anything to hurt.

Had Sarah felt that way about Angus? Had Angus felt that way about Sarah? Sometimes Chris heard other people talking about their growing-up years and felt only shock and disbelief. Weird words rolled from them so easily: dysfunctional, co-dependent, enabling . . . what Chris remembered was nothing like any of that. She remembered coming home from school to an empty house, sure, but walking in secure in the knowledge that Sarah would be there soon. All Chris had to do was change out of her school clothes and into her play stuff and do whatever was marked on the note on the table. It might say Chris—scrub spuds and carrots, Lorraine—add chopped onion to hamburger, but it would also say Love you heaps and bunches, see you soon, I'll do the cooking. Once in a while the note would say I'll be late, go to Auntie Prin's for supper, I'll pick you up there, love you like crazy.

Those times were when Angus was out on the *Sealkie*, working the fishing grounds, and who would expect anyone to just sit in the house waiting like some kind of fungus growing in the cool shade of another's absence? If Angus were home he'd have the world in his capable hands. There wouldn't be any note, just him: small, wiry, almost scrawny, with the vegetables ready for cooking and the meat loaf mixed and waiting to go in the oven.

They had disagreements, certainly. Angus could go up like a skyrocket over just about anything that stuck in his throat the wrong way. Usually he'd roar Bloody thundering hell and go into one of what Sarah called his perambulations. But however noisy he was, there was never the slightest hint that he was apt to take a swing at anyone, certainly not at Sarah. Sometimes Angus would hit the bar and come home more than half-packed. Sarah would shake her head and turn on a thick Scots accent copied from her parents, warning him he was on the road to perdition, and, worse, was wasting money. And then she'd laugh. Sometimes Sarah went to the bar with him and they came home with their arms around each other's waists, Angus roaring at the top of his voice "some had their boots and stockin's, some had nane at a', some had their big bare airses, comin' through McGrogan's draw . . ." and Sarah warning him he'd pay one day for his disreputable ways.

They could have moved to a bigger, more expensive house, but they didn't. They could have bought newer, more expensive vehicles, but they didn't. Nobody today lived in the same house for all those years! People traded up and traded down, signed mortgages and waited until the value of the place had gone up enough they could jump back into the Monopoly game and make a profit, biggest investment in your life, they said, as if that wasn't a bunch of bumph—the kids were, or ought to be.

And there had been money for a piano, and lessons, money for sports equipment, even money for the circus when it came to town. All those years, day after day, and Sarah working at the fish plant because, she said, she had always paid her own way and always would. Her one consistent piece of advice to her daughters: be sure you can feed yourself and your children.

Minnie stopped her streaking and racing, bounced up the stairs and jumped into a porch chair. Her mouth hung open, tongue lolling, and her sides heaved as she panted gleefully. Everything was as it was supposed to be. The lilac bushes would behave and stay put, the house wasn't going to break its concentration and wander off down the street, and the rose bushes had learned their lesson for the day. Minnie had done her job; now it was up to everything else to do its job, and do it properly.

Chris got up and went into the kitchen for a coffee refill. Her oversized T-shirt hung well below her hips, her big bare arse wouldn't show although she had to admit she had neither boots nor stockin's. She sipped the coffee but it was too hot. She put the mug on the counter and padded quietly to the bathroom. Her clothes were there where she'd dropped them, next to Annie's, near the tub where they had shared bath water and washed each other's backs. Chris hauled on her clothes, put Annwyn's uniform in the clothes basket, took her own toothbrush from Annie's holder, scrubbed her mouth and then got her hairbrush from the basket and tried to bring some sense and reason to her all-directions-at-once hair. She wasn't an envious person, really, but every time she saw Annie's curls, Chris knew all she would ever need to know about the sin of envy. And not just Wee Annie's hair. Anybody who had obedient hair could make Chris feel a pang. Neither she nor anybody else in the world had ever been able to "do" anything with her mop. Too many crowns, whirls, whorls and cowlicks, her very follicles in rebellion. Sarah said it was a sign of a busy nature.

Oh, God, Sarah, just hang on, please. Hang on and hang in. Dear God, please, she is too young to die. If you let her live I promise . . . anything!

Bruno Radonovich took the Rototiller back and put it in Sarah's garage, almost exactly where he'd found it. The gas tank was full, the oil topped up, all sign of dirt hosed from the tines and body. He checked the bag of cat food on the workbench. It was nearly full; the half-wild cats would be fine. Sarah, dear Sarah, if you didn't feed them they wouldn't hang around, having litters that would grow up counting on the steady supply of kibble in the garage, litters that would then have their own litters. When he'd said as much, Sarah had laughed. "Ah, but I've probably got fewer mice than anyone else in town, and no need to buy poison, or set traps," she said.

Unlikely. The cats were too well fed to need to go after mice. Bruno closed the garage door, checked the water dishes and walked to the back door. He took the key from his pocket and unlocked the door. "Chester," he called. "Come on, you've got your job to do. Unless, you dirty pig, you've jobbed the floor." No chance of that, he knew. Chester would split before he messed anywhere in the house.

The pig hurried out the back door, grunting and grizzling, arguing and bitching, scolding and nagging. He lumbered down the few back stairs, then ran across the grass to his current particular place. Oh, Sarah, Sarah, who else on the face of the gorgeous green earth would have a pet pig and let it sleep and live in the house? Bruno had been sure Sarah had, as they say, slipped the bonds of earth, or at least that part of earth directly related to reason and sanity, when she'd taken the pig.

"I'll turn him into sausage for you," he had offered.

"This pig has been through enough, he's not going through a sausage grinder, too."

It was true Chester had been through the wars. The scars on his thick hide told part of the tale. Chester wasn't a cute little pink living toy any more, and hadn't been for a year or more. Someone, some nameless, faceless one, had got Chester when he was a tiny baby. Probably ignored the advice to limit his food to a few ounces a day. Oh, he's so cute, here, give him a donut. Want to see something funny? Cut a piece of pie and watch this guy dig in! So Chester wasn't stunted, which is the only reason the potbellied pigs are miniature. Chester grew. And suddenly he was verging on enormous. What do you do with a nearly two hundred-pound pig?

Bruno wasn't sure what a person would do if the sausage machine was out of the question, but he was damn sure he wouldn't have taken the creature to the beach and turned it loose. Well, at first it hadn't worked out too badly. Chester mooched from picnickers. But as the weather cooled and the crowds shrank, Chester became desperate. He roamed further afield, and someone took a shot at him. Terrified and in pain, Chester raced off and got tangled in a barbed wire fence. Mighty Nimrod with the shotgun caught up to him, close enough to take another shot. Chester got through the fence and headed down the highway. Bleeding and out of his mind with pain and terror, he tangled with a motorcycle. The biker got to his feet, saw Chester, unconscious and bleeding, and hauled the scratched-up hog out of the ditch. "Jesus, it's Porky Pig," he muttered as he rode off to phone the police. They contacted the vet and the SPCA. The vet picked out the pellets of lead shot and disinfected the slashes from the barbed wire, and the SPCA phoned Sarah. "We need a temporary foster home," they told her, "for a very large badly injured pig."

"I can put him in the puppy shed," Sarah said.

Chester was in the puppy shed for several days. At first he cringed and shook with fear when Sarah went in to feed him. But he had memories of people, nice memories, going back to when he was a cute and cuddly baby. Besides, Sarah could probably walk up to a hyena and brush its teeth while it laughed. Chester started coming out of the shed and tagging along while Sarah did her yard chores. One day he matter-of-factly followed her into the house and lay down on the foot-wiper mat just inside the back door. Sarah phoned the SPCA and told them to stop looking for a home for Chester, he'd found one for himself.

The pig finished his job and romped, bouncing awkwardly, his straight tail switching with glee. What kind of a pig has small ears and a straight tail? Pigs have big ears and their tails curl and twist. But not Chester. Sarah said it proved he wasn't an ordinary pig, he was an inordinately fine swine. Chester started to eat grass, grunting happily. Sarah hardly fed him and he did just fine. Certainly he did a better job of fighting dandelions in the yard than any weed-and-feed a person could buy. He delicately nosed the budding flowers, then—*nip*—he ate them.

Bruno played with the idea of opening a landscaping business. He could "do" people's yards, mow their lawns, let Chester take care of the weeds. "You stay away from the flowers, pig," he called. Chester ignored him. But Chester could be counted on to ignore the flowers. He didn't set foot in the beds, and all Sarah had ever had to do was snap "No!" Maybe it was true pigs were as smart in their own way as people in theirs. Maybe smarter—pigs didn't shit where they lived.

Bruno went to turn on the hose and spray the hanging baskets that hadn't quite started to bloom. He pulled some grass from the flower borders, turned off the hose and went to check Sarah's garden.

Robins. Damn robins. They'd have the place ravaged if someone didn't take a hand. Well, he knew how to fix them!

Bruno hurried back to his own place, Chester ambling along behind. He went into his garden shed and got two big plastic owls. He then chose two of the poles that were neatly stacked against the far wall, screwed the poles securely into the holes in the feet of the pretend killers and marched purposefully back to Sarah's place, the sticks over his shoulder, the plastic owls bobbing, the pig grunting and trotting to keep up, pausing to nip the flowers off the dandelions growing in the boulevard.

"Hey, Bruno," David Morton called. "You going to apply for a municipal grant? Your pig does a better job than anyone else."

"Sarah's pig," Bruno answered.

"Yeah, but whose are the owls?" and David laughed again.

"My owls."

He put one at each end of the garden, the sticks firm in the dirt, the owls stuck threateningly in the air. Whistling between his teeth he checked the soil for dampness, decided against turning on the sprinklers, then left the garden and closed the gate. A person pretty well had to fence off the garden. The neighbourhood dogs respected no boundaries, often came just to chase the many cats. And the cats thought the soft dirt in the garden was there only to provide them with a place to scat! Chester was as good as he could be about chasing off the dogs, had gathered a few more scars squaring off against the German shepherd that lived on the next block.

One of the original cats—or what Bruno thought of as the originals, even though they were probably the great-grandchildren of the originals—twined herself in, around and between his ankles, purring loudly and clearly. "Won't do you any good at all," Bruno warned. "I'm a man with a heart of stone. Nothing you do is going to make me like you. If it was up to me you'd be heavier right now than you were when you woke up this morning. You'd have a hunk of lead in the middle of your brain. If you have a brain."

He hunkered down and stroked the cat, scratching behind the pointed ears. Sarah and her cats. My God, every time he saw a cat of any size, shape or description, he thought of Sarah and the big bag of kibble she bought every two weeks, took to the garage, laid on the workbench and then cut open so the cats could feed any time they wanted. Sometimes you'd see Chester, napping in the sunlight, with two or three cats curled up with him. Sarah laughed every time Bruno grunted and made the sign against the evil eye. He liked to hear Sarah laugh and even if he didn't give the first part of a good shit about any evil eye, he made the sign and pretended to grumble about the unnaturalness of cats cuddling pigs.

Sarah's grass needed cutting. There wasn't much Bruno could do to help Sarah, the fight was hers now. It was that same damn thing—alone when you come into the world, alone when you go out of it, and alone most of the time in between. But he could mow the lawn. He could even paint the porch and stairs. For that matter, he could make a project of it. Sarah wouldn't be home for quite a while, so he could get the wire brush and go over the old paint with it, then put fresh paint on the entire place. No worry about choosing the wrong colours, Sarah had never changed them. The house was white and the trim green, to match the roof. When— not if, when—Sarah came home it might give her a boost to see her house painted, her yard as neat and well-tended as when she went off in the ambulance.

He didn't know when he'd been so scared in years. Hell, he hadn't been that scared when people were shooting at him! Sarah Carson did not belong flat on her back in her garden, helpless, with the sun in her face and the flies walking on her flaccid arm. Sarah Carson belonged on her feet, her face shaded from the sun by the big straw hat she wore, the hat he had picked up from the dirt while the paramedics were carrying Sarah off on a stretcher. While they loaded her into the back of the vehicle, Bruno had stood there, as helpless as a baby, his huge work-hardened hands turning the hat, turning the hat, turning it as if any good would come of all the turning.

Well, he knew exactly where the wire brushes were. There wasn't anything he could do to help save Sarah's life, but there *was* something he could do, so might just as well go get ready to do it.

Bruno headed back to his own place, Chester and two cats following. Might as well buy a calliope and learn to play it, tum tum tiddly um tee tum tum tiddly, the circus parade is heading down Queen Street.

Sally and Lin stood at the foot of the bed, gaping in fear. Lorraine moved to the side of the bed, knew immediately she was next to

Sarah's good arm; the other one was swollen and discoloured as if a large, tight elastic band were gripped around it, interfering with the circulation.

"Momma," she said clearly. "Momma, we're here."

Sarah's eyes snapped open. She moved her head, as slowly as if a huge weight were sitting on it. "Rainey?" she managed.

"Yes, Momma. The kids are here, too."

The smile was one-sided, but it was a smile and Sarah tried to turn her eyes and find the kids. Lorraine gestured and the kids came to stand beside her.

"Hi, Grandma," Sally said, as if she lived right next door, saw her grandmother six times a day and had just dropped in for a drink of water. "Don't you worry, we're staying until you're better. I'll feed the cats."

"Yeah." Lin's voice was nowhere near as steady. "And I'll feed the pig."

"Rainey—" Sarah tried to move her good hand but the IV was in the back and a board was taped to her hand and forearm. She winced. Lorraine reached over and stroked Sarah's good arm. "Easy, Momma. No rush. We're here."

A nurse came in, all efficiency and starch. "Mrs. Carson is supposed to be sleeping. And visiting hours don't begin for another hour."

"Lady," Lorraine said civilly, but firmly, "I just drove from six miles past the last gate to nowhere. I'm very tired and when I'm tired I am not pleasant, okay?"

"Fine by me," the nurse laughed. "Just don't stay long. Mrs. Carson really does need to sleep. And I need to change the IV bag."

Lorraine leaned over, kissed Sarah on the cheek and whispered in her ear. "Duty has invaded. We'll be back. You do what Attila the Hun says and for God's sake, my darling, sleep or there's no telling *what* she'll do." Then, turning, she tapped the kids on the shoulders. "Come on, munchkins."

They followed, subdued. Lin's eyes were shiny and he blinked often but didn't reach up to wipe them. Well, why not? Sarah was their grandmother. And yet how often had they seen her? Almost never. The connection was through long-distance phone calls, cards and letters. And that incredible tribal thing kids have—you introduce them to someone they've never seen before, never even heard of, and tell them this is their cousin and just like that, as if they'd been living in each other's pockets all their lives, they're bonded.

The town had changed. It was at least five times as big as it had been when Lorraine had lived here. Streets headed off where before there had been bush, new houses stood where there had been bike trails, an entire mall was built on what had been the old landfill. She hoped the stuff dumped there had been relatively benign and that there wasn't an old hydro transformer dripping PCBs into the ground, to come up during the rainy season and contaminate that parking lot where people walked so casually, as if they weren't walking on tons of garbage.

But she had no trouble finding Sarah's house. They can't change the town that much. The old roads were there, would always be there, and those old roads led to the place that would always be home. She stopped at the supermarket and got several bags of groceries, winced at the dent it made in the money Wayne had given her. No Carson had ever been on welfare! But she was a McKye now, and God knows enough of them had nuzzled the public tit. She'd go see them tomorrow. No need to tell Sarah about it. No need to tell anybody. Bad enough that she herself would know.

She left the supermarket and drove north. She turned off the highway and slowed as she drove down Queen. New houses here, too. What had been pastureland, where people grazed their beef, had been cut into lots, and massive, ugly houses had been built there. Jesus, some of them looked as if they were built of solid concrete! Last as long as the cathedrals of Europe, without ever getting attractive.

Angus had bought two beef calves every fall, grazed them on Henderson's field, then butchered them and gave the Hendersons a hind quarter. He always called them the same names: Freezer and Sparerib. Now the Hendersons' field was gone, and three houses stood where the steers had grazed.

No sign of Christine's pickup. Where was she? Surely not on her boat! However short the season, you don't go out for days at a time when your one and only mother is fighting for her life! Not even Chris would pull a stunt like that, although some of the stunts she'd pulled were legendary.

Someone was scrubbing at the paint, scratching at it, the lawn and flowerbeds marked with flakes, some as big as saucers. Whoever it was had an old straw hat on his head. A pig was cropping the grass. Probably Chester, how many pet pigs could there be in the world?

"Chester!" Lin called, cracking open the door before the pickup was fully stopped.

"You be careful!" Lorraine snapped. "You'll fall out and break your silly neck!"

"Hey, Chester!" Lin was out of the pickup and running. The pig lifted his head, peered, then trotted to meet Lin as if they'd grown up together. Sally got there after Lin and hunkered down beside him, and they both fussed the big pink bulk.

"Rainey." The man in the straw hat put the wire brush down and moved forward, wiping his hands on the seat of his jeans.

"Mr. Radonovich," Lorraine blurted, and then her smile flashed. "It's so *good* to see you."

"Good to see you, Rainey. You look as if it was a long, hard drive. Come in, come in," Bruno said, as if it were his own place. "I'll make tea, you can sort yourselves out, get yourselves settled."

She moved her things into her old room and put Lin and Sally together in what had always been called the "spare" bedroom. She supposed Chris lived in her own room, even if it was long past the time Chris ought to have a place to herself. Lorraine had always thought Chris would be the independent one, the one who hiked off down the pike as soon as she got out of school, the one who headed to new places to see new people and do new and exciting things. But no, it was Chris who had stayed home, worked the boat with Angus until he died, then taken it over and run it herself. Her life had changed only in the smaller things, really. She passed her days doing what she had always done, surrounded by people she had always known, snugged into familiarity, into something that might easily be described as a rut.

When Lorraine went back to the kitchen, the grocery bags were on the counter and Mr. Radonovich was opening cupboard doors, peering in, figuring out where things ought to go, where Sarah had put them for years. Lorraine made ham and cheese sandwiches, and while she put the plates on the table, the old man got pickles and mustard from the fridge, hauled out a jug of juice and finally made that pot of tea. He seemed very much at home here. Some people had that talent. You could drop them on the back side of the moon and in no time at all they'd be settled.

"We went to see Grandma," Lin told Mr. Radonovich as if they were old buddies from way back. "But the nurse kicked us out."

"Never argue with the nurses," Bruno agreed.

"Visiting hours," Lorraine laughed softly, "don't start until one."

"Are we going back?" Sally asked.

"I am. Up to you if you go or not. You can stay here if you want, you're old enough to look after yourselves for an hour or so."

"I'm going."

"I'm not." Lin shook his head. "I hate it there! It stinks. And Grandma looks . . . scary. I'm staying. I'll help with the house. What are you doing to it, anyway?"

"First, scrape off the blisters and flakes of old paint, then make it look nice for when your grandmother comes home. Cheer her up, maybe."

"Does she know?"

"It'll be a surprise. So don't tell her, okay?"

"What if she didn't want it painted?"

"Everybody wants their house painted, boy. Houses and fences. Any time you want to do something real *real* nice for someone, remember that."

Sarah wakened with the unsettling feeling that she wasn't in her own bed, where she was supposed to be. In fact, she wasn't even in her own home. It took several moments for her to remember where she was, and why. Her memory was aided by the sound of Tess McFadden's voice.

"That's it, now you know where you are. I can tell by the expression on your face. Bit of a jolt when you wake up and you're not where you think you ought to be. But you're where you need to be, Sarah, and we'll take good care of you." Tess's accent was so braw you could have sliced it with the same knife you used to cut haggis. "Now, my dear, we're all of us here except Mike Casey's horse, and we're going to get you out of that bed and into this chair. I warn you, by the time we're finished you're going to feel as if you've done a marathon, but take my word for it, there's method in our madness."

"Tess . . ."

"That's me, Tess it is. Now, I'll just close off this wee bit of bother here . . . see what we did while you were sleeping? That's a permanentish sort of setup in your hand, we can unhook you and hook you up again without having to jab, jab, jab away at your puir flesh. So we'll take it off, and then down wi' the side of the bed. Now you have to trust us. I promise we'll try not to drop you to the floor. And if we do, well, you've been down there before now and if you try to sue us we'll all deny any such a thing happened. We'll tell them you're delusional."

"Nuts."

"Right. Totally nuts, your honour, we'll say. Right off her rocker and has been for a long time, anyone can tell you that."

The transfer happened so quickly and so smoothly Sarah hardly knew it was done. In no time flat she was out of bed and into the wheelchair, a blanket under her, the edges pulled over her shoulders, another blanket over her, tucked in around her.

"There, see. Amazing, aren't we? Skilled and trained to a fine fare-thee-well, and all this time you thought we were just coolie labour."

"No."

"No? Well, there. See how much smarter than most you've been? Now what we're going to do is give you a good wash while you're sitting in the chair. And while we're doing that, these others are going to strip down your bed and make it up with fresh linen. And then, my dear, the bed is going closer to the window so you can have a wee keek at the world. Honestly, when you think of it, the hundreds of thousands of dollars they paid some fool to design this place, and here we've got all the support equipment in the wall in exactly such a place as a body can't see out the window. They should have put the windows all the way to the corners of the room. And the oxygen and such could be in the wall, all right, that's a fine idea, but not smack in the middle of the damn room where you're midways between nowhere and no place."

"Men."

"Right you are, the whole lot of 'em were men. And more showers along the hall than a body can believe. As if everyone who came in were able to stand up and balance on a wet floor. Only one of them will allow a wheelchair in! They should all be plenty big enough for a chair, we could roll you in and just soak you completely."

Tess talked as if Sarah were fully engaged in the conversation and holding up her end of it instead of being able only to force partial words from her throat. The ones in the pink uniforms, whom she supposed were those they called practical nurses instead of registered ones like Tess, were busy with basins of warm water and soft cloths. Two others in pink were straightening the bed, changing sheets and pads.

"What do you want done with your hair, then, dear?"

"Brrr'ds."

"Birds, is it? Well, I doubt we know how to do that, but would braids do for the now?"

"Esss."

"Yes, is it. Well, fine then, that's what they'll do. Now, do you want them hanging down like Pippi Longstocking, or crossed on the back of your head, or up on top?"

"Ttt . . . p."

"Try to say it again, Sarah. I know you mean top, but you're having hell's own time with your vowels. Can you remember how to make it happen? You puff, dear. T . . . hah . . . p."

"T . . . *uh* . . . p."

"Close enough. You can be proud of yourself. You're doing very well, you know. Really! I'm sure it seems to you as if you've lost it all and you're doomed to life as a mute, but nothing of the sort. Not fourteen hours ago you could barely force a sound from yourself, and today, well, no denying it's fuzzy, but did I have any trouble understanding?"

"G . . . d fr . . . n."

"Yes, I am a good friend. You and I have been friends since before you and Angus got married. Now, my dear, the bed's ready, and so are you. We'll get you back in and I'll reconnect you to your little friend and then you are going to try a bit of lunch. Oh, don't look so frightened! Take a dare. Aster is going to help you. Don't wrack your brains trying to figure out if you know her family or not, because no, you don't, she's not been here long. Another transplant, the town's full of them. And don't you worry about not being able to swallow properly. We've got lovely big bibs to take care of the dribbles and drools, and Aster's trained to do what's needed if you start coughing or choking or whatever. And you might, Sarah, but I'm not fifteen feet down the hallway and you *know* I wouldn't let you get into trouble on your own."

She was so tired that by the time they had her back in bed and rehooked to her IV, she would much rather have gone to sleep than even to think, let alone eat, a bowl of cream of asparagus soup. She probably didn't get a half cup of it down. The rest wound up on the bib and the big towel Aster spread over Sarah's chest, but she was reassured to know that she had actual food in her stomach, and more reassured to know that it had got there with an absolute minimum of choking.

When Sarah ran out of energy, she ran all out. One minute she was coping and the next she was dozing. She felt a warm cloth on her face, opened her eyes and tried to speak.

"Yes," Aster smiled, "you did, you dozed off like a baby. Good for you. I'll just freshen you up a bit and then I'm going to leave you to nap until your family comes back. You're doing very well, Mrs. Carson. There, I'll just dry off your face and I think I'll put some of this nice cream on it. There's something about bed linen that just seems to suck the moisture from a person's skin."

The next time Sarah opened her eyes, Christine was sitting on a chair beside the bed.

David Morton planted the last of his beans, then went into his lath house to get the small cabbage plants he'd bought at the nursery. They'd been started in a greenhouse and he'd been told he should harden them off before he put them out, so they had spent their nights in the potting shed and been put in the lath house more each day until he'd felt confident he could leave them there, even at night. A week of that and they were as ready as they would ever be to go into the garden.

Every year David planted cabbage. He fully expected that sooner or later his would fail and he'd find clubroot, because it was moving down the street toward him. It had been years since Sarah had been able to grow cabbage and Marco had already said he wasn't planting any this year, he'd had several last season that had grown no bigger than softballs. The three houses in between didn't even plant vegetable gardens, although they were quick enough with their hands out and smiles on their faces whenever anyone had a surplus. Sometimes David dreamed of planting a dozen zucchini vines and flooding the neighbours with them. But then he thought of what happened if you missed one and it split, dropping seeds in the dirt. The following year you'd be buried. He agreed with Sarah, even one zucchini was too many.

Sarah grew the big pumpkins, Bruno grew the artichokes and elephant garlic, David went nuts with corn. He already had his crop-to-be started in his greenhouse, six plants per little peat pot. If it ever warmed up, he'd move them to their waiting space. He'd rototilled a half dozen times, he'd added fertilizer, manure, bone meal and trace elements and worked them into the soil, and at the rate he was spending money, he figured each and every ear of corn he grew would cost him about five bucks. He had early corn, he had mid-season corn, he even had late corn. He had white cobs, he had super-sweet, he had candy corn, he had red corn. David even had blue corn, which he planted in a different place in his yard; he didn't want it cross-pollinating with any of the other kinds because he would keep seed from it and didn't want to lose his blue strain.

There was no spoken agreement. They just trotted back and forth with bags of produce, not so much trading as sharing. There wasn't much in the world could beat a supper of Sarah's baby spuds with Bruno's rhubarb chard, and some of his own French beans. When the spirit moved any of them they'd have meals in someone's backyard, all of them arriving with their favourites. Sarah's mint sauce was unbelievable. Usually they invited Old Annie Daniels to join them, and she'd show up with a dessert fit for any king and a bottle of her homemade rhubarb wine. Some people grew tons of spuds, Old Annie grew rhubarb. "Well," she laughed each time she said it, "the blessed stuff as good as looks after itself, and there's no trouble at all to making jam, pies and wine. And them as loves jam, pies and wine seem to grow every-thing else a body could want."

Annie also grew cabbages the way David wished he could grow them. When he asked her how, she gave him a good ten min-utes on clubroot, maggots, wireworms and white butterfly, then extolled the virtues of a wood stove: that way you had all the wood ash you needed. "I've two patches," she told him, "turn about year by year, and in the one I'm not using, I put my ashes, work 'em in good, water it from time to time, rototill it to keep the weeds away. Not that much'll grow in so much wood ash. Kills off all manner of thing, including the mildew or whatever it is that causes the clubroot."

He'd tried it. He wasn't sure it was the reason he was the only one on the block without any sign of clubroot, but why take chances?

"And don't plant them out so soon," she'd warned. "I wait until about the time the carrot fly is finished. You put them out too soon and it's just inviting trouble."

It was just about impossible to tell what was "too soon." Some years February passed and spring moved in gently, each day just a bit longer, a bit sunnier, a bit warmer. Those years, when the rain fell it fell softly, like Scotch mist, too cheap to really pour. Other years, like this one, you began to wonder if the warm weather was ever going to come or if you were going to have to hold a survey, find out where it was and then drive out to visit it. More bloody rain this spring than a person could put up with! And not soft rain, but hard, driving downpours that turned the ground soggy and drowned or rotted everything put out in it. Cold? A person might as well move to Bracebridge, Ontario, as try to pretend this too would pass.

He finished putting out his cabbages, then went into the house, stripped off his gardening clothes, hung them on the hooks in the mud room, and walked to the shower. It wasn't until he felt the hot spray that he realized how chilled he was. Just sneaks up on you, sometimes. You get out there and get busy and you don't even realize you're one layer of clothing too few.

He stayed in the shower until the water started to cool. That decided it! First thing he was going to do was drive to Cranberry Sheet Metal and see about having a bigger hot water tank installed. Maybe he'd get a trade-in on the one he had, maybe not. If not, he'd keep it, have two of them. He was sick and tired of running out of hot water.

He got dressed and got on his motorbike. Then, as he had promised himself, he drove to check out the hot water tank situation. Fifteen minutes with the specs book and he'd signed on the dotted line. All they had to do was cut into the natural gas line he'd had installed when it went down their street. He hadn't gone to a hot water tank at the time, he'd stayed with his electric one, but better late than never. The one he'd settled on would give twice the amount of hot water with a recovery time of next to nothing.

He felt almost smug when he left the store and drove on to the hospital. He didn't take flowers or chocolates or even a book. He doubted Sarah was in any shape or mood for any of that.

My God, she looked sick. He'd been expecting her to look ill, but not to look like a little old lady who was teetering on her last leg. People like Sarah aren't ever supposed to get on their last leg.

"Da . . . id," she croaked.

"Hello, darling." He leaned over the bed and kissed her cheek. He'd never been so familiar with her before, but he needed that kiss, needed the time to fix his damn face so the shock wouldn't show. "Chris," he nodded, reaching out and shaking her hand. "Rainey." He shook her hand, too, and hoped she wouldn't notice the slight trembling. "How was the trip down?"

"Ghastly," she grinned. "Don't make a fourteen-hour trip with two kids in a pickup truck. Every second or third telephone pole winds up PeePeeVille."

"That's why I like my motorcycle. *Nobody* bums a ride!"

". . .uno?" Sarah managed.

"Bruno's fine, he's looking after your place. Or was, I don't know what's going to happen now that Rainey's here. Sarah, darling, you should have seen him heading down the sidewalk with Chester and a string of cats, all of them tails up, and him with a big plastic owl on a stick." David sat on the edge of the bed and started to spin the story. Well, they'd say, one thing about Dave Morton, he can tell you his grocery list and make it sound hilarious.

Sarah managed a partial smile and David felt as if his heart were chipping at the edges. Dear God in heaven, he started his mental letter, the closest he ever came to a prayer. This is me again. Picture me on both knees, tears on my cheeks, begging you to either let Sarah die or give her back her full smile. I don't care if she winds up needing a wheelchair, I'll buy her one of those motorized ones if need be, but please, Ma'am, if it's all the same to You, let Sarah have her smile back. The rest of us aren't going to be able to stand it if she's left with this pathetic little grimace.

"H—zzy?" Sarah tried. She shook her head impatiently and tried again.

"Busy," Chris translated and Sarah nodded, her eyes glistening with tears.

"Busy enough for a lazy bum like me," and he told her about his garden, his beans, his cabbages. "Tomatoes are started, but they look pretty spindly. I've decided I'll just grow them in the greenhouse this year. Too much like the Arctic outback to put them in the garden and if I keep them in those little pots much longer they'll stunt." Then he talked about work, about how some out-of-town yahoo had thought he'd challenge one of the locals, and words had turned sour so they went outside. "Used the time the mad pack was gone to get the table covers changed and the ashtrays all emptied."

"I think," Lorraine said boldly, "I've always expected you'd wake up one morning and decide to get into a different line of work. I mean, really, bartending?"

"Rainey, honey." He made his tone light and teasing, and passed it off as sincere. "You know I'm not just a bartender, although there's nothing wrong with being one. I'm a table waiter, bouncer, and general all-round factotum par excellence. In my spare time, that is. My real job is writing poetry and playing the guitar. One of these days the world will realize just what a treasure trove of talent they have in me and I'll never have to sling another glass of draft as long as I live."

Sarah made a sound and nobody understood it. She tried again, and this time tears slid down her face. She shook her head, tried a third time, then sighed the sound of heartache.

"We're wearing you out altogether," David said. "So what I'm going to do is bugger off for a while. I'll be back later, my dear. Is there anything I can bring you?"

Sarah didn't try to answer, she just shook her head. David stood up and nodded to Chris, then Lorraine. "If there's anything at all she needs, just let me know, okay?"

". . . iss," Sarah blurted.

"Any time my darling." He leaned over and kissed her forehead, then her cheek. "I'll be back in a couple of hours."

"Guitar!" Sarah said clearly, almost shouting, with a lopsided grimace.

He went into town and paid his phone, hydro and cablevision bills at the credit union. Every day in every way things get more convenient and less personal. Move in the technology and you can lay off everyone who used to work in the telephone company office. Then you can close the office. If someone wants a phone installed, why, there's a number that they can call. Want to pay your phone bill? Mail it in or go to any chartered bank or credit union. But do *not* expect the phone company to connect a human body or face to the voice that comes through the headset. He had photos at home, from the archives, of the BC Tel office in Powell River at the time his grandmother had been supervisor. Banks of boards, with little metal-lined holes, and half a dozen women sitting, number please, thank you, I'm sorry, that number is no longer in service.

Now the workers were no longer in service. Except for the linemen and repairmen, and they seemed to work out of their trucks. Oh well, they hadn't yet got around to putting beer bottles into dispensers, like the ones that spit out cans of pop. They hadn't yet got around to putting a gizmo on the keg and if you wanted a glass of draft you put in a dollar coin, if you wanted a jug of draft you put in five coins, everything automatic. It would come. And if the damn No Smoking by-law passed, they wouldn't even need table waiters to clear off the stuffed ashtrays and replace them with clean ones.

Who knows, maybe they'll make a machine that will listen to the many and various troubles the drunks maundered about: somebody done somebody wrong, who'd have expected it, and so I told the guy, I said, listen buster. The machine might even make the appropriate responses. More it changes the more it stays the same, eh buddy; comes at you from the most unexpected directions, for sure; proper thing, too. Throw in a few uh-huhs and a couple of you-don't-says and the only human you'd need would be the one to take the money to the bank. And if you did it the right way and put in a debit card machine, you wouldn't even need that.

Ah, but then who would vacuum the carpets and clean the toilets?

From the credit union he went to Mitchell Bros and got bacon, some of their nice made-on-premises meat pies, some fruit, a half pound of their cheese, which was the best he'd found, and a loaf of San Francisco–style sourdough bread. They didn't carry the brand of coffee he liked but he could get that at the Wildwood

Store, where he got his free-range farm eggs. He got his milk and cream from the dairy farm. All a person had to do was drive up to the house and there on the porch was a fridge. Open the door, pick what you wanted, put the money in the plastic box and leave your clean empties on the table, or on the floor if the table was full.

It took longer than shopping at a supermarket but he could get almost exactly what he wanted. Anyway, he was mad at the supermarkets ever since they hired some Yankee dude and he invented a contract that would have busted the union and wiped out years of benefits for the workers. When the workers refused to sign, the supermarkets pulled a lockout. Another little benefit of free trade with the fuckin' Yanks. Back to the old harmonization clause. Their social programs were virtually non-existent; a person could wind up bankrupt because of an impacted wisdom tooth and God forbid you'd think to have appendicitis. The chains had stores on both sides of the border, and so the same unions representing the workers. As soon as the Yankee workers started trying to "harmonize" with the Canucks, ho ho ho said Uncle Sam, and he hired some guy at six million a year, plus bonuses, stock options and profit wotzit that added up to thirteen million last year, and the buzzard turned around and tried to take away the extended sick benefits and the pharmacare insurance.

The fact was, they wanted to close down the current stores and open new ones, non-union ones, and hire new staff at minimum wage. Just like in the good old Hew Hess Hay. It's another way of waging war: invasion without guns. But if you told any of those nice people their government was an imperialist power they would be shocked, offended and deeply hurt.

Ta ra ra boom de-ay, down in the yew ess ay, we take their pay away, and skin them every day. A song for every occasion.

Christine parked at one side of the garage, leaving plenty of room for Rainey and the big pickup. After all, Rainey would be staying here, and with any luck at all Chris would be gone right after supper. Kids are nice, especially in theory; in practice they grate after a while, and the big difference between parents and non-parents is that the kids have so ground down the parents that they don't notice the stuff that drives non-parents halfway over the top.

But if you didn't know what she knew, or feel what she felt, you could be forgiven for thinking some part of you was melting. Bruno was up on the ladder and Lin was working on the bottom of the house, both of them busy, Lin with a wire brush and Bruno with some kind of attachment fitted to his electric drill. The lawn was confetti'd with bits of dried paint, and Lin's hair seemed to have changed colour, the dust drifting from the drill attachment making him seem preternaturally snowy-haired. He looked over at her and grinned, waving his wire brush. Chris waved back and took the huge package of chicken thighs with her to the house. Minnie was running in circles, hyper and excited and foolish, a stick in her teeth. Chris bent over and grabbed the stick and gave it a shake, and the terrier dropped her hind end, braced herself and half growled. Chris lifted the stick, the dog hanging off it, and Lin laughed. Even Bruno took time from what he was doing to watch, smiling that little half smile that made you wonder what was really going on in his head.

Minnie let go and dropped to the ground, and Chris heaved the stick as far to the back of the yard as she could. The dog was off after it, yapping, but not loudly and not hysterically. Lin must have played the legs off her before he got involved with the wire brush.

If the weather was nicer she'd have fired up the barbecue, but the wind was chilly and the ground cold, so she got out the big lasagna pan and lined the thighs up in it, slathered with sauce. What else—God, what do kids like to eat? Pizza, popcorn, what else? Well, they'd have to resign themselves to mashed spuds. There would be a sort of gravy from the chicken and sauce, and if that didn't satisfy their little souls they could put dabs of margarine on it. The sauce was going to be red, or at least reddish, so she should have a dark green vegetable. She didn't know if the kids would eat broccoli or kick up a stink so she decided to pass on it and go for green beans instead. What else? Where in hell was Rainey, anyway, she should be the one worrying about would the kids eat or wouldn't they!

Peanut butter, someone would have to be sure to get a big jar of that. Crunchy, probably. Someone had told her there hadn't even *been* peanut butter until 1949, that it was George Washington Carver who invented the stuff. He was trying to find ways to market what was, essentially, the only thing the poor sharecroppers could grow in soil depleted by generations of cotton. How many tons of goober peas went into peanut butter every year? And were they tons (two thousand pounds), or tonnes (two thousand five hundred pounds), what her dad had called tons or long tons? And what, pray tell, had kept body and soul together prior to peanut butter? What had nourished the under-fifteens of the nation before Dr. Carver got to work? What other things now considered to be staples were, more or less, "new"? Yogurt. She couldn't remember ever seeing, hearing of or tasting yogurt as a child. Now there were entire shelves of it in the supermarket.

So. Chicken, spuds, green beans and . . . what? A salad, probably. She'd be willing to bet five bucks Sarah had all the fixings in the fridge. Dessert? Oh, pee on it, they can have ice cream and canned fruit. She'd better check to see if there was ice cream in the freezer. There was sure to be canned fruit, and plenty of it, Sarah spent every September putting so much stuff in jars it was a wonder that the floor didn't give way under the weight of it all. Probably had canned peaches or plums from three years ago.

And if they were still hungry they could have sourdough bread and homemade jam. Minnie would be fine with some spuds, sauce and the skin off the chicken pieces.

Dear God in heaven don't let her die. Please please please please *please* don't let her die, or be crippled to the point she would rather die than live like that. Please God please God please God don't let me start crying!

3

David Morton sat on the floor, chin resting on his jackknifed knees, his arms wrapped around his legs, fists clenched together. The shower spray pummeled his head and ran over his face, sluicing away his tears as fast as they came. He didn't sob, he didn't sniffle, he just sat there, tears falling and mixing with the cooling water. Soon the water was cold, and still he sat there, mourning for Sarah, fighting the surge of emotion that had overwhelmed him since he had caught sight of Rainey. Maybe the next time someone started talking about how important, how vital it was that we all strive to be polite and civilized and soft-spoken and considerate at all times, maybe David would be none of the above and speak out, loudly, and tell the good folk what happens when you do that. God knows Wayne McKye could never have been accused of the mildest sign of civilized behaviour and yet he was the one Rainey ran off with, leaving David feeling as if all the sunrises and sunsets for the rest of his life had paled for the loss. Of course, one isn't supposed to display such emotion, not publicly anyway, or one becomes an object of ridicule: the scorned geek, the ditched jerk, the lovelorn lugan, the nerd.

So he'd gone about his life the way everyone expected him to. Off to university, got the education, the degrees, and came back home, the family pride and joy. Except with his training the only real job available to him was at the pulp mill. He knew when he started working there he would hate it, and he did. Maybe it wasn't the oldest but surely it was the filthiest pulp mill in the nation, and David had the education to know what the numbers meant, what the nature of the strange new combinations of chemicals meant to all manner of life, and what's more, he knew that the rest of them knew, too, and still they continued to mouth the company line, bafflegabbing the occasional reporter, being paid very good money to do their utmost to convince the rest of the population that "toxic" didn't mean what it seemed to mean, and that progress was the be-all and end-all.

He stuck it out. It was what he was trained for, wasn't it? What else would he do with himself and all that education? And the money was unbelievably good. He tried to move on in his life, making friends and dating other women, but none of them were Rainey. He was involved in what anyone would call serious relationships, he was sexual, and he enjoyed it, except for the nagging thought that it would be more, and better, and magical if only it was Rainey.

And one morning he couldn't do it any more. He got out of bed, same as usual. He had his morning coffee, same as usual. He showered, shaved, even began to get dressed, and then he absolutely could not make himself go out the back door, get in his car, drive to the pulp mill and report to work. So he phoned in, said he was ill and stayed home.

He found he was able to leave the house to go to the supermarket for food, he could go to the beach to watch the seals, he could take a walk along the paths that led from one lake to another. He could ride his bicycle and go to the rec centre to swim or work out in the weight room, or have a sauna or sit in the hot tub. He could go for a pizza, then to a movie. He could move around with no problem at all right up until the time he was supposed to take himself to work. And then it was physically impossible to get his feet to obey him.

He went to his doctor and got anti-depressants. He didn't think he was depressed, but he took them. Why not? You never know. He even went to see the local shrink, a disciple of Freud who probed for severe childhood trauma and seemed disappointed when he didn't find anything too traumatic.

And one day David wrote his letter of resignation. That day he had no trouble at all going out the door, getting in his car and driving to the pulp mill. And he had no trouble hand-delivering his carefully worded version of Take this job and shove it.

David had learned to play the guitar as a teenager. Who hadn't? He could chord, he could even play along with recordings of "Stairway to Heaven," "House of the Rising Sun" and "Deep Purple." He'd played at parties in university, but hadn't touched the instrument for months. The evening of the day he quit the mill for good, he got out his guitar and sat on his little porch for hours, practising, playing bars of music he had never heard before, snatches of sound that came from some place inside him, some place he had never explored.

A week later he got a job slinging beer in the pub. The money was a fraction of what he'd made in the mill, but plenty good enough for a comfortable living. His social life actually improved, his circle of acquaintances widened, the women moving in and out of his life were fun. He even convinced himself he'd "gotten over" Rainey, and began to consider the possibility that Rainey herself hadn't been the real reason for his disillusionment. After all, everyone gets dumped.

Except here was Rainey, back again, and here was David, blown apart, sitting on the floor of the shower stall, terrified by what had happened to Sarah, weeping for her, for Rainey, for himself, probably for other reasons he couldn't identify. Maybe he should go get some more of those anti-depressants, live his life zonked on pharmaceuticals.

Or he could just sit here until he developed pneumonia and died of it. They'd find him eventually, a pathetic huddled blue ball. Perhaps he'd have fallen over, blocked the drain and flooded the house. When the water started to pour out the windows and flood the yard, the sidewalk, the very street, they'd come looking to find out why and there he'd be, curled up like a booby, with nobody to blame but his own silly damn self.

What was the Springsteen song? Get over it? Yes, indeed, David, get over it!

Bruno came down off the ladder, his calves aching. Too old to spend an entire day perched on a narrow rung. Too old by far. But the house was as good as ready, and no doubt about it, the boy Lin had been a help. At least the boy knew he didn't know anything and was willing to be told what needed doing. Willing, too, to give it a try, which was more than could be said for some.

"You did a very good job, boy," he said.

Lin looked up at him and for a moment, Bruno felt shy.

"Can I help tomorrow?"

"Yes." Bruno began to wind up the extension cord. Lin immediately started helping, putting the wire brush in the cardboard box with the small paint chisel, the coarse sandpaper and other gear. "Tomorrow, if the weather favours us, we'll start the undercoat. We can go in to the rental place and get everything we need to spray paint the house. Probably take three days. Undercoat first. Then several coats of paint. Then the sealer."

"What about the windows?"

"Good boy." He smiled and Lin blushed. "I always cover the glass with newspaper or paint protector sheeting. And when the house is done, we can do the trim around the windows by hand, with brushes and rollers."

"Do people do this for work?"

"Yes, they do. Why, you going to be a house painter?"

"Probably not. It's hard work."

"You want a soft job?"

"I want to be Rapattack and jump out of airplanes to fight fires."

"Excellent choice."

The kind of choice he'd make himself if he were fifty or sixty years younger. Live life on the edge as long as you can, soon enough the arthritis will slow you down.

Sometimes, especially after a conversation with David, Bruno felt as if he wanted to atone for all those things in his past the nice people of his neighbourhood knew nothing about and, with luck, would never learn about. He daydreamed of going over the border to the US of A, where a person could buy just about any weapon of destruction the mind could imagine as easily as buying a case of beer or a new bicycle for the grandchild. Bruno would get some heat-seeking rockets. Stand on the hill above the mill, aim in the direction of the massive sky-scraping chimneys belching smoke, steam and waves of raw heat, then let fire. He could envision the rocket: slim, deadly, phallic, trailing a length of flame, rising up, finding the heat, following it down, down, into the dark maw of the stacks, and then *whump*, and the place would crumble.

Maybe then Bruno would be able to stop punishing himself for all those things that had seemed normal, natural, even appropriate at the time, things that would cause his neighbours to abandon him as a friend and spit on him when he walked past them. Better to jump out of airplanes and put out forest fires than wave the flag and commit obscenity in the name of patriotism.

"Better wear old clothes," he warned Lin. "We'll get covered with speckles of paint."

Rainey got back in time to apologize for being late, then sat at the table and poked at her food as if she were trying to eat cardboard.

"You okay?" Chris asked, on the verge of feeling insulted. You work to get a good meal together and people don't even have the respect to sit down and pack some of it away and at least pretend to enjoy it! God, Rainey, and wasn't it ever thus with you.

"Not really." Rainey blinked rapidly but managed a small smile. "I'm hungry, really I am, Chrissy, it's just . . . I'm too upset to swallow. All that damn driving and then . . . Momma, and . . . I'll get a grip, though, I promise."

"Please pass the sourdough bread," Bruno said, his voice calm and soothing. "Very good meal, Chrissy. You have your mother's touch with chicken. Sarah can take an old laying hen and turn it into a banquet."

"Thank you, Mr. Radonovich. There's plenty more."

"I believe I could," he smiled at her. "Perhaps after all these years we know each other well enough you could stop the Mr. Radonovich and call me Bruno."

"I don't know if I can," she admitted. "You've always been Mister."

The phone rang shrilly. Chrissy jumped up to answer it, her heart leaping to her throat. What if Sarah had taken a bad turn, what if they were phoning to say . . .

Rainey got it first. "Hello?" Chris sat back down, eyes wide, watching for any change in her sister's expression. And there was a change. Rainey suddenly looked firm, and grounded, and very sure of herself, determined and strong. "Yes, Wayne."

"Lin," Chris said, tapping him on the arm. "Run into Gran's bedroom and get the walkabout phone and take it to your mother. She might want some privacy for this call."

"Yes, I did. They're fine, they slept most of the way down and the trip was no worse than I expected. Mom? She's holding her own, and that's about all we can say right now. Could you hang on a half a minute? I'll get the other phone and . . . oh, here's Lin with it now."

She took the walkabout phone, hung up the old wall phone and left the kitchen.

"I hope Dad's not mad," Sally whispered. "He doesn't like anybody else to drive his truck."

"Too bad." Lin sat down and started eating again. "We couldn't have come down in Mom's old wreck, it would've fallen apart."

"But he might be mad."

"Nah. And if he is, so what? He's not here."

Wayne sounded subdued, even weary. At other times that tone of voice had melted Rainey, filled her with something close to pity, or a twisted compassion. And now, the flat out of it was she didn't care. If he was hungover, he had done it to himself. If he was tired, same thing. If he felt remorse, too late for that.

"So, uh, you, uh, had enough money?"

"Plenty," she agreed. "I did something I haven't done before,

I went into your wallet. Found enough there to take us to Alaska if we'd had to go there."

"Yeah. Well, uh, how long do you think you're going to be down there? Or isn't there any way to tell?"

"Right now we don't know how long this thing with Mom is going to take or how it's going to turn out. But I can tell you how long we'll all be down here, Wayne. We're not going back."

"Ah, Christ, Rainey, don't—"

"Don't, Wayne. You know and I know that you know what I know. I saw the rubbers in your wallet and I happened to notice the serial numbers on the money."

"I can explain."

"You think you can explain the black hole theory, but you can't. You can talk the birds out of the trees only so many times, and then it doesn't work any more."

"You don't just walk away from—"

"I didn't walk. I drove."

"In *my* truck!"

"Ours. Any lawyer will tell you that."

"Lawyer? If you think I'm spending good money to hire a lawyer you're out of your damn mind!"

"Fine then, don't. I've had lots of time to think about this, and here's what I've come up with: you can have everything up there and I'll keep what I've got down here. Seems fair to me."

"I'll fight you for the kids."

"Try."

"Rainey, listen—"

"Wayne, don't. Okay? Just don't bother. Instead of doing what everyone else does and fighting like ferrets until everything is ripped to shreds, including the memories of fun, and good times, and happiness, why don't we just tell each other the truth? Be a nice change for both of us, don't you think? We both know it's been going nowhere at all for a long time. So I'll take full responsibility for the kids. I do expect you to pay some child support but if you don't, I'm not getting into it with you over money, it'll be your shame and everyone will know you aren't supporting them.

You like it up there, I hate it. You like having pit bull dogs and a yard full of non-rolling stock, I hate it. I don't hate you yet, but it could happen. So the kids and I will stay here with what we brought with us and you can have all the rest. The cars, the dogs, the boats, the trailers, the motel, the fifteen acres of land, the whole shiteree. And instead of fighting we'll each of us take the time to calm down. When we get to the point where we can talk, really talk, fine. We'll do that. But no more bullshit from either of us."

"Rainey—"

"Why hang on, Wayne? Why cling to something you don't want any more, anyway? Think about it. You have more of a life *away* from 'us' than you have with us. And we have more away from you than including you. So let's do what each of us really, privately wants to do anyway."

"You don't even sound like you! You sound like someone else."

"I've been that someone else for a long time, but I don't think I knew it any more than you did."

"So your mind's made up?"

"So is yours, Wayne. You'll know that when you've had time to sit down by yourself and think about it. We know each other inside and out, right?"

"Yeah. Yeah, we do."

"Okay. It's not a hockey game, you aren't going to get ten minutes in the penalty box for not fighting me every inch of the way."

"I'm not going to fight you, Rainey. But, Jesus, a *note?* You couldn't *talk?*"

"I'm an awful coward, you know that." She laughed. "Chicken licken, remember?"

"There isn't a pit bull in the pen couldn't take lessons, and you know it," and he laughed, too.

"I'm going to hang up now, Wayne."

"Okay. Uh, Raine? I'll, uh, phone you in a coupla days, okay?"

"Sure. I'll give your love to the kids."

"Yeah. Uh, tell them, well, hell, you know what to tell them."

She went back to the table, and even though her supper was cold, she sat down and ate.

"Everything okay?" Chris asked.

"Hell no," Rainey said easily. "Nothing is the least little bit okay. My life's a bigger mess than it's ever been, I have absolutely no idea what to do about anything you might want to name, and you know something? I don't care."

"If I can help in any way . . ."

"Oh, you can be sure I'll ask! Haven't I always?"

"So who wants to come out in the boat with me?" Bruno asked suddenly.

"Me!" Lin nearly jumped from his chair.

"Me!" Sally agreed.

"Fine. Clear the table and do the dishes while I get the gear loaded. Your momma and your auntie will want to go see your grandma, so let's clear the way for them."

"You're not coming up?" Chris asked.

"Christine, my dear, if I was to go up there right now I'd take one look at darling Sarah and I'd burst into tears. Better I not intrude on her until I get myself under control. The painting I can handle, the children I can handle, but seeing Sarah the way she was when I found her, that I cannot handle."

He stifled the memories of things he had handled in his youth, things he had never discussed with anybody, not his wife, not the children, all of them, now, back in the old country, hating him even if they didn't hate the money that arrived every month. Marta wasn't well, he wasn't even sure she was still alive, and he hadn't seen his son or daughter since they were young. They didn't even write. And as for the victims, no way to atone, no way to apologize, no way at all to clean and tidy the past, make it presentable, make it acceptable, make it anything but what it was. He'd handled some outrageous and disgusting things.

But he couldn't handle the feelings that had surged up in him when he saw Sarah lying on that cold earth. He'd seen dead bodies on cold earth, he'd seen dead bodies on warm earth, lying in the mud, on the grass, and none of it had bothered him. But seeing Sarah, lying in her garden helpless and near death, ripped him apart inside.

He left the house, went out to the garage, checked on all of Sarah's damn cats and made sure they had food and water. He fed Chester and rubbed the soft skin behind the porker's ears, then walked down the sidewalk to his own place. He couldn't believe how chilly it was. Stupid old fool, to take two children out in an open aluminum boat in weather like this! So what if the sea was flat and calm, so what if there was no wind blowing? It was cold enough to do the proverbial to the brass monkey. And it was supposed to be springtime? Next thing you knew he'd be crocheting itty-bitty teeny-weeny afghans for the snowdrops and daffodils.

But he loaded his big tackle box into his small pickup, put in extra rods and made sure he had life jackets for each of them. He made a big thermos of hot chocolate, added a full package of Dad's cookies, pulled on his Cowichan vest and his windproof jacket, and drove the bit of distance over to Sarah's place.

Sally and Lin ran out of the house dressed for the Arctic. Of course Chris would know exactly how cold it was going to be! Smart woman, Chris. Strange woman. Well, maybe not strange as in weird, but different.

The kids were too excited to talk, and Bruno was glad of that. He got them to get out of the truck and stand out of the way, watching, as he backed down the boat ramp, then slid the boat off the trailer into the water. He tied the boat to a rock, drove back up the ramp, parked the truck and trailer well clear of the road. He carried the rods, tackle box, thermos, cookies, life jackets and the big waterproof flashlight down to the boat. Then he beckoned the kids to come over.

"On with the life jackets."

"Aunt Chris told us," Sally confided. "And said if we didn't she'd drown us herself. But she wouldn't, she was just saying it."

"And we're supposed to sit down and stay sat."

"Right. So in you go. Ladies first. Pull your toque down over your ears, girl, or they'll freeze and fall off. That's what happened to the seals, that's why they don't have any ears you can see. Froze and fell off."

"Yes, sir," she agreed, not believing a word of it.

They sat where they'd been told, they didn't squirm, wiggle or try to stand up. They did everything the way they were supposed to and Bruno knew they wanted to impress him so they could come out again.

"We aren't going to try for salmon," he told them. "Cod is what we're after."

"What's the difference?" Sally asked.

"Ah, I forget, you're not coast-raised. Well, the difference in the way you fish for them is as big as the difference in how they look and taste," and he was talking to them about cod fish, where they liked to feed, how they bred, the different kinds of them. "What we'll do is mooch." He handed her a tissue and she smiled thanks, dabbing at her nose. He demonstrated mooching while describing how they would troll for salmon, one day soon when it was a bit warmer, too cold for trolling now, the wind would freeze their fingers off.

Sarah was asleep when Chris and Rainey walked into her room. They sat quietly, watching the erratic rise and fall of her chest, feeling—something—in the room, something oppressive, something threatening. Chris almost imagined she could see the grim reaper: black cowl, huge scythe, red-rimmed eyes, body hidden in the dark folds of his drag, lurking in the corner, waiting, waiting for a chance to snatch Sarah's soul and take her from them.

The image was so strong, so upsetting that she left the room in search of something to read. Down the hall was a large room with a wide-screen colour TV, a fridge, an electric kettle and all the fixings for tea and coffee. And a wheeled cart loaded with paperbacks and magazines. She chose a couple of *Maclean's* and an *Equinox* and took them back to Sarah's room with her. She held the magazines out and Rainey chose the *Equinox*. Well, of course.

Chris was partway into an uninspired article about national

unity and the need for all Canadians to redefine themselves in the hope Quebec might condescend to remain part of the country, when Sarah wakened, coughing. Chris dropped the magazine, left her chair, put her arm behind Sarah's shoulders and raised her. The coughing continued. Rainey turned pale, the call buzzer in her hand. Then, blessedly, someone was there and so smoothly it seemed easy, she had—something—in Sarah's mouth, partway down her throat, siphoning—something—and the coughing subsided.

"There you are, love," the nurse said softly. "And aren't we getting slick at this."

"Lick," Sarah agreed, sounding so calm that Chris could have shrieked.

"If you're awake, maybe we'll just roust you out of bed and into your chair?"

"Air," Sarah nodded.

"Maybe your daughters would like to take you down to the lounge. They say a change of scenery does a person the world of good. And while you're gone, we'll get your bed changed and freshened."

"Osh?"

"Wash? Hands and face or all over"

"A . . . o'er."

"Wonderful idea. There's nobody in the tub right now, we can get you in there no trouble at all."

"We'll stay with her," Rainey offered. The nurse looked at her, then looked at Sarah, who nodded.

"You're sure?" the nurse asked. Sarah nodded. "Fine, then, wonderful. Some people are very shy about being seen in the tub by their nearest and dearest. Doesn't seem to bother them if it's us, virtual strangers. But . . . glad to see you've got better sense."

She looked so frail without her nightgown. Chris supported the affected side until the nurses somehow slid in and shifted her to the sidelines. She supposed they weren't allowed to let family do things like that. What if something happened and the patient wound up dropped to the tile floor by an unskilled relative?

"Unnafu," Sarah gurgled.

"Nothing like it," the nurse agreed. "You just let the water work its magic and they'll get your bed fixed and fresh. What say I rinse your hair? Or would you rather a complete special-treatment pamper and spoil-you shampoo?"

"I 'ot?"

"Why not, for sure. Go for the gusto, right?"

How could they understand the halting speech so well? Did they hear so much of it that the noises became another language, stripped of all surplus, honed down to mere hints? "I 'ot"? How long do you have to work with the afflicted before "I 'ot" becomes a valiant attempt at a joke?

Sarah was back in bed, wearing a fresh pale blue dicky gown, when David arrived with his guitar.

"Your every wish is my command, my love," he said, and Sarah laughed. Now how in hell had stodgy David Morton known what Sarah meant when she had, after so much effort, managed to blurt out "guitar"?

The very first song David played was "Bridge Over Troubled Water." Sarah closed her eyes and listened, getting answers to questions she had not yet formed in her mind, let alone struggled to put into garbled words. Of all the work and kinds of work she had done in her life, nothing had been more exhausting than trying to speak now. She had to use her entire body, inside and out, to force out even the raw burst of sound that meant thank you. Her tongue felt so thick it seemed to fill her mouth, and part of her face was numb, more numb than after the dentist had frozen it. Even her throat seemed thick, stiff and swollen.

David played the song through once, then started at the beginning again, and this time he sang the words, softly and clearly. Sarah had been quite sure for years that if he had wanted to make the effort and jump through the hoops, he could be a full-time professional, with tapes and CDs and, who could tell, maybe star status. She'd told him that and he'd just smiled and said even Jessie Winchester didn't seem too interested in hoop-jumping.

Chris wasn't surprised at the quality of David's performance.

She had heard him often, had even arranged to have one of the local sound engineers from the cablevision outlet set up his equipment and tape him singing. The tapes sold locally, enough to cover the cost of the studio rental and put a few dollars in the pockets of the friends who had helped. She had a copy at home, one at Annwyn's place and another on the *Sealkie*.

Rainey was surprised. She hadn't heard David sing for years. He looked as she would have expected him to look: the years had made predictable changes in the lines in his face, but he was broader across the shoulders than she would have expected, and his forearms looked as if he wrestled a chain saw instead of trays of pitchers and beer mugs. His hands looked ready to reach out and grip ax handles, but they weren't knob-knuckled or callused, and his short-clipped fingernails were clean, no sign of engine oil or the dirt of manual toil. When they'd gone together in high school, he would change the words of the old song and sing, "I'm in heaven when I see you smile, smile for me, my Lorraine." She wondered who he sang for now. Whoever it was, she hoped they appreciated it more than she had. David had seemed comfortable, safe and dull, like a worn pair of slippers. But Wayne—well, it had never been dull! Wayne was challenge and danger and excitement, not slippers but bright red dancing shoes with high spike heels.

But that was when she was seventeen, puberty hard upon her and no brighter than anyone else at the same age. And those days were long gone.

The next morning, Rainey enrolled the kids in school. For the first time Lin wasn't at the same school as Sally. He was still in elementary, and Sally was assigned to the middle school.

"It's not fair!" Lin looked about ready to turn on the faucet. "We didn't even bring our bikes with us and she gets to take a bus and I'll have to walk!"

"Put a sock in it, Lin," Rainey said calmly.

He looked at her and for a moment she expected him to go into the screeching fits he had perfected when he was about four years old. "It's got nothing at all to do with fair or not fair. She's older than you are, she's in a higher grade, and in this town that means middle school."

How do we manage to love our kids so much we spoil them rotten and turn them into the kind of little horrors give other kids the pip and make adults want to slap them?

They went out for school supplies and it took less than half an hour, but it took money, and there wasn't much left. She took them to Mr. Mike's for lunch, then up to the hospital for a brief visit with their grandmother before driving them home and leaving them in front of the TV.

Then Rainey drove back to town to the Human Resources to do what she had known she would have to do ever since she saw the condoms in her husband's wallet. It was one of the hardest things she had ever had to do in her life, even harder than packing their stuff into the back of Wayne's pickup and driving away from him, from their life together and all the years they'd shared. The leaving had seemed like separation; this other seemed like divorce. Rainey put herself and her kids on welfare.

She felt changed, in a way she could only hope and pray didn't show to the rest of the world. Easy to talk about it, even make jokes about it, but when she had signed on the appropriate line she felt as if she was agreeing to become someone she had never before met.

Sarah was terrified. She wasn't afraid of falling, or slipping, or landing on the floor, she was petrified she'd take some of the nurses with her, injure somebody, maybe seriously enough they'd have to take time off work. Or have a go-round with Workers' Compensation, which Sarah figured was a deal between the big bosses and the government, a scheme to keep workers from suing after they were crippled for life by sloppiness and stinginess and unsafe practices.

When she confessed her fear to young Annie, she was enfolded in a warm hug. "Oh, you dear dear soul," Annwyn whispered. "Not to worry, my fine old woman, not to worry."

But Sarah worried. Right up until David and Bruno walked in, all smiles and smelling of fresh air and fresh-clipped grass.

"Well, my sweetheart." David kissed her on the cheek, several times. "We're here to get you mobile."

"Very pleased to see you looking so well," Bruno said formally.

"Ih oo h'ink I ook wll oo ihn tttrbble," she said, pretending not to know how garbled she sounded.

"In trouble? Oh no, my dear, *you* are the one in trouble, no more lying in bed pretending you're the Queen Mom Of All."

"Annwyn told us you were worried you'd cripple her." Bruno managed a slight smile. "So we're here to dare you to try to cripple *us*. We're a pair of very strong fellows, you know."

"And stalwart to the very end," David agreed.

They found a walker and brought it back to Sarah's room, accompanied by an RN and a Practical. Sarah swung her legs over the edge of the bed and waited for the Practical to put her slippers on her feet and her bathrobe on to cover the back of her where the dicky shirt didn't close, then she pushed her hair back from her face with her good hand.

"Hur ee go," she blurted.

"Here we go," Bruno agreed.

Her dumb leg seemed ready and willing to hold her up; it was getting the stupid thing to take a step was the hard part. The walker was no help at all: they're designed to be used by someone with two good arms and hands, and Sarah couldn't quite see herself dangling from the frame by one hand, like Bonzo in his metal gym. She gave her good arm to Bruno and let David grasp the dumb one. After all, David was years younger and much less brittle.

She couldn't remember when she'd had to work so hard. Not in years, certainly. They made it down the hall to the nurses' station and then Sarah knew there was no way in heaven or hell she would manage the walk back.

"Hooped," she managed. She meant pooped, but hooped seemed to fit, too, and certainly they understood. The Practical grabbed a wheelchair and slid it into place, Bruno and David lowered her, and while Sarah caught her breath and tried to collect her wits, the Practical had the foot supports in place. "Oof," Sarah sighed.

"Want to go back to bed, or would you like a small tour of the outside of the place?"

"Rrrlly?"

"Really."

"I'll get a blanket." The Practical moved off, having decided Sarah would want to go. Sarah didn't, really, but everyone was so willing to go to so much trouble it seemed the least she could do was go along with them.

They went twice around the hospital, following the cement path past the beds of tulips, the displays of perfumed hyacinth. Forsythia bushes were in blossom, the clouds of yellow flowers catching the sunlight and glowing brightly. Sarah thought of her garden at home and her eyes flooded with tears. She wiped at her face and Bruno and David pretended they hadn't seen.

The breeze was steady but not cold, and spring songs were being sung by birds she couldn't see. In the distance somebody's dog yapped. It sounded like a small one. Children's voices rang clear and she pictured them playing with the little dog, imagined them throwing a ball for the dog to chase, barking happily.

Sarah was dozing when they pushed the chair back through the automatic doors and across the lobby to the elevator. She came awake when the elevator let them off on her floor. "Eeepy," she managed.

"You've done a full day's work." David patted her cheek gently.

Bruno watched and was filled with envy like he hadn't felt since he was sixteen and the prettiest girl in town was two years older, with more suitors than ducks in a pond. And she didn't know Bruno even existed.

Sarah managed to help heave herself out of the wheelchair but they had to pretty much lift her into bed. She felt she should apologize but knew they didn't think she had anything to apologize for, and would say so.

She tried to stay awake, she tried to visit, but oh God she was weary. She didn't even hear them leave.

Bruno didn't speak on the way home and David didn't expect him to. They were comfortable with the silence, and when they got back to David's place and the car was parked, David felt as if he had come to know Bruno better during the ten-minute silent drive than he'd done in all the years they had lived on the same street, practically side-by-each.

"She's going to make it, Bruno," David said quietly.

Bruno nodded.

"And if you've got any sense at all, old man," David dared, "you'll stop being such a formal stick and let the woman know you're madly in love with her."

"I didn't know it showed." Bruno felt his face going dark red, burning.

"Of course it does. It has for years."

Sarah wakened slowly. At first she had no idea where she was. Then she knew that it hadn't been a dream, none of it had, she wouldn't wake up and find it gone, it was real and it was worse than a nightmare. Her heart quickened. She almost yelled for help, then she grabbed the shattered bits of her own nerves and made herself calm down. She tried to sit up but at first she couldn't. So she grabbed the covers with her good hand, and used them to pull herself. She squirmed her butt, pushed with her good leg, got herself half-propped against the head of the bed, enough she could reach for her call bell and push it.

Annwyn came in, smiling, saw Sarah kilter-tilted awkwardly and hurried over to her. "Oh, my dear woman," she said, her voice as sweet as yam pie. "Here, just put your arm around me and hold on tight, I'll get you squared away in a minute."

"I nnneed," Sarah said slowly, but understandably, "a rrrope."

"A rope? To lasso a nurse?"

"Tttie to foot of bed. Hhhhaul me *uuupp*."

"What a wonderful idea! They've got a frame that goes over the bed, with a bit of a trapeze swing hangs down. It would work better than a rope. You could grab it and hoist yourself . . . you're a genius."

Annwyn raised the head of the bed, rearranged Sarah's pillows and got her settled in place, then brought a basin of hot water, a face cloth and Sarah's soap. She spread a towel over the bedclothes, and handed Sarah the wet, soapy cloth. Sarah washed her face, her neck and her dumb arm, then stared at her good arm. Annwyn reached for the cloth but Sarah didn't see. She lowered her head, grabbed the cloth in her teeth and managed to wipe it on her good arm. Annwyn said nothing, didn't praise her or let on she had noticed. She waited until Sarah dropped the cloth into the water.

"Would you like a bit of scotch broth?" she asked.

"Ppplease. In cup."

"Wonderful. I can turn on your TV if you want."

"No." Sarah lifted her dumb arm. "Wwork to do."

She sat in bed, holding her mug of soup in her good hand, sipping it and savouring the taste while staring at her dumb hand. She thought of her fingers, of the joints, bones, muscles, of how everything hooked up with everything else, and she stared at the red, white and blue ball that she was supposed to be squeezing and tried to remember how squeezing felt, and she tried to get her fingers to squeeze the ball. Nothing.

When her mug was empty she put it on the table and leaned back against her pillows. She was more tired than if she'd spent the afternoon spading in her garden. Why should she be tired? She'd had a nap, and all she'd done since then was stare at herself. But she was tired, no doubt about it. Even her dumb arm was tired. The muscles up near her shoulder practically ached.

She jerked with shock. She reached for her buzzer, pressed it, held it down, demandingly. Annwyn arrived at a run, her face tight with concern. Sarah tried to speak and all that came out was a babble. Finally she took a deep breath, reached up, touched her shoulder, felt her hand. "I *fffeeel!*" she crowed in triumph. And then she burst into tears.

"Come to me," Annwyn soothed, and she sat on the bed, holding Sarah tight, stroking her back, whispering in her ear. "Such a good old woman," Wee Annie crooned, "such a good brave old woman."

Annie Daniels' scalloped potatoes smelled almost as good as they tasted. Sarah almost started crying again as she ate. Old Annie smiled and nodded, sipping her tea. She ate her own supper and chatted, and when Sarah couldn't hold another bite, Annie tidied up the plates and cups, packed everything in the cardboard box in which she'd brought it, then got two water glasses and poured generously from a bottle she had brought.

"Nothing to finish off a meal like a good sip of huckleberry wine," she said, handing a glass to Sarah. "Remember our summer days? Out with the empty ice cream buckets, going from bush to bush, busy busy and nattering on about everything?"

"Ppppies!" Sarah blurted.

"Oh, the pies. You make a fine pie, Sarah. I never did learn to make crust like you."

Sarah sipped, licked her lips, sipped again, then stared hard at Annie.

"What, then?" Annie asked slyly.

"Nnnot sss'mer."

"Smer? What's smer?"

"Sss-*uuhh*-mer."

"Summer? Not summer? No, love, it's the following springtime. And a damn cold one at that."

"Th'ss wine not l'st—*lahst* sss-uh-mer."

"Is it not? You know what they say, when a body gets that expert it has to be because she spends all her time tippling."

"Not."

"You're right. It's from four years ago. To celebrate." She leaned over and patted Sarah's dumb hand. "When Annwyn told me you were here I got so cold I had to climb into a hot tub of water to keep from perishing. I don't have many friends. The thought of losing you was awful. Then they wouldn't let me come up to see you. Oh, I know, I could have phoned Chris or Rainey, but they aren't *you*, and it was *you* I wanted to see. When Annwyn finally said you could have a few visitors, well, I got the four-year-old out. I've been saving it for a special occasion, and this is exactly that. Now drink up, it'll do you the world of good. It's summertime, old gal, one entire summer, distilled and aged and full of what's good for what ails you."

Sarah nodded and drank some wine. Then some more. By the time Old Annie had left with her box of dishes and leftovers, Sarah was tiddly enough to giggle. When Annwyn came in to check on her, Sarah was glaring at her dumb hand, with the striped ball taped in place. Even from the doorway Annwyn could tell Sarah's fingers were twitching.

"Look," Sarah managed. "Move."

"Such a pair if ever I saw one," Wee Annie teased. "Drinking and carrying on, stuffing your faces and probably telling filthy jokes. If I find cigar butts under your bed I won't be surprised. And I suppose she's left you a bottle or two hidden under the mattress or somewhere."

"Tired," Sarah sagged.

"I'm sure you are. Here, love, finish your wine. Then you have yourself a little nap. It's only eight, you can snooze for an hour or two before bedtime rounds. I'll turn your light down a bit and I'll be back in time to get you all cleaned up for nighttime."

Chris checked the *Sealkie* and poured a half pint of homogenized milk into the enamel bowl on deck. Sally watched every move. "Why'd you put down milk?" she asked.

"Well, there's cats live on the docks," Chris told her. "And I don't want rats on my boat. So if I put milk down for the cats, maybe they'll keep away the rats."

"You could use poison."

"I could, but this boat fishes for food. You want rat poison near food? What if a rat ate the poison, then lived long enough to get into the prawn hold? What if it shit poisoned shit into the prawns? Or died there?"

"Yuck."

"That's it. We all leave something. The cats are very well fed. They get salmon heads, cod heads, prawns that have been crushed or cracked. But they do like their milk. Besides," she said, watching Sally's face, "this boat is called the *Sealkie*. You know what they are?" Sally nodded. "Well, they *love* things they have no way of getting out there. Milk, ice cream, fresh fruit, chocolate bars . . . and I leave something for them every night, whether I'm tied up or out there."

"They're a fairy story."

"Are they? You're sure of that, are you? Because I'm not."

Lin poked along the beach, turning over rocks and hunkering down to watch the small crabs as they scuttled off in search of another hidey-hole. Rainey watched him, and knew what Wayne had looked like when he was little, before she had met him.

"Nice kid," David said quietly.

"Yes. But spoiled. He's having a hard time starting at the new school."

"Kids picking on him?"

"I don't think so. I think it's just him. He doesn't like change."

"Do you?" he laughed. "It scares me all to hell."

"Really? If nothing ever changed, everything would have to stay the same. And if it had always been like that we'd be apt to be living in holes in the hillside, gnawing on roots and occasionally catching a mouse or something for meat."

"I'm sure there's some famous philosopher, or economist or someone has half a dozen books published saying just exactly that in big words and convoluted sentences, complete with arcane examples."

"What?"

"Exactly."

"You're a nut, you know that?"

"Yeah, I've been told that." He checked his watch, shook his head apologetically. "I'll love you and leave you," he said easily. "I've got to go get ready for work. You're sure Chris will be here to get you?"

"Sure as sure can be. Nice seeing you."

"Take care." He turned and ran back to his motorcycle, and as the engine roared to life Lin stood up and waved. The little tooty-tooty horn on the bike sounded, and then the gleaming black machine moved off down the dirt road, toward the highway.

Rainey sat down on a dry rock. The sun was setting, the sky beginning to show the stains of sunset. People said the incredible displays on that horizon were because of the pollution from the pulp mill. Rainey had never believed it.

The sky was still gorgeous when Chris and Sally arrived. Lin called and waved, and Sally ran down to the beach. Chris sat down beside Rainey; there was just enough room on the rock for the two of them.

"Seems weird to be here instead of with Mom," Chris said.

"I know. But I do think it will do her more good to have Annie Daniels visit her than for us to go up again."

"I know. And you're right. But it feels weird."

"Yeah. Me too."

"You think she's going to make it?"

"She's made it."

"You really think so?"

"I think so. I mean, there's no telling what shape she'll be in when she gets out of there. She isn't going to be the same, we have to get ready for that."

"I know. It's just—"

"Oh, God, Chrissy, you really are something else again!" Rainey leaned against Chris, putting her head on her sister's shoulder. "You're the oldest, *you're* supposed to babysit *me!* I'm the baby, I'm the one needs reassurance and bolstering."

"See, you got gypped all the way around!" Chris tried to laugh and managed only what sounded like a cough. "Your big sister is a wuss."

"You be careful what you say about my sister, see. I got friends in this town, see. I was born here, see. So you just watch it."

"Oh yeah?"

"Yeah." Then she dropped her silliness. "We'll make out fine, Chris, honest we will."

"If Sarah is half as scared as I am, she must be terrified."

"She's probably too busy staying alive and trying to get better to feel scared or anything else."

"My arse is starting to freeze, Rainey. You know what Momma said, if you sit on cold rocks you get hemorrhoids."

Sarah napped briefly after Old Annie left. She could still taste and smell the wonderful mixture of scents in the supper her friend had brought. It was reassuring, in ways hospital food wasn't. It brought the associations of years of her life, years of time when she could speak clearly, move easily. Her brief nap did more to help her marshal her strength than all the time she'd spent sleeping since what the doctor called her "cerebral incident."

She came out of her nap as easily as she had slid into it. The atmosphere on the floor had changed. Even from her bed, with virtually no view out the doorway, she knew the staff was busy, going from bed to bed, from patient to patient, getting them ready for the night. She turned her head to look out the window and blinked several times. In the glass she could see the reflection of her room, see herself in bed, her head slightly raised, two pillows under it; and beyond that, like a double exposure, she could see the bright streaks of sunset along the horizon.

They saved her for last. She wasn't sure if that meant they were dreading having to deal with her or if they were looking forward to it. She knew she was a lot of work. She was glad she wasn't a large, heavy woman. If she were, she'd feel even worse about needing to be aided and supported by young women, especially the slender ones, who looked as if they would break under a heavy load. She didn't remember anyone being that thin in her own youth. You don't pack buckets of water from a well and loads of stove wood from the pile in the shed and stay wraithlike.

But then modern women ate differently, too. Eggplant, now, she'd hardly even seen any, let alone tasted it, when she was young. And artichokes! She'd seen pictures in magazines and thought whatever they were they looked awfully like the heads of thistles. Now they were in the produce section of the Safeway. She'd tried them—once. A little pad of yellowish recipes hung above the display and she'd thought, why not? You could drop dead tomorrow and die without having any idea what these are like. She'd taken them home, followed the recipe to a tee, then sat for what seemed like forever dipping little petals into hot butter and garlic. A lot of work for next to nothing. Could as easily have made the garlic and butter and dipped homemade bread in it. A person would have to be on the verge of starvation to think of those things as real food. And if a person were on the verge of starvation, where would she get the butter?

Sarah lay in bed, a slight half-smile on her face, her imagination romping. Hordes of half-starved vagabonds coming in the dark of night to attack the town, going in windows, jimmying open doors, raiding refrigerators, their gaunt hands grasping, their skin-over-bones faces desperate. Then, pounds and half pounds of butter gripped in their fists, they left as they had entered and streaked back, away from town, away from danger and threat and cupboards full of food, taking the butter into the hidden places where the garlic and artichokes were waiting—just in time to save the lives of those who had been too weak to join the raid.

"Well, you're looking happy enough tonight. Feeling better?" Tess and Aster came in as if they'd been taking a walk, just happened to notice Sarah and stopped to pass the time of day.

"Old Annie was up. Brought scalloped spuds."

"Ah, that'll do it," Tess nodded. "How do you rate? I've prayed to the good lord above I don't know how many times and not once in my life has Old Annie Daniels brought me any scalloped spuds. I have to go to the twice-a-year Garden Club potluck and plant myself near the front of the line before I get any."

"Good friend." Sarah struggled to sit up and Tess waited, letting her push herself to the limit before stepping forward and giving her that last little boost.

"I'd not want to make you feel self-conscious, my dear, but do you know how much better your speech is already?"

"Concentrating," Sarah gasped. She gripped Tess's arm, steadying herself, already feeling as if she'd been at work for hours.

"Good. So we're hauling you out of bed again, love. Going to sit you in the chair with a blanket around you and take you down to the bathroom. And then, into the tub you go."

"Girls took me."

"I know," said Aster. "And we're taking you again."

"Think I'm dirty?"

"How could you not be, lying in bed, having to struggle just to move a bit. You've probably worked up a heavy sweat a dozen times today. Anyway, it's good for you. Cleanliness is next to godliness and whoever heard of a god—or a goddess for that matter—who had a gimpy leg?"

"Fingal the Fair had a club foot. It's why they made him the blacksmith."

"Fingal the Fair wasn't a god, he was a supernatural, and there's a difference. Here we go, love."

"Not so fast! Let me try."

It was hard work, and by the time she had managed to inch herself around and lower herself to the chair she was soaked with sweat and trembling with fatigue. God, it was worse than those few times she'd had to walk down the hall to the nursery, with her legs seeming double their real length and her belly feeling hollow and jiggly.

"I'm impressed," Aster said quietly. "You've got the determination of a pit bull."

"And the strength of a cairn terrier," Sarah agreed.

They wheeled her down the hallway and into the bathroom. The tub was waiting and they got her into it with much less fuss and bother than when Chris and Rainey had put her in. She wondered if they learned how in school or if it was practice, patient after patient needing assistance.

"Your back," she warned.

"I promise I'm careful," Aster laughed softly. "I've seen what happens to people who aren't."

"So, could you use a bit more water, love?"

"To my chin, please." Sarah tried to wink, and couldn't. "Might's well take a'vantage."

"Advantage, is it? We'll see who's taking advantage! Aster is going to stay with you and the rest of us are going to race outside, smoke cigars and play poker. We've got you where we want you, Sarah Carson, you're a prisoner now, and with the cat away in the tub the rest of us mice are going to slack off."

The idea of Tess slacking off was so ridiculous Sarah began to laugh. She'd never seen Tess McFadden moving at anything slower than twice the speed of sound. And it wasn't just random movement, twitching and fussing nervously. Tess moved with an economy of motion that was almost befuddling and she could get more work done in an hour than most people could manage in half a day.

It was nice in the tub. It was more than nice, it was heavenly. The water was almost hot, and the slope at the back of the tub was exactly what she needed. She could lie back and drift, turn her mind free, escape the limitations of her damaged body. If she wanted, she could go back to the time she was young and her children were babies, she could chase after them again, she could be strong and move freely.

She came out of it with a mental jerk. Somehow she knew, deep in the centre of her soul, that this was the road to crippledom. She couldn't really go back. But she could send her mind back there and forget she had mountains to climb in the here and now. And in no time flat, there she'd be, and a wheelchair would be a permanent part of her life.

She looked at her bad arm, her lazy one. It half floated in the water, her fingers taped curled around the little red, white and blue ball. She thought of the Visible Woman dolls she'd bought for the girls, the clear plastic figures with all the body parts visible inside. The bones were white plastic, the veins were red tubes and the arteries blue ones. There were layers of muscle in pinks and near purples, and—optional, at the discretion of the parents—a little pregnant uterus with a tiny flesh-toned plastic baby curled inside. She'd given the girls their dolls uterus inserted. One of the first things Rainey did was crack open the doll, remove the uterus, pry it open, take the baby out and store it back in the box. Sarah remembered her serious little face, the disapproving frown as she said, "Mine's not pregnant. She's not even married," and Chris laughing, but not mocking.

"They got along very well," she said aloud.

"Did they?" Aster answered softly.

"Always understood each other. Made way for each other's little strangenesses and weirdnesses."

"Your daughters?"

"Yes. You?"

"No. No children. Not until I can feel settled, and able to support them."

"Husband?"

"Not any more."

"Just as well."

"Just as well no husband, or just as well no children?"

"Either. Maybe both."

Sarah struggled to remember the way the muscles in the Visible Woman linked together, attached to the bones and made them move. It was hazy; she couldn't bring it into focus. But she could remember the old silly song about the shoulder bone connected to the arm bone and the arm bone connected to the elbow bone. There had to be muscles there or what would make the bones move? So, shoulder muscle connected to elbow muscle, to arm muscle, to back of the hand muscle, to finger muscle—*squeeze*.

She'd lifted her end of any number of sheets of plywood when Angus put the rooms in what had been the basement, and she hadn't had to strain this hard doing it. She'd lifted sheets of gyproc with no help from anyone and that too had been easier than this. Suddenly she couldn't do it any more. She was just too tired. She relaxed, and sighed. Sufficient unto each day the evil thereof. And the work. And the worry. And the fear.

And then she became aware that she was wiggling her toes. Not just on her good foot, on her lazy one, too.

"Can you see?" she almost whispered.

"I see toes moving."

"The foot?"

"A bit. More than when you started."

"Run outside and get the cigar smokers. I'm beat."

"No need to run. See this?" and Aster reached over, pulled a cord made of a length of gauze bandage. A buzzer sounded, and a red light over the door lit. "They'll be here in a moment."

Sarah almost drifted into another doze, but jiggled her feet while waiting. She felt as if hours, maybe days had gone by before Tess arrived.

"Look," she blurted. "Foot!"

"I'm proud of you, Sarah." Tess sounded almost smug. "I *told* you, didn't I, a good bath will do wonders for any woman."

"Tired, Tessie."

"I've no doubt you are. Well, not to worry, love, you're almost back in bed again. We'll let some of this water out and rinse your hair for you, and then into the chair with plenty of towels and the blanket, and back to your room for a clean nightie and a good sleep."

"Scared, Tess."

"Sure you are. I'd be terrified. It's a bloody betrayal is what it is. Oh, see now, the tape on your wee ball has soaked loose. Just hang onto it a bit longer, dear, and I'll fix it for you as good as new when we get you back to bed."

Startled, Sarah opened her hand, and the red, white and blue ball floated free.

"Surprised you, did I? Well, here, take hold of it again."

Sarah rode back to her room swathed in towels and blankets, as proud as any queen in her carriage. The little tri-coloured ball was in her hand, her fingers barely curled enough to hold it. But they were curled, and without tape, and she could wiggle her toes. "Behold," she yawned, "the power of scalloped spuds."

"You have to remember how you're doing it," Tess lectured, her tone stern. "You were wiggling those fingers just after suppertime, but then you went to sleep and when you woke up you'd forgotten you knew how to do it. Before you go to sleep, I want you to concentrate on how it is you're doing it, so that when you wake up again you'll remember. Promise me?"

"Anything."

4

Rainey was first up in the morning. She put on a pot of coffee, then set out bowls, spoons and juice glasses. She made oatmeal and wakened the kids. Lin was his usual cranky self, and sat glaring at his oatmeal, not even pretending to eat it, not even stirring it around, just glowering.

"Eat up," Rainey coaxed.

"I'm sick."

"No, you're not. You just don't want to go to school."

"I *hate* it!"

"Of course you do. You're the new kid. Everyone hates that."

"I don't see why we have to go to school!"

"Lin, listen to me. And listen good. You aren't a baby any more. So stop acting like one. I don't have time for this. I don't have the energy for this. I don't have the patience for this. Eat your breakfast."

"I *hate* oatmeal!"

"Eat it."

"I *hate* it and I *hate* you!"

She wanted to pull a Wayne, grab the kid, take him to the bathroom, drop his pyjama bottoms and warm his ass. She wanted to shake him until he had a good reason to snivel and whinge. Instead she turned away from him, went to the coffee maker, poured herself a second cup and left the kitchen with it.

She sat in the living room with her coffee, staring out the window at the front yard, the little fence, the sidewalk and the road. A few minutes later Sally came in with her bowl and sat on the sofa, spooning mush into her mouth. Rainey looked at her; Sally shrugged.

Rainey sipped her coffee, smoked two cigarettes, refilled her coffee and seethed while Sally got ready for school. The entire time Lin sat at the table, not speaking, and certainly not eating.

"Drive me to the bus stop?" Sally coaxed from the doorway.

"No problem."

She stepped into her sneakers, got Sally's lunch from the fridge and put it in her backpack, then put Lin's lunch in his backpack and put the pack on the table where he could see it. He responded by turning his head and refusing to even look at the pack.

Rainey was so angry she could taste it, that same bite as when you were a kid and you put a penny in your mouth. But she said nothing. Sally pulled on her windbreaker, picked up her pack and headed out to the truck. Rainey got her windbreaker and the truck keys, and on her way to the door she grabbed Lin's pack and slung it over one shoulder, then took him by the arm and yarded him off his chair. He was so surprised he didn't even squeak until they were out of the door and halfway across the porch.

"What are you *doing?*" he screeched.

Rainey didn't answer. She dragged him, barefoot and in his pyjamas, to the driver's side of the truck and heaved him in. He tried to scramble over Sally to the other door, but Rainey grabbed a handful of his hair and yanked him back, then pushed until his body folded and he was sitting in the middle of the front seat.

He wept, he howled, he yelled, he swore, he took a full-sized fit more suitable for a frustrated two-year-old, but Rainey did not relent. She let Sally out at her bus stop, then drove the half block more to the elementary school. She grabbed the pack, then took Lin by his wrist, opened the driver's door and got out, so angry she could split his head more easily than talking to him. She yanked Lin and his pack from the truck and pulled them to the sidewalk.

Sobbing and vowing eternal hatred, he slumped to the damp pavement, and Rainey got back in the truck and drove home.

She had the dishes done and the kitchen tidied when Lin came through the door, white-faced and trembling. She turned and looked at him. "Do I take you back in your pyjamas or are you going to get dressed?"

He didn't answer. He dropped the pack and ran for the bedroom. She waited two and a half minutes, then headed to the bedroom, prepared to drag him back to school if need be. He was sitting on the bed, tying his shoelaces.

"Brush your teeth, too," she said.

He nodded. The look on his face made her think of axe murders and evisceration.

"I'll drive you back today," she said, "but tomorrow you go on your own. You get up, you get dressed, you eat your breakfast, you brush your teeth and tidy your hair, and you go to school without any more of this babyish bullshit, do you understand me?" He nodded. "Do you understand?" she repeated stubbornly. He glared. "Answer me, damn it, Lin, or I'll hit you so hard you'll ache for a week!"

"I understand!" he yelled. "Okay, okay, *okay!*"

She took him back to school and let him off near the front gate. He slammed the truck door and stomped toward the building. She wondered if she should have offered to escort him in, then steeled herself. It was his pickle, he'd got himself into it, he could get himself out again.

Back at Sarah's house Rainey put in a load of wash, then finished tidying and dusting, and just when she was sitting down to a cup of fresh coffee, the phone rang. She answered, half expecting it to be the school with the news that Lin had pulled another stunt and was on his way back. If it was anything like that, she'd probably whip his butt, parenting classes or not.

"Rainey?"

"Wayne."

"Listen, Rainey, we've got an offer on the motel. S'help me! What do you think?"

"What do I think about what?"

"The offer on the motel. Should we sell?"

"How much is the offer?"

"We'll get back every penny we put in, and ten percent more. And that's *after* the real estate agent gets his cut! What do you think?"

"Well, you're the one wanted the motel in the first place, so really you should be the one to decide."

"If it's up to me, we'll sell."

"Okay then." She really didn't care what he did with it.

"And then what?"

"What do you mean, and then what? What are you asking?"

"Well, we could look for some other place to put the money into, or we could buy into a good business, a garage or something, or we—"

"Wayne, there is no *we*."

"Just listen, Rainey, don't get proddy. I could move back home, we could buy a nice house, maybe a few acres, get a few beef cows, fatten the calves up and sell what we don't need. I could get a job, easy, people know me. They know I'm a good heavy equipment operator, and we could—"

"Not *we*, Wayne."

"Don't you think you've punished me enough? Don't you think I've eaten enough crow, swallowed enough shit? Isn't it about time to stop sending me to my room on a time out?"

"That's not what this is, Wayne. We've tried that. We've tried couples counselling. We've taken courses. And it's always the same, it always winds up back at the same old thing, and it's not what I want. Not for me, not for the kids."

"Jesus Christ, Rainey! You could give lessons in hard-headed and shirty!"

"Is that what you consider to be conversation? It sounds like abuse to me."

"You don't know what abuse is. You've been babied and pampered and spoiled rotten all your life."

She could send him into a stuttering, stammering fury. All

she'd have to do would be put on her best-of-British hauteur and say something insulting like Oh, do tell, and what else have you noticed, great and wise one, which you feel ought to be brought to my attention. It had worked before, and often. For a long time making Wayne incoherent with frustration and rage had seemed like some kind of victory. It was her nuke, to be brought out when he said things that made her feel unreasonable and diminished, a force to reckon with and then some.

"Wayne, please try to hear what I'm trying to say. It isn't any one single thing. It isn't *only* because you've been screwing around for at least as long as Lin has been alive, it isn't only because of the gambling, it isn't only because you're seldom home and when you are you might as well not be. It isn't *only* because of any one thing. It's everything."

"And it's all my fault, right! You are the virgin queen, Joan of Arc, the long-suffering martyr, the—"

"No, I'm as much at fault as anyone in this. You never had any reason to take me or my opinion seriously because I didn't know a person had to find a way to be heard. I thought just talking would do it. But it takes more. We haven't been kind to each other for six years, maybe longer. You're no happier than I am and you haven't been happy for probably longer than me. You're saying some of the right things. You're willing to try again, and that's what we were both taught to do. But deep down, you don't *really* want to move back here. If you wanted to be here we'd have never left. If you really wanted to drive heavy equipment, you'd be doing it. So why not take some time and think about what you want in your life and out of your life and then go for what you want, not for what is supposed to be right. Think it over without the pressure of ohmigawd I have a wife and kids to feed and clothe."

"Rainey . . ."

"Wayne, why don't we just do it neatly?"

"Jesus, Rainey," and he was weeping.

"I'm going to hang up now."

"There's no chance?"

"None."

She replaced the receiver, went to the bed temporarily her own again, lay down and waited for a flood of tears. Less than half an hour later she was bored stiff and the tears still hadn't happened.

She got up, put the laundry in the clothes dryer, had a fast shower and dressed herself for a visit to the employment centre. She'd take anything, and if they were willing to send her back to school she'd do that, too. But she wasn't going to just rattle around with nothing but time on her hands, waiting for the kids to come home from school and give some structure, some meaning to her life. It was *her* life, damn it, not theirs!

Sarah turned her head and looked out the window at the world beyond the hospital. Morning sunshine, and it must have some heat in it—the lawn was steaming, the roofs of the outbuildings were steaming, even the walls of the brick buildings were steaming. She almost prayed. Spring was so late coming this year. She hated to think what the unseasonable frosts were doing to her fruit trees. Heaven knows it was hard enough to grow peaches and apricots without having frost on them this far along in the year. If the blooms weren't able to happen soon, the fruit would never ripen. Oh, you could bring it in green and put it on the windowsill, you could wrap each one in old newspaper, there were plenty of things you could do to make them ripen, but they didn't taste the same as peaches or apricots grown and ripened on the tree in the sun and heat. She wondered what it must be like to live in a place like, say, Georgia, where peaches were commonplace. She couldn't imagine becoming so used to an abundance of fruit that you'd have an orange tree, like people did in California, or down in the islands, the ones they used to call the Spice Islands. Imagine walking down the sidewalk and there on the boulevard are ripe oranges, fallen from a tree in someone's yard. Imagine grapefruit! She'd seen wild apple trees; were there wild grapefruit trees, wild lime trees? And would the wild fruit look the same or would it be shaggy, with tangled mane and tail, and a fierce bite to it?

She snickered at her own silliness. Wild grapefruit, indeed. Stomping their hooves and racing over hill and dale, no doubt.

"What's this I hear about someone wiggling toes and jiggling feet and holding her little ball all by herself?" Annwyn came into the room looking as if the night had been several hours too short for her. What kind of shifts did they make these young women work, anyway? Bad enough when a body had to deal with eight-to-four, four-to-twelve and twelve-to-eight, but split shifts and half shifts and short shifts and who knows what-all were criminal. And this new idea, the one being touted as an answer to anything a body could think of, the one where people work twelve hours a day for however many days, and then get extra days off, as if that was any help when anyone could see you'd spend most of your off time catching up on the rest you'd lost on your twelve-hour shifts! All those years of working, sacrificing, struggling for an eight-hour day and the wheel had turned again, only this time even the unions thought it was fine for a person to spend twelve hours at work.

"Fought I'd put out my own bideo," Sarah blurted. Then held up her good hand and tried again, more slowly. "*Thought* I'd put out my own *video*. Me an' Jane Ffonda."

"You're doing your *f* almost as well as my grandmother does," Annwyn teased.

"Lip. Like coming fffrom the dentist."

"So, let me see this trick with the ball."

Sarah deliberately dropped the ball to the bed, then, with a few misses and start-agains, she managed to pick it up and hold it, even managed to squeeze, although the amount of effort it took was huge in proportion to the result.

"You're a wonder. I'm going to tell Chrissy she's the daughter of Wonder Woman."

"Hard work, Annie."

"I know it is, dear, and it will get harder. We have to get something more happening with that hand and arm so we can get you in a walker and start working on that sleepy leg."

"Sometimes I want to cry."

"I'd want to cry, too. It must seem like climbing mountains or finding out you have to swim an ocean."

"Yes," and Sarah struggled to smother the sob she could feel rising in her chest.

"Well, we'll get you tidied up, and then, the bad news is, you start physio today. And no loafing in your own bed to do it, either. Your reward for doing so well with the ball and the foot is that you've skipped the entry level and you're catapulted into the general population. You, my darling yard bird, are going to take a trip down to the bowels of this fine institution."

"No candy?"

"I'll give you candy when you come back."

"Too Scotch."

"I know, you thought you'd get candy for the toes, candy for the foot, candy for the trick with the ball. But our bribes are different. We're into negative reinforcement. We'll make you so sick of physio you'll grab onto a walker and head off down the road with your dicky shirt flapping at the back and your bum exposed to the world."

"Cars in the ditch."

"You've got it. Cars in the ditch, drivers gaping, trucks loaded with canned pop overturned and entire tribes of dirty-faced children raiding the load. We'll probably make the six o'clock TV news."

The go-round at the bathtub was easier; Sarah was actually able to help a bit. But the time in the tub was shorter, and she felt cheated. She let them know it. "Need more time!" she snapped, feeling rushed and cranky.

"You'll get more time, dear, when you come back from physio. I promise. We'll put you in a nice deep tub and leave you there until you pull the cord to tell us you want out again."

"Bossy!"

"I am. No doubt about that. It's what they pay me for."

Physio was as close to hell as Sarah had come in her life. The physiotherapist was soft-spoken, she was kind, she was at no time rough, and Sarah would gladly have given her a swat on the head if she'd been able to do it. The frustration got in her way, she found it almost impossible to do things she knew she had relearned already, and that made her angry.

"Use the anger as energy, Mrs. Carson. I know this is awful. I know it makes you feel as if you're being treated like an idiot. I wish there was some other way to do the treatment, but if there is, I don't know it."

"Dumb!"

"It must feel that way, but really, you're doing very well. And, please, do try to believe that what I want is to be able to lend whatever help I can so that before too long you'll be able to walk out of here when you get fed up with me and my demands. Now let's try it again; push as hard as you can, try to send your foot and leg forward, try to push my hand back to my shoulder. And don't be afraid you'll hurt me. You won't."

And suddenly Sarah didn't care if she did! If the only way she could get out of this damn place and back to her bed was to shove the hand, or for that matter the physiotherapist herself, right through the wall, well, so be it. She felt as if she would burst with the effort.

The hand moved at least six inches. "Good," the soft voice said, and Sarah felt her fury explode. Good? Was that all it was? Good? As if she were two years old and being potty trained again? Sarah didn't care if she had a heart attack, she would push that goddamn hand back so far, so hard, so fast there would be no stopping her.

"Wonderful!" and the hand was gone, her leg was lowered, and the young woman was kneeling by the chair into which Sarah was safety strapped. She put her arms around Sarah and let her sob against her shoulder. She didn't pat Sarah on the back, or say Don't cry dear, or Everything will be fine dear, she just held her and Sarah sobbed. She wanted to apologize for her crankiness, apologize for the bursts of rage, apologize even for being there, and damaged, and a nuisance, and all she could do was sob.

Christine scrubbed the *Sealkie* with hot water, a medium-bristle brush and a soap that was formulated, or so the label claimed, especially for wood. Supposedly it was oil-based, and would give a special glow to whatever it washed. A special glow would be nice. A glow of any kind would be a welcome change.

She had finished the inside and begun outside when Tyrone Bentley came over to join her. He brought a case of beer. Christine was pretty sure there was more chance of a glow in the beer than in the wood soap, and gladly got up off her knees and went for the cushions that served her as deck chairs. When she got back with them, Ty already had two beer uncapped and his own sampled.

"How's your mom?" he asked, handing her the other beer.

"Hanging in." Chris took a good swallow, and sighed. "It's going to take a lot of physio, though, and they aren't giving anything you could even pretend was a guarantee. One entire side is affected—hand, foot, arm, leg."

"Pretty grim."

"Yeah."

"You heard they cancelled the opening?"

"I heard."

"Saw you doing housework here. That mean you're thinking of selling?"

"God, Ty, I don't know what to think! I think about it and think yeah, I'll do it, and then I get scared spitless. It's what I know how to do, eh."

"Yeah. Can't see myself in a polyester suit working in a bank, and I sure as hell can't see myself in clean jeans and one of those little polo shirts with the animal logo on the pocket, selling nuts and bolts and the very latest in electrical wall switches at the hardware store. I've been doing this since before I even quit school!"

"They wouldn't take me at the bank, they know how I handle money." Chris forced a grin. "But I expect the damn welfare would sponsor me for a job retraining thing. I could be a hairdresser, maybe. Or better yet, I could take the social work course and get a job with the whoofare just in time for the government to cut the budget and put me out of work again. Similarly, I could get a job as a teacher's aide and get put out of work by education cuts."

"No end to bloody possibilities, that's for sure. You hear about Ed Hanlon?" Chris shook her head. "Well, his back had been bothering him for a couple of years, right, so when they first announced the buy-back he figured it was as good an offer as he'd get and he sold out. So last week he sees the dork who bought it and he says come on in, I'll buy you a beer. They're having their beer and the guy tells him he just sold the boat. He got as much for it as he'd paid, so he didn't lose anything. But he sold the licence for ten times what Ed got. Ten times! Less than a year."

"I'd'a been tempted to pour the rest of my beer on his head."

"Well, hell, they got you coming and going. If you don't go out and fish as many days as they've decided, no pogey for the winter. If you don't catch as much as they think you should, your quota gets cut. They told Marty Hanlon he didn't catch enough prawns last year and so he can't fish prawn this year. Which means he sure as hell isn't going to be allowed to fish next year. So they don't even have to buy his licence back from him, they just disqualify him."

"How's Ed doing with his business?"

"How well would you expect him to do with a store that sells diving gear and fish bait?"

"And life preservers, you forgot the life preservers."

"Maybe I'll go down and buy me a couple. Wear 'em all the time."

"Well, they say it's good news that the fish stocks on the east coast have picked up enough the people's being given permission to go out and catch again."

"Ten each, I suppose."

"And a lobster, don't forget the damn lobster."

"So Fat Sam down at the Fisheries says to me, he says there's too many boats out chasin' too few fish. I said I already heard a politician on TV use them very words. But maybe you can explain to me why it is you're cutting down on the number of boats and putting the small guy outta business but you haven't cut down the total overall tonnage, which means the big guys just keep on, only without any competition. And he says to me, the bugger, I'm sorry you feel that way. I was so goddamn mad, Chrissie, I just bust out laughin'."

"There's the job they should give us."

"What? Laughin'?"

"No, fire Fat Sam and let you'n'me sit in his office and come out with stupid things. Shouldn't be hard to prove that between us, we can come out with the most stupid things they've ever heard. We got more imagination than Fat Sam. And you're better lookin'."

They laughed, and drained their beer. Ty put the empties in the case and hauled out two more full ones.

Chris looked at the bucket of now cool water and frowned. "This is the last one I'm having, Ty. I got a boat to scrub and I won't get that done sittin' on my cushion here."

"No sweat." He took his tobacco and papers from his pocket, rolled one and handed the makings to Chris. "Relax a bit. I'll give you a hand. It's not as if I'm rushed off my feet with things that need done. Joe Peters helped me scrub *my* boat yesterday and we did his last week. We're all busy, busy, busy doing bugger nothing, waiting for the chance to go out on the chuck and *really* lose money."

When Annwyn came home from work, Chris had supper ready; hamburger patties in gravy, mashed potatoes, steamed broccoli and a grated carrot salad.

"You spoil me rotten," Annie sighed, moving into Chris's embrace and snuggling.

"You get too spoiled and I'll turf you out the door," Chris laughed.

"Not this door, darlin', the lease is in my name."

"See what I have to put up with? Uppity woman."

Annie had a fast shower to get the hospital smells off her, then came to the table in jeans and a T shirt. They ate slowly and talked about their day, and when the meal was finished, Minnie got the leftovers added to her dog food. She carefully picked out the scraps and ate them, then licked the gravy off her kibble and spat the noogies onto the floor. "Damn dog," Chris muttered. "If it isn't human food, it isn't fit to eat."

"Well, darlin', would you eat it? I wouldn't."

They did the dishes together, then took Minnie to the beach to run her short legs off while they strolled, talking.

"So Fat Sam says to him, I'm sorry you feel that way about it, and Ty, he just bust out laughin'."

"So what *are* you going to do, Chrissie?"

"Annie, I don't know. If Ed's licence is worth ten times now what it was a year ago, who's to say it won't be worth twenty times by this time next year? Seems to me the fewer licences there are available for sale, the more they'll be worth. But . . . a bird in the hand, eh."

"We could flip a coin."

"We could. Then what do I do? Flip another to see what kind of life I'm going to try next?"

"Who's the person who spent most of last November lying with her back flat on the floor, her knees up on pillows, swallowing Tylenol?"

"I don't remember her name. Bad-back-Bimbo, maybe."

"Do you know one single fisher who doesn't have a lame back or a gimp leg or chronic bursitis or . . .?"

"No, only the in-breakers."

"So?"

"Yeah. Twelve years ago this job was fun. Eight years ago I really enjoyed it. Five years ago it was a good job. Last year it was goddamn hard work. This year? Well, I've probably got the cleanest damn boat on the coast!"

"If God came down from the clouds and looked you in the eye and said Chris Carson, your number just came up, either quit fishing *or else*—what would you do?"

"Twelve years ago I'd have said What's the *or else?* Now, well, I guess I'd just gulp and say yes, ma'am."

"So what do you think it's like for the ones who don't go fishing? The ones who help pack the clothes, help pack the groceries, then stand on the dock smiling and waving while half their life floats off into the unknown?"

"That doesn't answer the question of what next?"

"Oh, hell, Chrissie, you're as Scotch with your money as your mom! You've probably got enough stashed away to be able to— oh, I don't know, buy a bloody gas station or something!"

"Or I could sell the licence, keep the boat, wash and paint 'er some more, and do sports charters for the tourists."

"You could."

"I was joking."

"I wasn't. You keep thinking about jobs you can get. There aren't any. Face up to it. The only work you've ever done is fishing. You could take computer courses until you qualified for Old Age Pension and you'd be rotten at it. You don't think that way! You can't do office stuff, you don't walk like office, you don't talk like office, you don't dress like office and you don't think like office. You'd be a lousy waitress. The first time some ay-hole got lippy you'd dump his meal on his head and toss him out the front door. Any job you got, you'd lose. So, stands to reason, you *make* your job."

"You mean you can't see me in a tasteful little outfit?"

"Lord God. You and wotzisname the basketball player with the orange hair!"

The cab stopped in the driveway and Chris jumped out of the back seat and hurried forward to open the front passenger door. Rainey followed, and Bruno came out of the house, bringing the brand new walker frame. He had added some bright red ribbons, which fluttered and snapped as the frame moved.

Sarah got out of the cab carefully, face tight with concentration. She was so frightened she thought she might vomit. Bad enough to fall, but to fall in front of these people who loved her! They'd have her back in the hospital so fast the cab driver wouldn't even remember putting the thing in gear.

"Hang on, Mom," Rainey whispered.

"I'm hanging."

Bruno put the walker in exactly the right place. All Sarah had to do was reach out and grab it. She felt much more secure with the walker. She had practised with one just like it, up and down the hallway at the hospital. She had less practice gripping the arms of her daughters. In fact she had a lifetime of helping them, not the other way around.

The house was fresh-painted and she paused to admire it. And to catch her breath. "It's lovely," she said, and surprised herself with the strength in her voice. She had been afraid she would gasp and quaver like a little old lavender-drenched blue-rinsed lady. "Someone has done a wonderful job."

"Bruno did that," Rainey said. "That's how he works off his worry and his upset."

"Strong, silent type," Sarah agreed, looking at him and smiling.

Bruno flushed red with pleasure. His eyes shimmered with tears and Sarah knew everything he wasn't able to say.

"One of these days, when I can move around better, I'm going to catch him," she said clearly. "He's been running away from me for years. These long-time bachelors, you know. Skittish as wild cats."

"You don't have to chase me, Sarah. I've been caught tight for years. Now, into the house, my dear."

"Hear him? Bossy."

The irises were bright purple, sharp orange, clear white with stiff green spears of leaves. The first columbines were up, some of them in flower. The beds of bulbs were weeded, and someone, probably Bruno, had been in there with the little fork-dealie, loosening the soil, mulching with the almost decomposed leaves in the larger of several compost piles.

Step by step, carefully, Sarah moved to the doorway. The left half of the stairs had been modified, and there was a rubber-covered ramp for her to shuffle up—due, she was sure, to Bruno. She paused, catching her breath, and smiled at him. "Thank you so much," she said. "You don't know how much I've dreaded having to navigate stairs."

"I've put one at my place, too," he said. "Once I got this in and tried it out it was so much easier than stairs that I feel like a fool for having taken so long to figure it out."

Rainey dug Chris in the ribs with her elbow. "See? That's how the old folks flirt. She's hustling him."

"And what's more, he's putting the tap on her!"

The ramp conquered, there was the door to contend with. And when that obstacle was cleared, Sarah moved slowly across the kitchen, then down the hall to the living room. She turned, backing slowly until she could feel the seat of the recliner bumping against the back of her knees. She would have trusted to God and the saints and just let herself thump down and into the chair, but there were three of them falling all over themselves to help ease her down.

"A footstool, Mom?"

"Yes, please. Oh, my, hear me puffing and panting like a steam engine. Too old for all this, really."

"I'll get you a cup of tea. Would you like a sandwich, too?"

"No food, dear. But tea would be nice. Bruno?"

"Thank you, missus. Tea, yes."

"Missus? You know full well my name is Sarah."

The house hadn't been this clean since she could hardly remember when. A person doesn't pay as much attention when she lives alone. Things get put down where they seem most convenient, and then there's no reason to move them to a drawer, or a shelf, or a closet. Where they are is convenient, so leave them. But the place was spic-and-span clean, tidy, dusted, vacuumed, and she could even smell the faint after-scent of lemon oil furniture polish. She wondered if Rainey knew it was poisonous. But then Rainey's children were surely old enough to know better than to drink it, and she doubted if they went around licking the china cabinet, or sucking the sideboard.

One of the nicest things about Bruno was he didn't seem to feel any deep obligation to chatter. He could sit quietly without getting uncomfortable. Angus had been like that, too. You could sit on the same sofa with Angus Carson for hours, and from time to time he might look at you and smile, but he didn't seem to have to natter natter yat yat yat like so many do, giving opinions on the politics in places he'd never seen, deciding the fate of the world and the best policy for the government to boot. Bruno didn't natter either. He sighed, he settled back in the big chair across from hers, folded his thick-fingered hands together and just looked at her, smiling.

"You're a good friend, Bruno."

"I try, Sarah. I try."

She settled back in the chair, closing her eyes, feeling less at home in her own living room than she'd felt in the hospital.

"Are the children in school?" she asked.

"Yes. Of course they thought they should get the day off because Grandma was coming home, but we all said otherwise. Sally took it well, but . . . I'm afraid the boy was upset."

"How is he doing?"

"He's not a very nice child, Sarah."

"I know," Sarah nodded. "Too much of his father there."

"You believe in predestination?"

"God, no! But I do believe in role modelling. If the father gets what he wants by nagging, shouting, brow-beating and sulking, then the son, who's in training to be a father himself one day, will model his behaviour on what he sees. Personally, I'd have given him a royal boot up the arse years ago."

"The boy or the father?"

"Both. These parenting classes are all very well and good if you're looking for a social life. But I bet someone could draw a graph and prove that the more 'parenting' got done, the more kids became wretched brats."

"Beat 'em into submission?"

"No. Not beating. But I'd rather have gone to hell by a direct route than take orders from a person who didn't yet know how to tie her own shoelaces!"

She heard the tick tack tick tack of pointy little hooves coming down the hallway toward the living room. "There's my Chester," she said proudly.

"He heard your voice. He's very good company, Sarah. A bit stubborn, but . . ."

"Pig-headed," she corrected him. "Pig-headed and inclined to swinish behaviour."

"Pig!" Rainey snapped. "If you don't get your bulk out of the way I'm going to pour hot tea on you."

"That's the Chester," Chris agreed. "Get his big pink self in exactly the place you want to put your feet, then look innocent. Teasing is hard enough to put up with when it's done by someone who can talk."

They eased their way around the pig and brought the tea tray and a big plate of sandwiches into the living room. Chris put the food on the coffee table and Chester continued down the hall, his flat snout twitching, his sniffing audible.

"You're not allowed in the living room," Rainey warned. But the pig wasn't interested in anything she had to say. He wasn't even interested in the egg salad sandwiches. Yet. Obviously knowing he was going where he wasn't supposed to be, he lowered his head, squinted his eyes and just kept moving, through the doorway and across the carpet, his round body aimed at Sarah in her chair.

"Honest to God, Mom, couldn't you have got yourself a little poodle or something instead?" Rainey shook her head. "I mean, I try, but I really don't think a house is the place for a pig."

"Chester isn't a pig," Sarah said, reaching down and rubbing the bristly boar's head pressing gently against her leg. "Chester is my buddy. And you, you fine swine, why are you in the living room, anyway? Listen to you, wuf wuf wuf, as if you had every reason to think you're talking. Wuf wuf to you, too. Yes, I missed you. If you weren't so pig-headed they could have loaded you in the truck and brought you up to see me. That would have given them all something to talk about. But you have no reason to trust cars, or trucks, or any other vehicle, do you? No, and I wouldn't trust them either if one of them had nearly put my lights out for time and all eternity. No, I'm sure I wouldn't. Wuf wuf, there's a good old guy. Now you go mooch at Bruno, see if he'll give you a sandwich to take back to your blanket. You tell Bruno you particularly like egg, or failing that, cucumber. And ask Bruno who's been feeding you and spoiling you rotten—you're twice the size you were when I left. You get too fat your legs will give out. And take it from one who knows, that's a pain! Off with you, now. To your place, pig. To your place."

Chester grunted loudly, but turned and waddled from the living room, the noise coming from him enough to cause them all to laugh. He whined, he whinged, he grizzled and he bitched, but he plodded to his blanket and started the serious business of shoving with his snout until his bed was as he wanted it to be. As soon as he had settled himself, Bruno took two sandwiches and hunkered down at the pig's head, feeding him his treat.

"Damn pig will be the size of a freight car the rate he's going," Rainey said, but she was smiling, and her tone was almost affectionate. "Do you think he left because you said 'to your place, pig,' or was he ready to go anyway?"

"He understands." Sarah took the cup of tea Chris handed her, and smiled her thanks. "He probably understands a vocabulary of oh, I don't know, as much as a six-year-old at least. It's just that his mouth's the wrong shape to form words."

"Have a sandwich, Mom. Quick, before the pig eats them all."

"I'm not hungry, dear."

"Eat two sandwiches, Sarah," Bruno said firmly. "And then we'll set you up on the sofa for a rest. Unless you'd sooner get tucked into bed. We can do that, too, you know."

"Bruno, I'm too tired to be hungry."

"Drink your tea, you'll feel better."

She drank her tea and watched the others lunch on the sandwiches. She waited for the tea to perk her up, but it didn't, and she started yawning.

"That's it, into bed with you." Chris put down her half-eaten sandwich and went to take Sarah's teacup.

"I feel as if I've climbed Valentine Mountain," Sarah admitted. "It's been a big day."

"And it's not over yet, Momma. So off you go for a nap."

Her bed welcomed her back. Sarah snuggled under her own sheets, her own blanket, her own quilt, and she couldn't have kept her eyes open for a million dollars. This much of the house, at least, was still hers; here, only her own energy, only her own scents, only hers.

She slept like the dead for two and a half hours and wakened feeling better than she had felt in weeks. She got herself out of bed, grabbed her walker frame, and, using it for balance, got her sensible blue flannel housecoat on and the belt loosely tied. Barefoot, she manoeuvred to open her door, then made her way out of the bedroom. Chris heard her coming and went quickly to help. Rainey followed, anxious and uneasy. Only Bruno seemed comfortable with the new situation. He put down his hand of cards and went to fill the kettle.

"Now she'll be able to eat her sandwiches," he said, satisfied.

"I'll probably eat the hand and arm of the person who hands me the plate," Sarah agreed. Her speech, she knew, was slow, and her words sometimes slurred, but she could be understood. Enough, she knew, that once she had eaten, she would be able to phone old Annie and give her the news. "It's wonderful to be home," she said. She meant that she had enjoyed her own room, her own bed. The rest of it didn't seem much like home any more, and she had no idea how to tell them.

5

Rainey threaded her way between the tables, her tray balanced so skillfully that not one drop of draft spilled. The four-piece band was hammering out a not-so-good rendition of an oldie, "Me and Bobby McGee," and she could only hope and pray they contented themselves with playing it and didn't go overboard. The thought of the ferret-chinned blond who fancied himself the voice of the band letting loose with the words was just too much; if it actually happened she might just turn around and heave the tray. She liked the image: tray flying, beer splashing from the pitcher and glasses, streaming down the heads of the payday night crowd, like a cartoon drawing. And the tray winding up sideways in the open mouth of the crooner. That would stop the noise.

The table was cleared for her when she arrived, the empties held in the huge callused hands of the construction workers. She put down the tray and began to off-load the beer, and as the tray was emptied they put their dirty glasses on it, one by one, nodding politely, smiling shyly. One of them handed her a bill, and when she reached toward her apron pocket to make change, he shook his head and made a slight gesture.

"Thank you," she smiled. "Appreciate it."

It was the truth. She appreciated every tip she got, regardless of size. The wages here weren't bad, but the tips were what made it really worthwhile, especially since there was no way the damn federals could find out exactly how much she made, then tax it away from her. Grab grab grab, you wonder how they managed to eat with both hands shoved so far in her pockets. But maybe when you swill at the public trough you don't need your hands, you just shove in your face and gobble gobble slurp slurp like a hog, in it to your eyebrows.

Several guys got up from a table, weaving unsteadily. A chair tipped, then fell, but they didn't notice, they were so intent on making their way to the door. She righted the chair, then took the sodden terrycloth cover off the little table and put it—glasses, ashtray, the whole lot—on her tray. She set the tray on the chair. In her apron she had clean table covers, but first she used her clean damp cloth to wipe off the tabletop. No sooner did she have the table covered again and a clean ashtray on it, than several women came in laughing, and moved toward her. Rainey picked up her tray and moved quickly toward the bar. She put the tray on the top of the counter, and David took it and slid her a clean one. He put mugs on the tray, then tilted his head in the direction of a corner table.

"Maybe we should call in some help," he said softly, under the din from the so-called band and the crowd busily ignoring it.

"Getting kind of crazy in here," she agreed. She grabbed the tray and headed to the indicated table. If it was up to her she'd cut them off—they were already too drunk to be safe. One of them tried a bit of grab-assy and she shoved his hand away, looked him in the eye, smiled and said, "It's assault, mister, and I'm a very hard-nosed and cranky person."

"Assault, is it. Nice *ass*-ault."

"Want me to phone your mother and tell her how you act when you're off your chain?"

"Aw, don't be that way."

"I *am* that way." She put the mugs on the table, picked money out of the crumpled pile, made change, put it back on the table and left. Of course not one of them thought about a tip. That kind never did.

"Nice ass!" the idiot called after her.

She pretended to be deaf and continued doing her job. A very large guy in tight faded jeans, blue denim shirt and a leather vest with the Harley-Davidson eagle on the back stood up and moved slowly to the table Rainey had just served. Smiling slightly, he leaned over the chair of the grab-assy idiot and spoke softly.

Rainey didn't see it but David did, and he grinned. Every now and again God sends one of Her angels down to earth, and you never know when you're in the presence of one because they are very well disguised. This guy was one of them. At least as big as Arnie, and not as geeky looking, he could probably have sat on the sidewalk, pulled the parking meter out of its hole, then eaten it before parking his sickle. And he had obviously decided the waitress wasn't going to be hassled tonight.

"What's funny?" Rainey asked.

"You have a guardian angel, darling," he told her. "Big Pat just went over to have a chat with the guy with the untamed hands. Otherwise known as Lyle the Idiot."

"Here." She slid some coins across the bar. "Give me an extra mug of draft for Big Pat. Honest to God, that damn Lyle Collier, he was a nerd in school and he hasn't smartened up one little bit."

"Funny how that happens," David agreed.

Rainey put the complimentary mug on Big Pat's table and went on to take an order from a table near the bandstand. The tone-deaf had finished slaughtering Bobby McGee and were doing their best to chainsaw another moldie goldie. She wasn't quite sure what song it was supposed to be. She almost recognized it, but there were times you just didn't know, you know.

Lyle Collier or not—and the place had more than its share of the same type, different names—there were no fights, and no brave warriors suddenly deciding it was okay for 210 pounds of liquor-retarded creep to beat to a pulp 130 pounds of woman whose main sin was she'd been deluded enough to get involved with El Bravo in the first place. Rainey particularly hated those incidents, which she thought of as tragedies, not mere happenings. Some weekends she thought she might need anti-nausea pills by the handful. The band got no better, the crowd got no more sober, and the closest thing to real trouble was when some yahoo in cowboy boots and a hat too big for his head but too small for his ego went over to a table of women and started haranguing them about how they were all dykes and if they thought they were as good as men maybe one or more of them would like to step outside with him and find out exactly what it was they were lacking.

David was out from behind the bar in a flash, and before Rainey knew for sure what was trying to come down, David had Cactus Pete by the arm and was steering him away from the women.

"Take yer fuckin' hands offa me," the Rider of the Lonesome Plains slurred.

"Got a beer for you over by the bar," David smiled, but his eyes were starting to slit dangerously. "Compliments of the house."

"Those fuckin' bulldozer bitches!"

"Easy guy, easy, it's a free beer and then you go or it's tangle with me and go for good. I mean it, I'll have you barred."

"Me? You'd bar me? And let the perverts in?"

"I'll bar any troublemaker, Tex, even you, much as I like you. Come on, let's both of us just calm down here, okay?"

The fastest gunslinger this side of Egmont subsided, stumbled to the bar and stood sipping his free draft, while David talked him into grabbing a cab and going home while he could still remember his address.

By the time the place closed, Rainey's back ached, her legs were getting stiff and her feet were demanding she get off them. She went to the bar and did her thing with the money, and waited for David to close up the till and get the bank deposit bag ready.

"You want a beer?" he asked.

"I don't even want to smell the stuff. But I could probably drink a big glass of Sprite and then swallow the ice cubes. My throat is as long as a giraffe's and as dry as dust."

He pulled a Sprite for her and one for himself, then turned back to his books, checking and double-checking, sipping as he went. Finally he nodded and closed the ledger.

"How you holding out?" he asked.

"Okay. Actually, better than okay. Sally's doing great and Lin, well, he seems to be slowly getting the message. I didn't expect he'd leap through flaming hoops with joy and glee at the changes, but I didn't expect I'd have a full-scale rebellion on my hands, either."

"How's he making out with Chris?"

"Oh, well, that's another story, isn't it? I guess I'm worried she'll lose it and just give him a whack on the side of the head that'll rattle his gourd forever."

"Might not be a bad thing."

"You believe in whacking kids?"

"I think any kid over the age of five knows when he's pushing his weight around and kicking off power struggles. And I think talking only works with reasonable people regardless of their age. And if the little bugger is getting shovey, maybe what he'd understand quickest and best is a good shove back. Right now he can do just about any damn thing he wants and the only consequences are lectures and maybe a family round-table discussion. So if he doesn't give a shit about that, what good does it do? But getting dumped on his ass might make an impression."

"You don't think that's a bit like killing killers to prove killing is bad?"

"No, I think it's a bit like preparing them for the real world. Better he get bounced on his butt by someone who cares about him than turn into some kind of utter dick-head like Lyle. Because when Lyle pushes it too far he gets the supreme snot reamed out of him. Last time he was about a week and a half in hospital."

"Yeah, but did it do any good? He's still him."

"Right. But if it had been done when he was seven . . ." He shrugged. "Anyway, let me give you a ride home."

"You betcha."

David stopped at the night deposit box and carefully put the canvas bag through the slot. He waited until he heard the soft thump, then checked that the bag had indeed fallen inside properly. Rainey waited, yawning, feeling the beginning of that logey aftermath when the adrenalin quits pumping and the body begins to realize just how much energy has been expended. David got back on the motorbike and started it up, and they drove home.

Rainey stripped off her clothes and took them to the laundry basket, then showered the stale beer and cigarette smoke from her skin and hair. The warm spray washed the edginess from her body and she began to relax after hours of being pumped up and on the go.

Funny about a word like "productivity"; it seemed to be reserved for people who wore suits and had initials after their names, people who moved with a kind of grace, like dancers, as if they'd gone to school to learn how to do it, looking unhurried and maybe even elegant. Move like that, at that speed, and you'd have half the customers in the bar standing up and screaming for service. Casual? If she moved at a casual speed there'd be a small-scale riot. She arrived at work casual, but by the time she had her change-apron on and her float counted, the noise, the smells, the crowd—even if it wasn't yet a crowd but only a spattering of early arrivals, or afternoon hangers-on—would start to get to her, and by the time she headed out with her first tray, any sign of casual was gone, she was moving into gear. The more people, the more noise, the faster she moved.

At the same time she had to stay aware of who was ordering what, because not everybody wanted mugs of draft. Some people wanted it in bottles, and all those brands to keep track of—God forbid you'd give someone the wrong label. Plus run numbers through her head, add the total, take the money, make change, and get empty tables cleared, cleaned and reset before the next swarm of celebrants arrived. People wanted a clean table waiting. If she didn't get it done before they settled their bums in chairs, they started yelling. What the hell, didn't anybody come to work here tonight? What *is* this shit? As if they'd never seen empty glasses and bottles. Ten minutes later these people who wanted everything neat as a pin had slopped suds and beer and were busy turning their lungs to cinders so they could overfill the ashtray or, better yet, overturn it so she had to do the clean-the-table routine all over again. But this wasn't considered productivity. It was just menial work, and it got no respect at all.

Well, they could take their respect and put it where the sun had never even tried to shine. Rainey wasn't out looking for respect. She wanted money. And right now, she wanted hours of unbroken sleep.

She wakened quickly, jerked awake by the uproar in the kitchen. Lin was off on one of his soon-to-be-patented uproars. Rainey got out of bed, grabbed her robe and hurried, barefoot, to try to mediate. She got to the kitchen just as Chris was finally losing it.

Chris grabbed Lin and lifted him from the floor; then, so together Rainey knew she'd visualized this a thousand times, practised it in her head until when she finally did it, everything worked and it all clicked together. Chris took two steps, sat in a chair, tipped Lin over her knee, hauled his pyjama bottoms down and gave him six of the hardest whacks in the world.

"I'll tell my dad!" Lin screeched.

"Tell the queen for all I care!"

"I'll phone the police! You aren't allowed to hit!"

"Phone the police. Go for it. And be sure to tell them about *this*," and she was on her feet, shaking him.

Rainey went into the kitchen, got a mug and went to the coffee machine to fill it. Chris wasn't deterred. She didn't stop shaking Lin until she was good and ready. Lin ran to his mother, bawling. "She hit me, Momma!"

"Good." Rainey put out her hand to keep him from bumping into her and wrapping his arms around her waist. She sat down at the table, sugared and creamed her coffee and sipped it, while Lin sobbed and howled and bellyached, all of it at the top of his voice. "If you don't shut up," Rainey said when he had stopped long enough to draw a breath, "I'm going to cut loose on you, myself."

He screamed at her. No words, just raw, frustrated fury. Rainey took another sip of coffee and Lin continued to screech. Chris watched, ready to blow again. Rainey got off her chair, grabbed Lin by his arm, dragged him to the back door, opened it and shoved him outside. Then she closed and locked the door. He screamed and grabbed the knob, rattling it. Then he spun and raced for the front door, but Chris had beat him to it.

"Coffee?" Rainey asked, coming back into the kitchen.

"Yes, thanks." Chris sat down and reached for her cigarettes. "I think maybe we need some help with this kid," she sighed. "I'm not sure what the hell is wrong, but something is *not* working."

"David thinks he's on a power trip."

"What would David know about kids?"

"Well, he used to *be* one, if you remember."

Sarah came into the kitchen step-by-stepping it with her walker. Both her daughters jumped up, moved a chair so that she could just sink into it and helped get her settled at the table. Chris poured a cup of coffee for Sarah while Lin jumped up and down on the front porch hollering.

"What was this one about?"

"I don't know," Rainey shrugged. "It was going on when I woke up."

"He's late for school," Chris said, putting the coffee in front of Sarah. "Sally left about a half hour ago but mister wouldn't move on his own. Refused to eat his cereal, refused to eat toast. When I told him to get dressed he told me to go fuck myself, and when I said he would be late for school if he didn't hurry, he repeated the invitation so . . . I warmed his butt."

"How'd he get outside?"

"I put him there," Rainey admitted.

"Hmm." Sarah lifted her mug with both hands and sipped carefully.

"So here we are, two grown women, sitting with bated breath, waiting for words of wisdom and experience, and there you are, sipping coffee."

"I haven't got any idea what to do about it. Neither of mine acted like this at all. If they had, well—if I didn't kill them, Angus would when he got home."

"They don't let you kill them any more, Momma. They've got the Help Line and children's rights organizations and who knows what-all." Chris shook her head. "I'd lie down on the table and weep but he might see me through the window and consider it a victory."

"And he wouldn't eat breakfast?"

"No. Nor get dressed."

"Well, Minnie wants to go outside to pee. That's going to mean unlocking the door. That's going to mean mister charges back in here. So what do we do about it?"

"Ignore him," Sarah said calmly. "I think we should try really hard to ignore this nonsense."

"You think he should tell me to go fuck myself and I should ignore it?"

"No, I think when he tells you to go fuck yourself you should warm his butt and squirt detergent in his mouth to wash the filth out. When he starts this screaming routine, that's when you ignore him. I like the part about putting him outside, might give him the idea that in this house we don't put up with his stunts."

"He told me he wanted to live with his dad," Chris admitted.

"Good," Rainey said. "Let them do it to each other."

"You mean it?"

"Do you have any idea what his dad would do if he pulled a stunt like he's pulled this morning?"

"Beat him black and blue, I'd imagine."

"Exactly. And maybe mister would benefit from finding that out for himself, because I'm just about fed up. I am so sick of ass-holes!" She looked at Sarah and pointed her finger. "And I *know*, Momma, I helped make this one myself, I don't need reminded!"

"I didn't say a word," Sarah snapped. "If you heard someone say that, it must be the echo of your own voice in your own head."

"Great," Chris laughed. "Now we can quit fighting with the damn kid and fight with each other."

"I'm not fighting," Sarah said stubbornly.

"Neither am I." Rainey calmed down and patted Sarah's hand. "I'm sorry, Momma. Let's let the dog out and see what happens next."

Minnie went out, Lin came in. He went directly to his room.

Chris began to cook bacon and eggs, Rainey supervised the toaster and Sarah sat at the table sipping coffee and wondering why it was so many magazine articles made such a big thing out of "empty nest syndrome," and none of them even mentioned that the refilled nest brought ulcers and shattered nerves. Maybe she'd phone the Seaview Motel, see if she could arrange an off-season price if she guaranteed long-term occupancy. Nice view once you looked up, past the mammoth tank farm, the fuel oil company, the wrecking yard and the fish processing plant. Beyond that marring smudge the ocean beckoned, dotted with small islands and islets, and at night the bell buoy on the reef sounded regularly. Sometimes, before the incident, she had driven her car to the lay-by, parked and sat watching and listening, enjoying the peace. On nights when the wind howled like a banshee and the waves came in tall and heavy, smashing against the rocks and sending spray up over the lip of the bluff, she thought the storms were the most beautiful; on other nights, when the sea was like glass and the air was still, she thought the calm was wonderful.

Right now she would pay money for the chance to vote for the calm. It wasn't just Lin with his shenanigans; the truth of it was she just wasn't used to having a crowded kitchen, especially not first thing in the morning. Sarah liked to get up to peace and quiet. She liked to make her own coffee. Hers had more body to it than the coffee Chris made, which Sarah privately thought of as water bewitched and coffee begrudged. And the damn dog, too, ripping around the house yipping as if she were in hot pursuit of the last dragon in the world.

While Sarah sat at the table, face as calm as the unbroken shell of an egg, breakfast was cooked, the table was set and more coffee was made, this time by Rainey, thank God, who at least knew you had to use coffee to get coffee.

Lin came from his bedroom, fully dressed. He sat down at his place at the table and waited expectantly. Chris put the plate of bacon on the table; Lin reached and Sarah slapped his hand. He glared at her.

"You have better manners than that. And if you don't, you

should have. Keep your hands off the food. That's why someone invented forks."

"I don't have a fork," he whined. "I don't have a plate, either."

"If you're going to whine you'll have to go somewhere else to do it," she said, using both hands to lift her mug of Rainey's coffee. "I can't abide whining."

"What about *me?*" he yelped, realizing the others had plates and cutlery and he had nothing.

"A while ago you told me to go fuck myself," Chris said calmly. "Do you really think I feel like putting myself out for you? I don't think so, Lin. You get what you hand out. You told me to go fuck myself, so I'll tell you: go fuck yourself."

"Mom? *Mom!*"

"Won't do any good to yell at me. We've all talked about this. If you are nice, we are nice, if you're a pill, you're on your own."

Lin's eyes brimmed but the tears did not dribble. He got up from his chair, stomped to the cupboard and got himself a plate, yarded open the drawer and got a fork and a knife, then stomped back to the table with them. The plate of bacon got passed around but nobody passed it to him. When Chris had helped herself she put it on the table. He almost reached out and grabbed with his fingers, but he had the feeling Sarah would give his hand a good whack with her knife if he didn't take a telling, so he used his fork. The same thing happened with the platter of scrambled eggs; there was enough for him but he had to serve himself.

Chris spoke to Rainey, Chris spoke to Sarah, Chris did not speak to Lin. Rainey spoke to Sarah and Chris; she ignored Lin. Sarah talked to her daughters and didn't so much as glance at her grandson. Lin ate hugely and tried to pretend he didn't care if they paid attention to him or not. But he was starting to feel very much left out of life.

"I need a note," he snapped.

Rainey almost told him to go write it himself, but it wasn't Lin who needed the note, it was the school. So she decided to write one. But it wouldn't be the please-excuse-Lin-for-being-late kind. She'd let them know exactly why he was late.

"I need a ride, too."

"You have feet," Sarah said. "It's nobody's fault but your own that you didn't leave on time."

"I hate you all," he said, almost conversationally. "You're all assholes, every one of you."

That's when Sarah's good hand swung. She didn't hit Lin, she put her hand on his shoulder and shoved. The chair tipped, Sarah grabbed the back of it, gave a shake and dumped him off his chair onto the floor, where he sat, stunned.

"Don't talk like that at *my* table," Sarah said calmly. She righted the chair, shoved it under the edge of the table, then returned to her breakfast.

Lin wanted to tell her to go fuck herself, but he was sure more would happen than him getting dumped off his chair. He wanted to yell at her, but the last time he'd done any yelling he'd been as good as tossed out the back door. He would have flown at her and punched, but he knew Auntie Chris would get into it and all you had to do was look at the muscles in her forearms and you knew she could probably cream just about everybody in town.

He got off the floor and sat back on his chair to finish his breakfast. Rainey finished hers as if nothing had happened, then went to the jar where the ballpoint pens lived. She got a pad of paper out of the Hell Drawer and sat back down at the table to write Lin's note. "To whom it may concern: Lin is late this morning because he woke up with the idea he was the boss of the world and it has taken quite a bit of time to help him realize he's just a citizen like the rest of us. We've been having some real problems with his behaviour, and we were wondering if his wretched attitude is demonstrating itself at school as well. None of us are really sure what to do about it although we have all, at some point, wondered if it is still against the law to nail them to trees or tie them up and store them in the darkest corner of the basement. Thank you very much. Lin's mother, Rainey."

She folded the paper, took the writing pad back to the Hell

Drawer, got an envelope, put the note inside and sealed it. When Lin finished his breakfast, Rainey handed him the note. He stuffed it in his pocket and left the table, glaring at all of them. Moments later he left the house with his jacket and his pack, and hurried down the walk to the gate. Minnie ran toward him but he whirled and lifted one leg, ready to kick her, and the dog had sense enough to veer past him, out of range.

"That thing with the chair was a smooth move, Sarah dear." Chris poured coffee and took the pot back to the machine.

"I think it has to happen almost immediately to take effect," Sarah said, as if they were discussing African violets. "It's a bit like training a puppy. No sense raising a fuss an hour after the deed, they don't connect the two. Besides, it was that or pummel him and I'm in no shape to pummel a cat."

Sarah left the table and made her way back to her bedroom. The walker was going to wind up either her absolute enemy or her best friend; she would have to decide for herself which it was. She clipped the corner of the fridge and she bumped the edge of her bedroom door, but on the other hand she did not pitch onto her face or go down in a heap. She sat on the edge of the bed, planning ahead, trying to anticipate every move she would have to make to get her clothes from the dresser and closet and get them back to her bed so she could change into them.

"Need any help?" Rainey asked from the hallway.

"Maybe later. But I'd like to try on my own, please."

"You're the boss, darling."

But she wasn't. What was that poem, anyway, the one about being the captain of your ship, the master of your destiny. She'd thought it lovely. Now it seemed very much like hubris. Nobody was master of anything. Or mistress, either. All a body could do was try to cope. Sometimes, when Angus was half-packed and there were Yank tourists in the bar, and he was looking for a bit of excitement, he'd jump up, lift his glass high and holler "Remember the Alamo." Those who'd seen his act before would join him, cheering, and inevitably the Yanks would stand, too, glasses raised high. Then, just before the Yanks started sipping and toasting,

Angus would add, "If there'd been a back door on the bugger, Texas would be Mexico today," and he'd laugh and laugh and laugh. For lack of a back door a nation gets a crowd of heroes, and yet none of us had back doors, we all had to deal with whatever it was coming at us through the only door we had. What kind of mastery is there in that?

Getting dressed proved to be very hard work, but Sarah managed by herself—except for her laces. She was afraid to try walking with the laces undone and flapping, so she lifted the shoes, tied them together, draped them around her neck and padded, sock-foot, to the living room where Chris was finishing the vacuuming.

"I think I need the kind the kids get," she confessed, "with the Velcro."

"We could try Velcro or we could go for loafers."

"I haven't worn loafers in half a century," Sarah laughed. "Should I get brand new shiny pennies to go in the front part?"

"How's that?" Chris looked up from where she was hunkered, tying shoelaces.

"A bit loose-ish."

"Loose-ish? Is that like meet you at seven-ish?"

"I could probably push you over, too, you know."

"How's that?"

"Much better. And now I'm going for a walk. I barely got a glimpse of my yard yesterday, and I'm tired of being inside."

"I'll go with you."

"No, you won't. Minnie will come with me. If I fall, or if I need help, I'll tell her to talk. You'll hear her barking and know you're to bring a crane to lift me."

"Momma—"

"That's right!" Sarah snapped, suddenly very angry. "I am the momma. Not you. You are the child. Not me."

"I'm a very large child," Chris said mildly.

"Yes. A big baby," and then the anger was gone. "And mine, too."

She heaved herself up out of the chair and made her way to the front door. It wasn't difficult going out, she didn't have to get around the door, she just turned the knob, then kept pushing with her walker frame and her weight. The door opened outward and it was an easy matter to get past it to the porch. Coming back inside would be something else.

Chris hovered anxiously until Sarah got herself down the ramp. The walker was built so that Sarah could actually get inside it, and lower a seat, then walk in the little cage that formed when she did that. But even though it was Canada Standards Approved, Chris had to hurry down and check it. "I'm sorry I'm fussing," she blurted, "I just don't much feel like losing you."

"I won't have a fit this time," Sarah said, "but now that you know how it works, this is the end of it. I will not be driven to distraction by too much attention and fussing."

She sat, stubbornly refusing to take even one step with Chris standing over her, face tight with worry. "Go away," Sarah said, feeling her temper start to simmer again.

Chris left. As soon as the door closed, Sarah stood up and moved slowly down the walk to the bulb bed at the front of the house. The crocuses were still blooming; they'd hang on until the weather got too warm for them, then the white flowers would fade and the little round green seed heads would swell. Sarah loved crocuses. Even without the blossoms they looked like flowers. Some people snipped off the seed heads, some even took the lawn mower to them, claiming they drained the vitality from the bulb and made next year's blooms smaller, but Sarah didn't believe it. She let them do what they had been designed to do. There were cycles to things; why interfere? If the bulbs were in any way drained by the forming of seeds it got made up for when she put the beds to sleep and fertilized. Not only did she spread the well-rotted dark soil from her compost bed, she added rose food, convinced it helped with the colours of the tulips and hyacinths. She could smell the perfume of the hyacinths, and so could the bees—if bees could smell. Perhaps it was colour attracted them. They always seemed to go for the blue ones first. Blue hyacinths, but they seemed to prefer the yellow crocuses. Wouldn't it be lovely if just once in a lifetime a person could sit herself down and *talk* with a few bees, find out the how-come of their choices? Find out if they can smell the perfume or if they're just hard-wired to respond in certain ways. Find out if each bee has its own awareness or if each one is like one single cell in a big buzzy brain. And crickets. What new things would a person learn if just once, just one time, that person could discuss things with crickets?

The lawn was clipped and neat, the flowerbeds were well cared for and the rose bushes were pruned and trimmed, the buds beginning to swell. She couldn't have done better herself. Sarah sat on her walker seat and feasted her eyes. Out here, pretending the walker was just another chair, she could feel at home. The time she had spent in hospital seemed unreal. There were moments when it seemed like a nearly endless stretch of fear, boredom, and sorrow; other times, like now, it seemed as if she'd hardly been away from her own life, her real life. She tried to put it into perspective: when she was struck, the ground was cold, heavy with stored water. Even the weeds were still dormant. Then the incident, and now the flowers were blooming, the lawn was lush and the world was ripe with promise.

Minnie started yapping. Sarah jerked, wondering if she'd dropped into one of her not-quite-here fugues, released her grip for a brief span of time. But Minnie had another reason to be practically wiggling out of her tight skin.

"Bruno." She smiled at him.

"Good morning, my dear Sarah," he said, moving to stand beside her, patting her shoulder, even daring to rub her back.

"You've done a wonderful job." She looked at him, then at the flowers. "And the house is lovely. You're a good friend."

"Your grandson helped me," he said, stuffing his hands in his pockets and standing beside her, patient and calm.

"I was thinking of taking a walk," she said. "Mostly just around the yard, making myself at home where I can. It's hard to feel at home when the house is full of people I barely know."

"My children live in the old country," he said, sounding so smug Sarah had to laugh. "They detest me, and while it used to make me feel as if my heart was going to break, it now seems almost like the forgiveness of the Almighty."

"Detest you? They must be insane."

"Oh, they have reason. Or, just as important, they think they have reason." He looked around expectantly. "Where is Chester?"

"Ches— I don't know! My God! He's *always* in the yard!"

"Well, he's not in the yard now. Don't panic, I'll get the car. But first I'll check in the house. He might be—"

"He's not in the house, I was just in the house."

"Don't panic, my dear."

Bruno went into the house and came out seconds later with the keys to Rainey's truck. Sarah was already heading toward the garage, her walker feeling like an encumbrance even though she knew she'd pitch onto her face without it. Chris came running, Rainey right behind her.

"We don't all need to go looking for one pig," Sarah snapped.

"Just here to help you up into the seat," Chris said, forcing a smile. "Wouldn't dream of getting in your way, Momma."

Bruno backed the pickup out of the garage, parked it, got out, went around and opened the passenger door. With Chris helping, he got Sarah up onto the seat, then waited until she had her seat belt done before closing the door.

Five blocks from home, almost at the school playground, they spotted Chester coming down the sidewalk toward them, obviously headed home. And just as obviously, he was in no hurry.

"That scamp," Sarah laughed. "He's gone and followed Lin to school."

"While he's wasting time sniffing everybody's flowers through their fences, if you're at all interested, we can stop off at the store and have coffee. And anything else you'd like. Donut, or—"

"Why don't you teach me how to play that Keno game?"

"The pleasure, madam, would be mine."

"I'm not the madam," Sarah dared, "I just work here."

Bruno looked at her and laughed softly. "One of these days, my dear, you'll make a joke like that and I'll take it just a bit further. For example, I might ask you how much, or say something like, so let's go."

"You think you scare me? Wait until you do that and then hear what it is I have to say to you."

The late morning crowd was sitting with coffee, intent on the small console screen where the Keno numbers flashed. When they saw Sarah and Bruno they all smiled, forgot about the electronic game, and rearranged themselves to make room. Sarah manoeuvred her walker within reach of the round table, then checked to make sure the seat was in place before sitting.

"That's a good rig, you've always got your own chair," Tom Landry remarked. "I should look at them. What I've got now is a cane with this dealie on the bottom that's like a little box with four legs to it. Gives me more stability they say. Not that I've noticed much stability."

"How's your hip?" Sarah asked.

"Hah!" Tom shook his head. "They can say what they want about everything going better than they'd hoped. I grant you, the pain is gone, but the leg doesn't work worth a damn."

"There's no part of me works worth a damn," Caroline Blazer agreed. "By the time I get myself out of bed and start reclaiming all my bits and pieces—get my teeth out of the glass of water, get my wig, get this, get that—it's damn near noon."

"G'wan, you were the first one here this morning."

"I started getting ready for it last night," Caroline answered, and they laughed.

"Do you remember that old *Star Trek* program?" Sarah rested her lazy arm and hand on her lap. "The one about the guy who'd been burned to a crisp in an accident or something? What was left of him was connected to machines. He kind of poked up out of this box, nothing left but a badly scarred face and a few fingers on one hand? But they took him to this world where dreams and wishes came true? And he met this absolutely gorgeous young woman who fell madly in love with him? And he fell in love with her? And what she saw was this young, strong, handsome man, and what he saw was every man's dream, but what everyone else saw was the ruin he was and the gorgon she was?" They were all looking at Sarah, not a sign of pity or worry

127

or fear or uncertainty in their faces. "Well, I want that box he was in."

"The life support box?"

"Exactly. I'm still trying to figure out if it's more trouble to get my shoes on or to get myself to the toilet. With that box I wouldn't have to worry about either."

"Is that a pig walking down the street?" Tom asked. They all craned to look. "Is that your pig, Sarah?"

"That's my pig. My fine swine. We think he followed Lin to school this morning."

"Well, it's you he's following now. He wants in. Probably wants coffee."

"Chester doesn't like coffee. But he will do almost anything for a glazed donut."

"I'll get him one and lure him into the back of the truck with it."

"You can't lift him," she protested mildly. "He weighs at least two hundred pounds."

"I thought he was supposed to be a *miniature* Vietnamese potbellied pig," Caroline argued. "How does anything that big qualify as miniature?"

"A real pig can go a thousand pounds."

"He *is* a real pig," Sarah countered. "Unlike your hip."

"I never claimed my hip was a pig."

"No, and it's not real, either."

"Well, then, I don't know what to do," Bruno sighed. "You're right, I can't lift him in, and there's no ramp, and he doesn't seem interested in walking."

"He'll leave when we do." She rose, leaving her seat in place.

"Are you leaving?"

"No, I am not. I haven't learned how to play this game, yet. I'm just going to tell him to lie down and stay out from underfoot."

"Is she serious?" Tom asked.

"I don't know that Sarah is exactly serious," Bruno said proudly, "but I do know that pig understands just about every word she says to him. Sarah serious is not something I've seen much of, she's usually full of jokes."

"Damn shame about that stroke."

"She was so vital," Caroline added.

"She still is," Bruno said. "She's just a bit slower, is all."

"I'll be damned, look at that, the bloody pig is lying down to wait for her."

"That's my number!" Caroline turned her attention to her Keno card. "Look, I've got four out of six. That's better. Yesterday I got nothing worth getting all day."

"I spend a lot of time getting nothing, too," Tom answered, and Bruno giggled like a boy. "Go ahead. Gloat, you old bugger." Tom lit a cigarette.

"No gloating," Bruno said, reaching for one of Tom's cigarettes. "I live in hope. I just can't remember what it is I'm hoping for."

Rainey went back to bed. She didn't exactly get *into* bed, she was dressed and getting undressed seemed like something she was just too tired to do, so she lay on top of the bed, with the quilt pulled up to her hips, more for comfort than for warmth. She heard the phone ring but ignored it. It rang a second time, then didn't ring a third so she assumed Chris had it. It was probably for her, anyway, more business about selling the boat, which seemed to be an even bigger deal than selling a house.

She was so weary she couldn't even wonder how Sarah was or why she wasn't home yet. It was ridiculous, really. She had actually done more, and harder, physical work trying to keep the motel units vacuumed, scrubbed, aired and supplied with clean bed linen and towels because most of that led to other jobs like enormous laundry loads, and all the folding and putting away of sheets and pillow slips, the changing of vacuum bags, the go go go, steady but not slow. On top of which the yard, such as it was, and the driveway to keep free of ruts and potholes. And the damn dogs to feed! Mustn't forget the dogs. If they're hungry they might devour the children when they get off the bus from school. So if she'd done all that, why was she so worn to a nub with an eight-hour job? The motel had been a good twelve hours with the other twelve more or less on call, people as apt to arrive at two-thirty in the morning as eight o'clock at night. But she was tired, no doubt about it.

Maybe it was all part of the giving up of impossible things: a go-nowhere marriage and a business on the edge of bankrupt-cy—someone else's fantasy, really, not what you'd call a business. Make a body wonder why anybody would be willing to buy it, everyone should have known the new freeway wasn't going to change its route, the motel would always be faced the wrong way and awkward to get to, it was never going to fulfill any of the BS hopes he'd had. Maybe when you started to give away some of the load, your body decided it was going to give up on the hyper-energy, the ready adrenalin. Maybe once the body realized the race was over, it decided to get some of what it had been needing for so long.

She was pretty sure the fatigue wasn't depression. She knew some people dealt with—or, more to the point, didn't deal with—depression by sleeping. If you couldn't sing Stop the world I want to get off, maybe you snored a few choruses of Do what you want but do it without me. They said depression was just anger turned inward; that made sense except for the "just" part. "Just" means just a bit, just a tad, just a tinge. Delete the "just," there was never any bit, tad or tinge. Depression is anger turned inward.

Okay. She had ample reason to be angry, mainly with herself for hanging in long after it made any sense, but she didn't believe she'd ever been a person to waste time, and what was past, was, when all was said and done: past and passed by, passed on, passed away, gone. Can't alter one second of yesterday. Hardly control today. She didn't feel she was stuffing anger or fury or rage or even disappointment down where it could only hurt her, not against the bad luck, bad choices, dumbness of the past. She was just tired, was all.

And it hadn't helped any to be yanked out of slumber by Lin's tantrum. Well, she'd deal with that later. If she didn't stop fighting the very thing she most needed, she'd be in no shape to deal with Lin or anything else.

6

Chris hung up the phone, then went out on the back steps to smoke a cigarette and visit with Minnie. And wasn't that interesting. The school counsellor telling her he was surprised they'd had any kind of problem with Franklin because at school he was an absolute model. So what was that all about? If the kid was settled in at school, getting along with his peers, well liked by his teachers, who was the little horror who was making life miserable, and why?

Sarah and Bruno came driving slowly down the street, with Chester as honour guard, trotting along the sidewalk. Sarah's window was open and she had her head out, talking to the neighbourhood perambulator. They turned into the driveway and the pig raced for the back yard, woofing and grunting happily, and Chris went down to help Sarah from the truck.

Sarah didn't need any help. Bruno got out, went around, opened the door and Sarah put her walker down for Bruno to put in place and balance. She leaned forward and Chris's heart missed several beats. But Sarah got her hands on the walker frame and slowly let herself down from the seat and into position. As quick as a cat licking cream from its chin, Bruno had the seat in place and locked. Sarah took several steps, then sat down, pretending to puff and blow tiredly.

"That's a good trick." Chris patted Sarah's arm. "We'll see you on TV next on that circus program."

"I'm not taking Rainey's truck any more. A person needs an extension ladder to get in and out of it. They must make them for people with really long legs."

"How far did that pig go? You've been gone forever."

"The pig didn't go far. He was on his way back when we found him. We just stopped at the store for Keno and coffee."

"I didn't know you played Keno." Chris was aware how shocked she sounded, but she didn't care.

"I do now. Bruno taught me."

Sarah got to her feet again and moved her walker toward the house, Bruno walking beside her, Chris coming behind and being very careful to close the gate so the pig couldn't take another hike. She told Sarah about the phone call from the school, and Sarah nodded.

"He's always known, from the first day of kindergarten, that they just do not put up with certain behaviours," she said, her voice flat and certain. "But there hasn't been the same consistency at home. I think a lot depended on how worn out Rainey was, and a lot depended on whether or not his father was at home."

"You think Wayne cracked the whip?"

"No, I think when his father was home the child could get away with almost anything at all because his mother would turn herself inside out to keep things calm and pleasant. Instead of confronting him, she probably bribed him with a candy bar or something."

"I'll candy bar him," Chris promised.

Bruno insisted that Sarah take time for what he called a lie-down, and while she did that, he went out to the vegetable garden with the Rototiller and turned the soil again, breaking up and turning under the compost he'd spread. Rainey was still sleeping, and the last thing Chris needed was to tiptoe around the house so as not to awaken the snoozers while listening to the ungodly damn roar of the Rototiller. How many times was Bruno going to till the damn garden, anyway!

Chris whistled for Minnie, then got in her car and drove to Annwyn's place. She was in luck—Annwyn was just getting up.

"Mmmmm." Annwyn hugged her, kissing her warmly.

"Mmmmm yourself," Chris agreed.

"I've just made coffee. Want some?"

"Half a cup. I'm already pretty well topped up. God, it's a madhouse over there."

"That bad, huh?"

"Worse."

"Well, you should have moved in with me a couple of years ago, if not sooner."

"Huh?"

"I mean it. We should live together."

"Annie, darling, this place is barely big enough for—"

Annwyn was on her feet, her cheeks flushing. She picked up a chair, lifted it and slammed it back down on the kitchen floor. Minnie ran for the back door. Annwyn lifted one end of the table and slammed it back down, then repeated the move. "Is anything Krazy glued to the floor?" she shouted. "Is it? Look, Chris, the door that opened to let you in will open to let the goddamn furniture, such as it is, back out again!"

"Annie, please—"

"No! *No!* And no no no no *no*, Chris. Stop evading. Sometimes, honest to God, you're as slippery as a snake, weaving your way in and out and around and between and never actually doing or saying!"

"What?"

"I'll tell you what!" But Annwyn stormed out of the kitchen and Chris could only sit where she was, wondering what in the name of all that was holy was coming down on her head.

Annie returned, looking calmer. "Okay." She sat, no longer shouting or yelling. "Okay, here's my lease. See. All I have to do is give them thirty days' notice. I can leave this little pillbox any time at all. You're dithering away about what will you do with the money from the boat. I'll tell you what you *should* do, you should buy a house. I'll even tell you which one. Donnellys' place is going to go up for sale. You should buy it. It's big. Big enough for us to each have a nice big private space of our own plus a come-together space. I'll take the basement suite they built for Grandma Donnelly when she was still alive, I don't mind living in the basement. It's actually above ground, anyway. And twice the size of this place."

"And once I've sold the boat . . . what if I don't find a job? What if I'm S.O.L. and broke?"

"My rent will buy the groceries and any new jeans you might happen to need."

"Live off you?"

"Why not, I'll be living in your house!"

"But—"

"Do you want to live with me or don't you? Do you want this relationship to be a relationship or just an on-going casual-fuck affair?"

"Annwyn!"

"Get off the pot, Chris. Don't you know when you spend your life sitting on the fence you're in dire danger of getting the pointed end of a picket right up your fundament?"

"I just hadn't ever thought of—"

"So *think*."

"Annie—"

"No." Annie stood up, lifted her coffee mug and dunk-shot it across the small kitchen and into the sink, where it broke. "I'm going to have a shower. When I come out I'm going to get dressed. And then either *we* are going to go over to have a look at Donnellys' place or I, *alone*, am going to go check out an apartment. One where dogs are *not* allowed."

Chris sat, stunned and numb. She had never seen Annwyn so upset. They had known each other since childhood and in all that time Annwyn had never . . . except, of course, for the time she turned on Jerome Keatley and nearly ripped his face off because he'd dared to pat her on the butt and say "nice ass." The thing was, what would Chris do if she off-loaded the *Sealkie* and sold the licences? She might talk about buying a gas station franchise but she couldn't even begin to imagine herself doing that. She might joke about buying an ice cream parlour and eating up all the profits but that was a joke. Even at her most hard-headed, Annie wouldn't expect Chris to actually do that. And certainly Annie wouldn't expect Chris to open a cappuccino bar and sandwich shop. That too was a joke. People who went to cappuccino bars didn't eat, they all looked totally anorexic, as if they were trying to turn into the human skeleton like Nancy R had done. Well, if Chris had to live with Nancy R's old man she'd have felt too pukey to eat, too.

"Well?" Annwyn was standing in the doorway to the kitchen, her hair still wet and curling tightly. She was wearing loafers, white socks, jeans and a T-shirt with a Tiger Balm ad on the front. And Chris knew she'd give away every single thing she owned and then go live in a damp cave before she'd risk what they had in any way.

Donnellys' big old farmhouse sat on fifteen acres of land. The old Donnelly farm had been twenty times that big, but the bugger Elise Donnelly had married had nagged and bitched until she let him subdivide the place. No sooner had he sold off most of the land than he hit the road, leaving Elise with two kids, an enraged and aging grandmother, and less than a fraction of the money from the sale of the land. Elise had always been quiet, wouldn't say boo to a goose, but even the most spineless worm can turn if her grandma is chewing at her arse, and Elise had gone first to a lawyer, then to the police. Smart-arse was found in Vancouver. By the time Elise was through with him she had most of her money back, Grandma Donnelly was calmed down and pleasant again, and the first of several "Donnelly" men was installed in the renovated basement. It was one of them, probably the reddy-haired one, who finished the suite. When he moved on, Grandma Donnelly moved into it.

And now Grandma Donnelly had gone where all feisty women go, Elise's kids were grown and long gone, with families and lives of their own, and Elise had decided she was selling. "I have my eye on a nice condo in town, with a view of the ocean," she said placidly. "I've had enough of cutting lawns and pruning fruit trees."

"What about Walter and Jean?"

"Until I'm dead, it's my decision. Once I'm dead they can fight over what's left. And since I hate the thought of them fighting, I'll try hard to spend it all before I go."

The house was set back from the street, with more than an acre of land in front, all of it in grass. Chris had no intention of pushing a lawn mower around on that and started a mental list of things she would absolutely *have* to get if . . . It was only an if, but if, if, and if, then she'd want a ride-on mower. Although, really, what was wrong with long grass? Where was the law written that said you had to have clipped, fertilized, watered, green, lush, fast-growing lawns so you could spend hours of your life keeping the grass cut? Just a bit of fence across the front, to save the flowers and shrubs, and you could graze a weanling steer there, fatten it and then, come autumn . . . mind you, she'd have to see if she could get Pete to do the butchering for her, she didn't have any idea at all how to go about that.

In the back the fruit trees were leafed out and the last of the blossoms beckoned. The sound of honeybees seemed loud. "Are those your bees?" she asked, dreading the answer.

"No, they come from Thelma Grierson's hives. Every year she gives me several jars of the honey. I give her as much fruit as she wants. The bees, well, they do all that work for the chance to live in wooden boxes and get robbed two or three times a year."

"Do they sting?"

"I won't say they don't, but I will say I've never been stung. You just watch to see which direction they're heading in and out, stay out of their fly path and you're fine."

"Traffic problems everywhere," Annwyn laughed.

The house was neat and clean but just about ready for new wallpaper and paint. Chris extended her mental list. The traffic pattern showed on the rug, too. More expense.

"I haven't listed it with a real estate agent yet," Elise said. "I thought I'd give myself a month. If I haven't sold it myself by then, I'll call them. The price will go up then, because I know what I want to have in my pocket when I walk away from here and their commission won't come from me!"

A positively enormous flat-faced Persian cat leaped to the back of the sofa in the living room, arched its back and hissed at Minnie.

"You have to take the cat, too," Elise instructed, as if the papers had been signed and they were all in full agreement. "My daughter-in-law bought that thing for me for Christmas a few years ago—three, in fact. The last thing I wanted was a damn cat, but the grandchildren were certain I'd be overjoyed so . . ."

"What's her name?"

"Puss." Elise hardly acknowledged the animal's presence. "I couldn't be bothered to think up anything else."

"Is she spayed?"

"No."

"Has she had kittens?"

"She has them, I get rid of them as soon as I find them."

Chris couldn't help it, she added the cost of spaying to her mental list. There was no way she could kill kittens, and Annwyn wasn't going to be interested. Annwyn was a total softie, as bad in her way as Sarah was in hers, with a garage full of mostly wild cats she fed as faithfully as if they were prize-winning show cats.

Rainey wakened to a quiet house. She got up and got moving, then went to the living room to sprawl in a chair and enjoy the solitude. No sooner had she settled herself and yawned a few luxurious times than Sarah came from her room and moved to the bathroom with her walker. They smiled at each other, but did not speak.

Still yawning, Rainey rose and went to the kitchen to put the kettle on for tea. She toasted two slices of white bread, spread on margarine, then cut several slices from a block of cheddar and made a sandwich. Sarah came into the kitchen, still tousled from bed.

"Sandwich?" Rainey asked.

"No, thank you."

"You're sure? It won't take but a minute."

"No, thank you." Sarah looked out the window. "Bruno not here?"

"I don't hear him."

Sarah reached for the phone and dialled. She waited, then smiled as the phone was answered. "Bruno. Sleeping Beauty wakened herself."

She listened, said yes, then hung up the phone. "Bruno will be here in a few moments," she said, "and then he and I are going for lunch."

"For lunch," Rainey repeated, feeling totally stupid.

"For lunch. Pizza."

"Pizza."

"Yes. Tomorrow we'll try something different. One day he pays, the next day I pay."

Rainey finished her sandwich, then went to her room to make up the rumpled bed. She had grown up in this room. At first she had shared it with Chris, but then Angus got the addition built and Chris, being the oldest, got to choose between the new room or the old one. She took the new one. That was fine with Rainey. She didn't want to live out in the back of the house, where only recently there had been nothing but grass.

Now she shared the room with Sally, and Lin slept on the fold-out couch in the room in the basement. At one time the room had been called the rumpus room and the TV had dominated it. But after Angus died, when just Chris and Sarah were left in the house, and Chris was off fishing half the year, the new TV went into the living room because, Sarah said, she wasn't going to challenge the stairs just to watch the news. The TV still down in the room might be a genuine antique, if a thing with an electric cord can be an antique. It was still working, but it was a black-and-white. Watching it gave a person a very strange feeling, like stepping back in time—except for the program content. Rainey didn't remember so much pushing, shoving, yelling, shooting and car crashes from her youth, and she certainly didn't remember a time when socially inappropriate insults passed for humour. But don't we all carry our own editor in our heads, rewriting our memories each time we recall something?

She really ought to have done the laundry. There was still

time, it was energy and inclination that were missing. Tomorrow would be soon enough. She still felt as if what she wanted to do was curl up and go back to sleep. Maybe if she got some fresh air. Took a walk, perhaps, or did a bit of yard work. The thought of it made her yawn, but a person couldn't spend her entire life walking in a daze or lying on the bed sawing logs.

Bruno and Sarah headed off for a late lunch. It occurred to Rainey that neither of them would be very hungry at suppertime. Well, the kids could be depended on to consume plates of food. Maybe she'd do burritos. They could usually pack away an amazing amount if she spiced it up a bit and called it foreign food. She wasn't sure Sarah would care for it, but if not, she could fix something else for her. As for Chris, well, she might or might not be home for supper. Wouldn't you think she'd at least phone if she wasn't going to be there? Sarah didn't seem to notice or mind, but it ticked Rainey off to cook supper for three adults and two kids, and wind up serving it to two adults and two kids.

There wasn't a thing needed doing in the yard. Nothing Rainey could identify, anyway. Well, she could always stroll down to the corner store and get a couple of tomatoes for the burritos. What else would she need? Green pepper, maybe, if they had one.

She took her time walking to the store, and decided to have a cup of coffee while she was there. Several people were sitting at small tables, engrossed in the Keno machine. Their eyes flicked to her, then flicked back to the game. Rainey didn't know any of them. Not long ago she had known everybody in the neighbourhood, their children, their parents, the type and name of their dogs. Now entire bunches of people were strangers to her.

She was halfway through her coffee when David walked in. He saw her and waved. Rainey waved back and smiled.

"Pull me one, too," David called.

The coffee machine stood on the counter, a sign on it telling how much for a cup and how much for a refill. The mugs were laid out upside down on clean paper towelling, and little creamers were heaped in a bowl with ice cubes—small ones, no bigger than after-dinner mints. Rainey poured coffee for David, then set the mug of undoctored coffee beside her and moved the creamer bowl closer.

"Had lunch?" he asked as he slid onto the stool.

"Sandwich," she replied briefly.

"I just got up," he admitted, adding sugar and cream to his coffee and inhaling the scent. "First cup of coffee. Ambrosia."

"You're lucky!" She laughed shortly and told him about the morning uproar with Lin. "When it all calmed down I went back to bed, but . . ."

"I don't know how you do it." He shook his head admiringly. "I know I can't just crawl into bed and drop off as soon as I get home. I have to shower, shampoo, wind down, not only get the stink of the place off me, but get the rush-rush-rush out of me as well. Then when I do get into bed, I don't just drop off into dreamland, usually I wind up reading a couple of very boring articles in those good-for-you magazines, which are not to be confused with the other kind."

"I don't read in bed because Sally's in the room with me, but I often sit in the living room. I read the other kind of magazines, though. The kind with those articles like Can This Marriage Be Saved, and Do You Know Your Kids quizzes. If I'm lucky I've remembered to get a really trashy check-out counter one, with those articles on—oh, the woman in Brazil who gave birth to a child who had a face like a cat and when its teeth came in they were sharp and pointed. You know, that stuff that never happens here, always somewhere else. There are some very strange things go on in Italy, for example. Things like people locking their relatives in sheds for thirty years or chaining adulterous spouses to the bed for a decade or two."

"My favourite is the one about the woman doctor somewhere near Russia," David said. "She was driving down a lonely country road when she turned a curve and found the road blocked. So she had to stop and when she did, these two men jumped her and raped her. Repeatedly, of course. She pretended she enjoyed every minute of it and invited them to her place for a few drinks. Doctored the drinks, knocked them out cold, then castrated them.

Took them back to the place where they'd raped her, and dropped them out of her car."

"If she took them back, how did they ever find out who did it?"

"One of the rapists remembered the two-snake decal on her car, or something."

"So did they give her a Hero of the Republic badge or a jail term?"

"I can't remember. But I do remember thinking any rapist stupid enough to go to the victim's house for a few drinks deserved to be castrated."

"So now we know they have no brains and no balls. I guess they're ready to be made government advisors or something."

One of the men playing Keno broke out laughing. Rainey turned, surprised.

"Excuse me, lady, but eavesdropping is one of the big recreational pursuits in this place," the burly guy explained, still chortling.

"Woulda been a better story if she'd known, being a doctor and all, which nerve to press to paralyze them right then and there," another Keno player offered, "and *then* done a job on them. You know, like Spock's hold, where he just reaches out and that's it, you're out cold as a clam."

"Maybe those castrate-the-rapist stories are planted by the government or the police chiefs association or something," Rainey dared. "After all, if more and more people started doing it—"

"Less and less guys would be doing it," David agreed. "I hate the fuckers," he said conversationally. "They make it hard for me. I try to be friendly and the nicest women in the world reach for their pepper spray."

They walked home together in companionable silence. Twice they stopped, once to enjoy several flowering hawthorn trees, once to admire a huge lilac bush thick with purple blooms. "So what have you got on your agenda for this afternoon?" David asked, sounding almost uninterested.

"I'm going to start putzing around getting ready to make

burritos for the kids' suppers," Rainey answered, lifting her little brown bag of tomatoes and peppers and giving it a wiggle.

"Too bad," he grinned. "I was hoping you'd say 'Nothing,' and then I could say, well, why not come to my place and we'll make mad passionate love until it's time to get ready for work. But you'd rather slice and dice and lop and chop."

"I'm not saying I'd *rather*," she corrected him, with no hint of humour at all. "But when I do go to your place for an extended session of passion it won't be for a joke, and it won't be because I've got nothing better to do." He stared at her, nodded and started walking again. "Besides, I'm still married," she added. "Although I have to tell you that wouldn't slow me down much."

"Wouldn't slow me down at all." He reached for her hand. "And it's no joke. And I can't think of anything else I'd rather do. Or anyone else I'd rather do it with."

Lin walked in the house looking like someone caught halfway between insolence and total submission. Sarah sat at the table with a deck of cards as Rainey put a pile of chopped tomato in a bowl.

"Hi, babe," Sarah said, as if there had never been an uproar.

"Hi," Lin said ungraciously.

"Did you know Chester tried to go to school with you this morning?"

He stared and she knew he was expecting a blast for leaving the gate unlatched. "He was on his way back when Bruno and I found him," Sarah laughed softly. "You'd have thought he was paying rent on every house in the neighbourhood, just sauntering down the sidewalk on his trotters, sniffing flowers and ignoring the barking dogs. And they were all barking, he had them pitching fits. I guess they aren't used to having pigs promenading past their yard."

"I thought I closed the gate," Lin dared.

"It's a pain of a gate, anyway," Sarah agreed. "Maybe I should get a new latch for it and you could get Bruno to help you put it on."

"Don't need Bruno. I can do it," Lin blurted. "All you need is a wire loop-thing or a piece of rope."

"That would probably do it," Sarah agreed. "Look what your mother is making. She says you like it. I don't know as I've ever had any. Oh, by the way, Bruno told me to ask you if you'd mind going over to give him a hand. I think he wants to clean his basement and he needs someone on the other end of the box."

"Sure." Lin went to his room and came out again without his pack. "Can I invite him for supper?"

"Bruno? Well, sure, I guess so." Rainey looked at Sarah.

"Wonderful idea. Did you get smart at school or were you already smart before you went?"

"I wasn't very smart this morning." Lin dodged out the door and was gone before either of them could reply.

"Do you think that was an apology?" Rainey asked.

"I don't see why we should come to that conclusion. None of the rest of us have ever apologized for anything in our entire lives, why should he?"

Chris wasn't home by the time Rainey left for work, and not a word of explanation. Oh well, Bruno had come over, and anyway maybe it didn't matter. On the other hand, it would be nice not to be treated like a short-order cook.

David grinned and slid forward and inch or two on the bike seat. Rainey climbed up behind him, put on her helmet and steadied herself for the takeoff. The only thing wrong with a bike was you couldn't very well talk to each other, although they had helmets with built-in mikes and earphones. Probably cost an arm and a leg. And a few teeth, as well. But maybe part of the built-in feature was a little radio as well, so you could tune in to some music. Mind you, in a five-minute drive a person wouldn't perish for lack of rock and roll. Still, if you were to, say, go on a trip, it might be nice. Ah, but would it be safe? With the sound of the engine plus the radio plus any conversation you were in, you might not hear any other traffic. Of course the thing had mirrors.

Rainey wondered why she spent so much time gnawing away

on absolute inconsequentials and so little on trying to just simply enjoy the ride. Wondered, too, why her mind dodged away from any thought of David himself. She had enjoyed walking hand-in-hand with him. She supposed the neighbours would have a lot to say about it.

Bruno and Sarah played cards at the table. Sally concentrated on her homework. Lin did his compulsory half-hour of reading practice, then tuned in to TV until the program change told him it was time to run his bath. He put a tiny squirt of Skin so Soft in the water and lay back, soaking.

Nobody had made any mention of the uproar in the morning. That did not mean they had forgotten it, or that they were going to pretend it had never happened. Actually, he felt pretty crummy about it. Sometimes he had no idea why he did and said things. Sometimes it felt almost as if someone else was doing it.

"You going to be in there all night?" Sally called, rapping on the door.

"I've only been here a couple of minutes," he argued.

"You've been in there a good half hour!" But she wasn't griping, she was almost laughing. "Maybe you fell asleep and didn't know it."

"I'm coming, I'm coming."

"Leave the bathwater."

"You don't want *this* bathwater," he yelled. "I was filthy! Bruno has a spider farm in his basement."

He dried himself, hauled on his Toronto Raptors pyjamas, brushed his teeth and went into the kitchen to say goodnight. The little radio was playing old-timey stuff and Grandma and Bruno were having tea and still playing cards.

"I'm going to bed," he said.

"Not without spending some time on my knee cuddling, you're not." Sarah's good arm reached out, grasped his wrist and pulled him to her. "Mmmm, you smell good."

"I like it," he admitted.

"I do, too. Smell and feel. You have a good sleep tonight, and remember something, tomorrow is a whole brand new day."

"Tomorrow is the day that never comes," Lin smiled.

"Not so. Today used to be tomorrow. Have you ever heard the saying, Today is the tomorrow you worried about yesterday?"

"I like that. It's silly, but it's true." He kissed her cheek. "'Night, Grandma."

"Night-night, darling." she patted his tush.

"'Night, Bruno," Lin dared.

"Not so," Bruno put down his cards. "If you think you can just say night-night you're wrong. Cuddles are like candy. If you're going to share with your grandma, it's rude to leave me out of it."

"Guys don't cuddle guys."

"Yes they do. You see it at soccer games all the time." The hug was quick and shy. "Goodnight, boy," Bruno smiled.

Almost an hour later, Sally came into the kitchen for quick cuddles and cheek kisses. "You're all bristly," she told Bruno. "It's like kissing a hedgehog."

"Sign of a real man," he laughed.

"Sign of a real ape, if you ask me. Sign of a walking hair-brush."

They sat at the table, playing crib, time seeming to slow down to a crawl.

"I feel as if I'm stealing big pieces of your life," Sarah said slowly. "You've as good as babysat me all day. I appreciate it."

"I'm afraid," he told her, taking the pegs out of the crib board, effectively finishing the game. "I'm afraid if I leave you alone for any time at all, even a half hour, you'll go away."

"I'm not going to die."

"I didn't say 'die', I said 'go away'."

Rainey slipped quietly into the house. The clock on the back of the stove read five-thirty. She knew she wouldn't be able to sleep if she went to bed. She'd lie there, her thoughts churning, trying to sort out feelings, reactions, emotions, and keep them separate from neuroses or even psychoses. All those articles in all those magazines, and now you not only had to figure out if it was infatuation or love, you had to identify and discard codependency, enabling behaviour and learned response. Bad enough to make a mistake; worse to make it because you didn't take the time to identify past-life flashback or repressed memory. And what did any of that really mean?

They'd forgotten to set up the coffeemaker. Well, Sarah couldn't be expected to do it, but you'd think Chris would have had better sense—if Chris had even bothered to come home. She often stayed over at Annwyn's place. Behaving as if it was just a sleepover, a little girls' pyjama party extended into adulthood. As if the whole world, with the possible exception of Sarah and old Annie, didn't know full well what the truth was. And what must *that* be like? To know, even as a kid, that this huge, newly discovered wonder had to be kept secret?

Rainey remembered the first time she'd thought she was madly in love, forever and ever, amen. All she could talk of was Jerry Brankston this and Jerry Brankston that. Jerry is on the soccer team at school, Jerry can walk a half block on his hands, Jerry said, Jerry told me. With the inevitable result that when Jerry had fallen from grace, everyone in the house knew it because the eternal Jerry-did stopped. Chris hadn't been able to do that. Probably there'd been nothing sexual between her and Annwyn until after wee Annie came back from nursing school. And guess who was the first person got phoned once the suitcases and boxes were unloaded from the car and placed in the bedroom that had been waiting the whole time? And both Sarah and old Annie laughing and saying, Well, in spite of the two letters a week they've probably got a million things to say to each other. Saying things like Friends since the first time they met.

When the coffee was ready she sat at the table, sipping, trying to sort through the muddle of her mind. Well, she'd said extended period of passion, she'd said she wouldn't do it just because she had nothing better to do, and she'd said it would be no joke. For once in her life she was batting three out of three.

So now what should she do? Was she ready when the roof fell

in? There'd be hell to pay when Sarah found out, and Sarah would find out. Sarah had always found out where Rainey was concerned. Was she willing to pay hell? She could almost hear it now. Sarah would shit bricks because, after all, Rainey was still married. Made your bed, girl, now you lie in it.

But she wouldn't, not ever again. If she wasn't in her own bed, she'd be in David's, and that, as they say, was that. If, of course, David still wanted her there. How were you to know if what you'd felt was anything like what he felt? Maybe he was just being polite. A few of them might be, one could always hope. Maybe the illusion he'd packed around for so many years had been shattered. Maybe what he had anticipated had been ten, a hundred times more than what he'd experienced. How would a person know? What if it had all been such a letdown that he never wanted to try again? Could she deal with that?

Probably not. She should go into Tee Shirt City and get one made up, maybe a picture of a sphinx or something, with Queen of Denial (de Nile, get it?) printed in block letters. She hadn't dealt with much in all the years of her marriage. Oh, she'd worked like a galley slave making sure the laundry was done, the floors vacuumed, the windows gleaming. That was easy. It was a good way to stay too busy to worry about what was really going on with the cars in and cars out, boats in, repainted and back out again. She'd made sure she was too occupied with other things to have time to pay attention to other people's references to the chop shop. And those damn dogs! She'd worked overtime at trying not to notice the cuts, the tears, the sutures; they'd be fine when she gave them clean water at what should have been bedtime. Then he'd leave the place and load them, or some of them, into the big cage in the back of the truck. She'd go to sleep and when she got up in the morning, often as not, one or more of them would look as if it had taken a trip through a meat grinder. Of course he was taking them off to fight in front of a crowd of screaming mouth breathers. Of course he'd made money, probably lots of it, while the banjo pluckers from Deliverance bet money they'd made selling moonshine to each other. And of course the lawyers, bankers and real estate agents had put on their near-new jeans and five-hundred-dollar cowboy boots and joined the crowd, trying their best to look like good old boys, in spite of their expensive haircuts and clean nails. Oh, of course. And through it all, what had the Queen of Denial done? Why she'd done what she did best. And kept the motel clean, too.

She might try to deal with it now, but what would be the use? Face it—what had been the use, even then? Her mother's daughter to the core, she'd dutifully climbed every night into the bed she'd made for herself. And here she was, just out of another bed, and there'd been no hint of duty in that. She couldn't keep herself from smiling. David, you crafty dog, I would never have imagined it of you. And now I can't stop remembering, imagining, fantasizing, and wanting.

She had fresh-baked biscuits ready, with bacon and eggs, when the kids got up and came into the kitchen. They sniffed, they grinned and they hurried to the table.

"Is it a party?" Lin asked.

"Why not?" Rainey felt as if she had every reason to throw an absolute wingding. Except you can't tell your kids about things like that.

"Wow, Mom, this sure beats a bowl of dry cereal. Little bales of hay soaked in milk aren't really the blast to set off the day." Sally smeared a biscuit with margarine and took a bite, then almost groaned with delight.

"I know. And I can't promise I'll be on my feet turning out bang-up brekkies every day of the week because some mornings I'm just too tired to manage."

"You used to cook breakfast all the time." Lin sounded on the verge of tears.

"I know. But things change. You used to ride a three-wheeler and now you ride a two-wheeler with gears. That's a change. Your feet used to be so small they'd fit in a tablespoon and now we can hardly get them into the house. And I've got a job that keeps me up really late and makes me very tired. Changes."

"Lin," Sally said around a mouthful of crispy bacon. "Instead of feeling sorry about things that aren't any more, why not think about what's good? Before, we took the bus home from school and then there we were, miles from anywhere. Now you can go to the playground, you can play soccer, you can do just about anything. It's way more fun than it was."

"You're pigging all the bacon!" he protested.

"Well, if all you're going to do is sit and complain . . ." And then they were grabbing, snatching, pretending to fight, and laughing.

Rainey hoped it was the end of the family togetherness conversation. Maybe the reason so many of us spend so much of our time on the shores of de Nile is that it's a lot more comfortable, and at least it's something we know how to do.

She made lunches and the kids got cleaned up and dressed, then, finally, blessedly, left for school. Rainey was just finishing the dishes when Sarah and Bruno came in the back door.

"Good God," Rainey blurted. "You're up early. Been for a walk?"

"Ah, coffee. See, I told you there'd be coffee," Sarah said to Bruno.

"So what got you up so early, you pee the bed?" Then Rainey realized there was no way Sarah had been up and going for a walk before she had come home from David's. She gaped.

"I'll tell you what," Sarah said calmly. "You mind your business and I'll mind mine. You don't bother asking me where I've been and I won't bother asking how it is the motorcycle went directly to David's house and never did stop in front of this one."

"Mother!" And then Rainey was laughing. She pulled the plug from the sink drain, wiped her hands on a tea towel, then headed for her bedroom, still chuckling. She got undressed, climbed into bed and fell asleep to the soft sounds of Sarah and Bruno talking while setting the table for their breakfast. Bruno laughed softly. If Rainey hadn't been suddenly sleepier than she could remember being for ages, she might have laughed too. But she was too sleepy. Not tired, not worn out, just very very sleepy.

7

Chris couldn't believe how empty the house was even with all of her stuff and all of Annwyn's stuff moved in. Granted, she hadn't had much stuff. She'd never bought much furniture; she had no need of it while she was still living at home with Sarah, and even less use for it when she was out on the boat. She had her sound system, her camera gear, her clothes and a few books, and little else. Annwyn had furniture, but her rented place had been so small that there wasn't room for much. Now those extra bedrooms were empty, the little table and chair set looked lost in the huge, old-fashioned kitchen, and the living room seemed practically cavernous. Chris was more used to small places: her room at Sarah's, the confined space on the *Sealkie*, Annwyn's little rented house. Here, with all the high ceilings, the long hallways, the unfilled space, she felt almost agoraphobic. She didn't like the way her footsteps seemed to echo. That bothered her so much she got a pair of crepe-soled slippers to change into when she came in the house.

Annwyn loved it. She was as busy as Sadie the Cleaning Lady, even though the place had been spotless when they moved in. Chris was reminded of dogs peeing on posts, which was something Minnie was busy doing—she'd dehydrate if she wasn't careful. Not only fence posts, either. There were all those fruit trees in the back orchard, that alone could keep her busy for half a day.

Puss was at least over her hissy fit. When she'd realized the damn dog wasn't going to go away she'd gone into a tailspin, yowling and spitting, arched up like a Hallowe'en cat and threatening to spray in the house, to claim possession. The first time she took her position to spray, Annwyn grabbed her by the scruff of the neck, opened the screen door and fired the huge ball of fur off the side porch, fast way down, don't bother with the stairs, just get yourself to the grass. "If you think you're going to do that in here you can just get outside, you vile bugger!" she yelled. The cat landed on her feet, don't they always, gave a screech they probably heard in Bismarck, North Dakota, and streaked for the bush.

Wee Annie turned, saw Chris laughing, and snapped, "What's so funny?"

"I think what you said is along the line of those things they made us struggle with in school. You know: Lost, a dog by a man with a short tail."

"For sale," Annwyn laughed, "a chair by a woman with Queen Anne legs."

"If you think you're going to do it inside you can just go outside."

"Are you laughing at me? You? Daring to laugh? At me?" And then Annwyn was rushing her, jumping, wrapping her legs around Chris' hips, pretending to pummel her. They dropped to the floor, rolling around and laughing, until they were kissing and the laughing stopped.

"Guess what?" Annwyn whispered, "The neighbours are so far away I can *yell* if I want to and still not be heard."

"The neighbours never stopped you from making noise before," Chris teased.

"You think that was noise? Ho. Little do you know. Just wait until you hear me in *our* place."

"We could rent out the granny suite in the basement if you miss having an audience for your triumph."

"Dumb idea, my Chrissy. My, my, my, my *mine*."

By the time they were sane again, most of the day had slipped into one of the incredible sunsets that unfolded thanks to the tons of crud pouring into the sky from the stacks at the pulp mill. A person hardly dare enjoy them, knowing they came from the muck, mess and various airborne particulates. The effect was thrilling. A person could wind up thrilled to death.

What wasn't as thrilling was the reappearance of the god-damn cat, still with a hair across her arse. She came in the little cat door set inside the real one and crouched, eyes slit, ears back, all set to have herself another confrontation.

"Must be your suppertime, huh?" Chris went to the bag of kibble and looked at it doubtfully. "This doesn't look particularly appetizing, I have to tell you. Dry noogies, yuck. Maybe you'd like some of Minnie's canned meat. Want to try that, old Pussers? Minnie won't mind. Too much. How do you do with people food? Minnie would rather have people food than pet food. Here, try this."

The cat went to her dish, sniffed, curled back her lips, growled and practically dove into the dog meat and started doing the breast stroke.

"Jeez, look at her, she acts as if she hasn't eaten in a month!"

"Look at *him*," Annwyn said. "*He* looks as if all he's ever done is eat, eat, eat. He's as big as a pumpkin. He's bigger than Minnie. Heavier, too. And he isn't the same cat I fired outside."

"You're kidding me."

"I kid you not, that is a different cat. Puss is a female, remember? This . . . hairball . . . has definitely got nuts, you can see them when he walks."

"So—"

"So he's either a stray or . . . you know, if you feed him he's yours."

"Yeah, but look at him attack that stuff."

"You want to see something just as bizarre? Look at Minnie—she's got her head in the cat noogie bag!"

"I give up. They're obviously both suffering from identity crises."

"They're both pigs is what it is."

"Pigs? Chester is a pig. We didn't bring him." Chris put her arms around Annwyn, kissed her throat.

"Don't get started again, I have to have my wits about me for night shift in a few hours."

"Actually, I was just getting ready to bite you, is all. I'm so hungry I feel. . ."

"Me, too."

They opened a jar of old Annie's home-canned salmon. Chris got two large bowls from the cupboard, filled one with Minnie's dog kibble, then poured the fish juice on top. She put the salmon in the other dish. Annwyn already had the slices of sourdough bread buttered and was chopping green onion.

"So are we going to have a fight here or are we going to coexist?" Chris put the bowl of dog chow and fish juice on the floor. Three animals came forward, two of them spoiled creatures who approached the bowl from opposite sides. Both growled warning. Neither backed off. "You behave, now." Chris hunkered, stroking both at the same time, one with each hand. "Come on, there's lots. That's good ones, that's good critters. And you, Puss-impersonator, you'd better just calm yourself down and learn to behave because I can always get my Annie to toss you over the side of the porch."

Tentatively, emboldened by Chris's presence, Minnie stretched out her neck and began to eat. The Puss impersonator growled, but the smell from the fish juice was too much to resist. Even stuffed to the ears with dog meat, he had to try this, too. Within seconds the two overfed fur balls were eating from the same dish, each trying to out-gorp the other.

"Want to eat on the front porch?"

"Sounds wonderful. Tea, coffee, or—?"

"Or, please."

The table on the elevated porch was made of unpainted cedar bleached a soft pearly grey by years of weather. The chairs were white moulded plastic.

"I hate these damn things," Chris grouched.

"Me too. We can probably get picnic chairs that would match the table. Put cushions on them, too. I don't know whose bum these ones are moulded to fit!"

They ate slices of sourdough bread heaped with salmon and

washed it down with cold beer. "Don't you feel sorry for the poor Queen of England?" Annwyn asked. "I mean, there she is, and for a start she's got the job she's got, which I wouldn't want to have, believe me. Then, as if that wasn't enough, she's got that bizarre family of hers. On top of which she *isn't* watching the sky change colour and she *isn't* eating home-canned salmon."

"Poor bitch," Chris agreed lazily. "Did you see the article in one of those cheap things at the checkout? The one that said the old Duke of whatever, the one who used to be king but abdicated, had hooked himself up with what was really a man? In drag, no less, I guess."

"Jeez, how do they get away with printing stuff like that?"

"Maybe it's true. Maybe 'Wallis' was really 'Wallace.' Who'd know? Nobody sued them when they ran that spread that said that Dietrich was really a guy."

"Who'd sue? She was dead, she couldn't sue. No kids, they couldn't sue. Anyway, I thought it was Garbo."

"Maybe both."

The screen door squeaked and Minnie came out onto the front porch, followed by the cats. She lay at Chris's feet and licked her chops hopefully, just as the real Puss returned to the fold and jumped up on the porch railing as if she had never been away.

"Leave me alone," Chris muttered, tossing the dog a scrap of bread heaped with salmon.

"Why would she leave you alone when it obviously works so well?"

The hairy tomcat lay halfway between Chris and Annwyn and began to lick his feet clean. After a few minutes he began to purr. Minnie sat, then pulled her trick, sitting upright, front feet under her chin, begging.

"You'll burst," Annwyn said, tossing the dog a scrap. Minnie leaped, caught it in mid-air, swallowed quickly. "You didn't even taste that, you glutton."

"Go away," Chris waved. "Go lie down." Minnie moved, lay down, stared at Chris with reproachful eyes. "Doesn't bother me at all. Sulk if you want."

"Woman with a heart of stone," Annwyn agreed.

Puss came from the house, hissed at the tom and at Minnie; then, with what seemed like no effort at all, she leaped to the railing and sphinx-sat herself down, glaring at both women.

"She can curse like a dock walloper," wee Annie smiled at Chris, flirting openly. "Her opinion of us couldn't be lower. Who are we, anyway, to dump her outside, then let the woodpile-dweller in the house with that bloody dog? Who was here first, anyway?"

"Well, she can like it or lump it. At least the woodpile cat tries to be friendly."

Chris looked at Puss. "You might try it. Nobody ever tell you the old thing about catching more flies with honey than with vinegar?"

They finished their supper, drank the last of their beer and watched the colour fade from the sky. Then they cleared up, washed the few dishes, tidied the crumbs from the counter and went to bed to curl together like spoons and nap until it was time for Annie to start getting ready for night shift.

"Are you okay about this?" Annwyn asked, voice sleepy.

"This?"

"The whole house thing. Are you okay with it?"

"Yes," Chris said firmly. "Better than okay. It needs furniture, it echoes like an empty drum, I'm rattling around in all that space, but yeah, I'm fine with it. I love you, Annie-my-Annie. I'd live in the cat box with you if that's what you wanted."

"I love you, Chris-my-Chris. And *you* empty the cat box, not me."

Rainey half expected a go-round with Lin over who was going to get Chris's empty room. Instead, he helped Sally move her clothes into the closet. "You can still come down to watch TV in *my* room if you want," he offered.

"*Your* room?" But Sally was teasing. "Why don't you just claim the whole house while you're at it?"

"Okay. My house."

"My yard!"

"My truck."

"My driveway, go park your truck somewhere else."

Then they were whispering together, hatching some kind of plot, probably. Rainey supposed she'd no sooner than head off to work than they'd be back up again, making popcorn, watching unsuitable television or bopping next door to pester Sarah and Bruno. And wasn't *that* something to get your head around! Talk about you never know, you know. Not a word to anyone, directly. That pair, really. Oh, Sarah's bed was still in her room, and there were still clothes in the closet, but really she was installed in Bruno's house. And you couldn't just up and blurt into your mother's face the questions that so fascinated you, like: Mom, are you and Bruno just having a brief fling or is this going to be long-term? Or: Mom, are you going to go back and forth between two places or move in and shack up openly? After all, it *was* Sarah's house, she could do with it as she liked. And what difference would it make, anyway? Lin was fine in the room he was in, especially now that the fold-out and probably not-too-comfortable couch had been moved out and a new bunk bed installed, one with drawers underneath where he could keep his clothes, instead of having some cardboard boxes against the wall. Chris had given him her small colour TV; it sat on top of the old black-and-white. Often Lin had them both on at the same time, watching the same basketball game. He said the black and white had a bigger screen so he could see the baskets better, but the small one had colour, to tell the teams apart in mid-floor. What a nut!

She was paying rent now. Sarah hadn't wanted to take it, but it was important to Rainey. Of course she'd never get such low rent anywhere else in the world, which mollified Sarah, who hadn't wanted to take rent in the first place. My God, look at the time. If she didn't get a wiggle on she wouldn't be ready when David came to drive her to work.

She was in the tub, soaking and relaxing, when the phone rang. She didn't bother to get out of the tub. Either the kids or the message machine would take it. She heard Sally talking, then heard

David arrive. She couldn't still the now familiar lurch she felt in the pit of her stomach when she heard his voice after an absence, however brief. She hurried with her bath, dried herself quickly, hauled on her bathrobe and hurried to her bedroom to get dressed. Her bedroom. That was nice. Very nice.

He was in the living room with both kids, making up their own rules to Moot. He'd got them the game and had pretended it was educational and would help them with their vocabularies. Well, maybe. In the meantime it was the source of a great deal of laughter, and probably a few off-colour jokes. She and Chris had done things with Scrabble that would raise Sarah's eyebrows if she knew.

"I'm ready," she announced.

David looked up and smiled, but the kids weren't particularly pleased. They weren't even playing Moot.

"He's got someone living with him, you know?"

"Who?" Rainey felt almost physically attacked. She even felt herself take a step backward.

"*Him!*" Sally yelled. "Our supposed father!"

"Easy, easy, easy," David soothed.

"You shut up, it's none of your business, anyhow."

"Jesus Aitch Christ, does this have to blow up just as I'm getting ready to leave for work? You couldn't have this tantrum when there's time to deal with it?"

"What time? Now is when we found out!"

"Okay, listen. He isn't your supposed father, he is in fact your absolute-for-sure father. Believe me, if anyone would know, I would. So, if that's been bothering you, it should be settled."

"He's got someone living with him. A woman."

"Oh. Well. You didn't expect him to live all alone forever, did you? You didn't think he'd slump in a heap and suffer until he was an old man?"

"But I heard *kids.*"

"Oh. Well. Yeah. That's different."

"And he wants us to go up there for summer holidays. To meet everyone, he said." Sally's face twisted with anger. "Meet everyone. Everyone? There is a *world* of everyones out there that he hasn't even met. Like *us*."

"Jesus."

"When did he ever spend any time with *us*? And now all of a sudden it's time for the family hour?"

"I'm not going." Lin sounded very calm. "I'm staying here, where there's a big beach and Bruno can take me fishing and I won't have to get used to a whole bunch of strangers who think they're all of a sudden part of my family."

"They might be real nice kids," David said softly. "They might be just as upset as you are."

"They're little kids." Sally sounded calmer. "Real little."

"Well, little kids are usually pretty nice."

"He said this person is going to be our stepmother." Sally's voice shook with insult. "And when I said I didn't need one, I had a mother, he laughed and said, well, now you've got two. A person doesn't *get* two mothers."

"Sally, honey, you know he's apt to say the first thing that comes into his head. You know a person can have step-parents as well as real ones."

David stood up, reached down and took Sally's hand. "Listen. The timing on this whole thing is really lousy. We've *got* to get to work."

"I know. I'll be okay."

"Babe, I never doubted that for a minute," he said. "It's *us* being okay has me worried. A person gets . . . kind of nutsy, I guess . . . whenever someone they love a lot is having a bad time. And I know this is a bad time for you and that makes me feel really pissed off and shitty. But we're only going to work, doll, okay? We aren't leaving you. Or you, either, McGillicuddy. Sometimes when I'm in a snit, it helps me to write letters I know I'm never going to mail. It helps me stop stuttering and stammering and makes things seem clear. I'd come over after work and read it if you wanted to share. You could leave it on the table in the kitchen."

"We'll get home as soon as we can, love, I promise."

"Are you coming straight here or are you going to David's place first?"

"Straight home," she swallowed, hoping there was nothing in her face or voice to betray what she was really feeling.

Halfway to the motorbike she lost it. She grabbed David, buried her face against his leather jacket and let it go. Shoulders shaking, she finally managed to lift her face, place her cheek against his. "So are you coming home or shacking up again?" she whispered, trying not to guffaw loudly.

"Yeah, Mom, eh? Like, you know, I mean, hey, eh?"

"I never even dreamed they'd noticed."

The bar was full. In fact, if the fire marshal had come in he'd have made at least two dozen people leave. Before her shift was even half over, Rainey had to duck into the back room and change her shirt, she was slick with sweat and so thirsty she gulped the Sprite David handed to her through a crack in the doorway. "How close to full moon are we?" he called.

"Thank God for that full-strength deodorant."

"Wonder if the kids will notice?"

She went back to work still chortling to herself about Sally's little bomb. Some role model. What a pair of role models. Grandma is shacked up and so is Mom. Was there anybody who didn't know?

Someone opened the fire door and propped it with a chair. Rainey was tempted to rush over and stand in the space, enjoying the breeze. The cigarette smoke whirled, and moved in visible ribbons toward the opening. Thank you, dear God, maybe if I can breathe I'll last the shift.

Just before closing time, Chris came in. She waved and moved to an empty chair. The chair was empty only because the guy who'd been in it all evening had gone to the john to drain his bladder, but Chris didn't care about things like that. It was empty, she took it. Rainey hurried over, put two draft on the table, shook her head no when Chris reached for her wallet.

"The kids are fine," Chris said. "Lin phoned me and I went over. Mom was already there. And Bruno."

"I thought they were okay when we left."

"Sally phoned him back. Ripped an unholy strip off him, from what Lin says. And you know your ex, nobody talks to *him* that way!"

"Maybe I'll run away from home."

"You already did, remember? That's how you got here."

"I seem to have brought home with me; now I want to run away by myself."

"Well, from what I hear Lin ran over to get Mom while Sally was still yelling into the phone. Mom got there before the call was finished. What she overheard was prime."

"Did anybody come to work here tonight?" someone yelled. "Come *on*, eh? We're dry over here!"

"Gotta go." Rainey moved quickly.

Chris sipped her beer. Chummy came back from the men's room and gave Chris a sideways look when he saw her in his chair, but before he could say anything, someone else got up to go to the john so Chummy sat down there. Chris supposed they could play musical chairs for the rest of the night. She pushed the spare draft over in front of Chummy. He looked at her, then at the beer. He nodded, lifted the glass and drank deeply. "Busy night," he grunted. Chris nodded agreement.

"Last call," David yelled. Chris burst out laughing as at least half the patrons stood up, holding their glasses high, and began to sing "Time gentlemen, please, it's time to drink up your beer; time, all you drunks, please, we want to get the hell out of here."

"See you." Chummy put down the empty glass, stood up, and wove his way toward the front door.

Rainey dropped off another draft and Chris sat sipping it, waiting for the room to empty. When the customers were all cleared, David pulled two Sprite and sat down with Rainey and Chris. "Mom and Bruno were already there when Lin phoned me. I waited until Annie had gone to work, then I went over. I was worried about Mom—I mean, you know, she's not exactly sixteen any more."

"Was she okay?"

"Oh, Sarah was great. I take it she had a word or two with your ex as well."

"Poor guy, he really walked into it this time."

"We'll be lucky if he doesn't arrive on the noon boat tomorrow," Chris agreed. "Anyway, I thought I'd drop by and let you know it's all calmed down. They're in bed, they're asleep." She looked at David and grinned. "And there's a humungous heap of scrawled paper on the table waiting for *you*, mister! And if that makes you feel good, forget it, because one of the things Sally yelled at her dad was she didn't need him any more, she had you, and you were more of a dad than he'd ever been. So when the noon boat comes in, you're due for a bop on the beak."

"Not me, I'm leaving right after I drop Rainey off at Sarah's place. I'll be gone when Blood and Thunder gets here." But David was laughing, and already getting to his feet to get on with the cleaning and closing up so he could get back to the house and read Sally's screed.

Rainey looked at Chris. Chris looked at Rainey. And then they both started to laugh. It was like kids-again time, sitting in the shallow water at the lip of the lake and splashing each other, laughing and hooting for no reason other than they could, and wanted to, with the heat on their skin and the sunlight making diamonds on the water. How many times had they lain on their backs, kicking like fury, sending up gallons of spray that made rainbows before it fell back down on them, laughing and yahooing just for the sheer joy of doing it.

"Why don't we all leave?" Rainey managed.

"Because my Annie won't want to go. She hasn't quite finished scrubbing every inch of the place—roof, grass, orchard and all. She's gone insane. She's going to drive *me* insane. Scrub scrub scrub, Dora Domestic, busy busy, she'll have the place worn out if she keeps it up."

"Ah, listen to you, you love every minute of it."

"She's got this soap, some Irish name. Murphy, maybe. Or Flanagan, or Harrigan or Hoolihan or Clancy. I don't remember.

But it's a special soap for scrubbing wood. Makes the place stink like a church!"

"What would you know, you haven't been in church for so long you don't even remember what it looks like, let alone smells like."

"So yesterday I come home from town where I've been grocery shopping, and what greets me? Wee Annie, spattered from head to toe, pointing into the bathroom and singing. Remember that old joke song from the British Music Hall show on the radio, the one Dad always listened to? Remember the one—I painted it . . ." Chris started to sing loudly and Rainey laid her arms on the table, her head on her arms, laughing helplessly. "I painted it, up the middle and down the back, every cranny and every crack, I painted it, painted every part, and though I'm not an artist, it looks a work of art."

"And had she?"

"Had she ever. I never expected to live in a house with a bathroom with lavender walls."

"Well, at least it fits." Rainey stood, leaned over the small table and kissed Chris on the cheek. "You're lucky she didn't decorate it with pink triangles."

The mass of pages was waiting on the kitchen table. Rainey made tea while David sat, reading. Several times he frowned, but then he started to grin, and by the time he had finished reading, he was smiling broadly. "You should read this," he said softly. "Right at the end she writes, 'you can show this to Mom if she's interested'."

"Mom's interested." Rainey sat down to read and David sipped tea, ate the sandwich Rainey had made for him, and waited.

"Oh, wow," Rainey breathed softly when she had finished. "She covered all the bases, didn't she."

"So, did you know your ex, or soon-to-be-ex, had been . . . otherwise involved?"

"I didn't know specifics, like who or where or exactly when, but yeah, I knew he was messing around. He was gone more than he was home."

"Do you know this woman?"

"If Sally's right, and she's nineteen, she's hardly a woman. Or at least she wasn't when the thing started because the oldest one isn't even four yet, so she was sixteen when he was born. That's pretty sick. It means she was fifteen when she got pregnant. He was messing with a child."

"You were a child when you started hanging around with him. Maybe he got a taste for it."

"Sick," she repeated dully.

"I like the part toward the end where she writes that she isn't interested in spending the summer cleaning motel rooms and babysitting." He picked up the letter and scanned the last page. "'Because I have my own life, now, thank you, and my own plans for it'."

"Would you very much mind staying here tonight?" Rainey looked exhausted. "It's not him or his cradle-robbing has me upset; it's Sally. I don't want her here by herself. She might wake up and need to talk or—"

"You don't have to explain. Of course we'll stay here. But I positively demand the chance to shower off the stink of that damn bar." He took her hand and squeezed gently. "Want to be a good little environmentalist and share the water with me?"

"Only as a means to save the planet." The exhausted look was fading, the up-yours look that was so much Rainey was trying to establish itself. "But first I have to go in and check my kids."

Lin was asleep, a lump under the blankets, his bed rumpled and scattered with magazines and books. Rainey lifted the covers, made sure he wasn't in danger of suffocating, and stroked his cheek. His eyelids flickered but he didn't waken. She turned off the light and went back upstairs. Sally was lying awake, her eyes seeming huge.

"Hey, you'll be a mess in the morning." Rainey sat on the bed, and bent to kiss her daughters' cheek.

"It's Saturday, no school, I can sleep forever."

"In this house? Good luck. You okay?"

"Just angry is all. Did you know? About her, I mean."

"Didn't know it was *her*. But I knew he was . . ." She searched for a word that wouldn't sound harsh. Maybe if she could make it out to be no big deal, Sally would be spared some upset. But did she want her daughter to grow up thinking it was no big deal when an adult man became a sexual predator on young girls?

"I'm not going up there for holidays," Sally warned.

"Hey, babe, I'm not the one you're fighting with, okay? I'm not the one you have to convince." She gathered Sally in a hug, stroked her back.

"Momma," Sally said clearly, "you stink."

"I know," Rainey laughed softly. "Gross, eh?"

"I'm not working at that job," Sally yawned. "I want a job that won't make me smell like an old ashtray."

"I do too. It's just that there aren't very many and what I'm doing pays better."

"And I'm *not* going to hang out with some old guy, either. I know her sister, you know. She was a grade ahead in school. The whole family is stupid."

Sarah made her way carefully down the sidewalk from Bruno's place to her own front yard, her cane tapping softly. Maybe one day she'd be able to use a less obtrusive one, an ordinary one instead of this awkward model with the four-tip base. But it was stable, no doubt of that, and she still needed the extra support and balance. Her bad arm and hand were improving daily, she had more control, more movement, but no strength yet. Certainly not enough that she could use two ordinary canes instead of the one she called her upstanding friend.

The lawn chair was damp and she couldn't wait for the early morning sunlight to dry it, but she had a nice thick towel in her shoulder bag of goodies and needfuls. She spread it on the seat and lowered herself carefully. Ah, that was welcome. If a person has to be temporarily inconvenienced with a bit of paralysis it should happen when you're young enough to not be exhausted by the strenuous effort it takes to heal and recuperate. There was no rhyme or reason to it, either; some days she could putz and putter around for hours and not feel worn out. Other days, like today, a little stroll left her trembling and sweaty.

Tigger, the striped tabby with medium-length fur, came to twine around her feet, purring loudly. As long as she made no move to pat him, stroke him or pick him up, he would visit with her. Sometimes he even jumped to the back of the chair and rubbed against her head and neck, but only if she sat still and let him make all the overtures himself. Toe, the striped short-hair tabby with bits of white on his feet, was bolder. He jumped into her lap and nudged her hand with his head, not so much inviting as demanding her attentions. Little Louie-Louie Babalouie, the tiny black female with the crooked tail, sat gazing at Sarah with what seemed to be adoration, but she was too shy to come close enough to touch or be touched.

"Ah, Louie-Louie, how's my sweet one today? What have you been up to since last I saw you?" The cat opened her mouth in a silent meow, then lay down on her side and played floozie, rolling and flirting, but always from a safe distance.

The breeze on Sarah's skin was warm, and heavy with the scent of roses. Some of the fancies had no perfume worth mentioning, but the old pink climber more than made up for the lack. Every year the bush was covered thick with blossoms, the heads smaller than the hybrids, but what they lacked in size they more than compensated for in numbers. And the perfume, especially first thing in the morning and in the cool of evening, was heady and rich. The other climber, supposed to be a hedge rose but really nothing more than a rambler, was white and had only a faint scent. A person had to be near it to smell the perfume. Some years the blossoms had a faint pink blush in the centre, probably thanks to the bees. When Angus was alive he had put little bags over the blossoms to keep the bees from cross-pollinating them, but what was the use of having flowers if you could only see them by removing a bit of a bag?

The rose bush Chrissy had given her for Mother's Day four years ago was in blossom, a strange deep purplish colour. It bloomed later than the ordinary ones and its flowering season was shorter, but for the time it was at its peak, it was striking.

Her favourites were the Joseph's Coat of Many Colours. She had planted three of them along the front of the house and trained them up the trellises in such a way they made a wall of crepey blossoms. First ones to flower, and last ones to pack it away for the autumn. Sarah supposed sooner or later she'd have to prune them back with the hedge clipper. She wondered if she'd be able to use it one-handed or if that was another thing she would have to let someone else do for her. Seems as if it's the things you most enjoy doing are the most affected by whatever the devil has dumped on you.

She heard Chester before she heard the back door. He was making his *rumf rumf rumf* sound, the one that wasn't really a complaint, more an acknowledgement of some kind. She heard his hard, pointed little hooves scrape scraping on the concrete stairs, then along the sidewalk heading toward her, and the noise he was making changed to a friendly *hmph hmph*. When he caught sight of her he quickened his pace, tippety tappety tippety. He stepped off the sidewalk and headed across the grass toward her.

"Chester, my good friend." Sarah held out her hand and he moved toward her. Toe leaped to the grass and streaked away, followed by Tigger. Louie-Louie stopped flirting and crouched, alert and suspicious. "See what a fearsome creature you are!" Sarah rubbed the pig in the soft place between his ear and his skull. Chester lowered his head and made happy little grunting noises, nudging at her with his rock-hard muzzle. "Easy there, don't love me so much you do me an injury or it's bacon on the barbie for you. Stuff you with sage and onion dressing, cook you slowly, invite the neighbours over for supper."

"Invite you for coffee." David spoke quietly.

Sarah jerked with surprise and knocked her cane to the ground. "Oh, drat!" she muttered.

"Here you are, my princess." He put the mug of coffee on the wide arm of the chair, bent and picked up the cane and put it near her good hand where she could get it if she needed it. "Top of the morning," he teased, toasting her with his own steaming mug.

"When I was younger," Sarah said, lifting her mug carefully and sighing happily, "we played a game called Musical Chairs."

"Shocking, isn't it," he agreed. "Is it any wonder the younger generation is going to the dogs?"

"Doesn't surprise me at all. Is Rainey upset about Bruno?"

"I don't think so. What about you? You upset about me?"

"No," she patted his hand. "But I'm glad you haven't moved in full time."

"If I did that, my darling, I'd have to—well, wind up like some kind of authority figure or something, co-parent, stepfather, whatever. And from what I've seen, that's when the bullshit breaks out with the kids. And when that happens, well, all the allegiances get pulled and stretched and tugged out of shape. I figure if I *don't* move in full time, I can be good old Dave, everybody's friend. And," he grinned, "I'll always have someplace to run to when it's time to hide."

"I'm all in favour of demilitarized zones, myself. If you show up at your place and find me already there, you'll know why."

"How are you doing? I mean really."

"Some days I feel so cheated! Other days, most days—well, you know what they say, any day above ground is a good one."

"Do you know how much progress you've made? Sometimes people get so focussed on where they want to go they don't notice how far they've come."

"I try to keep that in mind. It's just so . . . slow. And I miss my independence. I know there's no end of people who are more than willing to drive me anywhere I need to go, but lord, I long for the days I could drive myself! Never happy, I suppose." She lifted her mug and sipped.

"I was thinking of getting a big piece of rubber matting, like they use in horse stalls and such, and cutting it to a manageable size," David said to Louie-Louie, who was once again playing the floozie on the lawn, flirting with both of them while keeping an eye on the grazing pig. "I thought I'd also get a bell, like a cow bell, or one of those bulb-ended a-ooga horns they make for kids' bikes."

"Is this conversation going somewhere?"

"Oh, yes, my queen. I could take the rubber mat to the flower beds, put it on the grass near the border, then you could hold my arm while I lowered you down to it. You could putz and putter until you had things the way you wanted them and when you were ready to move to another section, why you could a-ooga a-ooga and I'd come out and shift your mat to another spot."

"It still leaves me totally dependent." Sarah could feel the tears prickling at her eyes.

"I thought of that. And what I thought was that whatever it is you're doing, you're more or less dependent, anyway."

"The kindness of strangers," Sarah tried to smile.

"No, just a very minor expression of the love people feel for you. And if you're going to be more or less dependent regardless, then you might as well be doing something you enjoy as just sitting. Which is, my love, something at which you were never particularly skilled."

"I don't mind the getting old part of things, David, but I do detest the being gibbled!"

"Any day above ground . . ."

"Yes. I think it's a good idea. Until the rubber mat arrives, do you think a thickly folded towel would do? Mustn't get my backside wet on the dewy grass."

David was gone, taking the empty mugs with him. Sarah sat in the sunlight, talking softly to Louie-Louie. Toe returned, and so did Tigger, and when David came back the cats did not streak away as if terrified.

"What about a thickly folded flannelette sheet?" David smiled. "And where would you like to start?"

"I'd like to do something in that columbine bed. You have to be very careful with them or they'll just go rampant and take over the entire yard."

"I'll get your gardening tools." He folded the sheet and put it on the grass for her.

"Don't forget the nippers, please. These roses need some work." Sarah felt more alive than she'd felt in days, months. There was a world of people whose help would make her feel diminished, but David wasn't part of that world, he was part of her world, and she knew he had spoken the truth when he said his help was an expression of love.

But when he lowered her to the folded sheet, Sarah felt awkward, clumsy, stupid and very very shy. He seemed to intuit her discomfort, and once he'd moved her refilled coffee cup within easy reach, he left her alone. She picked up a clod of earth and kneaded it in her fingers, crumbling it, enjoying the feel of it and the scent of it. And so if she did have to depend on David to come and help her move on to the next clump, so what? She was, for the here and now, doing something that had always made her feel content.

She worked hard and when she had finished with that clump of columbine she sat back, as sweaty and content as if she'd been working all day, accomplishing great things. She looked around and saw Toe watching her, his eyes half-slit against the brightness of the morning sun. Beyond him, Louie-Louie Babalouie was stretched on her side, half asleep. Sarah considered hollering for someone to come and help her move along the columbine bed, then defiance rose in her. Instead of shouting, she grabbed at the edge of the folded sheet and, with much squirming and wriggling, lurching and muttering, got herself moved. The sheet under her was bunched and wrinkled, nowhere near as comfortable as when David had so carefully spread it for her, but she wasn't the princess who slept on a pea.

David came out some time later with another mug of coffee for her. He was surprised and impressed to see how much she had done and how far along the bed she had managed to move herself. He plopped to the grass beside her, slopping some coffee on his hand. "Stubborn old bezom, aren't you?" he teased.

"Do you know what a bezom is?"

"A crone, I thought."

"A broom, my dear sir. You have just called me an old broom."

"Hey, it's better than calling you an old boot."

The cats withdrew, Toe moving to crouch under the quince bush, Louie-Louie hiding behind the lavender. Sarah sipped her coffee and enjoyed the feel of the sun, the smell of turned earth, the faint scent from the leaves and blossoms. Someone in the house called something, and David got up and went inside to see if he was needed. Sarah wanted to do more work on the beds but she knew she couldn't, and, more important, shouldn't. While she was trying to figure out how to crawl back to her chair and haul herself up into it, Toe came over and pressed against her, rubbing his head against her arm, then finally licked her hand with his rough tongue. She made her bad hand obey her, reached out and stroked the cat's head, told him he was a good friend, a good cat, a nice fellow, and totally beautiful too. He purred, agreeing with her every word.

"Can we put you in your chair?" Rainey smiled, her face still pink and flushed from the shower.

"Oh, I'd be ever so grateful," Sarah agreed. The last vestiges of resentment about her semi-helplessness were fading.

"Good lord, woman, just look at what you've accomplished!" Rainey blurted. "I guess I should come down on the kids' heads and get them busy out here."

"We'll see," Sarah said evasively. "It's a bit much to ask of a child, and anyway, what else am I doing with myself?"

"There we go, my dear." David helped her turn, then held the chair firmly while she sank into it.

"Thud," she laughed. "As graceful as a pregnant sow on a sheet of ice."

"Is there anything we could get you?"

"I think I'm going to catch my breath and then toddle back to my current residence." Sarah adjusted her hat so the brim shaded her eyes. "Oh, my, that's more work than I've done in months. It feels good."

"Sneaky woman," David chided, "inching your way around from clump to clump on your own, too proud and stubborn to give a yell."

"Ah, but it felt good," she breathed.

It all felt good. The breeze on her face, the warmth of the sun. She sighed and closed her eyes. David put the sheet over her legs, tucked it in between her hips and the armrests of the chair, and she heard them leave quietly. Then there was only the whisper of the trembling rose leaves, and the tickle of flyaway strands of her own hair brushing her cheek.

She napped and didn't know it, wakened only when Toe jumped to the back of the chair and began to rub his head against hers. "Ah, and is it a wee bit of loving we're seeking?" she whispered. She moved her head in rhythm with his, imagining two cats sitting in the sun, grooming each other, comforting each other. He began licking her hair, then the side of her face. His tongue against her skin made her own tongue feel itchy, the inside of her cheeks puckered involuntarily. She was about to speak to him when Louie-Louie leaped up and landed in her lap. Sarah didn't dare move. She waited until Babalouie was settled in the sphinx pose, paws out, tail wrapped around her body, tip under her chin. "Well, then, and this is a whole new chapter in life for you, Babalouie my dear. What is it, a case of when the mountain could no longer go to Mohammed, he decided to go to it? Well, as the old song says, all or nothing at all, I suppose." She moved her hand and gently laid it on the cat's body, her fingers moving slightly. Babalouie squirmed and rolled, then started to purr, a rusty sound, but definitely friendly.

Chester came back down the sidewalk, hooves trip-tripping, moving his bulk with ease. He reminded Sarah of an old British Navy ship in full sail. He left the walkway and moved across the lawn to stand by her knee, nudging her gently.

"Yes, Chessy," she said, "and I'm sure it's a puzzle for you. Sorry, old friend, but, as the song says, gone art the days."

"Chester," Rainey called. "Hey, Chester, come get 'em. Scraps, Chester."

The pig turned and hurried toward the back of the house, his loyalty tested beyond his abilities.

Rainey came to Sarah's chair and put one hand on her mother's shoulder. "Could I talk you into a change of location, my dear?" her tone was soft, her love evident. "We could move you and your chair to a shaded spot. You're getting a bit pinkish." The cats ripped off, unwilling to accommodate someone other than Sarah.

"Pinkish is it? Pinkish? Well, better than puce-ish or something even worse." It was an effort to get out of the chair, and a bit of a fumble to get the cane and position it for that first important step. "It is," Sarah said clearly, "more than a bit of a pain in the arse."

"I'm sure it is. I wish I could—"

"Yes, and I wish I could, too," Sarah laughed, with only a trace of humour.

"We're taking the kids to the lake. It would be lovely if you'd come with us."

"The lake? I'm not sure I could—"

"No, we're not either, but we'll never know if we don't try."

They left a note on the table for Bruno to find when he came back from his morning fishing, and they headed off to the lake in Sarah's car. David drove and Sarah sat in front with him. Rainey rode in the back seat with the kids. Sarah wondered why everybody, including herself, had assumed David would drive. There had been no discussion about it; they took their places as if it had been rehearsed a hundred times. She knew what Chris and wee Annie would say about it—socialization and conditioning and so on. She might even agree with them once in a while if only they would talk about it in plain English.

She could hear her wheelchair rattling slightly in the trunk. On a short trip it wouldn't bother her, but she made a mental note that if they were going to be in the car again for any length of time, she wanted the chair covered with an old quilt and then tied in place. Chinese water torture was child's play compared to something metal clittering against something else metal.

They went down the switchback hill, took a sharp left off the highway and drove past the lakeside pub to a large parking area. Sarah got herself out of the front seat and was steadying herself with her cane when David and Rainey got to her. She grinned as if she had just leapfrogged up the Matterhorn. "Gotcha!" she crowed. "Did it myself."

"Want to try walking down the incline on your own, or do you want to glide down like the queen in her carriage?" Rainey asked.

"I'll start down like the queen," Sarah decided, "and if the sun sets on the empire, I'll finish the trip like Cleo in her barge." But before they got the chair out of the trunk, she had started down the hill, picking her way carefully.

She left everything for the others to manage. There was absolutely no chance of her being able to take care of anything more than herself and her upstanding friend. Oddly, it didn't bother her at all. She who had lugged, toted, carried, packed and arranged so much for so many others most of her life, handed over the responsibility gracefully. Actually, she thought, she had just let the damn thing drop with a thud and a small sigh of relief. Their legs were much younger than hers!

Even loaded down with a cooler packed with food, two blankets, towels, swim fins, snorkel masks, a huge thermos, lawn chairs and the wheelchair, they got to the flat area before her. The walk down was on a slight incline, not really a hill, but definitely a challenge. Sarah knew each and every one of them wanted to hover, to fuss, to hold her arm, even put an arm around her waist, and she was quietly grateful they had acted as if there was no need for concern because Sarah would manage.

And she did. It wasn't easy, she had to take it very slowly, and once she stopped to catch her breath, but she made it on her own. And possibly the best part of it all was that when she got there her good old Rolling Thunder was waiting. She sank into it gratefully, knowing her face was flushed with exertion, her hair damp with sweat. "It's like that old joke—now it takes me all day to manage what I used to enjoy doing all day."

"You coming swimming, Gran?" Sally invited.

"Not today, my dear. And probably not for quite a few days. But I promise you, before this summer is out I'm going to do everything I can to make sure I get in at least one good swim with you."

Rainey opened a small bottle of juice and handed it to Sarah, who nodded thanks, smiled her lopsided appreciation and drank thirstily. A few drops dribbled from the not-working side of her mouth. She considered feeling embarrassed, then thought, so what? Would the world end because an aging woman had two or three damp spots on her dress?

"Not too hot?" Rainey asked quietly.

"Nice," Sarah nodded, still short of breath. "Very nice. The breeze off the lake is soothing."

"Hungry?"

"Tired. Sleepy." She held out the nearly empty bottle and Rainey took it, smiled at her, then adjusted Sarah's hat to shade her face. Sarah tried to say thank you, but she knew she was slipping to that other, welcome place. She picked at her dress, trying to spread it over herself like a lap robe in the chilly breeze. Rainey got the big towel with the Star Trek ship on it and laid it over Sarah's lap. Sarah nodded, her eyes drooped, and she was asleep.

Rainey was filled with the same kind of surging love she had felt when she first saw each of her children. What she had felt for I-refuse-to-even-think-his-name had been different from anything she'd known until then, an aching emotion ripe with feelings of desperate insecurity, the need to clutch, to grab onto, to hold, to do anything—well, almost anything—to keep. It was like something that had to be fed. Day by day, bit by bit, she had tossed fragments of her very self into the ever-starving maw until there was so little left of her she didn't know who or what she was any more, until the only way to save herself was to leave. She couldn't imagine ever feeling like that again, couldn't imagine ever again letting herself be subsumed by someone else's whims and vagaries. She remembered when Sally was born, remembered the sweat pouring from her own body, remembered the smell of antiseptic and disinfectant in the room, remembered even the touch of the nurse's hand on her arm. And then, through the terror and the pain, the sound of that first astonished yelp, and the soft relieved laughter of the staff. She wasn't sure what had happened for the first few minutes, she felt half out of her body, felt suspended somewhere, dizzy and disbelieving; the pain had been so much a part of her that when it was gone it was as if she had almost gone, too.

And then they handed her the naked baby, laid her infant daughter on her bare skin, and Sally had wiggled and squirmed as if trying to get back inside, back to where she had been comfortable, and warm, and at home. Quite simply, Rainey had felt as if she would explode with the feeling that grew inside her. She had placed her hand on Sally's back, felt the insubstantial soft bones, the velvet smoothness of the brand-new skin. Then felt the rise and fall as the child breathed. All she had been able to do was soak it up, let the tears slide down her face, and all she had been able to say was "Hi, bub." They had laughed again, softly, gently, not at her but with her, sharing a fraction of her joy.

Of course good old wotzisname hadn't shown up for hours, and when he did he reeked of booze. But at least he remembered to bring flowers. Maybe he had tried harder than she had known.

And then with Lin, that same overpowering feeling, the one that very quietly and matter-of-factly said she would die to protect him. But by then things with *him* had changed, and they both knew it. Oh, she had still felt almost everything she had ever felt, it was just that she no longer expected to get back any of what she was giving, she knew it was a one-way street.

And now here it was again, and it was her own mother brought that rush of emotion. She wanted to sit with Sarah on her lap, cradling her, rocking her, as she had cradled and rocked her babies. They had snuggled closer, wanting more, more, more, but she knew Sarah would struggle, would say Here you, give over, you're smothering me. And so Rainey did what she could, she covered her mother with the Star Trek towel and patted the weak hand, moved it a few inches so it rested on Sarah's lap without pressing against the side of the chair.

David and the kids were diving off the floating raft, Lin yelling and laughing, still so much a little boy. From this distance, Sally looked like she could be any age. The little girl was gone; those long legs belonged to her and she moved them with grace.

God, how had she changed so completely from child to almost-woman without Rainey noticing it before now?

And how in hell did they manage to cavort and splash in the water this early in the season without freezing to death? It wasn't even "the season" as far as Rainey was concerned—there was snow on the mountains and the lake water must be bone-chilling. She had no more intention of going in there than jumping in the air and biting herself on the butt. She looked at her book but didn't want to read it. She looked at the food basket but didn't want to eat. All she really wanted to do was sprawl here and watch the fools in the lake, watch the napping old woman who was her mother, watch the far-off blue of the sky, the clouds drifting across it.

"So nice to have you home," Sarah said clearly.

Rainey jumped, sat up and gave a small laugh. "I thought you were asleep," she blurted.

"Maybe I am," Sarah agreed. "Maybe it's all a dream. I hope not."

"Well, if it's a dream, maybe when you wake up you won't need your chair, or your cane. Maybe nothing will have happened."

"It happened. They told me there's a fifty-fifty chance it might happen again. They didn't say, but I expect if it does it'll kill me."

"Mom, don't!"

"Now, now, dear. Best we face the truth. I'd rather spend my last bit of time being totally honest than pretend . . . anything."

"Mom, I—"

"If we wait until I'm dead, even with my will, things get complicated and the government winds up skimming off the cream. If we do things before I'm dead, well, they'll have to go skin some other poor soul. It's not complicated. You get the house, Chrissy gets the bank accounts. I can live on my pension and it dies with me. It's . . . I worry about Chester. The vet says they can live up to thirty years and he's not exactly . . . well, he is, after all, a pig."

"Chester is fine," Rainey laughed." And don't tell him he's a pig, he thinks he's the kids' full-time babysitter. Their Asian nanny."

"We talked about it, Chrissy and I. The house is worth more, but there's three of you. She's fine about it."

"She going to buy another fish boat?"

"No. No future in that. Besides, it would keep her away from wee Annie. Oh, don't look so surprised, dear. I've known longer than you have."

"Does it bother you? Did it?"

"I was too busy being worried about you being stuck up a back road trying to make a go of what so obviously wasn't go-able."

"The motel? Well, until the new highway—"

"Not the motel, dear," Sarah laughed softly. "My heavens, *look* at those children, they'll be blue as ancient Britons if they don't get out of there soon."

As if they had heard her words the kids stroked for the shore, came out of the water shivering, picking their soft-footed way over the pebbles and harsh gritty sand and dirt.

"The funnest!" Lin dropped to the grass, hugging himself. Rainey handed him a towel, he wrapped it around his reddened body.

"If you were to haul off that wet suit," Sarah said clearly, "and get yourself as dry as possible before putting on your clothes, you'd warm up much more quickly."

"In a minute," he chattered. "Out of breath."

"Is there food?" Sally looked hopeful.

"Only for those people who have dried off and got dressed." Rainey reached for the food basket. "Hurry up and it'll be waiting when you're done."

"Look at *him!*" Sally laughed, pointing. David was coming from the water, shaking his head, his hair spraying droplets. "He's purple!"

"So are you, dear," Sarah said.

They rushed to change and ate as if they hadn't seen food in a week. But the swimmers couldn't stop shivering, so once their bellies were full they started packing up the picnic leftovers. David pushed Rolling Thunder up the hill, got Sarah settled, then started the car and turned the heater on full. While he was storing the chair in the trunk, the others arrived with the rest of the gear.

"Mom and I will probably perish in the heat," Rainey groused. "It's like a sauna in there."

"Barely tolerable," David contradicted, grinning widely. "It's because the kids and I are health nuts. We'll sacrifice anything, even your comfort, in our quest for fitness."

"Nuts, for sure. Fit? Fit to be committed."

They piled in the car and David drove them home. Sarah fell asleep, lulled by the heat, the sound of the motor and the movement of the car. She was still groggy when they got home and she stumbled on her way to the house. Immediately Lin had her by one elbow and Sally by the other.

"Thank you," she managed. "I thought I was about to take a good close look at the pavement."

"Don't bother," Lin told her. "I saw it up close when I fell off my bike and it's nothing, not worth the trip."

Sally shook her head. "Not worth the trip? You sound more and more like Auntie Chrissy all the time. Easy, Gran, watch the stairs here . . ."

Sarah managed the stairs, made her way to her bedroom and lowered herself to the bed. She sighed wearily. It had been nice by the lake, but she was glad to be back where she could lie down and rest. Was that what she had to look forward to for the rest of her life? Little increments of pleasure between longer ones of exhaustion? Well, at least there were the pleasures. Be nice if she could go back to when she was, oh, eighteen or twenty years old, spend some time talking to her young self, explaining how it was going to be, asking the girl Sarah to please take time to pay attention to her enjoyments.

Sally came in and helped lift Sarah's legs and feet to the bed. "Want me to slip off your shoes?"

"Please. And if you would sort of flip the bedspread over me? I can't sleep properly if I don't have something over me."

"I like to be so warm I'm almost-but-not-quite sweating," Sally smiled. "Mom says it isn't healthy."

"Healthier than not being able to sleep," Sarah yawned. "Oh, my, excuse me."

She slept then, a deep, rich, two-and-a-half-hour visit to a dreamless and peaceful place she didn't want to leave. But finally her bladder demanded otherwise and she awoke unwillingly, reached for her upstanding friend and padded slowly to the bathroom in her bare feet.

When she was finished in the bathroom she went to the kitchen, put the kettle on and got herself a cup and a tea bag. Sometimes she could do the whole teapot routine; other times, like now, she knew there was no way she would manage. The tea tasted better from the pot, but she wouldn't get to taste any of it if she spilled it on the floor or, worse, down her own body. It was that damn one-arm business! She didn't much like padding around barefoot, either, but the day was too far advanced for her to be able to manage her laces. First thing in the morning she was fine, even one-handed she could get it done. A fine trick, that. You'd think some one-armed person would invent a new shoelace. Or even a new shoe. Maybe she'd go looking for penny loafers, they don't need laces. Her pride would not allow her to even consider sneakers with velcro straps. Not yet, not by a damn sight!

She made her tea and got her cup to the table without spilling. That meant she had to move a chair halfway between stove and table, then get herself well balanced and hang the cane over the chair back. She moved her cup from the stove to the seat of the chair, got her cane, took a step, propped the cane against the end of the table, got the cup, moved it, and when she was certain it was settled properly, she used the cane to hook the chair and drag it back to its place at the end of the table. There she sat, shaking her head at the bother of it all. Such a go-round! What was needed here was a little wheeled thing, a table or a chair, or something—almost anything. This other business was not only unsatisfactory, it was boring. Bruno had an electric kettle, so she could sit at the table, teapot ready, and plug in the kettle in the outlet under the window, behind the table. When the water was boiling, voilà, she could make her tea right there.

So what did that tell her? It told her that as soon as she had her tea she was getting herself over to the other place, barefoot or not.

8

Chris was reasonably content in the new place for the first month and a half. There was enough to do to keep her busy—not run off her feet, but not merely puttering and filling time. The roofs on some of the outbuildings were demanding attention, some of the fence posts had rotted in the ground and needed replacing, the holes and ruts in the driveway had to be dealt with, the clothesline sagged, and in the big shed that begged to be used for something, several panes of glass were cracked or missing. And, of course, the flowers and roses refused to be ignored.

She could hardly believe the masses of them. She began to feel she could confidently tell people that they could name any annual and they would find it in the yard. Wee Annie was thrilled, and old Annie, predictably, wanted cuttings, rootings and bulbs to take back to her own place. In return, she brought colour varieties and hybrids that hadn't been present. "Oh," she waved casually, "just muck 'em in anywhere, they'll take. Things are tougher than some would have us believe. Just remember to water them. Nothing likes to be thirsty. Just don't," and her tone changed, "water the roses in the heat of the sun, and never *ever* spray the bush, you'll get all kinds of grief if you do. Water the roots, soak 'em good, but do *not* spray them. Unless you do it in the evening, when the sun is off them, to get rid of the dust on the leaves."

Old Annie loved to come for supper. She who had seldom

shown her face at the little rented place, now came at least twice a week, always bringing something, usually dessert.

"Pineapple," she told Chris. "The secret to almost anything is a can of crushed pineapple. You could take a roll of toilet paper, give it to the kitten to shred, then put it in a bowl with a can of crushed pineapple and that child would sit down and eat it with a grin on her face. When she was wee I'd sometimes sit her down for lunch and put a bowl of Wonderful in front of her. Cottage cheese with crushed pineapple." She paused, her eyes blinking rapidly, staring at something only she could see. "The year she was nine— well, you were at the party, Christine the Pristine—do you remember the cake? Wee Annie was so happy! And all it was, was a shortcake recipe with two cans of pineapple, one crushed, one sliced, and whipped cream until hell wouldn't hold it."

"I remember." Chris put the cup of tea where old Annie could reach it. "That was the year you got her the tea set."

"Well, I never had one when I was small. I have one now. In fact I have several. And I never use them!" she laughed. "Two or three times a year I take them out of the china cabinet and I wash them, rinse them, dry them and then put them back again. But many's the time I have stood in front of that cabinet and just looked at them. There might be people think I'm a poor old woman but I've got my tea services. And silver cutlery too, although I don't use it." She laughed softly. "I saved and saved for it, promised myself that when I got it I'd use it every day. So finally I got it, and you know what? It makes food taste funny, especially cabbagey things. I don't even bother cleaning it any more. But I've got it."

"It's probably worth a fortune by now." Chris sipped her tea and looked over at the side yard where the dog and cat were curled side-by-each in the shade.

"It was worth a fortune then," old Annie corrected gently. She sipped her tea, then put the cup down. "Why is it every time I come here you make me a pot of tea? In this heat? Don't you have any beer?"

"Beer?" Chris gaped, then laughed heartily. "Here I was

bending over backward and turning myself inside out to make it a good and proper visit, with tea and little cookies and the folderol, and now you tell me you'd sooner have beer!" She picked up the cups, grinning widely, and went into the house. She came back with chilled brown bottles and two of her best beer glasses.

Old Annie ignored the glass, took the bottle, already beaded with condensation, and smiled hugely. "To your very good health, my dear," she winked. "And a lifetime of the best of the things you wish for yourself."

When wee Annie came home from her shift at the hospital, supper was almost ready. The table was set on the porch and dessert was in progress. "Looks good enough to eat," she said, bending forward and sniffing. "Mmmm, my favourite."

"All it is," old Annie grinned, "is a bowl of whipped cream with crushed pineapple in it."

"What a life." Wee Annie snuggled her grandmother, holding her close and placing her cheek against the old woman's face. "My two favourite people and dessert too."

"You know the whole damn town is talking, don't you." Old Annie sounded almost stern. "They've nothing else to do, summer is always the silly season, yap yap they go. It's as if their minds, such as they are, can only deal with the short days of winter, and when summer comes and the days are long there's all this time for them to fill and no wit or wisdom to fill them, so they gossip and yap and involve their silly selves in what's none of their business. This year it's you and Christine."

"My dear old woman," wee Annie said, assuming her grand-mother's lilting accent. "To quote my grandmother, do I give the first part of a good goddamn? Have I ever?"

"Not where Christine is concerned, no. But there's awful stuff can fester in the minds of the stupid. There isn't much in the world more dangerous than a bigot, especially if the fool can be told God Almighty is on his side. There's a group gets together down my way—it's not a church, but they give themselves airs—and they've got this full-blown moron set up as their preacher, or something. I can't figure out if they think they're fundamentalists, evangelists or charismatics, but there they are, and every one of them old enough to know better, down on their prayer bones asking for the wickedness to be struck from on high, to perish in the flames of righteousness. They haven't yet mentioned either of you by name, but they're on about abominations and unnatural practices and if I was you I'd top up my fire insurance. Might as well make a bit of cash, just in case they come with sheets and torches."

"If they do," Chris said quietly, "maybe a few of them won't leave. I could put up a sign like the one in the sporting goods store. These premises protected by a twelve-gauge shotgun three nights a week. Guess which three."

"It talks like a good joke, but could you?"

"I'd bet on Friday, Saturday and Tuesday nights," Wee Annie laughed.

Chris made flower boxes for the huge front porch, using cedar planking from a pile out behind one of the sheds. She filled them with a mix of potting soil from the nursery and composted manure from yet another pile behind what had once been a barn. The petunias and begonias, trailing geraniums and fuchsia did so well she made hanging baskets and hung them from tree branches and set them on fence posts. She was such a regular at the nursery that before he advertised his closing-out sale, the owner gave her a deal, the kind that happens only once in a lifetime, and then only to a few luck-kissed people.

"It's the wrong time of the year to be planting trees," wee Annie protested.

"It's the time we got the trees, though," Chris said agreeably. "The ones in pots I can hold on to and plant when it's cooler, but these are going to go into transplant shock no matter what I do with them. I think—I hope—if I put a soaker hose on them, dribble water to them all night . . ."

"Cross our fingers, pray to God." Annie looked at the small tree doubtfully, then shrugged. "Well, as you said, now is when you got them."

"He said not to fertilize them. Said that would only force them to make new growth at a time when they'll be too weak to keep it alive. Said to give them at least six months to settle in before even starting to think about doing anything more with them. Which will be easy. You know me, off to a great start but easily distracted."

"Oh, such a damn lie! You're the original two-legged pit bull!"

"No, I'm easily distracted. Like right now. You've got a few little beads of sweat on your top lip . . . I'd love to lick them off . . . then . . ."

"Plant the trees, Chris. I'll help."

She teased Chris later that it was a good thing she hadn't been as easily distracted or the carload of good-natured women who came by would have been shocked speechless, and disappointed in their quest.

"The man at the nursery said we should try here," one said.

"He doesn't have any left," another added.

"We need four," the heavy one said.

"One each," the short one added.

They were looking for hanging baskets. They left with six baskets and a cardboard box in which nestled a dozen of the bedding plants Chris hadn't planted simply because her tilled areas were already full and she had been too busy digging holes for the fruit trees to till a new plot or build more flower boxes.

She looked at the money in her hand, then shook her head slowly and handed the cash to wee Annie.

"Maybe you should go talk to Conrad," wee Annie said softly. "He might be open to an offer he can't refuse."

"Damn shame," Chris frowned. "The guy's been in that same place for as long as I can remember and then all those assholes build their fancy schmancy houses and start complaining about the traffic and the smell of fertilizer, and they get the zoning changed, and . . . it's not as if they didn't know he was there before they started buying up what used to be the gravel pit."

"So go talk to him. You'd be safe here, they've just had the zoning changed to small holdings—that's about as close to protected farm status as you can get. Surely to God if they'll allow pigs and chickens they'll allow roses and plum trees."

Chris chewed on the idea for nearly a week. Then, on impulse, she put a few beer in a bag and headed to the nursery. Conrad looked as if he'd rather get a diagnosis of testicular amputation than the news he'd been getting. The place was as good as stripped, not a bedding plant to be seen, although there were still plenty of rose bushes in pots, as well as azaleas, rhododendrons and small ornamental evergreens.

"Hi, Chrissy," Conrad nodded, but couldn't muster a smile. He sat on a big rock near the concrete pond he'd had constructed years earlier, and which now was filled with water lilies, water iris and goldfish of all sizes.

"Hi, Con." Chris pulled over a wooden lawn chair, took out two cans of beer, handed one to Conrad and pulled the tab on her own. "Fuck 'em," she toasted.

"And all their relatives, too," he agreed, pulling his tab and drinking thirstily.

"So, what are you going to do?"

"Damned if I know." He looked around and sighed. "See that white house up there, the one made out of fuckin' cement? Well, Chummy there is a real estate salesman. He came over last night and he was all smiles and grins and yah yah old buddy bullshit, and he made me an offer on this place."

"Oh yeah?"

"Fuckin' insult. He's sittin' up there on a half acre of what used to be a bloody gravel pit, and he offers me about twice as much for ten acres of improved good soil as he paid for his rock heap. I was so mad, Chrissy, I couldn't even be bothered cussin' him out. But today . . ." He drank again, deeply. "If I'm not careful I'm going to wind up sitting over there under those lileodendrum trees I haven't been able to sell yet, bawlin' like a baby. What does he care that two full-timers are on the unemployment, what does he care that three seasonals got nothing to look forward to, now? Oh, he says, I have to understand it's going to cost a lot to get in equipment and an operator and get rid of all the . . ." He waved at his grove of ornamental trees. "Bloody things are worth eighty to a hundred bucks each and he wants to bulldoze them!"

"What are you going to do, Con?"

He shook his head, baffled and miserable.

"Wee Annie and I have fifteen acres," Chris said, sipping and reaching for her cigarettes. "And we're zoned small holdings. I guess you heard I sold my fish boat . . . damn government and their BS go-rounds with the industry. So I've been keeping an eye out for, well, like a job, you know? But," she grinned, "you have to admit I'm not exactly good secretary material—computers and all that stuff—and I've got some money put aside . . . and wee Annie says she's got some . . . and, well, I don't know zip-all about the business, but you do, and . . ." She let it hang and smoked her cigarette.

Con reached out, took Chris's cigarette from her fingers, took a deep drag on it, then handed it back.

"I quit ten years ago," he laughed shortly. "Mostly I just quit buyin'. Now I only puff at other people's."

"I always knew you were Scotch."

"Know what I'd like to do? *Really* like to do?" He was sitting straighter on his rock, and the dullness was gone from his face. "I know that son of a bun up there wants to—you should excuse the expression—develop this chunk. I mean, hell, look at the view, for a start. He could get, oh, probably a dozen houses here, or an apartment, maybe a couple of them, then just sit back and grow fatter and fatter. And me, I'd like to take me some time to really look into it, figure out the best of the best. Maybe put in, oh, I don't know, miniature fuckin' golf or something . . . a theme park, maybe, or a water park or . . . something noisy . . . drive the bastards crazy . . ."

"Go-karts," she agreed.

"Something. I could likely get in touch with one of those development companies. You know, you always see their names up in front of condo developments and such . . . make them a deal, partnership or something. I put up the land, they dance through the zoning legalities. They got lawyers on staff for that, eh? Be kind of nice if they put in, oh, family condos or something, have some kids whipping around yelling." He drained his beer and handed the empty back. Chris brought out two full ones. "So what you got in mind?" he asked, smiling.

"I don't really know, Con. It was Annie's idea to start with. Those women who drove up looking for bedding plants kind of kicked it off for her, and she put the bug in my ear and I've been sort of gnawing on it ever since. I mean it would take some time and some money . . . no sense moving the lileodendrum until the weather cools . . . be a bitch getting that fish pond moved . . . stuff like that needs time, but, well, there's outbuildings and sheds that can be used, and I guess things like the watering system can be disconnected here and put back over there and . . ."

"Fifteen acres, eh? Well, you'd need some of that to live on. House, driveway, some privacy and all. But maybe I'll get in touch with Larry Bridgehouse, see what he'd ding me to use his equipment to start moving some stuff. What did you have in mind, a fifty-fifty split?"

"I hadn't thought that far, honest to God. Maybe talk to Annie, or a lawyer or . . . what do you think?"

"I think fifty-fifty. You've got the land, Annie had the idea, yeah, I think fifty-fifty, with some kind of option to buy when I decide to take the money the development company throws at me so's I can run away to Reno or Lost Wages and blow the whole lot of it in one night. Come home broke, show up begging you to hire me on at minimum wage." He laughed. "Let's go see your Annie."

"She'll be home from work at about six. You can have a look around the place, start planning the layout in your head."

"Fuck 'em." He stood up, lifted his beer in the direction of the big new houses perched on the hill behind what had been his life's work. "And the foundered horses they rode in on, eh?"

"Doubles," she agreed.

Con followed Chris in his own battered pickup, and she knew it wasn't just two beer had taken the slump from his shoulders. There ought to be a law against taking people's lives away from them, she thought. Bad enough when you fudge and fart around and take away jobs, but when you take a life's work you take people's dreams, and if we aren't allowed to have the shy little dreams we cherish, what's the use of even bothering to feed the kids once they arrive? Might as well let them go immediately as keep them alive to face a life without dreams.

She'd heard him when he said "your Annie." Your Annie. It was an acknowledgement, which in no way denoted oppression, or ownership, or control, or anything the least bit negative. Your Annie. And she was Annie's Chris. And while old Annie was probably right about the wailers and moaners being on their knees praying for some mandrake or warlock or minor devil to take an eraser to one out of eight people on the face of the globe, there were others more than willing to live and let live. Others who would probably just spit and say, Well, never did me no dirt. Pay their taxes, on time and in full, get themselves out to vote like we should all do, don't get in my way, what do I care about the rest, it's none of my business.

When Con saw the soaker hose set up at the base of the newly planted fruit trees he didn't say anything. He just nodded, as if that said everything. He looked at the ones in pots, set behind the big shed with the newly installed replacement panes, another soaker hose running along the tops of the big plastic tubs. Again he nodded.

He went into the big airy shed, stood looking and grinning widely, his head bobbing, nodding, nodding. Chris went with him to the old orchard, where he examined each tree as carefully as if he were a pediatrician examining a three-year-old child with a fever. "Need to do some curative cutting on some of 'em," he said softly. "Wait until mid-winter to do it, though. Some real pruning, too. My God, these things must be as old as Christ's kneecap. A lot of these are as good as rare, you know. We could, if you're agreeable, get rootstock and graft onto it from some of these old-timers. Make some of those speciality things, you know, four or five kinds of apples coming from the one rootstock. People like that. You got 'em coming ripe all through the season instead of getting hit with two hundred pounds of all one kind and most of them not keepers, at that."

Chris nodded. She was already learning how to communicate with Con.

He grinned and nodded back. "You know what you got over there?" He pointed. "Them's what my mother called egg yolk plums. Can't hardly find them any more, not even from the specialty growers. You go out when they're just about ripe and stand under the tree and there they are, sort of on each side of the branch, if a branch could be said to have sides, like golden balls, so heavy the branches droop and you have to prop them up so's they don't crack off. And there you are and the sunshine coming through, and they look like some kind of jewels."

"So would those props look kinda like a two-by-four with a big notch cut in at one end?"

"Exactly. We'll put 'em in place soon's we can. No use straining the tree any more than it already is. Dig out those suckers around the roots, too; some of 'em might shape up and actually be a tree, with fruit one day, but most of 'em's like mules, and all they do is take energy from the tree. That old pear tree there, now, it's got rot in the trunk, probably fulla bugs. We'll clean 'er out, put in some fungus and mildew killer, then mix us up a batch of concrete and pour it in the hole, get another forty years out of it. Not that pears turn into much here on the coast, but damn, the blossoms in the springtime, eh."

When wee Annie came home Con had the table set and the potato salad made, and Chris was laying the prawns on the barbecue. "Just be a minute or two," she promised. "And there's cold beer in the fridge."

"Hi, Con, good to see you. How's things?"

"Looking up, our Annie," he nodded. "We're open for suggestions, ideas and plans, with plenty of room for dreams and someone to do the bookwork."

"You want bookwork done you should recruit my grandmother. But not me. Chris says I'm so Scotch she can't believe my family comes from Wales."

"Get her and Sarah and Bruno involved," Con laughed, "first thing you know they'd have themselves a fruit and vegetable stand set up near the parking lot."

"That's a damn fine idea," wee Annie said seriously. "I'm

going to get a piece of paper and write some of this down. Otherwise, we're all sure to forget. Kids'll probably want to sell hot dogs and popcorn, Sarah and Gran will have jam and jelly, Bruno will have strings of European sausage hanging with screens to keep away the flies, and . . ."

"Don't forget the lineup of Brinks trucks," Chris called, "ready to lug all that cash off to the bank for us."

Rainey listened to the plans, wondering which of them had gone totally insane—Chris for daring to jump into something like this, or herself, still raw and stinging from the auto court venture. "A lawyer," she said firmly. "Not just one to steer you both through the hoops. You each get your own. Then the two sharks can make sure every wrinkle is ironed out and that each of you is totally protected, no matter what."

"You really think so?"

"Please. Chrissy. You're the big sis and I'm the little sis and you've always been quick to jump up to defend me. Let me do the jumping up this time. It'll cost you a couple of hundred dollars, and pray to God you never need the protection, but on the off-chance you do, you won't be hung out to dry. Please."

Rainey knew Conrad. Most people in town knew him, except perhaps one or two come-latelys, the kind who do their shopping out of town, then complain about how few stores there are and how poor the selection is. She'd seen them coming back from the city with their vans stuffed with discount supermarket groceries and nursery stock packed in, so proud of themselves because hey, just take a pencil and paper and figure out the savings. If they did, they'd find they had actually spent more than if they'd shopped at home, once they added in the gas, the meals, the hotel room, the parking and everything else.

Conrad's father was the one who had started the nursery. Later, about the time Rainey was starting grade one, the old man retired and Con and his wife Trish took over the business. The old man chuckled, rowed his funny little green-painted wooden boat out from shore, stowed the oars and sat happily mooching for cod and telling anyone who stopped their own boat to visit that the new brooms were busy sweeping clean and he couldn't stand the dust, ha ha. The new brooms enlarged the greenhouses, brought in more stock, put up a brand-new sign inviting customers to come in and browse, and changed the old man's years-old tradition of closing on Sunday, the Lord's Day.

Trish was a year or two older than Con, and one of those people who didn't have an enemy in the world. She'd been born an O'Reilly, and like all of them she played at least two instruments, sang, danced, and probably laughed more in a week than most people managed in a month. Con had worshipped her. She was pregnant with their first child and driving home from her prenatal visit with the doctor on the day that Percy Whitmore, drunker than any person had any right to be, went through an intersection as if the stop sign weren't there, and ploughed right into the driver's door of Trish's car.

Con was in the courtroom when Percy went up in front of the judge. He sat there in the same suit he'd bought for the funeral, his big tanned hands resting on his knees, his hair freshly cut but still showing the indentation where the band of his hat fit, and every time the judge looked up, the first thing he saw was Con's face. Even so, Percy got six months. His driver's licence was already suspended so the judge extended the period of interdiction and ordered Percy to attend defensive driving courses. Con sat quietly, his face expressionless. Percy headed off to the pokey, did his time, came back and went on a toot. Six years later he took his wife's car off the road and into the lake. When the tow truck hauled it out, Con was one of a large group of people standing on the bank watching. He shocked some people when he showed up at the funeral and stood, hands clasped in front of him, as silent as Percy himself. He was the last person to leave the cemetery.

Rainey didn't want to pee on Chris's growing dream, but the whole thing seemed too off-the-cuff to be trusted. It wasn't as if Chrissy had spent her entire adult life immersed in flowers and ornamentals, it wasn't as if she had been the one to prune the rose bushes. Chris didn't even have a pot of nasturtiums on her boat.

And suddenly, out of the blue, the farmstead was to be turned into a nursery?

Still, the enthusiasm was contagious. Larry Bridgehouse put his trucks to work and the greenhouses were taken apart, loaded and transported, and the bits and pieces were piled up where Con indicated. What took a week to move was going to take six months or more to reassemble, and Rainey wondered if any of them had given a thought to where wee Annie was supposed to sleep when her shift brought her home at about the time the hammering and banging, bashing and slamming started.

"I'll be sleeping at Gran's place," wee Annie answered. "I get my old room back. It's quiet there and I'll be fine, but thanks for being concerned about it."

"Annie, are you okay about this nursery business? I mean—"

"Rainey." Annie blushed slightly, then became very interested in the coffee in her mug. "I *hated* it when Chrissy was fishing! Not just because it's so dangerous, but there I'd be, standing on the bloody wharf, waving goodbye with a big smile on my lying face while half my life floated off on the tide. Each day she was gone seemed longer than the one before, and each time there was a storm I was sick to my stomach. When the Search and Rescue helicopter took off I could hardly breathe. Each time I was sure it was Chrissy. I hated it. And I knew she loved the life! Maybe that was the hardest thing, knowing that if I kicked up a stink she'd try to live on the beach, and all the best of what we have together would be ruined." Annie looked up, her gorgeous eyes brimming with tears. "I felt like a traitor when all this buy-back stuff started and the regulations were changing and bit by bit by bit the smaller boats were getting squeezed out, and that included *Sealkie*. And while Chrissy was worrying and trying to find some way to keep on fishing . . . I was practically praying *against* her. I felt like a traitor. I still feel . . . not good about it. And I know she was looking for some kind of work that wouldn't bore her stiff, and I know that's why she was so busy with flower boxes and hanging baskets and . . . and now she's busy, she's making plans, she's . . ."

They sat in silence for several minutes. "The thing was," Annie went on, "that because of how things are, still, and probably for a long time yet, there wasn't anywhere to go with what was boiling in me. There'd be, like, picnics or potlucks or something . . . the 'wives' of the fishermen would get together . . . if there was a big storm they'd get together, and—" She looked back down at her coffee mug, turned it slowly, tried to smile. "And I didn't do anything to include myself. Because as lonely as it was to feel excluded, it would have been even worse to feel I was there on sufferance, as if I was . . . pretending, or . . ."

"Jesus," Rainey breathed. "I wish . . . well, that's dumb, eh? Can't go back to change things. And a good job, too, or we'd be so busy going back and changing we'd have no time or energy to go forward!"

"What would you change?" Annie dared.

Rainey got up, took their mugs to the sink, emptied out the cooled coffee, rinsed the mugs, then refilled them and took them back to the table. Both she and Annie knew she was really stalling for time, going over her life, trying to pick and choose.

"Change? The thing of it is, Annie, that if I changed anything, I wouldn't wind up where I am right now, and where I am right now seems fine to me. Better than fine. This feels as if it's where I'm supposed to be."

"And Wayne?"

"Oh, yeah, right, there's still that," Rainey laughed, with no trace of bitterness. "Well, Wayne . . . He's decided we have to sit down, face to face, and talk. Usually that means he talks and I listen, or worse, he talks and I block it all out and stare at the floor. I suggested he put it in a letter and I promised I'd answer. He said no, he hated writing letters. I suggested his lawyer could talk to my lawyer. He said no, he didn't have one and wasn't going to spend money on one unless it was someone right here, in town, where his kids are, so the guy would be johnny-on-the-spot if anything came up."

"That sounds reasonable."

"You think so?"

"Well, sure. If his lawyer is to heck and gone up in Duck's Arsehole or wherever it is he lives, then the whole weight of it comes down on you. You'd be the one had to phone Wayne's lawyer long distance, you'd be the one doing it all. Or worse, your lawyer would phone his lawyer and the cash register would sing, ka-ching ka-ching ka-ching, with you picking up the tab. If his lawyer is here in town, you can. . . drive through his front window and park on top of his computer and yell in his face."

"Well, anyway, he's coming down. And of course he's bringing the whole clanjamfrie with him. Child bride, infant children, and for all I know the damn dog and a litter of half-grown snarling pups."

"I can't offer to have them at our place. Chrissy would strangle him, put him through the brush chipper, add the pulp and mush to the compost heap and use him as fertilizer next spring."

"How interesting." Rainey did not smile. "I didn't know you had a brush chipper. May I borrow it?"

And then they were both laughing, and a place inside Rainey that she hadn't even known about relaxed.

Sarah heard them coming and composed herself, making sure the expression on her face was pleasant, although she was getting a bit tired of that, too. She didn't always feel pleasant, or cheerful, or even very patient. And why should she? And why should she care if any of them, strong and healthy and mobile as they were, got upset if they saw her impatient or frustrated? Who said she had to baby them for their entire lives?

"Hey, there." Rainey smiled and kissed Sarah's cheek. "How are you, dear?"

"I'm in a bitch of a mood if the truth be known," Sarah said clearly.

"Good. That makes for a full crew." Rainey sat and sighed deeply. "Brace yourself, my dear, in about—" She checked the clock on the stove. "Oh, an hour, unfortunately probably less, we are about to be visited. It would seem Sally's strip-ripping had some effect. Not the one she intended, probably, but—"

"Oh my Christ." Sarah shook her head. "Maybe I'll become a complete invalid, unable to even rise from my bed. I just *know* my speech is about to deteriorate, I won't be able to carry on a conversation of any kind."

"Right. I think I'm going to be struck with a sudden bout of premature senile dementia. I won't be able to hear or understand either."

"I'm going to Bruno's place." Sarah stood up and Rainey laughed.

"If you wait a minute I'll get your shoes."

"I need loafers," Sarah blurted. "I'm sick of fighting with laces. Or sneakers with velcro tabs. I'm tired of dependency."

"You were right, Momma, you are in a bitch of a mood."

"I warned you."

"Warned her of what?" Sally came in with a bag of groceries.

"I'm as snarly as a bear with a toothache."

"Me too. Did you hear the great news? And *she*," Sally glared at Rainey, "says we can't stand in the front yard with a wheelbarrow full of rocks to throw at them when they drive up in their brand-new camper-van."

"You can come over to Bruno's place and throw them from there. That's where I'll be."

"No you won't. *She* says we're going to have a family barbecue, with wienies for the little kids and—"

"Well, then, *she* can make it happen. I'm off."

"I'll put the groceries away, Gran, and then I think I'll need to come over to check on you and make sure you're okay. Okay?"

"I won't be okay. You may have to spend the entire evening taking care of me. I can feel a bout of total helpless dependency coming on."

She stumped her way back to Bruno's place slowly. Had some part of her heard enough of the phone call that her subconscious had figured out enough to wake her up in a foul mood? Why should she look for reasons to be in a mood, wasn't she entitled to one without an excuse? God knows everybody else was moody enough! You'd think they were an opera company full of prima donnas. Well, she'd had practice with that kind of emotional blackmail. Angus, dear, darling, much-missed and still-loved Angus had been a man of extreme moods, practically legendary among his peers for his ability to leap into a fight, any kind of fight, anybody's fight, words or fists, and just keep at it until he was satisfied it was over and he'd won. Was it any big surprise Rainey had got herself entangled with the same kind of personality?

Except that Angus had been willing to work. Maybe he looked on that as just another kind of combat, him two-fisted against the unfairness of the world. Wayne seemed to think that someone, somewhere was serving free lunch and if he just looked in enough places, eventually he'd find it. And a pity, too, because he had a way with machines. If he'd only find a way to settle himself down, to function the way most of the world did, he could have a job, a good one, with decent wages and . . .

And with no more divine intervention than that would take, Chester could probably learn to figure skate.

Bruno was cleaning fish on the back porch. He looked up and smiled at her. "You've had a full day." He came down the steps, offered her his arm. She took it and he reached for her cane.

"You're all fish guts," she said, shaking her head. "You'll stink up the foam tip. I'll go down the street followed by stray cats and hopeful dogs."

"Sorry, didn't think." He smiled again.

"I should warn you." She heaved herself up the stairs slowly. "I am in an absolutely foul mood. Small children and helpless infants are not safe."

"I take it you've heard we're about to be visited."

"I was in a foul mood before I heard that bit of news."

"I used to look over from my place to your place and wonder," he laughed. "I'd see you puttering in the yard or working in the garden or . . . I remember one time I looked over and you and Chrissy were talking together and then you both started to laugh. You were facing each other, both bent forward from the waist a bit, almost nose-to-nose and both of you laughing, and I thought,

God, I'd sell what's left of my soul for that kind of . . ." He shook his head. "And now, my dear Sarah, I wonder how you managed to find the laugh."

"Mostly by doing my best to pay as little attention as possible to the bloody soap operas they think are their lives," she snapped. "And *you!*"

"Me? Me what?" He stood waiting as she lowered herself to the chair on the porch.

"You and the fish for the family barbecue," she laughed. "Why are they doing it?"

"You know them better than I do." He turned back to the small table and the fish. "If we have to endure this, at least we can eat well. I got two nice salmon and a lovely big rock cod."

"I'd rather shove them up than watch him swallow any of it."

"I'd pay to see that," he agreed. "Maybe make it an Olympic sport."

"I suppose I should *do* something toward it," she fretted.

"Why? All this fish, it's more than enough. It's Rainey and David decided to set some kind of standard of coast hospitality, let them do the running around for it."

"I suppose he thinks they're bunking in, too."

"He's got his new camper-van." Bruno rinsed the fish, then gathered the guts and heads into the colander. "But I imagine he'll need a place to park it. I am quite certain there won't be room for it in our driveway."

"No," she agreed, nodding firmly. "We have to keep the driveway clear, Bruno. After all, we never know when I'll take a turn for the worse and need to be rushed to hospital. No time to waken people and ask them to move their camper-van."

He chuckled and nodded, took the colander of mess to the back of the garden, dumped it and made the *ch ch ch ch ch* sounds Sarah used to call the cats. To her total surprise, they streaked over and clustered around the pile, not even snarling or hissing at each other. Bruno turned on the garden tap, rinsed the colander and his hands, then poured handfuls of water over the tap itself to rinse it.

"Lovely evening," he told her, coming back with the colander and a small bucket of water. He slopped water on the small table, and scrubbed at it with a brush. "Messy kind of a job."

"I don't suppose Sally will allow him to park in that yard, either."

"We'll be lucky if Sally doesn't set the new van on fire. I'd supply the matches."

"I have to tell you, if David invites them to stay in his house, I'm putting the entire lot of them up for adoption. In my day . . ." She shook her head.

"My hands are clean." He turned, smiling at her. "Could I get you a cup of tea?"

"No." She reached for him. "Just come with me to bed and convince me I'm not ready for the grave yet."

"My my. And you the mother of grown children!"

They heard Wayne and his current troupe arrive, but there were more important things to attend to, and by the time they got themselves sane and dressed, and went over with the fish, the first awkwardness was over. Sarah nodded politely but did not smile, and there was no thought of her offering to shake his hand. She gripped her upstanding friend and he accepted that. She might have felt sorry for him if he hadn't so thoroughly messed up the lives of her daughter and grandchildren.

Wayne knew he was about as welcome here as the town whore at the church picnic, but he was nothing if not stubborn and he had things to discuss with Rainey, whether she wanted to talk to him or not.

The current companion was tall, rake thin, and just about as smart as a sack of rocks. Her smile was tentative, and her hands, with the fingernails gnawed down to the quick, fluttered nervously. Her butter-blond hair was parted in the middle and hung straight and long, almost to her waist. Both little boys had the same colouring, but their hair was still dandelion-fluff white. They looked at Sarah with wonder, their eyes bright blue and shining with excitement. None of it was their fault, any more than it was the fault of Sally or Lin, and Sarah smiled at them.

Sally touched Sarah's arm and smiled. "Would you rather sit in the house or outside?" she asked softly.

"I think I'd like to sit in the back yard, dear," Sarah answered. "The air is warm and you know I do enjoy the flowers. You might take those too poor wee boys for a bit of a walk, maybe to the playground."

"Gran!"

"And what part did they have in any of this, my darling? Look at them. If you didn't know all the things you know, you'd probably like them."

"But I *do* know!"

"Yes. Still, it's not as if they've done any of it."

Sally didn't answer, but she didn't stalk off, either. She accompanied Sarah to a chair and stayed with her until Bruno appeared with two cans of cold beer. He handed one to Sarah.

"To you, my dear." He tinked his can against Sarah's and smiled.

Sally watched them intently.

"Questions, Sally?" Sarah said quietly.

Sally blushed, looked away, then shook her head jerkily.

"They don't touch on it on the TV." Sarah avoided looking at her granddaughter and concentrated on the roses against the fence. "We're old, yes. But not dead. Yet."

"I'm sorry," Sally whispered. "I didn't mean . . . I mean I didn't . . ."

"It's like a fire," Bruno said. "And when you're young, a teenager, say, it's like when the cedar kindling catches, and the fire crackles and sends sparks flying. Then later, when you're, oh, say mid- to late twenties, young still, and searching, it's like when the bigger pieces of cedar and alder get put on, and they burn bright and hot. Later on there are coals, and you aren't putting cedar on, and the alder and maple and sometimes even fir are in bigger chunks, the flames are steady, the heat is less intense but it doesn't falter. And then you get to where Sarah and I are, and all the madness is gone, you've got a huge bed of red-hot coals, not many flames but good steady heat. And later, if anyone as young as you can believe there will be a 'later' for your grandma and me, the coals will be like a wonderful, comfortable warmth, maybe not exactly *heat*, but wonderful all the same."

"So, is it, like, is it love?"

"Oh, yes." Bruno's face glowed, his eyes twinkled. "For a long long time I have had what you'd probably call a crush on your grandma. I'd watch her when she was working in her garden or busy with her flowers. Found more reasons than you'd believe to go over, ask if she needed anything, ask if there was anything I could do to lend a hand. If I couldn't think of an excuse, sometimes I'd pace around in my kitchen and give myself long lectures about being an old fool."

Sarah laughed softly, sipped her beer, then sneaked a look at Sally. The girl was watching Bruno intently, all sign of embarrassment gone. Bruno was so frank, so open, and so matter-of-fact that there was no place for shyness or false modesty.

"And you're in love with my grandma?"

"Yes. I love her, and I'm in love with her. You're too young to understand the difference, but you will."

"Too young!" Sally laughed suddenly, and pointed her finger at Bruno. "You, too! *Everybody* tells me I'm too young. Right up until the point where they tell me I'm too old! Too old to dunk my crusts, too old to nag and natter at Lin, too old to have a temper tantrum, but too young to do anything interesting."

Chris and wee Annie arrived with a huge bowl of fruit salad and another of whipped cream. Wayne started to move forward, his hand already reaching out to take Chris's, but when she turned away as if he weren't even there, his hand fell, limp and homeless. Then he blinked, and in the blinking his eyes lost the off-balance ill-at-ease trying to be friendly look, and assumed that flat blankness that meant he was tallying up the score, just waiting for the chance at payback.

Chris took the dessert into the house and came out with two cans of beer. She opened one and handed it to wee Annie, then opened the other and sipped. Wayne looked at wee Annie, then at Chris, and then he laughed, once, shortly. He turned to the nervous youngster who had left her given name, Linda Janice, far behind her and was now calling herself J'neesa.

"Want anything?" he asked.

"If there's a Coke or something . . ."

"If there isn't, I'll go get you some," he said gallantly. He went into the kitchen as if he were the one who had paid off the mortgage, and came out with a beer in one hand and a can of Sprite in the other. "No Coke." He held out the Sprite, unopened. "This do?"

"It's fine." She pulled the tab and sipped thirstily. "Ah, nice and cold."

Sarah watched the currents swirling, the interplays and inter-actions, and kept as much of her own feelings from her face as she could manage. She was almost thankful for the stiffness that remained in one side of her face. If anyone saw a look that puzzled them, she could bring out the invisible tear-drenched hanky and do the poor-old-soul routine.

The two little boys stuck together like glue and watched everything. Heaven alone knew what tales of horror they had overheard or what they had made of them. Wayne was as casual and uninvolved with them as he had been with Lin, but J'neesa kept a close eye on them and communicated with little smiles and nods, or sudden slight frowns.

Lin came out of the house with an armload of his precious bright yellow-painted metal trucks, bulldozers and loaders. The little boys brightened immediately, looking hopeful, and one of them even took a step or two forward. "Comin'?" Lin asked, and both little guys looked quickly at their mother. She nodded but did not smile, and they hurried after Lin. A patch of grass and clover had been cleared from the back yard, near the fence around the garden, and the dirt there was dry and light. Lin put the cher-ished toys down, then hurried back to the house. The two little guys stood for a moment, unsure, then the two-and-a-half-year-old hunkered suddenly, set a truck on its wheels and brushed dirt off the cab. The three-and-a-half-year-old sat with that boneless *plop* of a young child and tried out the levers on the earth-mover, lifting the bucket, dumping, lowering it. Lin came back with his gravel scoop, set it near a heap of dirt, then spoke to the boys, who listened. The older one took the small backhoe, vroom-vroomed it over to the heap of dirt, played with the levers until he had managed to scoop a bucket load, then vroom-vroomed over to the scoop and filled one of the buckets. The thing worked like a ferris wheel, and when the bucket was full, Lin worked the handle and the bucket lifted up out of the way and an empty bucket slid forward to be filled. The little boy watched closely, and before Lin could explain it to him, he had the big Euclid model, vroom-vroom, pushing it forward, backing it, three-pointing it until he had it parked on the other side of the gravel scoop. The buckets were brought forward and filled, then moved up the metal frame, went over the top and started down the other side, touching the back of the Euclid and dumping the dirt. When the truck was full, vroom-vroom-vroom, it headed across the patch of bare dirt, three-point turned, and then the little boy worked the turnkey and the bed of the truck rose and the dirt dumped to form a new pile. The two little guys looked at Lin, then at each other, and they laughed. "Works good, eh," Lin said proudly. "David gave me the gravel scoop and I had the truck from before."

Wayne was drinking his beer and talking to J'neesa, but his eyes were on David, who was checking the temperature of the barbecue. "Need a hand?" Wayne asked, knowing it didn't take two grown men to read a temperature gauge.

"I'm fine. But maybe later you could help carry the fish out."

"You got any wieners? Kids have never had fish. Not that I know of, anyway." He looked at the teenager questioningly, and she whispered something to him. "We got some in the van," he said. "There's a bit of a fridge in there and she's got some stored there." He set his empty beer can on the steps and moved toward the large, expensive, brand-new vehicle. J'neesa watched him go, sipping at her Sprite with little bird-sized lip-wettings that shouted to the skies how frail and uneasy she was.

Wayne came back with the wieners just as Chris walked out of the house, looking back over her shoulder and laughing. She stepped aside quickly to avoid bumping him and her foot came down on his empty beer can. For a horrible moment it seemed as if Chris was going to crash down the few steps and fall on the concrete walkway. But her reflexes were good, she stumbled and had to two-and-three step it to keep her balance, but she stayed up. "Ever graceful," she joked. "Here she is, the prima ballerina doing her version of the dying duck."

J'neesa darted forward, grabbed Chris by the arm to steady her, whispered an apology, then snatched up the crumpled can and took it into the house. She came back out again, her face beet red and miserable. ·

"My fault," Wayne said, actually making eye contact with Chris. "I left the can there when I went to get the wienies."

"That's okay, I think I just learned something about looking where you're going instead of where you've been. Thanks, Jan. Could I show you around the yard? Mom's got some great roses. On the other side of the house she's even got one gets almost green flowers."

"Green? You're kidding, right?"

"Come see." Chris sauntered off, J'neesa following. Wayne watched them go, then took the wieners into the house, came out with another cold beer and sat in a lawn chair, looking totally relaxed.

The salads, stuffed eggs, pickles and chutneys were on the kitchen table with a stack of dishes and a pile of cutlery. They set up the little guys first, with bowls and spoons and permission to pick up their wienies with their fingers. David put a small piece of salmon and another of cod in each bowl and told them they didn't have to eat it. "We're having a party," he winked, "'cause this is the first time we met you guys and we really like you. So the rules aren't like at home at a regular meal. You don't have to eat it all, you don't have to eat what you don't like, and if you don't finish your supper you still get dessert. Okay?"

Lin watched and listened with no sign of jealousy and sat on the grass with the little guys to eat his own meal.

Sarah would rather have been at Bruno's place, watching the

goings-on from the back porch. But no one in the yard could tell, and later, only Bruno got told.

Chris did her best to stay away from Wayne and he did his best to not laugh each time he saw her talking to wee Annie. David behaved as if this bizarre gathering weren't the least bit odd, and Rainey might have been at the Governor General's annual tea party. Sally spent most of her time near Sarah and Bruno, and when she wasn't with them she was talking and laughing with wee Annie, who was fretting because old Annie hadn't yet arrived.

"Relax, darlin'," Chris soothed. "You know she has to get the chores done before she can leave."

"She's too old to make all that work for herself," wee Annie protested. "Three cows to hand-milk, then feed and fuss, then get the milk to the house and do that boring thing with the separator, and her customers coming sauntering in as if the whole thing happened by magic and she had all the time in the world to jaw with them, and I haven't even mentioned her damn garden!"

"You know it's what keeps her alive and perky."

"I know it's what's going to kill her! She's five-foot-sweet-bugger-all and I bet she doesn't weigh ninety pounds. And she's *old*."

"How do you think she got that way?" Sarah interrupted. Wee Annie looked at her and hesitated. "That's always been her life. All she's doing is living it the only way she knows how, the way that keeps her happy. She'll be here, wee Annie. She isn't lying dead on the floor of the barn with the milk cows licking her face."

"I know. I mean, I'm sure of that. And still, lately, right out of the blue there's this feeling of . . . dread."

"Then talk to her about that. You're not the only one in the family is Welsh, you know. Old Annie is too. She's always said some feelings are second sight and should be shared. Maybe you're being told something she isn't."

"Dear God, Momma," Chris protested. "You're going to scare the devil out of her!"

"I certainly don't intend to," Sarah replied placidly.

Chris shook her head, reached out and touched wee Annie's arm and smiled at her. Wayne looked away, a slight frown wrinkling his brow. Sarah promised herself that if he said as much as one word she would kill him and plead brain damage in court.

David offered to take the kids to the beach for a quick dip and paddle and a chance to watch the sunset. J'neesa smiled and went to the van to get a sweater. Wee Annie looked at Chris, who nodded, and they headed for the kitchen to do dishes. Sarah looked at Bruno, who immediately stood and offered her his hand, helped her up from the chair and made sure she had her cane firmly gripped in her good hand. The little boys trotted off to the van carrying trucks. Lin didn't take a toy but stayed with them, big brother on guard. Sally, who had no interest in the beach, the sunset or the chance to paddle her feet, went to the kitchen to help with the dishes.

Rainey sighed. No way out of it. Everyone had drifted off, leaving her with Wayne, giving them room and time and space for the "talk" Wayne had driven from up-country to have. She wished she had to go to work, she wished she had to go to the dentist for a root canal, she'd develop a fast case of pilonidal sinus if she only knew how.

"Got some papers for you and your lawyer to look at," Wayne said, looking at her like a spaniel puppy that has just had its backside slapped and doesn't know why. "There's business stuff. I guess it's what they call division of assets."

"Where's that damn dog?"

"Diamond? She's in the kennel. She's due to pup again soon, and I didn't want her doing that in the van with the kids being the midwives. Why? You want the dog? You know she's my dog!"

"No, no, Wayne, no quarrel there. She's your dog, she's always been your dog, I wouldn't in a million years get into that one."

"Thanks, Rainey." He tried a smile that didn't quite fit. "That's damn decent of you."

"And your uh, classic cars," she went on, keeping a straight face. "I'm not making any claim on them, and I won't, not now, not ever. Could you believe me if I promised, cross my heart and hope to die?"

"I believe you. You don't have to promise. So what these papers are about is this. It's the motel, and your equity in it, and you're not to sign a thing until your lawyer has checked it all out and made sure it's tickety-boo. I think it is. I tried real hard to be fair about things. I mean, it's all gone for shit, I know, but . . . I don't want a fight, okay?"

"Fine by me."

"So . . . you shacked up with that faggoty David?"

"Faggoty?" she laughed. "Wayne, you're no judge of character."

"Never liked anything about him. He always did hang around like a damn egg-sucking dog."

"Don't get started," she smiled, her eyes narrowing. "You said you didn't want a fight."

"Okay, okay, just askin'. So, are you? Shacked up with him?"

"The kids and I live in Mom's house," she said. "He has his own house."

"And your mom's shacked up with that old Polack guy or whatever he is?"

"Bruno. Yes."

"Christ," he grinned widely. "He must be one helluva man. Either that or he don't expect much."

"Jesus, Wayne, you're all charm tonight."

"Yeah, well, anyway the motel is as good as sold. All's it needs is your signature. Tony Poirier is gonna buy it. You know Tony."

"I know Tony," she agreed, and kept to herself her opinion of the drug-dealing scum-sucker.

"He's gonna put in one of them destination casino things. All the stuff that went against it as a motel is like a bonus for a casino. Close to the freeway, but far enough away from it there'll be parking and privacy and like that. Gave me—us—a good price. We get back what we paid plus what works out to ten percent profit. So what I figured was we split the value of the original purchase fifty-fifty, and the ten percent goes to you as a catch-up on child support and such. Plus, of course, for the stuff that we had, no sense trying to ship it down here, freight costs probably wind up more than what the stuff is worth. Unless there's something you want, like sentimental stuff or something? And the ten percent, well, that'll help pay divorce costs and like that."

"You want *me* to get the divorce?"

"Yeah," he shrugged. "Me, I got no grounds. You never once stepped out on me, or crossed any line, or anything."

"The papers?"

"I'll go get them." He got up and headed to the van.

Rainey sat empty-handed and quiet, waiting for some kind of reaction. This was like the sound of the bugle playing that sad music at the Remembrance Day ceremonies. Every time she heard it she imagined a voice, a woman's voice, singing the same three words, over and over, Rest in Peace, Rest in Peace. She hoped it would, this frayed, dead little remnant that had once been the most important thing in her life.

Wayne came back with a sheaf of legal papers and handed them to her. Rainey tried to read them, then gave up. It was that same ridiculous wherefore and whyof and pursuant to and blah blah that passed for language. She looked for the money and read that part.

"Fuck, Wayne, you don't really expect me to pay *all* legal costs," she said wearily. "I mean, I can see paying for the divorce, okay, no problem. But you get your half untouched and my half pays the commission and the legal shit?"

"Well, you're getting the ten percent."

"Wayne . . ." She took a deep breath, ready to dive into a real go-round.

"Okay, okay! Jeez." He shook his head. "I didn't take you for that kind of person, Rainey. I mean Jesus, you get the truck! *My* truck!"

"Don't start," she said flatly, "or I'll make a counter-offer the court can't refuse. I'll point out there were four of us in this 'family' whose assets we're dividing, and I'll ask that the kids be included too. That means half would go into trust funds, then you'd get a quarter and so would I."

"There's *four* kids!"

"No. The court won't see it that way," she sighed. "Wayne . . . no stunts, okay? No bullshit. You guys, honest to God, it's like some kind of game, winning is all that counts. No matter what kind of big bozo you wind up as, no matter how badly you screw your own kids, you, by God, won the game and that'll show the whole friggin' world!"

"You keep beatin' me up with the kids. The kids, the kids, the kids, and meanwhile whatever you get out of this, that goddamn David is probably going to—"

"Oh, fuck that, Wayne! You want me to start in on J'neesa, or whatever in hell her name really is, and those two little cot-tontops—who, by the way, you were spending money on at a time when the rest of us were cutting every corner we could find and pinching pennies? Anything you get and a lot of stuff we didn't get went to her and them, but you're going to have a shit fit because David might sit in a chair or watch the TV? It's not *your* money, okay? If I want to take it all down to the friggin' food bank, it's not your business. If I rip it into little pieces and paste them on the wall it's no skin off your backside one way or the other."

"Hey, hey, hey, get a grip here."

"You get the damn grip. You got your shirt in a knot? Well *you* got it in a knot and it's *your* shirt and *your* knot, so *you* get your head around it and leave the rest of us alone! You're worried someone might be climbing *your* apple tree and stealing *your* apples? Well, it's not your tree. It's none of your business, okay?"

"Jesus, Rainey, you get more and more like your bloody sis-ter every day! You think I like the idea of my kids being influenced by a couple of—"

"Watch it," Chrissy said from the doorway. "You don't want to kick it off with me, little man."

"Oh, great." Wee Annie's voice came from behind Chris.

"Now we can have a real dustup and maybe even throw things at each other."

"No," Rainey started laughing. "No, there isn't going to be any dustup. My lawyer will talk to his lawyer and then the lawyers will get all the money and there won't be anything left for us to fight over and the kids can, oh, I don't know, live on welfare or something."

"Shit!" Wayne got to his feet and began pacing angrily. "Okay, okay, I was out of line, all right, everyone satisfied? Okay, Christ, fine, you pay for the divorce and I'll pay the other stuff!"

"No reason we can't split both. I'm not looking to skin you. But I'll rip out your throat before I let you skin me. Stay up front, Wayne. No sneaky moves just for the thrill of winning something, because nobody will win except the bloodsuckers."

He stuffed his hands in his pockets and glared at the toes of his cowboy boots.

"Get you a beer?" Chris asked.

Wayne nodded.

When the rest of them came back from the beach, Wayne, Rainey, Chrissy and wee Annie were drinking beer and old Annie was eating hungrily and grinning.

"Sold the cows," she told Sarah proudly. "Been thinking of it for a while now, but I didn't want to send 'em off to the auction or like that. They're used to being family cows, not just milk machines. Young people from up the road bought 'em, no argument about the price, just handed over the money and smiled from ear to ear. They got kids. Found out the dairies put formaldehyde in the milk to keep it from going sour, decided it was next best thing to poison. Kids think the cows are the best thing since sliced bread. You should have seen old Blossom, been in love with kids most of her life, standing at the fence and mooing as the kids head off down the highway to catch the school bus. I've already started telling my customers they'll have to go to another place to pick up their orders."

Sarah sat beside her friend, patted old Annie on the knee and smiled at her. "What are you going to do with all your spare time?"

"Oh, I'm going to drive the rest of you around the bend. I'll be running the roads, dropping in for tea, showing up for lunch, there'll be no end to the social life."

"Did wee Annie tell you she's been getting the heebie-jeebies about you?"

"Mom!" Chris blurted.

"Really?" Old Annie looked at her granddaughter, then held out her hand. "Come tell me, wee Annie."

"Now you've done it," Chris glared.

"I know I have," Sarah smiled. "The thing is, if there's anything in any of it I don't want wee Annie beating herself up by saying things like I should have told her, and I didn't and that means it's all my fault."

"Sweet Christ," Old Annie said mildly. "We're all on edge tonight, aren't we?"

Both little boys were dragging, worn out by long hours in the van and all the excitement and anxiety since their arrival. Without knowing exactly how it happened, Rainey set them down at the table with bowls of familiar and reassuring Rice Krispies. "Then you can climb into the bathtub," she promised, "and get all that itchy sand off you and then, if it's okay with your mom and dad, you can maybe ask Lin if you can lie on his bed and watch some TV for a while."

"This is too weird," Sally said softly. "This is really all just too weird for me, Momma."

"Darling," Rainey said, putting her arms around her daughter and holding her close, "it's so flippin' weird for me I don't even know what I'm supposed to be doing! And so I do what I know how to do, what I've been doing ever since you were an eight-pound bundle, and I look after the little ones. Anything else is apt to send me screaming off across the landscape."

"I'll go with you." They cuddled, then Sally laughed. "So I'll go hunt up some bathtub toys, right?"

"You're a darling."

Wayne walked into the kitchen, a smile on his face, and sat down at the table as if he had gone into a café and was waiting for the waitress to appear. When Rainey made no move to get him a cup of coffee, he went to the cupboard and got two mugs. That's when she knew there was another shoe to drop.

Sally came back in the kitchen with some float toys. She put them on the table and the snap, crackle and pop crowd grinned.

"Boy, you guys are sure lucky," their dad told them. "That's some big sister you've got, eh? The best!" He turned his smile on Sally, upping the wattage, surrounding her with the glow that Rainey had found so impossible to resist for so long.

"You're sure you don't want to come with us?" he said softly.

"I'm sure."

"Positive?"

"Sure, certain, positive and convinced." She took a step closer to Rainey.

Wayne handed Rainey a mug of doctored coffee. She curled her hands around it, then said quietly, "Do you think you could start the water in the tub, Sally, please?"

"Got it!" Sally left, grateful for an excuse.

"What do you have on your mind, Wayne?"

"Me?" He looked so innocent she could have shot him. "Just making sure, you know how it is, doesn't hurt to check. Lin says he's not coming either. Says he's got a job picking berries. Says he's going salmon fishing with wotzisname, the Bohunk guy."

The sound of water running in the tub came to them clearly. The two cottontops looked at each other, then picked up their bowls to drain the last of the milk.

"Don't you spill that," Wayne told them, "or I'll leave blisters on your asses."

"Not in this house you won't," Rainey smiled.

"There, see, even Auntie's on your side. What a spoiled pair of little monkeys you are. Don't get carried away with it or I'll rip off your ears."

Giggling, they scooped the float toys and started for the bathroom. Then they stopped and looked questioningly at Rainey.

"That's right," she told them. "Just around the corner.

Follow the sound of the water. Sally will help you with your laces."

"She's good with them." Wayne sipped, then pulled out his cigarettes. Before he could offer one to Rainey she had her own out and lit. She didn't offer her lighter to him. "I was hoping she'd come with us. Woulda been nice to have someone along to help look after them. Give J'neesa a bit of a break."

"Wouldn't have been much of a break for Sally, though."

"Change is as good as a rest, that's what they say." The zillion-watt smile was turned on Rainey. She had no trouble at all resisting it. "J'neesa is pretty well worn out right now. She's been having hell's own time with her family, as if she wasn't legal age and had the right to make her own decisions. They'd keep her tied to the sofa for the rest of her life, if they could."

Rainey let it pass. Wayne had his own way to approach anything, and it was seldom the direct and unvarnished way.

Sally came back into the kitchen, grinning from the frolic in the bathroom. Loyally, she sat at the table, near Rainey, and smiled determinedly. "They're having a wonderful time," she said.

"So, I was wondering if you'd like a summer job for a couple of weeks," Wayne said to her.

"Job? Me? I've got a sort-of one. Bruno said I could use his mower and do people's lawns. I've got eight customers already."

"I had in mind a babysitting job." Finally he put it on the table, where it squirmed and slithered and hissed. Rainey had to swallow hard not to burst out laughing.

"I already told you, I'm not going camping with you guys. I've got my lawns to mow, I've got softball practice during the week and a game every Sunday, and—"

"I was thinking maybe the boys could stay here and you could babysit them while J'neesa and I—"

Rainey lost it. She didn't throw her coffee in his face, she didn't leap up and plunge a butcher knife into his throat, she didn't run for the gun she didn't have anyway so as to blow him to hell. She did something far more damaging. She burst out laughing, and couldn't stop. Wayne stared at her, shocked. Sally, who hadn't had time to answer Wayne, started to grin. Within seconds she was laughing, too, almost as hard as Rainey was.

Rainey left the table, and headed out the back door, still howling with laughter. Sally stayed at the table. David looked up when Rainey went out on the front porch, tears coursing down her face, laughter still bubbling up from her belly. The others turned to her as well, their faces puzzled.

Chrissy began to smile. "Share the joke?" she asked.

"He . . ." Rainey choked, coughed a few times and started laughing again. "Oh God, he asked Sally . . ." She couldn't continue. She went down the steps, laughing.

"You'll make yourself sick." Sarah wasn't smiling. "You have to get hold of yourself, Lorraine, or you'll be on your knees gagging."

"Oh, Momma!" Rainey threw her arms around Sarah and buried her face in the curve of her mother's neck. "Oh, Momma, sometimes, honest to God, it gets chronic."

Old Annie laughed, rising from her chair. "Chronic is it? I've heard that word before now." She reached for Sarah's cane. "Might get myself one of these. I could use an upstanding friend of my own." She grinned at wee Annie. "I'll be over at Bruno's place," she said. "But I'll drop by to see you on my way home. I want to see what you've accomplished so far. You never know, I might get an idea or two for myself."

Rainey stepped back and patted Sarah's face. The laughter had stopped, but she was still smiling widely. "He wants to leave the boys here, have Sally look after them while he and J'neesa holiday," she explained.

"My dear lord in heaven," Sarah said mildly. "Doesn't that man get some of the oddest notions."

For a moment, Rainey thought the guffaws were going to start up again. Then Sally came down the stairs laughing and went over to kiss her grandmother goodnight. When Sarah was sufficiently smooched, Sally turned to Bruno and gave him a long cuddle. "See you in the morning."

Sarah patted Rainey's arm again, then started carefully down the walk, her good arm grasping Bruno's, her lazy arm hanging, swaying slightly. Old Annie walked behind with the cane. She stopped to examine the rose bush at the corner of the house, nodded approval, then looked more closely. Minnie was lying behind the bush, her muzzle on her feet, pretending to be somewhere else. "You'll be fine, dog," old Annie almost whispered. "The wee ones are in the tub and they'll be asleep soon. Oh, it's a terrible thing, isn't it, the way things change and alter and no sooner does a poor brute get used to things than it's time to get used to something else. They aren't staying, dog. Life will become what you're used to. I won't tell a soul where you are."

Lin went into the house and a couple of minutes later Wayne came out, looking as if everything in the world was exactly how it should be. J'neesa looked up at him and Rainey could have wept when she saw the young woman's expression. She remembered it from the other side, when she had been the one wearing it. Most of the world would have thought it a happy smile. Oh aren't you the most wonderful thing in my life and aren't I lucky you even pay any attention to me! No wonder the poor kid needs a holiday.

"How are they?" J'neesa asked, on the verge of anxiety.

"No sweat. They're scrubbed, dried, in their jammies and down watching TV with Lin," he told his child bride, as if he had done it all and not sat drinking coffee while Sally and Lin took care of the boys. "They'll fall asleep down there and later on I'll take them to the van and tuck them in."

"If you want to get a good camping spot," Rainey said, her tone as friendly as she could make it, "you'll have to leave soon. There's a ferry coming in about half an hour from now and it'll be packed with tourists. If they get to the campsite first you'll be out of luck."

"We could just stay where we are." He was daring her and she knew it.

"Why would you want to park in a driveway when J'neesa can wake up tomorrow morning not two minutes from the beach? You're such a tease, Wayne!" She turned to J'neesa. "We'll help you round up the kids' stuff. And you should take some of the potato salad and the last of the salmon with you, your kids loved them. And there's got to be at least six wienies they could have for breakfast. You're on holiday, you don't have to do the cereal and poached egg thing, just put ketchup on a paper plate and hand them that and the cold wienies and they'll be fine."

"Listen to her, she's got my life planned for me." Wayne rose, shaking his head and smiling, and for once Rainey had no idea what he was up to. "So what's the decision on the job offer?" he asked Sally.

Sally gulped and composed herself. "Can't do it," she said clearly. "Just don't have the time."

He pressed on. "Think Lin would be interested?"

"He's busy, too." Sally's voice had hardened.

Chris looked at her. "They're kind of busy," she said, taking a hand. "Both of them have part-timers with us, getting the bedding boxes whacked back together, sifting top soil, grunt work like that."

"Can't have little kids ripping around a construction site." Rainey picked up Sarah's chair and headed to the porch with it. "I'll get the salad and salmon and maybe Sally could scoop up their clothes."

The boys walked to the van sleepily, each carrying a brightly painted metal truck, presents from Lin. J'neesa carried the bag of clothes and grubby little sneakers, and once she was in the van Rainey handed her the foil-wrapped fish and a tub of spud salad. "You enjoy yourself," she said, smiling. "Have a good vacation."

"Thank you," J'neesa said clearly. For a moment she looked as if she had more to say, but then she retreated back into her silence.

Rainey closed the door of the van and walked back toward the house. When she heard the van start up, she didn't turn to watch it leave.

"What was that all about?" Chris asked.

"Sally'll fill you in." Rainey sounded exhausted even to herself, and she didn't care. "Just more of the same old same old."

Chris and wee Annie went home, Sally and Lin went to bed,

Rainey and David sat in the living room to watch TV but it was stuffed with pap.

"Fifty channels and nothing worth watching," David sighed.

"If I start to cry you mustn't get upset," Rainey blurted.

David smiled at her, then reached out and took her hand. "If you start to cry I will get upset," he corrected her. "But I won't *act* upset, okay? I won't say a thing. I'll just hold your hand and mind my own business."

"I don't know how I did it for so long."

"The amount of energy it must have taken could have lit up New York," he agreed. "Why don't you wiggle a bit closer and let me put my arm around you so you can lay your head on my shoulder and tell me all kinds of lies."

"What kind of lie would you like to hear?" She moved over beside him, bodies touching.

He slid his arm around her shoulders and hugged her closer. "Oh, you could try telling me those romantic lies, you know, how you love me so much and how we'll have a good life together and only be truthful with each other and always have respect and . . . that kind of lies."

"Ah, listen to you. The problem is, you see, you asked me to tell you lies, and if I tell you all that stuff, I wouldn't be lying. So what do you want? The lies, or that stuff?"

"I'll take that stuff. Any day or night of the week."

"So he says to Sally, he says, Oh, I thought maybe they could stay here with you and the two of us could go off on our own."

"Are you serious?"

"So then he says, as they're getting into the van, that maybe he and Janice or whatever won't go anywhere on holiday, after all, maybe they'll stay down at the campsite so—get this—the kids can get to know their big brother and big sister. You know what that means? He'll be showing up, dropping them off, sponging babysitting . . ." She wiped tears from her face. "Jesus Christ, but I am tired of it all."

"Yeah," he agreed. "Me too, and I haven't had years of it. Oh well, at least they're nice little guys."

"Maybe his mother will fall madly in love with them. Maybe she'll want them with her twenty-four hours a day, seven days a week. She never did really cotton to my two. Maybe these ones will be more to her liking."

9

Bruno made a memory board for Sally's room, a simple foot-square piece of soft pressed cardboard, white-painted, framed by strips of well-varnished finishing board. To this she pinned her ribbons from track and field and a black-and-white copy of the picture that had been in the local paper, of her in mid-air, body straining for what would be the winning attempt in the long jump. She had other photos, of Sarah and Bruno getting into his aluminum boat to go fishing, of Chris, Rainey and wee Annie cleaning fish and laughing, and one of Lin sitting with one arm draped over Chester's bulk, the pig's face turned toward Lin, his mouth partially open. It looked as if the two of them were sharing a wonderful joke. She had a photo Chris had taken of Sally and David on the motorbike, and another picture of Sally and wee Annie talking together. Bruno said it was about the best photo he had ever seen, and Sarah liked it so well she got two enlargements, framed them and gave one to old Annie.

Wayne's mother, Edna McKye, had ignored Rainey and the kids for years and hadn't so much as phoned to see how Sarah was doing, although she must have known of the stroke—everyone in town knew and spoke of it to each other. Edna might have dropped off the face of the earth for all anyone saw or heard of her. But then, Rainey hadn't burned up the phone lines with the news of her arrival or with catch-up stories about the children, and she certainly hadn't bothered to drop by with them. Wayne himself waited almost four days before getting in touch with his mother to let her know he was in town, parked at the municipal campsite.

Edna invited him for supper. Wayne said he'd come if his "new family" was invited as well. Edna said don't be silly, of course they are.

Wayne and J'neesa arrived with the boys and a potted begonia they'd picked up at the supermarket. Edna took one look at J'neesa and her sons and knew everything Rainey hadn't bothered to phone and tell her.

"Well," she said. "And what's *your* name?"

"Ricky," the older cottontop said, obviously frightened. "And he's Randy."

"Ah. Ricky and Randy. Well then, let's put this lovely flower in the middle of the table so we can all enjoy it while we have supper. Do you like roast pork?"

"I don't know." He looked on the verge of tears.

"What about creamed potatoes?"

"Yes."

"And green beans from the garden."

"Yes."

"And pickles?"

"Yes."

"Well, and just in case you aren't too fond of roast pork, I've got some brand-new pizza slices I can warm up for you."

The boys sat at the table and ate hungrily, hardly saying a word. J'neesa ate, but less hungrily, and smiled nervously whenever Edna spoke to her or even looked at her. Wayne talked as if he had never been away, had never neglected to phone her, write her or visit, as though years of silence had not gone by. Edna caught him up on the small news and listened while he talked of his "investment" in the motel and how it had "paid off" the way he had known all along it would. J'neesa's gnawed fingernails spoke more loudly and honestly than Wayne's shallow chatter, and Edna was forced to re-examine a mountain of things she would have preferred to continue to ignore.

"And so are you heading back up there soon?" she asked.

"Well, the thing of it is, J'neesa kind of likes it down here. I've told her winter isn't the same as summer, we can't just park on the beach and stay on holiday forever, but you know how it is when these drylanders fall in love with the coast."

"It rains something horrible all winter," Edna said directly to J'neesa, who blushed a near-maroon colour, swallowed with difficulty, then sipped her water before speaking.

"I don't mind rain," she said, her voice almost a whisper. "It snows up there, snows lots. And it's real cold. Perishing cold. And there's no work."

"Not a lot of that here right now, either." Edna watched as Wayne glared at Ricky, then tapped the child's plate beside the small helping of sage and onion dressing. Ricky's eyes flooded but he dutifully took some of the dressing, put it in his mouth and chewed. The boy was trying hard not to gag. Edna glared at Wayne until she caught his attention, then she reached over, spooned the last of the dressing off her grandson's plate, put it on her own and winked at him. Randy looked hopeful. Edna took his dressing, too. J'neesa's eyes grew wet and she blinked rapidly.

"Gonna spoil 'em rotten," Wayne warned.

"Wayne Franklin," Edna snapped, "you were probably ten years old before you decided you liked dressing. And you decided on your own. Nobody ever stood on you and poked anything down your throat with a stick. There's no need for them to get sick on something they don't like when they've done such a good job of eating the rest of their dinner." She might have told him more, but he grinned at her and she almost sucked her teeth with anger. His brother was like that, too. Just had to have someone to boss and bully, and if you gave in to him he'd take it all the way to the wall, but if you stood up, even a little bit, he slithered sideways with that I-know-something-you-don't-know grin.

"I guess waterfront property is real pricey," J'neesa dared. "Wayne says only dentists can afford it. But there's other land for sale . . . and I like all the trees. Not many big trees up there. Wayne says they're all just sticks, and I didn't know what he meant until we came here. I like it."

"So what do you think?" Wayne said to his mother.

"What do I think about what?"

"Well, you've got twenty acres."

"I've got twenty acres, yes. And I've got three children. Your sister gets the house and two acres of land, you and your brother split the rest. But not until I'm dead and I don't plan on dying any day soon. Talk to your brother, settle things between you, then I'll give you two acres ahead of time." He nodded, smiling. "But," she warned, "you sign a legal undertaking. You get a job, you build a proper house inside of two years, and you guarantee and promise if you ever sell, the money gets shared between these two and Rainey's two."

"What?" he gaped.

"You heard me."

J'neesa finished the small portions on her plate, then turned her attention to the two boys, either of whom had eaten more than she had. "Had enough?" she whispered. Randy nodded. J'neesa took her plate and his to the counter by the sink. Ricky finished his potatoes and beans, then carried his own plate to the sink. J'neesa returned to the table and sipped her tea, smiling at Edna. Wayne concentrated on his food, taking more pork, more gravy, and more dressing. Edna finished her meal, got up, took her plate to the sink, then went to the fridge for dessert. The little boys watched her hopefully.

"Do you like blackberries?" she asked.

"Yes, ma'am," Ricky answered.

"And do you like whipped cream?"

"Yes, ma'am."

"You might call me Grandma."

"Yes, ma'am. Grandma."

"Good boy. See this? This is blackberry grunt." She smiled at J'neesa. "You just make yourself a shortcake, same as for strawberry shortcake. Or, if you don't happen to care for shortcake, an ordinary vanilla or white will do. Put your berries in the pan first, the more the better, then pour the cake on top, bake it the regular way, be sure to let it cool a bit, then serve it up and bury it in whipped cream. And eat until you grunt. Sometimes I don't bother with the cake, I just go down to old Annie's, get a couple of pints of cream, whip it up and then put in half the berries, whip that, and ladle it over the rest of the berries. And it's good for them. Full of vitamin C. And," she smiled again, "mustn't forget all the calcium in the whipped cream, right?"

J'neesa smiled, a timid, almost trembling smile. Dear God in heaven, how young is she, poor overwhelmed little thing? And what was wrong with Wayne that he would go fishing for minnows? Had Rainey assumed Edna knew more than she did? Or was Rainey unable to pretend everything was fine and unwilling to disillusion her mother-in-law? Was this one of the reasons for Rainey's stubborn lack of communication? For that matter, what were Edna's own reasons?

Wayne packed away his second helping and started right in on his dessert. While J'neesa and Edna packed the dishwasher, Wayne took the boys outside and walked slowly with them, looking at the land, already picking which of the acres he wanted, figuring out how much the second growth would be worth, how much of it he could use for the house, how much he could sell.

"No," Edna said flatly, "no damn trailer houses! They look like hell."

"Well, what about those modular ones, you know, pre-made, but they look like real houses?" he bargained. "I could get a foundation poured before the end of next week, set the modular on it, then add on . . ." He talked easily, smoothly, and Edna watched him. It all sounded fine. But this was, after all, Wayne, and he might start off by raising hell and propping one corner of it, but he didn't have an impressive record of finishing.

"I don't want a yard full of dying cars, either," she snapped.

"Maybe I'll just buy a couple of acres," he said coldly. "At the other end of town. Might be better all round; I never did like you ordering me around, running my life."

"Don't be foolish!" It was easy to laugh. "Nobody *ever* ordered you around, nobody *ever* got to run your life. And you have never, not one time, bought and paid for something you could scam for free."

He laughed too. Edna wasn't sure she liked the sound of that laugh, but she knew her lawyer could draw up a fine undertaking paper. She could probably anticipate almost any stunt he might pull, cover it before he even tried. Maybe she'd phone and invite Rainey and the older two for lunch. Rainey would know better than anybody what sort of enterprises Wayne might take it into his head to try.

"J'neesa's been thinking of taking her high school upgrading," Wayne announced, as if he and his mother were on the best of terms. "She's got this idea she might like to take some kind of training. Think Sally'd want to babysit after school?"

"Probably not. Besides, after school for Sally would be after school for J'neesa, too. What you need is someone to look after them during the day."

"You looking for a job?" he dared.

"Looking after youngsters? Not even the ghost of a chance, Wayne. But your sister-in-law might, if you paid her in full and on time. She's looking after your sister's youngsters, another couple might not make much more work."

"Looking after Jeannie's kids? How come?"

"Jeannie's busy." Edna smiled triumphantly. "Been a lot of changes while you've been gone. Jeannie's got her own company now. Does deliveries. Got a truck with a closed box and a van, got someone running the phone and doing the books. Doing fine, she is."

"Maybe I'll hit her up for a job. I'm a good mechanic and a damn fine driver."

"You can try."

But they both knew the chances of Jeannie giving Wayne a job were the same as the chances of a snowball in hell.

Wayne would have parked the motor home on the piece of land he had in mind that very night, but J'neesa whispered something to him and he nodded, then drove back to the campsite by the beach. Edna observed it all and wondered, not for the first time, how it was the clinging types seemed to be able to handle those scruffy pups an ordinary person could never get around.

Chris was up every morning at six-thirty, sitting on the front porch with a mug of coffee and her cigarette pouch and rolling papers. At seven, Con arrived in his battered pickup and joined her for a coffee and sometimes a warmed-in-the-nuke muffin, usually a lemon-with-cranberries. Then, with a thermos of coffee to keep them pumped, they started putting back together the oversized jig-saw puzzle Larry Bridgehouse had transported from the nursery. After eight but before eight-thirty the work crew arrived: Larry's gormless brother Mike and two of Larry's cousins, who Chris privately nicknamed Feckless and Witless. She called them by their real names and she even managed to remember which was Carl and which was Thomas, but when she thought of them, it wasn't by the names their parents had given them.

"At least they can manage to get the framing done," she muttered. "But Jesus, Con, go behind them and check to be sure they remembered to put in the nails or the whole thing will blow over in the breeze."

"Amazing, isn't it?" he agreed. "And they expect to get paid same as someone who knows what they're doing."

For three full days after the new framing was finally done, Gormless, Feckless, and Witless blundered around putting the glass back in place. Chris was dumbfounded when they managed to get it done without smashing anything. She had fully expected at least one of them, possibly even all three, to come hurtling through the roof at any minute.

But then the greenhouses were done and the work crew, such as it was, was paid and off down the road smiling. Chris and Con began the work of reinstalling the plastic piping for the overhead watering system, and when that was done, there were the heat cords to install in the bedding boxes. Every day was packed with work, and by late afternoon, when Chris went into the house to start supper, she was tired. She was using a different combination of muscles than she had used on the *Sealkie*, and it took time to get herself in the kind of shape she'd need to be in for so much hard work. At night she slept as if she'd been hit on the head with a brick.

The people she considered her *real* work crew dropped in to help as their personal schedules permitted. Bruno went salmon fishing every morning, often with Lin, sometimes with Sally, and increasingly with Sarah. Rainey and David usually dropped by for several hours in the afternoon, to lend a hand and a lot of moral support. Old Annie showed up every morning and appropriated the job of watering—not just the plants in the lath shed, but the flower boxes, hanging baskets and borders. Chris waited to feel some kind of proprietary jealousy, she being the one who had planted it all. But she was too busy with too many other things, and anyway, old Annie knew better than Chris did what needed lots of water and what only needed some.

Rainey was so surprised when Edna McKye phoned to invite her to lunch she couldn't think of even a bad excuse. So she accepted. When the day came she checked Sally and Lin from head to toe to make sure they were spic-and-span clean, neat, tidy and presentable. Then had Sally check her as well.

"God, mom," Sally pretended to moan, "it's not as if we were having lunch with the Empress of China."

"The Empress I could handle, it's your grandmother McKye scares me."

"Why? Is she so . . . tough?"

"I don't know. I hardly know the woman."

"How come?"

"Your father and I ran away together. We headed off, as far as we could, and your grandmother McKye never forgave me for it. Maybe she thought if we'd stayed here things would have worked out better, been more . . . normal."

Edna smiled easily, spoke as if there had never been one single moment of strain between her and Rainey, and looked at Sally with such raw hunger Rainey felt ashamed of herself for not visiting sooner.

Wee Annie went to old Annie's place when she got off shift in the morning, but if she was on afternoons, she came home well past midnight and crawled into bed with Chris and snuggled close. They made jokes that their sex life had died when the first of Larry's trucks had arrived with all that work.

In spite of the work, the hammering, the moving of this and shifting of that, the trying out of something else, wee Annie managed to sleep until nearly noon. Once awake, she made lunch and they ate it in the shade, with jugs of chilled juice or cans of cold beer. Con lost the haunted look he'd been wearing when Chris first drove up to talk to him about wee Annie's idea. "Gonna be so fat," he said happily, "they'll have to roll me down the hill. Haven't had so much good food since who can remember when."

"Listen to you," old Annie laughed. "All's this is, fool, is ham sammich. Bit of spud salad. It's not as if it's patty de foys grass, you know."

"Did you eat this much when you were at home on your ownsome?" he replied placidly.

"No," she laughed. "But we were talking you, not me. Usually I just sort of grabbed something. Anything. On my own, it's just fuel."

"Are people still alive out there?" Chris yawned. "You know, beyond the fence, in those houses I can see on either side of the road? Are there still people? Doing people things like just sitting on their arses in the shade?"

"Don't even get started," Con sighed. "But I have to tell you I've enjoyed just about as much of this frenzied activity as my personal mental health can tolerate and if I don't get to a beach pretty damn soon there's going to be real trouble for all concerned. I have been known to sulk when deprived of the beach."

"Don't bother," Wee Annie laughed. "We'll have supper there tonight. Promise. *If*, and only if, someone can wrestle that propane barbecue into the truck."

"No problem," Con nodded. "Guess we should let the others know, huh?"

"Listen to the man." Old Annie began to pick up the leftovers. "Not a month ago he lived all by himself next to the lake and now, all of a sudden, mister sociability, laying claim to the whole damn family. You'd think we'd adopted him or something."

"You did," Con agreed. "What does that make you, my sister?"

"Sister? I'm old enough to be your mother!"

"Okay, Mom," he winked, then joined her in the cleanup. "Sit, sit, sit," he said hurriedly when Chris made a move to help. "Just sit yourself for a while, Mom'n'me can do this."

Wee Annie watched, then smiled as Con hurried to catch up to old Annie. "Ah," she sighed, "we are actually sitting here in the side yard, in the shade from the house and that prehistoric apple tree and we are alone. Alone, my Chrissy, alone! Can you believe it?"

"No." Chris rolled two cigarettes and handed one to wee Annie. "I have to tell you I'm getting goddamn sick and tired of never being alone with you when we're both awake. It's like a circus around here!"

"Yeah, well, it can't last forever. And I'm starting days off. Do you realize what that means? It means that when we get back from the beach we have some small tiny chance of being alone. And I am going to have me a lukewarm shower, then I am going to lie stark naked on our bed and send frantic prayers to the ear of the goddess. If she hears, and if she answers, you'll come in still a bit wet from your shower, and you'll drop your towel in a soggy heap on the rug and get on the bed with me. Naked as a jaybird. And then . . ."

"I'll probably die," Chris warned. "I'll probably overload completely. Just poof, that's it, all she wrote. And why is a jaybird any nakeder than any other kind?"

"I don't know. Oh hell, here they come, and don't they just look all primed for another few hours of unremitting manual labour. What are we supposed to do this afternoon?"

"*You* aren't supposed to do a thing. *You* worked until two in the morning, remember? You've already done your shift for today."

"Piffle." She raised her voice. "Gran? What's on for this afternoon?"

"The good Lord will provide something," old Annie answered.

The propane barbie stayed in the bed of the pickup and they cooked on it there, parked tail-to-the-view, their lawn chairs, blankets, towels and beach bags down on the beach. Minnie chased sticks, chased tennis balls, chased rocks, swam until her legs were trembling, her tongue hanging loosely.

"No more," Sally said firmly. "You're not even having fun any more. You're nuts."

"She's obsessive," Chris agreed. "I really do think if we took turns throwing things until our arms were numb she'd keep on chasing right up until she pitched a heart attack and dropped dead."

"Come here, moron. Too bad we can't get Chester trained to ride in the truck, he'd probably be a hoot at a picnic."

"Probably would. I've half considered getting a baby one, using it as advertising or something for the nursery. You know, petunias, pansies . . . those are the kinds of names most people give them."

"It'd probably eat everything." Sally grinned at them, and Chris wondered who the kid was going to look like when she got all her bits and pieces firmed up. Right now, looking at her, you knew what Sarah had looked like when she was young. Almost. But the eyes were different, more like Gus's had been, and yet enough like Wayne's mother's you couldn't deny she had contributed. "But they've got these plastic ones at WalMart, and not small, either. They're a couple of feet long. A pig lying on its side, holding its head up with one front trotter. You could get a half dozen of them, set them, like, on a display thing? With bedding plants around them? The Reclining Swine nursery. Maybe get some of those plastic flamingos too."

"Listen to you," Chris grinned approvingly. "Gonna hire you out as an advertising consultant."

"Yeah? Well, they've got these toads. You can, like, fasten a garden hose to them and they spray water. And other ones, they're like motion detectors, you walk past them and they croak. If you put one in with, say, the fancy iris, you know, the expensive ones? With some pictures of what the iris are going to look like? People would start to walk past them, the toad would croak, and most people'd stop just because of the noise. Once you've got them stopped, and they see the iris, you know, those browny ones, or those other ones that are almost black? Bet you'd sell way more than you would if you didn't have the toad. Can I have a part-time job?"

"You talk to your mom about it?"

"She says I have to keep a B-plus average."

"Okay."

"You're easy."

"Yeah. I am. But not cheap!" and she laughed softly.

And then suddenly, blessedly, the endless muscle-wrenching work work work was done. And that as good as caught them all by surprise. They had been so focussed on doing they hadn't really noticed how much they had done, but there it was, middle of August, the blackberries coming ripe, and the greenhouses were up, the bedding boxes in place, the mess left behind by construction was raked into a pile and waiting for the Hallowe'en bonfire the kids had planned.

Con looked at what they had done and nodded slowly. "I didn't think we'd make 'er," he admitted. "Two months of the hardest damn work I've ever done in my life. But . . . we're ready for business."

"About time, too," old Annie snapped. "I was starting to think I'd never get any berries picked. Garden at home looks like hell."

"Ah, but the gardens here look like something out of a seed catalogue," wee Annie flarched. "I've never seen begonias like these ones. Even yours at home aren't as good as these."

"They are lovely," old Annie bragged happily. "Wait until next year! I've got great plans for next year. And while we're talking about next year, where am I supposed to store the manure?"

"What manure?"

"Well, we can have just about as much of it as we want. And of any kind you want. Amazing the number of animals working day and night to provide us with fertilizer!"

"I thought out back, well clear of the house," Con took off his ruin of a peaked cap, wiped his sweaty forehead with a big faded hanky, put his cap back on, then took it off and tossed it aside. "Too wet," he muttered.

"I should hope to God well clear of the house." Wee Annie pretended to scold. "And let's pay attention to the prevailing winds, too, because I do *not* want to have to deal with aroma."

"I wouldn't mind aroma, it's the shitty stink gets to me," Chris agreed.

"Well, then, when's all this crap due to arrive?"

"Whenever you want it. As much of it as you want. If we put it on top of that knoll, it has some chance of draining. Nothing worse than a manure heap that's waterlogged."

"Put down a concrete pad, put up a roof, maybe use some fibreglas panels for walls," Con said.

"And we just finished bragging about how all the work was done," wee Annie laughed. "Personally, I'm going to get something cold to drink and then I'm taking it with me to the beach."

"I'll get some clean pails," old Annie said. "Maybe get some berries picked before we have to leave. Might even get enough for a pie or two."

"I can pick berries," Con offered. "Used to pick for my mom."

"I can't," Chris blurted. "All I can do this afternoon is laze around like a slug."

"I'm all for lazing," wee Annie nodded. "I bet I'm lazier than you are."

"Bet not."

"Well, then," old Annie grinned, "why don't Con and I go

berry picking in his truck and leave you two to do the lazing for all of us."

"Phone over, tell them over there that we're going for berries," Con said. "I bet there's tons of them down the back road to Brewster's Bay."

"Lord yes," old Annie agreed, "and there are always acres of the ground-hugging kind, doing their best to cover the mess the clearcutting left behind. I could do with some ground-berry tarts. Maybe even get enough to make a pot of two of jelly, it makes nice solstice presents. Now you be sure to wear long sleeves," she lectured as they moved away together, "and get yourself another hat. The August sun can burn your ears crisp in no time flat. It's not as if you had too much hair, you know."

"Grass doesn't grow on a busy street," he replied.

"No, nor on a brick, either."

Chris sighed, and wee Annie laughed softly. "Jeez," she drawled. "I'm feeling *so* lazy."

"I'm so lazy I probably can't even make it to the beach," Chris agreed. "Do you think they're doing it on purpose?"

"I know for a fact they are. Now let's pray like mad fools that old Annie decides she's going to do her baking and jamming at her own place. I'd *love* the chance to be alone, with you, in our house, without having to do a thing except smooch smooch smooch."

"Not to lazy to smooch?"

"Annwyn, if it was anybody other than you I'd probably just flop on the bed, close my eyes and snore snore snore. Nobody but you makes these things happen inside me. Nobody but you makes me think of. . . all kinds of beautiful, wonderful, wet, damp, slippery . . ." Chris grinned. "But it isn't anybody else, it's you, and we have a chance of being alone and all I can think of is that even on a hot hot day, when you take off your shirt and sit smiling at me, your nipples pucker and stand up and yell me, me, pick me. And there's this spot, in your low back, right in between those two dimples, and the skin there is, like, fuzzy, and when you lie on your belly and I kiss you up and down and up and down and the fuzz is so soft, and if I look I can't see it, but when I lick, I feel it on my tongue and—"

"Shut up. Shut up or we won't even make it to the house. And I do *not* want to get deeply involved out here, practically in the driveway. What if, God forbid, we start to get customers."

"Piss on 'em." Chris stood, held out her hand.

Wee Annie reached up, took Chris's hand, pulled herself to her feet and they looked at each other.

Slowly, wee Annie's face pinkened. "Oh," she said softly, "oh, you just wait, are you ever going to pay for what you're doing to me out here. You just wait, I'll have my revenge, I vow to God I will."

Bruno and Sarah shared a blue plastic pail that had once held vanilla ice cream. They also had empty margarine tubs hanging from their necks by lengths of strong twine. Into these they put the huckleberries they picked, and when the margarine tubs were full, Bruno took them over and emptied them into the ice cream bucket. He could pick more quickly than Sarah, and it was much easier for him to walk back and forth than it was for her. The ground was rough and thick with salal, Oregon grape and ankle-grabbing ground blackberry vines.

"Not too hot for you?" he asked gently.

"Not yet. I'm enjoying this. I like the smell of them. If I was struck blind I'd know someone had brought me here just by the smell of ripe berries."

"Sometimes, even after all these years, I am surprised all over again by the amount of free food in this country. There is no way we are going to be able to pick all of these berries. A hundred old Annies couldn't even make a dent in them."

"She tries, though, God she tries! It would bore me half to death to spend as much time picking as she spends; hour after hour, day after day. She'd be here week after week and month after month if the season lasted long enough."

"A person could set up a cannery," he teased. "Hire pickers, hire other people to turn the berries into jam, or put out our own line of pie filling or . . . no end to the possibilities."

"No end at all," she agreed. "Wind up so rich we'd be exhausted just lugging it all to the bank."

After a while Sarah began to flag. She found a place where she could sit, her back supported by the bole of a large stump. She sat in the shade, slowly eating the huckleberries in her margarine tub. After a while Bruno came and sat beside her. He took a handful of berries from his tub and dropped them into hers.

"I can hear the others," he said quietly. "It sounds as if Sally and Lin are doing more laughing and joking than picking."

"You're good with them," she said. "You must have missed your own family something terrible. I can't imagine what my life would have been if—"

"Ah, but things here are different." He ate some berries, stared out across the mess of clearcut, ate a few more berries, then sighed deeply. "Life over there is so different from life here that it doesn't even seem like the same planet. The big war ended and, for most, there was what they called the postwar boom. Back there, the boom was because of things being blown up."

"Oh my." Sarah couldn't remember hearing this tone of voice before, and Bruno's accent was thicker than usual, too. "How dreadful."

"If you picked ten of us off any street anywhere and asked what it was all about, how it had all happened, you'd have at least ten versions, maybe even more." He lit a cigarette, the smell of it harsh and biting. "And so," he said tiredly, "for us, there, the war was not over. Those of us who had lived together for years, fighting a common enemy, were suddenly fighting each other. We were already . . . hard . . . all those years of hiding, years of killing, of seeing our friends killed, finding our families slaughtered, and we did things to each other worse than anything the foreigners had done. Much worse. Entire villages, from the oldest to the newborn, were butchered and their bodies thrown in the well, or buried in a pit, or . . . To some people I was a hero. To others . . ." His sigh was like a shudder. "I had a wife, I had two little daughters. I met my wife during the big war. She was a guerrilla, like me, a brave, brave girl-woman . . . but then, when there was no common enemy, and everyone went insane, and vengeance was what ruled our hearts and our heads . . . and it wasn't my group who did it but it was a group of my 'kind' of people and . . . in one of the villages 'we' attacked, her father and brother were killed. Tortured first. Brutal torture. Terrible. And even though *my* particular squad was not involved . . ." He shrugged. "And no way to convince her there had been any . . . reason? Any need? Any excuse . . . no way to make her believe her brother had commanded a group that had massacred the patients in a hospital, no way to make her believe her father had . . . all she knew was *my* kind of people had killed *her* family."

"Oh, my dear." Sarah could barely speak. Instead of clearcut and fern, salal and huckleberry bush, she could see in sharp detail the pictures on the TV news, of the many, many bones that had been uncovered.

"And then the communists . . . more foreigners . . . and I had a price on my head. And they had recent pictures . . . and they put up posters . . ."

"They got the photos from—?"

"Yes. She, too, needed vengeance. I understand that."

"My God!"

"And so I left. I had to leave. There was no longer any chance of hiding, or of surviving or . . . and my real name, my dear, is not Bruno Radonovitch."

"Oh, I knew *that*," Sarah smiled. "None of you are who you say you are. Everyone knows that. For all you know, none of us are who we say we are, either. Or if we are, our grandparents weren't."

"All I know about the real Bruno Radonovitch is that he was several years older than I was, but dead in a concentration camp by the time he was twenty-two. A patriot. A good man. Dead before being a hero became the same as being a monster," he added bitterly.

"Does it matter?"

"And I sent money. As soon as I got work, here in this country, where the earth has never been soaked in blood, I sent money.

To a friend, at first, because I wanted no link between my wife and Bruno Radonovitch, and I did not want her to supply them with a name the way she had provided the photographs. But she knew, she always knew. Every month I sent money. More money than any working person there could have made. She and my girls lived well . . . lived very well, and . . . even after she married again, I sent money."

"Oh, Bruno." Sarah mourned with him.

"I have never gone back. I would be arrested and shot. But I have . . . friends. . ."

"Why are you telling me all this?" Sarah wiped tears from her face.

"I learned yesterday my wife has been dead for two years. My daughters are married. They have made their choices. I always let them know—indirectly, but they knew—if they wanted to come here I would . . . but they hate me, too. How could they not? The way their mother felt about me they couldn't help it. I feel I have more than filled my responsibilities. They have better educations than they would have had if . . . and I just wanted you to know . . . wanted to know if you think I still owe them?"

"Oh, Bruno." She reached over, took his hand and squeezed gently. "Do you mind very much if I keep on calling you Bruno? I don't even know whoever the person is who had a different name. And yes, you've more than fulfilled your obligations. My heavens, how old *are* those daughters?"

"They have good jobs, their husbands have good jobs." He smiled, even laughed a bit. "And they are *very* well established. After all, they've had all this money arriving for years."

"One does wonder, though," Sarah said quietly, "how much of it they actually got."

"They must have received most of it. There are several houses. They own land . . . in fact they are quite well off, so . . . But you're right, of course, probably everyone dipped their beak, including the government."

"I've eaten all my berries."

"Would you like mine?"

"Just a handful. A person gets so thirsty in the heat!"

Later, as they lay naked together, with only a sheet over them and the window open to invite the night breeze, Bruno sighed. It sounded as if it came from a place so deep inside him that it would be impossible to map the geography, find the source.

"I did not dare hope," he whispered, "you would even want to speak to me once you knew."

"So foolish," she yawned. "How could I stop what I feel? Why would I even want to?"

On Grand Opening Day the plastic pigs and flamingos were in place, and if there were no bedding plants, the bulb display was magnificent, the rose bushes and fruit trees offered an incredible selection, and within an hour of opening they had seventeen customers signed up for the Opening Special. Chris and Con would go to the home, examine the yard, make a note of what was already planted, then plan, prepare and plant an easy-care personalized display. If the customer requested, and paid for it, they would also come to weed and prune. Special discount for old age pensioners and disabled people.

"Seventeen?" Old Annie shook her head. "That's half a full work week, girl. How are you going to run this place, do the work, and still find time to drive around town mowing lawns and weeding petunia beds?"

"Prioritization." Chris tried to keep a straight face and couldn't. "Besides, once the things are established the slave labour can do the upkeep."

"That's me," Sally said firmly. "I'm the slave labour."

"What are you going to do with your money? Buy a fire truck?"

"No. I'm going to buy a greyhound dog," Sally answered. "Do you know that more than twenty-five thousand of them are put down every year? Just because they aren't winning races any more. Twenty-five thousand. Perfectly healthy, young purebred greyhounds. I'm going to buy one. I'll have it de-trained, and then I'm going to make sure it has the very best life a dog could have. Bones to chew, balls to chase, the whole thing."

"Twenty-five thousand?" Old Annie shook her head. "The things a person learns that she didn't really want to know."

People bought bulbs—not just a few, but dozens. Other people chose rose bushes, wisteria, clematis and honeysuckle vines. Sally's idea of a computer-generated six-page mini-catalogue was a hit. No pictures, but descriptions of twenty-four plants and the care, pruning, and fertilizing of them.

"It's working," Sally whispered excitedly to Sarah. "I knew it would. See? People take one, look through it, and then the next thing you know, they're buying something they hadn't thought of, because now they know how to take care of it, see."

Two days after the big opening, the Clip Joint swung into action: the lawn-mowing business was off to a belated but enthusiastic start.

"Actually," Con told Chris, "I think the big deal for the kids isn't the money they'll make, it's the chance to ride the mower."

"I hope they still feel like that when the grass starts growing again in the spring. Right now things are slowing down, getting close to autumn and all. The only reason people are having the kids do it is they're fed up with it after all the back'n'forth. Personally, I don't understand the whole lawn thing, anyway."

"Don't let any customers hear you say that. They'll stop buying all that lawn fertilizer and lawn seed. You sure we've got enough?"

Even after Labour Day long weekend, even with the kids back at school, the orders for mowing continued, and the stream of customers at the nursery remained steady.

"It's how people are showing their support for Con," wee Annie yawned, her breath warm on Christine's cheek. "Has he said what he's got in mind for the other place?"

"Those arseltarts are trying to get the zoning changed down there. They want residential only. That would shoot down any chance of a go-kart track."

"Con isn't serious about that. He's still got some incredible trees there."

"Can't move them until the rains start. Some of them, as far as I'm concerned, shouldn't be moved even then. He's had them since forever, at least."

10

Edna watched carefully as the forms were laid, the concrete poured and the first floor/basement was built. She'd given in on the modular home and even she had to admit Wayne was working, and working hard. When the first floor was ready, the company brought in the modular on a specially constructed flat-deck. The house actually came in two pieces, and was lifted, one side at a time, by powerful machinery.

And still Wayne was up early in the morning, working hard, working steadily, finishing the first floor, setting up the family room with a TV and video games in it, a secondhand sofa and two chairs, and a free-standing propane heater. The washer and dryer were downstairs, along with the freezer and the furnace. There were two rooms that could be used for anything, but Wayne told Edna they were bedrooms for Sally and Lin.

"They'll need their own space; they'll be coming for weekends, for holidays."

Edna sighed. "Wayne, when they were here for lunch it sounded as if they have their time pretty well filled. They've got jobs, they've—"

"They're mine. Maybe before, when we were still up there, I might have gone along with them when they said no, they didn't want to go up for a visit. But we're here now. There's no excuse for them not to stay over."

Edna expected all hell to bust loose. She was sure Sally would invite Wayne to visit the beach and pound sand up his arse. She was also sure that Wayne would go up like a helium balloon, and she was prepared to intervene if he whipped off his belt to teach Sally a lesson, or swung his callused hand at Lin.

But none of it happened. Sally and Lin arrived after school on Friday in Bruno's pickup, bringing their bikes and a potted magnolia. Bruno stopped on the highway at the foot of the driveway, got out, lifted the bikes from the truck and waited for the kids to take them. Edna watched as, one at a time, they went over and gave Bruno a long, gentle cuddle. Sally put the magnolia bush in the carrier, took the bike, said something that made Bruno grin widely, then started up the driveway. Lin hugged Bruno and the old man ruffled the boy's hair, patted his cheek and said something to him. Lin nodded, his face serious, then another hug and he took his bike, and moved to join Sally, waving, watching over his shoulder as Bruno got in the truck and did a fast three-point turn, then drove back the way he had come, blipping his horn a few times.

The kids pushed their bikes up the gravel and lay them down in the grass near Edna's house. Lin looked nervous, but Sally looked as if she had been coming here once a week for her entire life. She moved toward the house, graceful as a ballet dancer, avoiding the hug Wayne tried to give her. She went right to her grandmother and handed her the plant, pot and all. "It can stay in its pot until things cool off and the rains start," she said quietly. "If you decide to plant it now, be sure to water it really well in the early morning and again after the sun goes down in the evening. Auntie Chrissy said to tell you it gets a purple flower, shaped like a cup. Old Annie says not to give it any fertilizer until springtime or it'll sprout new growth that will be too tender when the frosts start to happen."

"It's lovely. Where do you think it would look best?"

"Well, old Annie says it'll do better if you've got a protected place. She said if it was hers and she lived here she'd put it at the side, near your bedroom window, where that addition you put on a while ago sticks out and will stop the wind. Old Annie says the wind dries them out, says it does more harm than the frost alone."

"If old Annie says she'd put it there, then that's where I'll put it. She knows her plants."

"We could dig the hole," Lin offered. "If you've got a shovel."

"I've got shovels," and Edna laughed.

"If you guys know how to use shovels," Wayne laughed loudly, "boy, have I got work for you!" He put his arm around Lin and hugged him. "We can put in a few hours tomorrow, filling in the ditch from the septic tank to the drain field."

"Have to do it tomorrow after work," Lin said calmly. "We're due at the nursery at nine."

"What due at the nursery? You're here for the weekend."

"When we're not at work," Sally said quietly. "I'm not losing my job."

"But—"

"I would have been at work tonight but I'm here. That means someone else is doing my job. Someone else is getting paid what ought to be my money. Since this is the first time . . ." She shrugged. "But next time, if you want me here, you have to come to the nursery, pick me up and give me a ride out. I can ride back on my bike in the morning. I'll take it to work with me Friday after school."

"Sally, we better clear up a few things."

"No." She turned away from him and smiled at Edna. "We've already talked to the lawyer. And he says if Wayne isn't willing to co-operate then we don't have to come at all."

"I don't have anything to do with it," Edna said slowly, "but if anybody asked my opinion I'd say you had your job before your father decided you were to visit, and jobs aren't all that easy to find."

Wayne looked at his mother as if he had never seen her before. Edna knew he would find a way to pay her back. Wayne always evened the score.

Edna served supper and watched as Sally cut the meat loaf

into bite-sized pieces for both little boys. They stared at her with big blue hero-worshipping eyes.

"Maybe after supper," Sally suggested, "you could help Lin and me dig the hole for Grandma. And maybe when we're not here, you could, like, stand in for us and help Grandma remember to water the bush."

"Grandma lets us help her in the garden," Randy whispered. "And she takes us for walks in the bush. We picked berries."

"Two kinds," Ricky added. "See, my fingers are still kind of blue."

"Mine, too." Lin showed his stains proudly. "Mom made jam."

"So did Grandma!" Ricky looked surprised. "I didn't know anybody else knew how to make it but her."

"She showed Momma how," Randy said firmly. "And Momma said next time she'd be able to do it her own self."

"Then we'd better get busy tomorrow," Lin laughed. "I only have to work until lunchtime. Mom says when I'm older I can work a full day."

"And us? Will we be able to work at the nursery?"

"Probably not," Lin shook his head. "Probably you'll get other kinds of jobs. If your dad will let you."

"He's your dad, too," J'neesa said gently.

Lin looked at her and smiled, even nodded, but his eyes were focussed on the wall behind her.

The last day of summer was warm, the sky a soft blue with sweeps of feather-plume clouds. Customers arrived steadily, buying chrysanthemums, buying decorative kale and ornamental cabbage. The kids rushed home from school, changed into their work gear, jeans and T-shirts with Clip Joint printed on the back. Con loaded the ride-on mowers in the back of his pickup and drove off to deliver the kids, unload the mowers, check with the customers and, in the process, get three more orders for pruning and dormant oil treatment. He came back and refilled the display of purple mums, and the Bobcat arrived on the back of Larry Bridgehouse's flat-deck. Bruno waited while Larry unloaded the machine, then rode on it to the area they had decided was the best place for the trees when they arrived. He left Larry busy digging a deep trench and walked back to the nursery, to refill the bulb display.

Boxes stacked in rows, with other boxes stacked on top, and each box had a sheaf of flyers fastened to it, on which was a colour picture of the type of plant and instructions on planting, fertilizing and taking care of it. Only three King Alfred daffodil bulbs were left. He took them from their box, put them in his shirt pocket, removed the last couple of flyers, folded them and put them with the bulbs, then refilled the box with narcissus, the old-fashioned Poets, with the white petals and the little red circle at the base of the trumpet. One or two of the bulbs looked small and irregularly formed. He took them out of the display and put them in his shirt pocket with the daffodil bulbs. He refilled the other boxes, noted on his little pocket-sized pad that he needed to order more King Alfreds, need-ed more anemone and squill, then took the wheelbarrow full of sacks of bulbs back to the work storage area. He wasn't ten feet away when Emmie Fletcher noticed the Poet bulbs and began to count two dozen of them into one of the brown paper bags.

In the kitchen the jam factory was in full swing. Sarah and Bruno, old Annie and Rainey did the jars, lids and rings, David did the lifting and most of the peeling, and young Annie worked as overseer and slave driver out in the orchard, with half a dozen kids busy picking fruit, eating fruit, laughing and teasing each other. They were getting paid by the hour, which Con thought was ridiculous—he had wanted to pay them by the bushel.

"And have them picking so fast they drop the fruit in and bruise it?" old Annie nattered. "I'd sooner have unbruised, if it's all the same to you. Bruised is fine for jam, but not for preserves."

"Besides," Sarah said, siding with her lifelong friend, "we want them to show up again tomorrow. If they feel cheated we won't see them again."

To be sure the kids came back, each of them was paid in cash and given a jar of jam to take home.

"And tell your mothers," Sarah smiled, "that if they want to bring some jars and lids with them tomorrow and make a bit themselves, we've plenty of fruit and room on the stove, as well."

"How much?" a dark-haired boy asked carefully.

"Oh, son, your mother will know what it's worth," old Annie smiled. "We're not looking to skin anything except the apples for the jam."

Chris felt as if she were running on an empty tank. If one more person started to chat with her she thought she'd just screech in their faces. She had too much to do to hear about this and that and nothing at all. She was beginning to wonder if she had made a silly choice. She was used to long periods of time with nobody else around, time when she could concentrate on her job, do what needed to be done without interruption or distraction. Maybe all this customer-is-always-right stuff wasn't for her.

She'd tried to talk to Con about it but he'd just grinned at her and said there would be plenty of time to be all alone once the weather changed.

"Don't think of them as customers," he told her. "They're friends. After a while you'll get to know things about them. Who likes the kind of yards that require some daily puttering, who wants to just go out once a week and get it all done. Some are half daft for roses and they'll be out every day or two deadheading and training, dusting for this, spraying for that and taking pH tests; others want miniature evergreens they can plant and as good as forget. You'll know who can be guaranteed to kill every single hanging basket they buy, who is like old Annie and will have baskets so full they have to reinforce the sundeck to hold them. Part of how tired you are now comes from it all being new. Just relax with it."

Relax with it. Sure. Five people with bags of bulbs, and you had to check each bag, make sure the bulbs were prime, and while you were at it count them just in case there were eleven instead of the ten the customer claimed.

"They dust them with a sulphur powder at the wholesaler's," she told one woman, "but we made up these little packets of the same stuff, and we recommend you store the bulbs in the fridge until planting time, and shake what's in the envelope on them so they're still absolutely at their peak when you put them in."

"How much?" the woman demanded.

"Complimentary," Chris made herself smile. "You know us, we're the ones will probably never make it into the black because we're too busy spoiling our customers and making sure they get full value."

"Thank you," and Chris was rewarded with a grin. "Will they need fertilizer?"

"In the springtime. You don't want to encourage them to put out any growth at all this time of year, that's why you should keep them in the fridge until the weather changes and the ground is cold. That way they'll stay dormant. If they start to grow they can be damaged when things get cold. You might want to put a good layer of mulch on them when the night frosts are hard but the ground hasn't yet frozen. Maple leaves are what my grandmother uses in her beds. A good thick layer of them. And," she winked, "the nice thing about them is that you get 'em free of charge, we go down to the beach, rake them up under those big vine maples, fill the bed of the pickup. You just stuff them into garbage bags and take them home in your trunk. Or pay the neighbourhood juvenile delinquents to do the work for you."

"The same ones who are so busy picking fruit for you?"

"The very ones. They're good kids. And fun to have around."

"I'll take some of those plums, too, please. The purple ones. Would you have enough for me to make a dozen pints of plum jam?"

"I can have them brought down for you. Would you rather have them in a bag or a box? The box isn't exactly spiffy clean, but you'll want to wash the plums when you get them home anyway. We don't use any kind of sprays or weird poisons, but there's always the bird do-do, and the bee do-do."

They discussed the price of plums, and of apples, and pears, then Chris phoned up to the house and spoke to Sarah. Con was getting ready to go find the kids, load the mowers and move them to the next neighbourhood, and he waved as he drove off, grinning. Chris sent the woman up to the house to pay and get help loading the fruit. No sooner had that customer left than Chris was busy with the next one, who had already eaten three of the plums on display and wanted another dozen to take home for the rest of the family. She sampled an apple and took ten of those as well, and by the time all the customers were taken care of the fruit display was a thing of the past and two other cars were up at the house buying by the box, for canning and jam.

Chris closed the nursery at seven, locked the doors, locked the gate, then walked up to the house. She sat on the back steps, lit a cigarette and sighed deeply. Even her bones were tired.

Soft, strong hands pressed into her shoulder and neck muscles and began to knead, gently, firmly.

"It's been a day," wee Annie whispered. "And it isn't finished yet. They've just about got the kitchen cleaned and tidied, and Gran says the roast is almost ready. She'll be making gravy in about ten minutes. Sarah says you're to just sit here and relax, you've done enough for one woman today. Bruno is getting ready to whip the spuds and Gran says you should get this into you; says it will probably save your life." She kissed Chris on the curve of her neck and then her skilled hands moved, one of them rub-stroking Chris's back, the other reaching forward and dangling a bottle of beer in front of her.

"Ah, Annie-my-Annie," Chris sighed. "You're an angel."

"Not really." Wee Annie sat down beside Chris, still stroking her back. "I'm actually a woman. A very earthy one, at that. I've got earth under my fingernails, earth on my jeans, probably have it in my hair. I need a bath."

"Ah, but you have to consider the necessity for conservation," Chris lectured. "There may be a water shortage one day. They're thinking of passing a federal law, nobody can soak in a full tub of water unless they share it with a friend."

"And turn off the overhead electric lights, too. Candles, I hear."

"I heard that, too, so it must be the way it is."

The next morning the canning display was in place, each bottle sparkling in the sunshine streaming through the window, the jams, jellies, preserves and chutneys as brilliant as any jewel. Old Annie brought a load of her own canning, some of it from the previous year. They set that to one side with a sign stating it was "Vintage" and sold it for twice the price of the fresh. The pickled beets were such a hit they were gone before coffee break, and the zucchini chutney lasted only an hour longer. Up at the house the food processors were lined up on the counter, busy whirring and whining, turning more zucchini into chutney, turning corn into relish and slicing cucumbers and beets, beets and more beets. Sarah's fingers were so stained with beet juice they were purple, and David complained he'd lugged so many boxes of vegetables and fruit his arms had stretched to the point his fingers were dangling in the tops of his rubber gumboots. Bruno made another trip to town for more jars, lids and rings, and for as many pounds of peppers as he could buy.

"Doesn't matter if they're green, yellow, orange, red or purple," Sarah crooned in his ear, hugging him with her good arm. "Your cheek is bristly already. And I know you shaved this morning, I sat there and watched you."

"It's a sign of masculinity." He kissed her in the little hollow just above her lips and under her nose. "What they call secondary sexual characteristics."

"Secondary is it?" Her voice was low, her breath warm on the wrinkled leathery skin of his neck. "You watch where you take that secondary stuff."

"You two stop it!" old Annie snapped. "The next thing you know the lot of you will be paired up all over the place, smooching and flirting and getting ready for God knows what and here I'll be doing all the work by myself."

"Jealous bitch," Sarah laughed.

"I have a friend," Bruno offered. "Nice guy. New car, lots of money, real fancy dresser."

Old Annie guffawed. "I don't have the time. Unless he can run these damn noisy machines and fill jars for me."

They worked until eight that night and quit only when wee Annie started to yell at them that she'd had enough, she wanted her house to herself.

"Look," she said, unable to keep up the pretence of anger verging on insanity. "I've got sandwiches made, canned salmon with lettuce and green onions. I've got a salad made. I've even got seventy-leben gallons of tea, your choice of hot or iced. Now for the love of Jesus who died on the cross for your sins, will you call it a day!"

"Don't you just love a forceful woman!" Chris pretended to swoon. "Makes my heart go all pitty-patty."

At ten the lights were out, the big house was silent, and Chris and wee Annie were together somewhere out in the ozone where there was no thought of beets or onions, no thought of zucchini, squash or pickled peppers. Con was asleep on his couch, the TV still playing some hysterical show. David and Rainey were at work, doing their best to cope with a pub full of people who showed every sign of being frantic. Perhaps they were dying of thirst, perhaps they were merely crazy. Sally was asleep. Lin was watching a space shoot-'em-up with Chester. The boy sat on the braided rug, his back against the aging sofa in the downstairs TV room and the pig lay beside him, making soft snuffling noises of appreciation each time Lin held out a few kernels of fresh popcorn. All Chester had to do was open his mouth and Lin carefully put the popcorn in on the thick, pointed little tongue. "Num num," Lin said each time. Chester grunted agreement, then smacked his jaws together, his long, curved bottom tusks glittering in the light.

When Rainey and David came home from work, even the TV room was dark and silent. Rainey checked on the kids. Sally was sound asleep, her homework and textbooks neatly stacked on the floor beside her bed. Lin lay in a heap and tumble of blankets, one arm hanging over the side of the bed, his fingers brushing Chester's burly shoulders. The pig opened his eyes and watched as Rainey pulled the quilt over the boy.

"You," she whispered, "are supposed to sleep in the hallway, on your blanket. Sarah has never allowed you in the bedrooms."

Chester grunted agreement, snuffled and then made wet smacking noises with his mouth. "What was it tonight? Peanut butter sand-wiches? Cereal? You're going to get so huge we'll have to put a skateboard under your belly so it doesn't drag on the ground and get road rash."

Sarah rolled to her side and lifted her lazy arm enough she could lay it over Bruno's belly, her numb hand cupped over his pelvic bone. "The only other man I've ever been with was Angus," she said to Bruno, her voice deep and almost purring, "and he was as hairy as a human could be. Like a pelt, it was, starting at his ankles and wrists. He had to shave his throat so the fur wouldn't stick up out of his collar. I thought all men were like that. You're so smooth it's almost like touching another woman. You've got less hair on your arms than I have."

"Ah, but mine is long, dark and wiry, yours is soft and fine as baby hair."

"Is it long, dark and wiry, indeed?" she laughed softly. "It didn't feel like that to me. Long, yes, and thick as well, but dark and wiry?"

"Delilah, that's who you are. Delilah."

"Not so. She sapped Samson's strength, if you remember. And whatever else you may be, bohunk that you are, sapped doesn't seem to be part of it."

"I've been saving it. Like putting money in a bank. Years and years now, all I've used it for is to pee. But now, lucky man that I am, you're in my bed, which is exactly where I've wanted you for years. I was still a young man when I started lusting after you."

"Oh, away with you now, you'll talk the potatoes out of the ground before they're ready."

"It's true. The first time I saw you was when I was looking around at houses. You had on a dress, a summer house dress. Pale blue, no sleeves. And you were busy in your garden. When you stood up I could see the shadow, the outline of your body, dark in the light blue of the dress. You had a bucket of something, I don't know what. And you called out something, and Angus came from the house to take the bucket. As he turned to go back he patted your bum and I was so jealous I could have eaten a hole in his throat."

"Oh, listen to it," and she wriggled closer, pressing against the length of him.

"That's why I bought this place."

"You bought it because it had a big back yard."

"And I could stand in the back yard and catch sight of you."

"You'll go to hell for lies like that."

"I've already been in hell. It's not much."

"Poor Angus," she sighed. "I've missed him."

"He was a good friend. Once I got past being jealous of him."

"I always thought he'd die at sea. I had this horror of them not finding his body and of me never really knowing . . ."

"It happens. But not all the time. Would you like a cup of tea? A glass of beer?"

"A loaf of bread, a jug of wine and thou beside me . . ." She sat up, patted his chest. "I could make you a sandwich, and a pot of tea."

"I'll make the tea." He patted her leg. "I still don't trust you with boiling water. You'd use your lazy arm as an excuse. Oh my, the poor man, think how much it must hurt to be scalded there. I didn't mean it, but you know how it is, my arm and hand don't work as well as they once did, it was an accident, will they have to amputate . . ."

From the kitchen window they could look over and see the light in Rainey's kitchen, see her and David sitting at the table, with mugs of something, talking earnestly, both of them looking serious. Bruno cut four slices from the loaf, spread them with margarine, then went to the fridge for the cold meat. Sarah rinsed the teapot, filled it with hot water, put it to warm through and reached for the tea caddy. The water in the kettle was singing but not yet boiling, so she got the mayonnaise, mustard and cheese from the fridge. Bruno sliced cheese, Sarah put sliced ham on the bread, cut up some green onion, put that on the meat then went over to empty the water from the teapot and put in the tea bags. Bruno lifted the kettle and Sarah went back to the counter to lay slices of cheese on the green onion.

"Mayonnaise or mustard?" she asked.

"A bit of both, please."

Sarah spread mayonnaise on the bread and mustard on the ham. Bruno grinned, put the lid on the teapot and reached up to get the sandwich plates from the cupboard.

"Here, the living room, or the bedroom?"

"Living room please, love. I *hate* crumbs in the bed."

"Your every wish, my dear." He got a cookie sheet from the cupboard, put the plates, cups, sugar and cream on it and carried it one-handed, the teapot in his other hand. Sarah followed him slowly, minus her upstanding friend, her good arm and hand touching the wall for balance.

"My my," she muttered. "Pegleg Pete."

Sally's greyhound arrived by plane two days before Christmas. Chris picked her up at the airport and took her home, to the total disgust of both cats and the wary suspicion of Minnie, who was quite prepared to fight for alpha spot but didn't want to go up against Chris, who made it clear the new beast had every right in the world to her crate, her dish and her blanket. Minnie glared, walked stiff-legged and curled her lip a few times, baring her teeth, but the greyhound showed no inclination to challenge anyone. Even the cats quickly learned the new animal was timid and submissive.

"Poor thing," wee Annie crooned. "You don't have the slightest idea what's going on, do you? It's all so strange. Nothing is the least bit like you're used to it being, and you just don't know what's expected. Well, you'll be fine soon. You'll just mark time here for a couple of days and then, you wait, you'll just *love* your Christmas present. Oh, yes, you'll love her! And she's going to go absolutely insane when she sees you."

"Not very affectionate, is she?" Chris worried. "She's about as standoffish as an animal can be. Might be a bit of a disappointment for the kid. Maybe we should have got her, I don't know, maybe a cockapoo puppy or . . ."

"She wanted a rescued greyhound, Chrissy. The rescue part is really important to her. She'll be fine, you'll see. And this pretty girl isn't the least bit nasty, she's just very very shy. Give her time to relax."

Chris and the greyhound were the last ones to arrive at Sarah's house, now Rainey's because Sarah was full-time at Bruno's. Even her clothes and embroidery basket had moved there. The opening of presents hadn't begun and the kids were just about jumping out of their skins, trying to eat breakfast calmly, trying to contain their excitement. Chris left the dog in the truck and hurried to the kitchen, apologizing for being late as she went to get a cup of coffee.

"Chores took longer than I thought they would," she lied.

"Can we?" Lin fretted. "We're all here now. Can we?"

"Will you bring my coffee for me?" Sarah stalled.

"Yes," and he was off his chair, his cereal three-quarters untouched.

When the stack of presents had been distributed, opened and exclaimed over and the excitement had begun to wane, Chris excused herself and left the living room. She went past the bathroom, through the kitchen and out the door, and she returned the same way, but not alone.

The greyhound was trembling, more nervous than usual. She walked, tail tucked between her hind legs, at the end of the brand-new purple web leash that matched her new flat web collar. Chris walked over to Sally, handed over the leash, then sat on the couch next to wee Annie. Sally stared at her dog. The dog sat. Then the dog lowered herself to a crouch position, put her head on Sally's outstretched legs, and sighed. Chris sighed with relief.

"Hey, you," Sally said softly, her eyes glittering with tears. The long, skinny tail wagged slowly and the pink tongue flicked, licked the black nose, then licked again.

"What's her name?" Lin asked, watching the dog.

"Queenie," Sally answered quickly.

"The papers they sent with her say—"

"Queenie," Sally smiled, her tone firm. "That other name was for a dog who lived in a kennel and had to chase a mechanical rabbit. And was going to be killed. But Queenie is the name of a dog who goes for walks with her person, only runs when she wants to, isn't going to be killed, and is going to learn to run alongside my new bike when I take it on the trails. And she's going to be spoiled, and she's going to get fat, and she's going to sleep on my bed."

"Beside your bed."

"On my bed."

"In her crate beside your bed," Rainey repeated. "With her own blanket, which you will toss in the washer every couple of days."

"Will I be allowed to play with her?" Lin asked.

"No tug-of-war games," Sally warned. "The lady at the kennel says they're a dumb thing to do with a dog, it's how people get bitten and it also teaches the dog that you only think you're the alpha one."

"What's the alpha one?"

"The boss."

"Then Chester's the alpha one," Lin laughed. "He thinks he's the boss of the whole world."

"Chester knows who he is," Bruno agreed. "And now that he's got two yards to patrol his world has doubled in size."

"I'd rather have a horse," Lin declared. "And anyway, that dog shakes all the time."

"You'd shake too if you were in a room you'd never seen before, with a bunch of people you didn't know," Sally defended.

"And," Sarah added, "if you had a long tail and there was a rocking chair almost on top of you."

"Where's Minnie?"

"She's at home," Chris laughed. "I didn't think we needed a me-me-pick-me competition. Not this morning, with everything all topsy-turvy. Her nose is a bit out of joint."

"I'd play with her. You know I would," Lin frowned. "It's Christmas! She should be here."

"What does a dog know about Christmas?" Chris laughed. "She's probably overjoyed to have the intruder out of her kitchen."

Sarah gladly walked back with Bruno, then sat in the blessed quiet of his living room, more than content to let her daughters do the dinner preparations. She had worried she would feel resentful or cheated, because for all the years of their lives it was Sarah who had stuffed and trussed the turkey, Sarah who had done the cooking, baking and fussing. When old Annie arrived to join her in a glass of ten-year-old huckleberry wine, Sarah sighed. "I thought I'd feel cheated," she confessed, "and instead, all I feel is relief."

"That's two of us, then," old Annie agreed. "And if I nod off in this chair ye're not to waken me until it's time to eat."

"I'd better set the alarm clock." Bruno eased himself into his recliner and sighed happily. "I'm probably going to doze off myself."

"Well, before you do, get yourself a glass." Old Annie lifted the wine bottle. "I understand you Europeans grow up with the taste of fine wine on your tongues and know it when you sniff it. And this is fine. Too fine for the likes of those beer guzzlers in the other house."

"Thank you, ma'am." He rose again, went to the kitchen and came back with a glass. Annie filled it. He sat back in his recliner, sniffed, smiled, then sipped appreciatively.

"What do you have where you're from?" old Annie asked. "For Christmas, I mean. It was hard for me to make the switch from goose to turkey. I'd held out for goose for years, but then my Annie-wee-Annie came to live with me, and she was one hundred percent Canadian, wanted turkey. And the goose you buy in the stores now is all grease and no taste. I used to raise my own, but they're a bother, always making noise, always racing off to defend what doesn't need defended."

"Mostly," he winked, "where I'm from, we devour our young."

"I've heard they can be tasty," old Annie nodded. "But often quite scrawny."

"Very scrawny," he agreed. "This is indeed fine wine . . . If I should start to cry you're not to get upset," and he seemed unaware that the tears were already dribbling down his face, and unaware that he was beginning to pick up Sarah's speech patterns, the almost singsong rhythm of her words. "This is, without doubt, the happiest Christmas I've ever known. And I know I do not in any way deserve what I have."

"None of us do," old Annie said. "But I'm damned if I'm going to feel guilty about it."

"Oh, fuck guilt," Bruno said casually.

"Oh, no, not guilt, too," Sarah sipped her wine. "I don't have time to fuck guilt. Nor the energy," and then she and old Annie were braying with laughter, two old bizzums who were more than their daughters or granddaughters would ever suspect.

Bruno took a clean hanky from his pocket, wiped his face and watched them laughing together, spitting in the devil's eye.

When David drove Sally and Lin to Edna's house for a Christmas visit, Sally took Queenie with her. Edna McKye had never had a dog in her house. Ordinarily the mere idea of dog hair in the kitchen would have been enough to send her into orbit. But she opened her door as wide as it would go and stepped aside to allow her grandchildren to enter, with the obviously nervous dog. She didn't even ask if the animal was properly house-trained.

"Merry Christmas, Grandma McKye!" Sally smiled, kissed Edna on the cheek, then moved aside so Lin could do the same.

"Your father and that lot have gone back up there to have Christmas with her family," Edna said as they walked together from the kitchen to the living room.

"You don't have a tree!" Lin blurted.

"No," Edna smiled. "I haven't had one for years. So much bother putting it up, then it drops needles, then you have to take it back down. So for a long time now I've not bothered. I get a new poinsettia plant every year, that's my Christmas tree."

"Golly." He moved to where two long coffee tables had been pushed together under a side window. "Look at them all!" He put the two big brown paper shopping bags beside the display. "And look how big this one is."

"That's the first one I kept," Edna said easily, as if she and

Lin had been close friends since the day he was born. "I got that one the year Sally was born. That's the first year I decided against a tree."

Sally moved to a big chair and sat down. The dog sat obediently, trembling slightly. Sally removed her jacket, dropped it on the floor and snapped her fingers. Immediately Queenie lay down, her front paws on the jacket, head up, alert, her snake tail wagging slightly. "I could have brought you one of the special poinsettias we had at the nursery," she said to Edna. "Con had about a dozen of them shipped in; they've been grafted, or something. Got some deep red flowers, some white ones, some yellowish ones, even got some that are sort of speckled red and white. Con said the speckling is actually from some kind of virus or something. You'd think when you grafted them all onto one basic stem the entire plant would get infected, but so far they seem to be holding true. If you want, I could bring you one anyway. We've still got a couple of them. They're kind of spendy and I think people had the idea they'd hold off on buying them until after Christmas, figuring the price would go down."

"But it won't," Edna guessed.

"No. If anything, it'll go up. They're big, too. Not as big as your big one, but bigger than most of them usually are."

"I'd love one." Edna felt as if the rest of her life wouldn't be long enough to spend as much time as she wanted with these two. "But you must let me pay for it."

"Oh, don't be a McKye," Sally blurted.

Edna laughed heartily. "All right then. And don't you be a Carson."

"I promise. There's something for you in those bags."

"And something for you, too, under that coffee table."

"We brought the little guys presents." Lin dropped to his knees and began to pull packages from beneath the table. "We didn't know they'd gone up there, but we figured . . . you know . . ."

"You're very good to them." Edna lowered herself to the floor, halfway between the two. Lin's bum was up in the air, and without even thinking of what she was doing, Edna leaned over and slapped it gently. "Gotcha," she said.

"That's it. Child abuse," Sally chortled. "We're going to sue you, Grandma. Sue you for everything you've got."

Lin sorted the gift-wrapped packages and put some of them back under the coffee table, a pile for Ricky and a pile for Randy. He emptied the shopping bags and added packages, several each, then put two other packages together, but to one side.

"What did you get your father?" Edna asked as casually as she could.

"They had these sets in WalMart," the boy answered easily. "Soap on a rope, shaving cream, after-shave and deodorant, you could get different smells of them. We got the English Leather one. And they had these other sets, for ladies, we were going to get one called Rain for J'neesa, but then Mom made us take it back because she said it was too much like her name, so we got the one called Olde English Lavender. And we got her some school stuff, too. Because she's doing that upgrading thing?"

"Your father will probably smell like a flower," Edna smiled. "I got him half a dozen T-shirts, some winter socks, and some men's cologne. Not English Leather, though, I got something else, I don't know what, the young man at the store recommended it to me. Said it was what he was wearing. He smelled nice, so . . ."

Lin took most of the packages from the shopping bag to where his grandmother McKye was sitting.

"For me? All this for me?"

"We're flarching you." Sally sounded so matter-of-fact Edna couldn't help but wonder if she was telling the truth. But then she saw the twinkle in those eyes, and she laughed softly.

"You," she said, not aware that she sounded as if she were on the verge of singing, "are an awful tease."

Edna made a pot of tea and brought out a plate of shortbread and another of mince tarts. Sally knew the shortbread had been bought at the Scotch Bakery because she'd helped old Annie deliver several containers of it. The mince tarts had probably been made at home, and they were good, but she ate only one of them, and one piece of the shortbread she had helped make.

"Is that all?" Edna sounded disappointed. "You'll never get fat that way."

"No, ma'am," Sally agreed. "But wait until I get turned loose on dinner. I'm saving as much room as I can for that."

"Yeah," Lin laughed. "They're cooking up a storm at home. David said his fingers were going to look like bleached prunes by the time he got all those Brussels sprouts washed and cleaned."

Sally excused herself, and Queenie as good as glommed onto her left ankle.

"That's a very loyal dog," Edna said quietly. "Sally must spend a lot of time training her."

"No, she only got her today." Lin was sitting cross-legged, almost cuddling his new outfit. "I think the whole bunch of them chipped in to get it for her. It's one of those rescued ones. I guess you actually get the dog for free, but then you've got the de-training to pay for, and the dog's room and board while they get it trained away from being a racing dog, and then you have to pay for the plane trip, and . . . you know, like that."

"Really?" She watched his hands, so like her brother's, square across the back, the fingers short and thick. He was stroking the nylon, tracing the brand name embroidery, and he looked as if the angels had answered his prayers. Thank God for the young man at the store, the same one who had recommended the cologne she had bought Wayne.

When Sally came back into the living room she was grinning from ear to ear. "My grandma Sarah says that you're to come have Christmas dinner with us," she announced. "She says she's got your place set at the table already. And my mom asked could we please borrow your big platter. If you don't mind, that is."

"Big platter? Oh, of course. You're sure?" Edna couldn't believe how eager she felt. She also couldn't believe her McKye stiff-necked pride wasn't jumping up to bite her on the nose.

"Mom said you'd know the one she meant."

"I know exactly the one." Edna got to her feet and amazed herself by petting the dog on its long, skinny head. "Would you excuse me for a few minutes while I tidy myself a bit? And I think I'll use some of this lovely perfume you got me."

"Old Annie said you'd like it."

"Yeah," Lin blurted, "we had to order it sent in, they didn't have it in town. We almost got ulcers worrying it wouldn't be here in time."

"It's wonderful."

For Edna McKye the feeling of being pushed aside and left out that had haunted her for so long was beginning to evaporate. She had no idea how Wayne was going to react when he found out she had as good as joined the other camp. And she realized she didn't really care.

Sarah was surprised when Edna McKye drove the kids, and the dog, home for dinner. She and Edna probably hadn't said four civil sentences to each other in more than a dozen years. They'd never been friends and they moved in very different circles, but when Sally had called she had supposed, without knowing why, that Edna would say thanks but no thanks to the invitation. You'd think she'd have had other plans: dinner with her other son, or with her daughter. But here she was, smiling as if they were all on the very best of terms, and holding out the platter, which sported a big stick-on bow and a tag.

"Merry Christmas," Edna said, handing it to Rainey. "I ought to have given this to you years ago. I gave Jeannie hers when she got married, and I gave Peter's wife hers a good six or seven years ago. I just didn't want to ship this one. You know how they are, whether it's the pest office or the freight company, as soon as they see the Fragile sign they start using it for a rugby ball." She smiled at Sarah. "They were my grandmother's. She had a good half dozen of them, and when she died I got them all. You can't get them like that any more. I got her big bowls, too, but nobody else is getting any of them until I die."

"Shouldn't say that out loud," Sarah warned. "Those bowls

are so rare, and so good, they're apt to put ground glass in your gravy just to get them."

Edna smiled. Then her smile died and she stared, speechless, as Chester waddled into the kitchen, moved toward her, making his chuntering conversational noises.

"Christ almighty!" Edna blurted. "Is that a *pig?*"

"His name is Chester," Sarah said easily. "Don't worry, he doesn't bite."

"A pig," Edna repeated. "In the house?"

"He's very clean," Sarah smiled. "He's probably cleaner than any cat or dog you ever had."

"I think I've seen everything now."

"Well, no, dear, you haven't. Wait until you see him with his Christmas dinner."

"At the table?" Edna's voice squeaked on the last word.

"No. He's too big and fat to fit on a chair and too low to the ground to just stand, but he gets his own Christmas dinner. What's more, he knows it's special. You'll see. "

"Give the woman a glass of huckleberry wine," old Annie told Sally. "Before the poor thing faints with the shock of it all."

"I wondered what I'd have to do to get some of that wine," Edna smiled at old Annie. "I got some of your shortbread from the bakery. I really do think you get better each year."

"Don't buy any next year, I'll set a tray aside for you." Old Annie lifted her own glass of wine. "Mud in your eye."

"And in your own, I'm sure."

They visited, they drank more huckleberry wine, they chatted about absolutely unimportant things, and then Sarah moved to make up Chester's plate of Christmas dinner.

"Will your dog like gravy, do you suppose?" she asked Sally.

"I suppose so." Sally put the brand new plastic dog bowl on the counter. "But please don't give it to her until after we've finished our meal."

"Chester eats at the same time we do."

"I know, but he's Chester. The book says I should feed the dog *after* we've eaten."

"That's mean!" Lin snapped. "Real mean."

"It's because of their pack instinct." Sally wasn't arguing, she wanted her brother to understand. "If you feed them at the same time as you eat, or if you feed them before, they think they're the boss. In a pack the boss ones eat first, and all the others get what's left. So we're her pack, now. And we're the bosses. That's what it says!"

"Yeah? Still seems . . . you know. . . especially with Chester getting his."

"And no bones," Sarah said firmly. "I'd bet this dog has no idea at all what to do with them, for one thing, and I'd bet, just from looking at her, that she'll have a nervous stomach for the first few days. So trembly."

Edna could hardly concentrate on her meal for watching Chester with his. "I suppose I thought he'd make a dreadful mess. Pigs aren't known for their table manners." She still didn't feel right about having a pig in the house, and it showed.

"It's their jaw," Sarah explained. "Most animals, and people, chew in a sort of a circle? But his jaw isn't built that way. He can only chomp up and down. That's why he makes noise when he eats."

"I didn't know they could do that thing with their tongues. And I didn't know their tongues were, well, pointed."

But before long she shifted her attention from the pig to the turkey, and by the time the meal was half over she no longer felt she was trapped in a bizarre situation comedy. Her grandmother's platter looked totally at home on Rainey's table, and both Sally and Lin piled the stuffing high on their plates and ate it happily.

"The best part of this," Sally sighed, "is tomorrow. I can hardly wait for the sandwiches."

"She's gross," Lin added. "She puts white meat on the bread, then she piles stuffing on it until you'd think it wouldn't fit in her mouth, then it's mayonnaise, and the other slice of bread. It's like a bread-and-bread sandwich."

"She'll have to fight me for it," Chris warned.

"I doubt there'll be any stuffing left over," Con laughed. "I'll probably just pig it all down before I go home tonight."

Sally waited until the first load of dishes was done before she put Queenie's bowl on the floor and snapped her fingers. Queenie answered the snap, and stood, looking at the bowl. Sally hunkered down, tapped the rim of the dish with one finger and petted the dog.

"Yum yum," she crooned. "Yum yum for groceries."

The dog ate daintily and slowly. At first her tail was down between her back legs, but slowly it rose, then began to wag.

"She's an odd-looking thing," Sarah said. "You're sure this is what you want? Because we still have time to get you something that's more . . . usual."

"What would anything usual do in this family?" Sally asked. "Something usual would probably take one look at the pig and run off down the street going ki yi yi."

She filled the sink with hot water and detergent. "And trust David," she nattered in mock anger. "Buys a dishwasher for the house for Christmas, then tells us the plumber can't get here to install it until after New Year's. By then I'll have dishpan hands. By then I'll probably have dishpan arms!"

"Nag nag nag," Sarah laughed. "Nag nag."

When Edna drove home she felt full, and not just with turkey, mince pie and whipped cream. Jeannie and her three had gone to Comox to ski Mount Washington, and this was the year it was Pam's parents' turn to have her and Peter and their two. Well, turnabout is fair play, but it had looked as if it would be a cold Christmas for Edna. Instead she'd had a fine meal she hadn't had to cook, and a lovely afternoon and evening with people she could have been friends with for years, if only things had been different.

11

February arrived, soggy, dark, gloomy and as nasty as it always is on the coast. The shortest month of the year, and yet ask a dozen people how they feel about it and hear a litany of woe.

"Everything rotten that ever happened to me in my life happened in February," wee Annie said quietly. She was lying on the floor with her feet resting on the coffee table, her eyes mildly glazed with codeine as she did what little she could for her agonized back.

"Let me get you something," old Annie fussed. "Are you warm enough?"

"I think so. I'm just feeling sorry for myself, is all."

"You're to find yourself another job of work."

"Yes, Grandma."

"You say that every time this happens, but you don't do anything about it. Name me a nurse who doesn't have a back that aches and acts up on her. I knew there was some reason I didn't feel right about you going off to nursing school!"

"You didn't feel right about it because I had to go out of town to do it," wee Annie said placidly. "You didn't want your little baby heading off into the bright lights of the city."

"They're talking of starting up a nursing course here, at the college. You got the best marks anybody ever got, they even said so and gave you that special gold pin."

"Gold-plated, is all."

"Gold. As soon as you can, you go into your boxes and bring out all your papers, your transcript of marks, your commendations, the whole thing. Then apply for a job as an instructor. And if they do their usual thing and only hire their friends, well, at least it's a start. You should quit and run the counter, you'd be good at that, everybody likes you."

"Yes, dear."

"Listen to you. Yes dear. As if you were an obedient child. As if you had *ever* been an obedient child. I should have put blisters on your butt when you were still small enough for me to do it."

"You never put even one blister on my butt."

"I know, and see what came of that!"

Old Annie went back to the kitchen to continue making lunch. She had a pot of baked beans in the oven and cornbread almost ready to go in. The cats stayed well away from her feet, having learned the quick and startling way what would happen to them if they twined themselves around her ankles. They watched her from a safe distance as she cut the trimmings of the pork into bite-sized pieces.

"Not in the house," she told them firmly. "Not a chance."

She opened the door and tossed the bits over the side of the porch and down to the wet ground. The cats yowled their displeasure but went after the food. "Greedy guts," she said pleasantly, closing the door. "Nothing to either of you but an overactive digestive system."

Con and Chrissy came home for lunch. They were soaked to the knees and red with cold. "There's dry clothes set out for you," Annie pretended to scold them. "Chrissy in the upstairs bathroom, Con downstairs. And if you both try to take a shower at the same time one of you will get scalded."

"I'm first," Chris shivered. "But I won't be long."

"That wind," Con complained. "The older I get the worse it gets."

"Here, have yourself something to put a smile on your face. It's what I did with the windfall pears," and she poured him a half glass of something not quite yellow. He sipped, and smiled at her. "Now he doesn't mind waiting for his shower," she nodded. She put the cornbread together, stirred efficiently, and before he had finished his drink she had the johnnycake in the oven and the pot of beans on the stove, lid off.

"Smells wonderful."

"It will be. Give you some pneumatic lift when you're heading up the ladder."

"Going to need some pneumatic lift. Getting too old for this, Ma."

"We were *born* too old for that kind of work. God must have her hat on backwards or something. She designs us a body that's the most beautiful thing you could ever imagine, then makes us ruin it by working."

"I blame Eve, myself."

"Well, she's an easy one to blame. Mind you, if Adam hadn't been such a damn bore Eve might have been too busy taking care of business to get herself involved with the serpent."

"You figure he was boring?"

"Well, Lilith left, didn't she? Said a magic word and flew off to the Gulf of Aqaba, to consort with fallen angels."

"Lilith wasn't in the Bible they made me study."

"No, and don't you ever wonder why? Hurry on, now. Get yourself warmed and into dry clothes. And leave those ones near the washing machine, I'll get them done this afternoon."

Chris helped wee Annie up off the floor, walked with her to the table and hovered until her precious was seated, pale-faced but smiling.

"Gran's beans," Wee Annie sighed. "Nobody makes them as good."

"You always say that." Old Annie put the cornbread on the table. "Ever since you were barely high enough to have to duck to walk under the table. This was the first meal you ever had in my house."

"I know," wee Annie nodded. "I remember. Maybe that's why I love your beans so much, they made me feel so *safe*."

"Ah, darling." Old Annie reached out, touched her granddaughter's cheek. "Had I but known."

The phone at the nursery was set on the answering machine and the calls came in steadily, everyone leaving a name, number and address, wanting trees pruned and dormant-oil sprayed. Those not busy with the actual pruning and spraying took turns on the phone in the afternoon, returning the calls, marking the names of the customers in the new appointment book.

They ate hugely, then sat at the table over fresh tea and checked the afternoon schedule. Wee Annie began to fade and Chris walked with her to their bedroom, helped her onto the bed, tucked a pillow under her knees. "Oh, darlin', I hate to see you hurting like this."

"Grandma says I should pack it in."

"She's right."

"You, too? I'm good at my job. I *like* my job."

"Then we're going to have to find some way to do something about this back."

"I've been thinking of just getting drunk and staying that way for the next twenty years or so."

"I'll plant a few extra grapevines." Chris kissed Annie's forehead, then her nose, and finally her lips. "I love you, Annie Daniels."

"I love you, Chris Carson."

When Chris got back to the kitchen, Con was washing dishes and old Annie was sitting in her chair with a cup of tea, a cigarette and a look on her face of such peace and contentment she seemed borderline smug.

"Dishwater looks good on you." Chris picked up a tea towel and began to dry.

"I'll do anything to keep from going back out in that mess."

"Why don't you take the afternoon off? I can—"

"Just shut up, okay?"

"Okay."

After they left, old Annie settled herself with the answering machine and the appointment journal. The names were written in the order they came off the tape. When she had the names and numbers written down, Annie started phoning. At least three-quarters of the calls connected her to a machine. "This is Annie Daniels phoning for the nursery. We'll be out next week to do your trees. You don't need to be home, we'll slip the bill in your mail box. It's twenty dollars a tree up to a total of a hundred dollars, then ten dollars a tree after that. And if you're an old age pensioner, like myself, you get a fifteen percent discount."

The calls that were answered by actual human people took longer. There were rituals to get through, niceties to exchange, gossip to be caught up on, and some jokes and teasing. "Bulb bed, too? That will be extra, of course but I can promise you won't be sorry, they do a very good job. As part of the package they'll work in some of our special composted muck, it'll give the bulbs a real boost and you'll get blossoms like you haven't had in years. Now did you have any trouble with rootworm last year that you know of? What we do, see, is go in and very carefully lift up your bulbs, break off last year's babies, dig in the muck, and then, if you need it, we'll dust the bulbs, nothing toxic, but it'll get rid of those ugly little things that eat holes in them. No extra cost—this year. It's by way of being a free sample for next year. Then we'll want a mortgage on your house and the heart of your firstborn child. While they're there they'll check your rose bushes, and let you know what might need done to them. And if you've got a special composter for snippings and trimmings and such, be sure to let them know; a note on the back door will do if you aren't going to be home. Some people don't like their yard trimmings going into the regular composter; I know I don't. I don't use chemicals in my vegetable garden, but I'm not too proud to use them on my displays, so I try to keep the two separate. They'll have a grinder-machine on the back of the truck so they'll pulp everything; it will compost very quickly. Of course, if the branches are too big they'll have to take them away, no charge for that."

Every afternoon, without fail, Sarah and Bruno went to the Complex. Three afternoons a week Sarah had her stroke recovery class and the other days they swam, they visited with others, they sat in the hot pool and then swam some more. At three they left the pool, then went to Bruno's for what they called their rejuvenation nap. Some afternoons they actually slept, but more often they lay cuddled together, kissing each other, fondling and smooching.

"I feel as if I've known you this way most of my life," Sarah sighed. "And yet, you're a mystery and a marvel to me."

"Tell me," he whispered.

And she did, in graphic detail.

They could have gone to Rainey's for supper every night, but seldom did. Bruno loved to be alone with Sarah, and they both enjoyed making supper. "I love them as if they were my very own," he told her, "but my God in heaven they never do quite shut up, those kids."

"No wonder Rainey is always eager to go to work," Sarah agreed. "It must seem next door to heaven, only two hundred people talking at one time, with music blaring and glasses rattling and not a child in the place."

When the worst of the cramping in wee Annie's back eased, she began going to the Complex with Sarah and Bruno. First she went to the fitness room and did her weight work with a trainer, then she changed into her bathing suit and joined them in the hot tub. In March she went back to work and she fit her trips to the Complex into her shift schedule. If she was on days, and home for supper, she and Chris often went together; then Sally and Lin decided to join them.

Old Annie wouldn't go near the place. "Not me," she snapped. "I don't invite the whole town to get into my bathtub with me, either."

"You don't fool me," Sarah laughed. "It's because you're afraid you'll get swarmed by a horde of impassioned old geezers."

"It's hell being an international sex symbol," old Annie agreed. "Been a problem all my life. And," she added, grinning wickedly, "it's not the old geezers keep me away, it's all those young men wanting to find out if it's true what they've heard about older women, and all those years of experience and practice."

No sooner had they finished the pruning and dormant oil of the fruit trees than they were into the rush of getting ready for spring fever. The first bedding plants arrived and had to be examined, treated for bugs and travel damage, hardened off and eventually set out on long display tables. Young fruit trees arrived, their roots wrapped in dirt and burlap sacking, and were set in windrows of sawdust. The lilac, forsythia and clematis arrived in pots and it, too, had to be fussed, hardened off and set in place. Their workday began at seven in the morning and each day seemed to last just a bit longer.

Even Wayne had to give in and pretend he was a reasonable person. "No," Sally said softly, "we can't get there until probably eight-thirty, and I have to be back on Saturday morning, there's a ton of stuff for me to do."

"Well, for all we'll get to see you—" He was angry but working overtime to ensure nobody else knew it. "We might just as well not bother. Maybe we can change your overnighter? Maybe you could come on Wednesday nights and go to school from here?"

"I work after school every night," she said.

"I'm not sure I think it's a good idea."

"You had after-school jobs. Grandma told me so."

"The boys really miss you."

"The boys hardly even know me."

"Don't worry," Lin soothed. "I'll be there. Mom won't let me work any extra, she says I have to do better in school first. Sally can do it because *she* hauls in B-plus and A-minus and *she* always has her homework done. Mom says when I can do that, I can work extra but until I can, I'd better be studying. With Bruno running herd."

"Well, I'm damned," Wayne muttered. "That old bohunk sees more of my kids than I do. Fine state of affairs."

"Dad," Sally said, looking him straight in the face, "when we lived up there we hardly ever saw you."

Wayne's face flooded with colour. His eyes squinted a bit at the corners.

"We could have been such good friends," Sally said. "When we left and came down here you hardly even called or spoke to us. Now all of a sudden there's this . . . this *push*. . . and it doesn't fit."

"You're my kids," he said sullenly.

"We were your kids before, too."

"And the little ones . . ."

"Stop it, please." Sally looked so much like Sarah, sounded so much like Edna. "I'll see you as much as I can but I have my job, and my life, and I am *not* coming out here on those nights you're on afternoon shift. If you're not going to be here, I'm not going to be here. Twice last month—"

"I came straight home from work!"

"You got here at two-thirty. I could have worked, and instead I was trying to think of something to say to J'neesa."

"Well, at least you got to visit with the kids."

"I can live without that. Let's not fight." Now she sounded like her mother. "I'll come visit when you're here, as often as I can, and you will phone once in a while, for no reason other than to say hello, how are you. You don't, you know. You don't phone between visits. You don't say hey, if you're off work and got your homework done I'll pick you up and we'll go to the Complex, or fishing, or just go for fries and coffee. It's all up to me."

"I don't phone because your mom might answer and get upset."

"My mom goes to work Tuesday to Saturday. After supper. She can't answer the phone when she's not there. And if I'm at work and nobody answers the phone, it only means Lin is over at Grandma and Grandpa's place, and the number is in the book and *he* would love the chance to, oh, I don't know, go skating with you and the boys or—or swimming, or fishing, or just walking down to the playground."

"Oh."

"He'd *love* it if you'd phone and ask Grandma nicely, then come and pick him up and bring him out here for an hour or two. Especially if he got to see Grandma Edna. And *she'd* . . . you know? I mean, think about it, we've got cousins we hardly even know! You could take him over to visit them, or arrange for them to be at Grandma Edna's place when you brought Lin over. You know?"

"Jesus, Sally, you've got a rough tongue. You're taking strips off me. You're making me look real bad here."

"Ah, g'wan with you." She hip-bumped him, catching him off-guard and off-balance. "Nobody could make you look any worser than you make yourself look when you get all McKye and stubborn."

"Listen, Carson—"

He grabbed her, intending to tickle her, but Queenie launched herself at him, and the roar coming from her throat was not the sound of the shy and obedient animal she usually was.

"Je-*zuss!*" Wayne leaped back.

Sally grabbed the collar, restrained the dog. "Easy, easy, easy," she soothed. Queenie stood trembling, expecting all manner of punishment to fall on her head. "Daddy? Daddy, can you just talk to her? Please? Tell her you're not mad at her?"

"Here, girl," and Wayne hunkered beside Queenie. "Here, now, it's fine. Good girl. Good dog. Yes. Good you. Come to me. By me, dog, that's it. By me. Now, then, fine brave girl. We're play-ing. Queenie play? Play, girl!" He stood again and smiled at his daughter. "Sal? Maybe we should teach her to play with us. Want to? I'll hold the leash."

"I don't know how."

"I do," and he grabbed her suddenly, lifted her, tickling. "You think I had those dogs just for the chance to shovel poop?"

Queenie yelped, trapped between her obedient disposition and her need to protect Sally.

"Come on, Queen." Wayne jiggled Sally, placed her belly down on his shoulder and started bouncing. "Come on, Queen. Play!" and he put Sally on the ground, waited until she had her balance again. "Let's play tag," he suggested. "You take her leash, I'll run, you chase me and then I'll turn around and go at you and you be sure to laugh, okay, because if you screech she'll put a hole in my face."

They were both out of breath and red-faced with laughter by the time Queen caught on and began to play. Edna watched from the kitchen window. She could hear Wayne's pit bull barking, barking, barking, and she hoped the chain would hold and the animal not launch herself into the game and kill the greyhound. It was true that the dog had never so much as snapped at anyone, and the little boys played with it for hours at a time. Still, you hear so much about them, about how unpredictable they are, how vicious, how dangerous.

Her timer dinged and she took the banana bread from the oven. When she looked out the window again the pit bull had become part of whatever game was being invented. Wayne had a softball bat and ball, Sally was wearing his old glove and both dogs were pacing eagerly. Wayne hit the ball. It flew over Sally's head and she jumped up, arm extended, and sniped the ball, then threw it back to Wayne. The dogs raced after the ball. Wayne got it and batted it, and it flew past Sally, both dogs following. Queen was running, her body stretched and lean, moving smoothly, gracefully, and much faster than the pit bull ever could.

"If the silly buggers had a lick of sense," Edna said to the faucet, "they'd have those creatures chasing softballs instead of mechanical lures. And if whoever used to have her could see her now he'd want her back again. She probably never moved that fast before."

Con brought the big ride-on roto-vator from the nursery and did the garden plot in Rainey's back yard and Bruno's yard too. When he had driven off to go to old Annie's place to do her garden, Bruno took Sarah's Rototiller and went over both plots again, then a third time. Lin and Sally wheelbarrowed muck from the pickup to Sarah's garden and spread it everywhere except the area marked off for potatoes, and when the thick black stuff was in place, Bruno did one last pass with the machine, mixing it with the fine soil. "You kids keep an eye on your grandmother," he told them. "Don't you let her work too hard. I'm off for more of this muck."

"Grandma said she was just going to measure out her rows," Lin said easily. "So you know what that means."

"Knock her to the ground," Bruno instructed. "Then sit on her until I get back."

When he got back the rows were marked, but not planted. Sarah was sitting on her backyard chair, sipping a mug of sweetened tea. "I thought you'd have had it planted," he teased, "and have your jars washed and sterilized, ready to start canning it all as fast as it grows."

"Daft man," she smiled at him. "The children want to do the planting. Well, really, what they want is for me *not* to do it, but I make out as if I don't know what they're really up to. It makes them feel good to think they're outfoxing me. Besides," she said, staring into her cup as if rainbows lived in it, "I can't do it, Bruno, not really. I'd wind up flat on my face again."

"I'll help." He patted her shoulder. "We'll get by, my dear. There's a lot you can do, and you know you'll do what you can."

"I thought I'd try some container planting this year. I think I can handle a good show of begonias and fuchsias, and I know I can do roses. I was wondering how you'd feel about a few of them along your front fence."

"*Our* front fence, you mean?" He took her mug, sipped and returned it to her. "I'm not much good with roses. I do better with vegetables. But if you tell me what needs done . . ."

"And I thought it might be very good advertising for the nursery if we put in a plot of, oh, salad stuff of various kinds. There are some amazing new kinds of things, not lettuce, but, well, like it. And . . . you're laughing."

"I am so," he agreed. "Between you and old Annie I'm going to be worn to a nub."

Bruno and the kids moved the muck from the pickup to his garden, then he did the Rototiller routine again. "We'll plant yours, too," Lin offered.

"Thank you, boy," Bruno nodded. "Nice to have a young back or two when you get as old and as feeble as I am."

"What he means by that," Sally laughed, "is that he'll plant his in less time than it takes both of us to get Gran's planted."

"Bet not," Lin answered calmly.

After lunch, both gardens planted, Sarah went to bed for a nap. Bruno lay down with her but as soon as her eyes were closed he was up again, and busy digging the sod from along his front fence line. Sally was off on her bike, gone to the nursery, and Lin had headed off in the truck with Wayne and the two little blond boys.

David came over to help, bringing two cans of cold Orange Crush with him. "I've been thinking," he said quietly, "of renting out my place. Then I thought maybe I should sell it. Then I thought maybe I should talk to someone who might know more than I do. So . . . that's you."

"Rent it out," Bruno sipped the cold drink. "The rent will cover the taxes and repairs, and there's enough of us to help with any upkeep needs done. You don't need the money right now. If a time comes you need it, well, you can sell then."

"Guess I should repaint and all."

"What you do is you do a scrub-out. Then advertise. And when the new tenants come, you tell them they can pick the colours themselves. People like to do that. Makes them feel the place is home. Then we'll paint before they move in."

"Thought I'd give the furniture to Chrissy and Wee Annie. Some of it, anyway."

"What we ought to do is have our first barbecue supper. Then do the great furniture switch. There's some of Sarah's stuff I know she'd like to have, and there's some of yours I'm sure you'd like. We'll run around moving this out of my place and that out of your place, and . . . and we should videotape the whole thing and send a copy to that TV program. We might well win the ten thousand-dollar prize."

"Yeah, and we can watch from our traction beds in hospital while our backs heal."

"Sarah wants roses along this fence."

"You could take the sods down to the nursery. People buy them, you know."

"Well, then. There's a career I hadn't thought of." Bruno shook his head, drained his pop, tossed the empty can into the wheelbarrow. "Then when people said, Hey, old man, getting lazy aren't you? I could say, Me? Don't be a fool, I'm just sitting here in the shade guarding my crop. What crop, they'll say. Sod, I'll say, I'm a professional sod plucker."

They dug a strip of Bruno's carefully tended lawn away from the fence, removed the sod in foot-long sections, and piled them in the wheelbarrow. David took the wheelbarrow to the driveway, lifted the sod a piece at a time into the bed of the truck and went back for another load.

"Going to need topsoil," Bruno muttered. "And plenty of sterilized steer manure and at least two loads of muck, and shredded peat moss and . . ."

"Don't forget the rose bushes."

"Sarah will have her ideas about them. Might even be nice if I took down the fence between the two places."

"Don't do it," David begged. "You know what will happen if you do. She'll want to put roses in the fence post holes."

"Now there's an idea."

When Sarah wakened from her nap, she and Bruno drove the sod over to the nursery. Chrissy helped unload it onto a big blue tarp, then watered it liberally.

"Bet you it's sold before this time tomorrow." She sprayed her head, shook and laughed softly. "If we get any busier, I might just scream and run off down the road."

"I don't think I could run," Bruno answered.

He backed the truck as close to the muck pile as he could get and Chrissy used the tractor and bucket to fill the bed. She tossed two bales of peat moss on top of the muck, then shook her head. "Have to bring the topsoil later on."

"We're having a furniture switching barbecue for supper tonight," Bruno told her. He explained the plan. "That way nobody will throw anything away that someone else wants."

"All these arrangements are getting . . . permanent." Chris rolled a cigarette and handed the makings to Bruno.

"Well, we've been . . . not exactly camping out but . . . long enough."

"Tsk tsk tsk, such goin's-on." She lit her cigarette. "And we'll all wonder where we went wrong when the kids start moving in with their boyfriends and girlfriends. We'll be busy decrying the collapse of the moral fabric, moaning about how family values are disappearing. Tsk tsk."

"Yes, I suppose so. And no telling what *their* kids will be like. Sad thought."

Sarah watched Bruno, David and Rainey as they spread the peat and muck along the fence line. She would have given almost anything to be able to work alongside them.

"Got your plans made?" Rainey asked, wiping sweat from her forehead. "Are you going to do different kinds or—"

"I thought I'd just continue what's already there." Sarah shifted her weight on her chair. "I'm actually excited about this. It's going to take at least two, possibly three years to get them established but after that they'll look as if they've been there since forever."

"Bruno said something about containers?"

"Yes. Mixed fuchsia and begonia."

"Where are you going to find the time?"

"I have nothing but time," Sarah said, her voice firm. "Lots of it."

"You're sure?"

"Oh, very sure. Very sure, my dear. And I want you to know I do not expect you to keep things the same in your yard as I kept them. It's your yard, now."

"Thanks, Momma. I don't think I could even begin to keep it the same. I'm not as dedicated a gardener as you are."

"Your father used to tease me about it. He'd say I was more avid than Ava." She waited, but there was no grin of recognition on Rainey's face. "Ava Gardner?" Sarah urged. "The actress?"

"Oh," Rainey nodded. "I see. I think."

"Yes, well . . . I guess time has taken the funny out of it. Or the wry."

"Rye? At this hour of the day? A bit early, isn't it?"

"Groan! That's more a Chrissy kind than one of yours."

"I'm working on it, practising as much as I can."

The topsoil arrived after the nursery was closed and locked. David and Rainey had already left for work but there were plenty of willing hands to unload and spread, and other willing hands to run the barbecue. The rose bed was done, hands washed and plates filled, and they sat on Bruno's back steps eating and relaxing in the fading light. When the phone rang, nobody bothered to get up and run for it.

"Pork chops," old Annie said contentedly. "I always did love a good pork chop."

"Sssshh, don't let Chester hear," wee Annie warned.

"Let him hear? My dear, he's eating one himself."

"Yes, but he thinks it's giraffe. That's what I told him."

"When should we start the furniture switch?" Bruno asked. "It's going to take us a full day, at least."

"There goes Sunday," Con sighed. "And I was so looking forward to going to church."

"You set foot in one and God Herself will faint with the shock of it," old Annie said.

"Oh, well, we can't have that. I'll be sure to stay away."

They teased and laughed, chatted and joked, discussed the how and why of the furniture swap, then discussed whether or not they were going to stay open on Sundays now that the soft weather had settled in on them.

"I think we should," Chrissy said. "Lots of people only have the weekend off, and if we're shut we'll be sending a lot of business to the competition. It also means we're as good as taking money out of our pockets and putting it in his."

"I agree," Con nodded. "I stayed open on Sundays for exactly that reason. That, and the convenience to the customers. People seem to need Saturday for shopping and nobody is going to browse, saunter and enjoy if they know they've got the back of the station wagon stuffed with food. And it's the browsing and looking around that really sells your specialty stock. People come in knowing they want six begonias from the bedding plant table. They go have a look, see what we have, then say oh, look, they've got this or that and go have a look. Inside of ten minutes they're down in the shrubs and when they leave you've sold them two rhodies, an azalea, a Japanese willow and their begonias, if they remember them. But it won't happen if they have to rush."

"I'd like the extra work time," Sally said.

"If you want the extra time on Sunday you're maybe going to have to slow down after school," Sarah suggested. "You haven't left yourself time for softball. Or much of anything else."

"I'd rather have the job."

"You might be able to arrange both."

"And you're the one told me you can't have everything," Sally teased.

She picked up plates, took them to the kitchen and started filling the sink. Lin came in with cutlery and more dishes, put them on the counter and went out for more. They had the dishes almost done when Wayne arrived in his new crew-cab long-box four-wheel drive. He parked in the driveway and walked around the side of the house.

"I phoned," he said, already on the defensive. "Nobody answered. But I figured you'd be here. Or next door. You kids want to come to the Complex? We've still got a few hours we can swim."

"Hey, great!" Lin ran for the new gate between the two places to get his suit and towel.

"Get mine, too, please?" Sally called. "I'll take Queen to the house."

"Queen's fine here," Chrissy laughed. "She and Minnie are sniffing each other out and not a hair is raised. Ah, Min, you're getting mellow in your old age."

"Are the wee boys in the truck?" Sarah asked.

"Yeah. But they're fine." He was still defensive. "It's such a hassle getting them in and out, everything takes forever, you'd think there was some kind of challenge to getting into a car seat."

Lin raced back with both swimsuits and one towel. Sally

rolled her eyes, opened her mouth to ask him if he was too dumb to count, but Sarah made a quick shushing noise.

"Get one from the cupboard," she said quickly. "And don't leave it down there. They've got enough towels and such to keep the secondhand store supplied."

"As if." Sally kissed Sarah's cheek, then ran to get a towel. "You're such a dipper, Lin," she said cheerily.

He looked at Sarah's towel, then shrugged. "What can I say," he mugged, "the woman tells the truth."

Ricky and Randy were in car seats in the small crew space. Sally and Lin sat beside Wayne in the front.

"J'neesa's not coming?" Lin asked.

"School," Wayne said briefly, starting the engine. "Every time I turn around it's school. How *you* doing with it?"

"I'll pass," Lin said. "But *she's* probably going to get an award. *She* has no trouble at all."

"Maybe because *she* does her homework," Sally answered.

"I don't think they should be allowed to give us so much," Lin replied. "It's not fair. If I did all my homework I wouldn't have any time for anything else. Hours and hours of it. So I only do some."

"We didn't get a lot of homework when I was in school," Wayne said. "Except around exam time, then we got stuff like review."

"We get a lot," Sally said. "It's a drag. It's not too bad for me, I'm lucky, I'm a fast worker, but if a kid was having trouble, hey, he's right."

"I guess they figure if a kid is having trouble they need the extra practice."

"At alternate school they do it differently," Lin said enviously.

"You aren't going to alternate school, so just give up on that one. You'll wind up with a tutor and no part-time job before you get to alternate school. You're probably going to wind up with a tutor anyway if you haven't pulled up your socks by Easter time. You know what Mom said."

"If they try to make me do that," Lin said defiantly, "I'll just go and live with you, Dad. You wouldn't make me have a tutor, would you?"

"Would so," Wayne answered easily. "If your mom says tutor, we'll toot. Get one for both you and J'neesa, she's having some trouble, too. Math mostly."

"I hate math!" Lin was on the verge of sulking. He stared at Wayne as if the betrayal were too much to bear.

"So does she. But," Wayne laughed, "*she* does her homework." And before Lin could respond, Wayne grabbed him just above the knee. "Gotcha!" he said loudly. "Horsebite!"

Lin was still giggling and squirming when they got to the Complex. Sally wasn't surprised when Wayne went right to the hot tub and lay back in it, leaving her and Lin to supervise Ricky and Randy in the baby pool. She almost said something about it but didn't, mostly because Lin was having such a good time being big brother to the adoring younger ones. When Wayne finally joined them, Sally left the small pool and went to the big one to do some laps, but shortly afterward Lin was stroking along beside her, telling her it was time to leave. "The sibs are tired," he laughed. "Rick's almost asleep in the water."

"So, want to get your toothbrush and jammers and spend the night?" Wayne asked them on the way home.

"Yeah! Great!" Lin cheered.

"Can't," Sally smiled. "Too much to do tomorrow. Maybe next time. He," she pointed at Lin, "should take his homework with him, he hasn't even started on it."

"Well, then, bring some of it with you and you can do it tomorrow when J'neesa is doing hers."

"I'll do it when I get back. After."

"Nope, you'll do at least some of it while—not after, while. We won't run off and do anything special without you."

"Aaaah—"

"Well, it's *your* homework. Why should your mom have to bother about it when it isn't her work? Don't be a pill, Lin."

"I guess," Lin said clearly, glaring at Sally, "some people just can't keep their mouths shut."

Sally laughed, which brought on the sulkies again. But Lin took his socials homework with him when he headed off for the overnighter.

"One day," Sally said, sounding so much like Chrissy Sarah almost laughed, "Lin's going to clue in. The only reason Dad took us was he needed someone to be with the two little guys. I bet Lin winds up babysitting."

"Lin's too young to babysit," Bruno grumbled. "He's hardly able to look after himself."

"On the other hand," Sarah tried to calm the waters, "he might grow up a bit if he has some responsibility. I was hoping his part-time job would—"

"He can do some of the work." Sally hung the damp towel on the outside line, then began fussing her greyhound. "But he has to have someone there to remind him of what needs done. And to make sure he does *all* the job. He's kind of forgetful. Or something."

"He's actually quite young," Sarah said quietly. "And I know when you were his age you had to keep an eye on him, but it isn't his fault he was the baby for so long. That isn't something you just make up your mind to change. It takes time."

"I just worry," Sally blurted, "that he's going to grow up to be just like dad. You know, kind of . . ." She shook her head, unwilling to put into words the things she felt and feared.

"My dear dear dear." Bruno reached out, took Sally's hand and pulled her onto his lap. "You must not do this to yourself. You are a girl. You are a young lady. A *young* lady. Please. Being young is so precious and so fleeting. Do not cheat yourself of your youth. He is your brother, not your child. And the other one is your father, not your responsibility. You are not expected to fix everything."

Sally was weeping and Sarah wanted to console her, wanted to take her from Bruno and cuddle her, but instead she sat quietly and watched. It might well have been the second hardest thing she had ever done in her life, just behind getting herself halfway mobile again.

"Either Lin will realize or he won't. It is between him and his father. Their relationship is their business, their problem, and not yours. Perhaps they will be friends. Perhaps not. But all *you* have to take care of is yourself and your dog. And the best way to do that is to learn to let go. Learning to let go is so hard."

"I just . . . I just wish . . ." And she turned on his lap, wrapped her arms around him and sobbed against his shirt. "Oh, Grandpa, I just wish life wasn't so *messy!*"

Sarah laughed then. Easily and from the belly. Before long Sally was laughing too. Laughing wetly, laughing tentatively, but laughing.

"You know what I mean!" she accused.

"I know what you mean," Sarah agreed. "And you're right. The word for it is messy."

They watched TV until David and Rainey came in from work, then watched Sally and her Queen walk through the new gate and up the steps to what had been Sarah's house.

"Such a treasure," Bruno sighed, and Sarah thought he meant her granddaughter.

Later, in bed, snugged as close to him as she could get, Sarah licked the salt taste from his white-fuzzed chest. "They say," she told him, "an orgasm has the same cardiovascular fitness results as a five-mile run. And at the rate you're giving them out, I'll soon be using both legs, both arms and both hands, and be ready for the Senior Citizens Olympics."

Bruno kissed her cheek, his hand stroking her hip. "I didn't know they had medals for this."

"They don't. They want us to keep it a secret. Otherwise all those youngsters will get jealous. I'd be fighting off a mad horde of thirty-year-olds."

"I wouldn't even get to see you for the crowd of twenty-five-year-old young men clustered around you."

"Young men," she said, nuzzling his nipple and sending ripples up and down his skin. "I don't want a young man. What would we talk about? Not that you and I do nothing but talk."

"I think we should get married," he told her.

"No," she yawned. "I much prefer living in sin. I spent a lifetime being very very good. Then I died. And when I was reborn, everything was different. I'm not going to go back to being good because then I might have to go back to being dead, and I'm not ready for that. I'm going to live a long, full and very sinful life from here on in."

"You? How are you going to be sinful when you're asleep?"

"I'll think of something. Erotic dreams, perhaps."

"But you won't marry me?"

"Not a chance. I might debauch you, but not marry you."

"What word is that? Debauch. The only word I know that sounds anything like it is botch, and that means to ruin."

"That's it. Ruin your reputation, ruin your morals, lower you to my level. Botch you right up."

"Not tonight, my dear. After what you just did to me there's no way I'm going to get 'right up' again. It may be days before I get 'right up'."

Sarah nodded, drifting into sleep, knowing tomorrow would be another day, another messy day.